Praise for *La*

"Life, death, religion, and the best and worst of humanity clash in Forbes' darkly comic novel...Forbes has crafted an insightful, witty, and grimly humorous tale of life, death, and the great beyond. The narrative is well plotted and evenly paced, and the characters, from rigidly religious folk to hopeless romantics and jilted lovers, are thoughtfully complex...readers see a vision of humanity in all its brutality and beauty. An irreverent, funny, heartwarming, and heartbreaking novel."

—*Kirkus Reviews*

"*The Lawnmower Lady* is the rare page-turning novel full of suspense, intrigue, and romantic desire that also succeeds as a literary work of art—masterfully crafted and resonant with insight. Forbes writes with the authority of a well-informed and gifted critical thinker with astute observations to offer. With her complex, nuanced characters she illuminates the human condition and its brilliant, messy struggles; captures the quirks and charms of rural Vermont town life; celebrates the transcendent power of music; and acknowledges the tensions inherent in faith traditions without ever pontificating. Her elegant prose, steeped in vivid sensory detail and effective analogy, is a joy in itself, but it is her wisdom that shines brightest. I fell in love with her characters who delight, frustrate, and surprise, and wanted to linger a long while in their quite beautiful, mucky world. What an authentic, life-affirming, and hope-restoring gift!"

—Marjorie Nelson Matthews, author of *The Red Wheelbarrow*

"Chilling, hilarious, irreverent, and fun, Forbes' bighearted novel defies classification. Love story, thriller, satire, and mystery combine to make this piece of rural New England life a universal and fun exploration of death and life everlasting."

—Marguerite Graham, retired educator

"*The Lawnmower Lady* had me from the opening scene. This hard-to-put-down story follows the spirit of Fay, known in her small town as the lawnmower lady, as she observes the reactions of her friends, acquaintances, and family to her death and the life she lived. We are taken along on this wonderful ride, with all of its twists and turns, as fellow flies on the wall. Highly recommended."

—Peter Collier, retired clinical social worker and musician

THE LAWNMOWER LADY

A NOVEL

EDITH FORBES

Montpelier, VT

The Lawnmower Lady ©2025 Edith Forbes

Release Date: March 10, 2026

All Rights Reserved. Printed in the USA.

Paperback ISBN: 978-1-57869-216-3

eBook ISBN: 978-1-57869-225-5

Library of Congress Control Number: coming 2026900160

Published by Rootstock Publishing
an imprint of Ziggy Media, LLC
Montpelier, VT 05602

info@rootstockpublishing.com
www.rootstockpublishing.com

Book formatting by Eddie Vincent, ENC Graphic Services.

Author photo by Flying Squirrel Graphics.

Cover Design by Vance Kiviranna, www.kiviranna.com.

This is a work of fiction. Names, characters, businesses, places, events, and incidents are either the products of the author's imagination or used in a fictitious manner. Any resemblance to actual persons, living or dead, or actual events is purely coincidental.

No AI training. No part of this book may be reproduced or transmitted in any form or by any means, electronic or mechanical, including photocopying, recording, or by an information storage and retrieval system (except by a journalist or reviewer who may quote brief passages in an academic or editorial review) without permission in writing.

For reprint permissions, or to schedule a book club visit or author reading, contact the author at her website, www.edithforbes.com/contact.

For Ruth, with love.
And to answer your question: I used to hope so,
but now I'm not sure.

Chapter 1

For years after I died, I thought the uselessness of my existence might kill me a second time. If I noticed a bolt coming loose on the tractor, or a broken board on a fence, I couldn't pick up a tool to fix it. I could only hang there like lint, watching, as the bolt fell off and the machine broke, or the piglets found the hole in the fence and trampled the garden.

As deaths go, mine had been as good as I could have wished. A massive stroke dropped me mid-stride, moments after I emptied a bucket of outdated milk and bruised produce into the trough for my pigs. I died on the spot, on the floor of the shed, with my last breath inhaling the scent of manure and my ears tuned to the grunting of mealtime contentment. Fortunately, I was out of sight of any humans who might have felt obliged to call an ambulance. I could slip away quietly, unbothered by debates about the state of my brain function and the definition of death.

The timing of the event, in late November of 1999, suited me very well. Besides being spared one last unnecessary winter, I had made a grateful escape from the arrival of the new millennium, an era that to my eye promised more disaster than otherwise.

Until Dryden found me, I was not sure that I *was* dead. Perhaps I had merely fainted. Perhaps it was a dream that I could see my body lying in the dirt, with my pigs on the other side of the fence jostling for position at the trough.

Then I was jolted by a shot of adrenaline. A thought flashed: *Fay! What happened!*

Our dog Scollay bolted across the barn toward my body, with Dryden close behind. Her thoughts tumbled in confusion, *No, please, let her be alive, let her be OK...*

She knelt beside my body and peered at my face. Scollay circled us, whining.

"Pulse, wait, see if she has a pulse..."

She yanked off her gloves and felt my wrist. Her fingers fumbled among the tendons.

"Fay, please... Maybe my hands are numb. Calm down, Dryden. Think. Try the throat..."

Her hand shifted to my throat, searching for the carotid. Her fingers found neither breath nor pulse. Only stillness. Her adrenaline subsided, and in its place came a numb recognition that the coolness she felt on her fingertips was not her own chilled skin, but mine, cooling with death.

For a long time, she didn't move. She pulled off my wool cap and sat next to my body, stroking my hair, vaguely watching the pigs. Now and then she moved her hand from my head to stroke Scollay, who was pressed against her side.

I, meanwhile, was buzzing from the shock. I wasn't sure how a dead person could feel a buzz but that was how it seemed. As if I'd grabbed an electric fence wire, thinking the juice was off, and found myself knocked backwards by the full five thousand volts.

Being dead didn't shock me. I was prepared to be dead. I'd been airing out the guest room for years, ever since I turned seventy-five, figuring death might turn up any time. What shocked me was that I was still here, in my own pig shed, watching my niece stroke what used to be my hair, and not only that; I could also *feel* her doing it.

The sensations weren't coming through my scalp, though. My scalp was meat, inert and nerveless. What I felt instead, as distinctly as if the sensations were my own, was the texture of my hair, the wiry bristle of it, sliding across the skin of Dryden's fingertips.

What next? Was this a temporary state, a moment of transition? Or was I here to stay?

Already I was outside any theory I'd ever had about my death. For the sake of open-mindedness, I had considered the possibility that one or another of the institutional dogmas was right, that I might spend an eternity of torment in the company of the unrepentant or be reincarnated as a city park pigeon, but the future I had thought most likely was oblivion. I had expected that one day my pupils would fix and dilate and that would be the end of me. Curtain closed, game over and what comes next is not for me to know. It never occurred to me that my heart would stop, my brainwaves go flat, but here I'd still be, right where I'd always been, not a memory or opinion the less, only the power of action gone.

I wanted to protest. I never asked for this. The world is too full of human chatter as it is. It doesn't need me hanging around, like the interminable dinner guest. I was anticipating peace and quiet when I died. I was ready to be done with the human calamity. What had I done wrong, that my part in it was to be prolonged?

If I did imagine an afterlife, I imagined it only for my body. If I wished for anything, I wished that my flesh might not be rendered toxic with embalming fluid or squandered into the atmosphere by a crematorium in one final punctuating belch of greenhouse gas, but instead might be fed to the ravens and coyotes and eventually be shat back onto the soil to bloom as a trout lily somewhere deep in the woods.

I'd said as much to Dryden, sometimes when we were butchering a hog, more often when I'd been to a funeral. Funerals had been an increasingly frequent event in my life and they left me irritable. I'd come home sputtering, "If I could have my way, I'd have someone drag me out in the woods and leave me for the scavengers. It's a damned waste, pumping us full of poison and locking us up in a casket. I don't want to be toxic waste! I want to be food!"

"Coyote lunch, huh?" she said one time, and I instantly felt better.

"I know, I'm asking the impossible. What if everyone wanted that? There aren't enough coyotes left on earth to eat us all."

She smiled more. "If everyone wanted it, some company would see a market and make a business of it. High-end fertilizer."

"Right," I said. "Freeze-dried and packed in five-pound bags. Perfect for the ornamental shrubbery."

"Humus sapiens," she said.

At moments like that I thought my heart would burst, from love and worry. She had come to me so late in my life. Lovers may be harried by time's winged chariot, but how much more so is a woman who first feels mother love at grandmother-age? With every twinge that shot through my joints, I felt the approach of the day when I was too feeble to look out for her. With each new talent and quirk she revealed, I was reminded of the span of her life I would not see.

As far as money went, she'd be fine without me. I came from the New

England tradition that planned for death the way people used to plan for winter, putting by firewood and potatoes, and I was passing on the same comfortable cushion I'd received from my forebears. Part of the money would go to Noah for his lifetime, but Dryden would have the rest, and also the farm, which I'd bought at a backwater price in 1956, long before interstate highways and high-speed chairlifts transformed cold rocky hillsides into "view potential."

Some other worries were not so easily managed and the biggest of them was Dryden's mother. I first met Anita at a gathering of my extended family, probably someone's birthday. Even then, in her twenties, she was a powerful presence, a tall blonde with elegant facial bones and a confident handshake. With Charlie following her in a happy daze, she had circled the room introducing herself, finding charming things to say to one after another of my sedate, bookish relatives. Wherever she went, the conversation got louder and livelier and the effect lingered a bit after she moved on.

She seemingly intended to marry Charlie and I wondered how my brother had attracted such a dynamo. He was neither handsome nor enterprising and she didn't need his money, such as it was. Her own father and uncles had made a fortune in packaging and cosmetics.

In time, I realized that Charlie had something she could neither buy nor build for herself. He had blue blood. One of our grandmothers was descended from a signer of the Declaration of Independence. Our ancestors had fought in the Revolutionary War and the War of 1812. They had been governors in the colonies. Anita didn't care that our eminence was ancient history and we now lived modest and unremarkable lives. She may even have thought it would be pleasant, to come home to someone who didn't strive.

As a parent, she was a conundrum. She had been tireless in her devotion to Spenser and Sidney, her two blood sons, but then, having made the choice to adopt a daughter, she could not bring herself to like the child. Almost from the first moment, her interaction with Dryden had been a battle of wills.

I still remembered a Thanksgiving weekend at their house in Arizona, one of the rare occasions when I visited them after they left the East Coast. The weather was incongruous to me but normal for the desert, brilliant hot sunshine. Dryden was thirteen. Her brothers had come home for the weekend, one from college, one from law school. For dinner that Saturday, Anita had invited three other couples from their social circle, people whose opinion counted.

The adults were gathered in the living room for cocktails. Anita and the people who mattered were having martinis. Charlie and I had glasses of wine. It was very good wine. Anita did not allow anything that wasn't good into her house. The living room decor was regional, from whitewashed adobe walls and Spanish colonial furniture down to the last detail of iron candelabras and mantel ornaments. My two nephews were handsome, blond and polite, as were the daughters of the guests. Apart from my own faded but serviceable dress, purchased decades earlier from L.L. Bean, the tailoring in the room was expensive and sophisticated.

Then in walked Dryden, wearing blue jeans and a casual cotton shirt, bright cardinal red. Anyone else in our family would have looked dreadful in that red. Our northern pinkness of skin would have blushed to ruddy alcoholic splotches; our blond or sandy hair would have dulled to anemia. Dryden, with her black hair and warm brown skin, looked splendid.

At the sight of her, Anita recoiled, but she took a moment to wind up her conversation before gliding across the room to where Dryden was standing with Charlie and me.

"Dryden, those clothes are inappropriate," she said quietly. "They're garish and slovenly. Go and change."

Charlie, who loved Dryden in equal measure to Anita's dislike, was gazing at her in awe. He offered a tentative protest. "But she looks love—"

"She looks cheap," Anita said.

A couple of the guests had paused from conversation to glance our way. Anita made a smiling shrug, as if to say, "Teenagers, what can you do?" before speaking to Dryden again.

"The way you dress tells people who you are. I don't want our guests thinking you're someone we hired to play the marimba."

Her voice was edged with scorn but she kept it low, avoiding a scene.

"At least Dryden can play something worth hearing," I said. "Unlike the rest of us."

Anita chose to ignore my remark. She turned away to rejoin her guests and soon the room was loud with talk about places not yet spoiled by holiday crowds. From Charlie, I caught a look of gratitude. Though he and I were opposites in many ways, we both felt a disproportionate fondness for Dryden, the child not of our own blood.

Dryden, meanwhile, had shown no reaction, either to Anita's remarks or to mine. She simply shrugged and went to change her clothes. Already, at thirteen, she had acquired a demeanor of calm inscrutability that I found unnerving. It belonged to someone decades older, someone whose fading energy and brittle bones compelled them to pull inward.

When she reappeared a few minutes later, she was wearing one of Anita's tailored beige business suits, which looked ridiculous on her, but could not be faulted as garish or cheap. She had guessed, correctly, that she would not be scolded for taking the suit. As long as Anita could pretend that her daughter was now behaving properly, she would not want another awkward moment. A flicker of irritation crossed her face as she registered the sarcasm implicit in Dryden's attire, but she did not pause from conversation.

At the time, I thought Dryden was as indifferent to my defense as she was to her mother's criticism. Then, a year later, during a December storm of sleet and freezing rain, my evening reading was interrupted by a knock on the door. I opened it and found Dryden standing in the slush on my doorstep. Her hair was dripping; her sneakers were sodden. She was carrying a daypack and her saxophone case, nothing else.

"I want to live with you," she said.

Even at that age, she said what she meant.

Are you crazy? I thought. I'm a grouch. Generally speaking, I don't like people. If you and I see too much of each other, I might stop liking you, too.

"Come in," I said. "Get warm."

To buy time, I asked how she got here.

"By bus, mostly. I've been saving up money. I got as far as Pennsylvania and then I hitchhiked. It was easy, except the last guy kept singing ABBA songs and he was way out of tune. But then he drove an extra hour to bring me to Gilham. He was worried some creep would pick me up."

"Were you worried about that?"

"Not really. It's like Mom says, I look like a plow horse. What are the odds I'd meet someone so desperate he'd act creepy with me?"

How did one answer such a remark?

"I'm afraid you're a good nine hundred pounds short of a plow horse," I said.

Her face lit with a grin. "You use tractors anyway, I bet. So can I stay?"

This time I didn't pause. "I'll talk to Charlie," I said. "I'll see if I can work it out."

Two minutes of conversation and the idea of having her there had taken root like a bittersweet vine, weaving itself through every crevice in my psyche. I wanted to know her better.

Later, when I'd had time to reflect, I thought I must be the crazy one. For decades, I'd been happy living alone. Even in the first flush of my love for Noah, when we drove through any weather to share a bed, I'd been glad to have a place away from him. Yet when Dryden repeated her request to stay, it didn't occur to me to say no. My gut said yes, while reason was still fumbling to find its bifocals. It seemed a mere detail that I'd have to persuade her parents.

Charlie was reluctant to let her go, but it was Anita's view that counted. After taking a few hours to think it over, she called back to say she would ship Dryden's clothes to my farm, because the alternative was probably a military academy.

That night I woke up sweating. What had I done?

What if Dryden drove a car off the road? Got pregnant? Got hooked on drugs? Fell in love with a weasel? Or a drip? Or never fell in love at all?

What had possessed me to take this on? I didn't know the first thing about being a parent. All well and good, to want to look out for Dryden, but I had no skills. Dryden wasn't a lawnmower to be tinkered with until I learned how all the parts worked. I was as ignorant as a teenaged mother, but without the resilience in my joints.

But Noah had skills, I thought. He knew how to handle kids, I thought.

Except that I had not consulted Noah yet. He was in Virginia, taking advantage of the school vacation to visit his sister. I had thought of calling him, but didn't do it. I told myself I didn't want to trouble him. The truth was, I didn't want to give him the chance to tell me I was crazy, or, as his more delicate style would have put it, "should consider all the ramifications."

Just before daybreak, I finally fell into a restless sleep. When I woke, the sun was up and shining on an inch of new snow. I quickly dressed and went to check if Dryden was awake. Finding her door open and her bed empty, I felt cold. Had she changed her mind and gone?

I hurried downstairs to the kitchen. It was empty.

Never before had the stillness of my house felt hollow, but then it did. I could hear the tiny clicking from the wall clock. My late sleep had let the woodstove die down to a few embers and the sunlight coming through the window was a pale winter trickle.

I looked for a note, but there wasn't one. Then I thought, where's the dog?

At that moment, the door opened and Dryden came bouncing in, shedding blobs of snow and mud from her sneakers. My old collie trotted in after her, scattering grit from his fur.

I thought of the towel hanging on the porch, for wiping the dog's feet, and the tray for muddy boots beside the door. As the adult, I knew I should instruct her in their use, but my throat was so full of relief, I couldn't speak. In any case, Dryden was already talking, with an exuberance I'd rarely seen in her.

"Did you know that pigs are smarter than dogs?" she said. "I've been throwing snowballs, and this guy will go after them, over and over, and never figure out why they disappear, but the pigs figured it out right away. They followed the first one and after that they just looked at me, like I must be really dumb to think they were that dumb. But you're more fun, aren't you!"

She put her face close to the dog and let him nose her, trading drip for drip.

"Could be he's dumb like a fox," I said. "Could be he's figured out that if he earns his keep by being amusing, he won't have to earn it by getting eaten. Same with horses. Better to carry a load than be made into stew."

"Huh, I wonder..."

She flopped onto the floor, as if to ponder the question from a dog's perspective. He curled against her and she stroked him, oblivious to the muddy snowmelt her jeans were soaking up.

"Maybe it's about dignity," she said. "Maybe pigs would rather die and get eaten than make fools of themselves. Maybe horses and dogs don't mind being servants, but pigs refuse to grovel, so they look right at us and say, 'no way' and get shot."

"They're eager enough when I bring the slop bucket. They don't say 'no way' then."

"That's in their own interest. You're waiting on them."

I laughed. "They leave a darned good tip, in the end. Want to come help me wait on them?"

As she scrambled to her feet and headed for the door, I stopped her and pointed at the boot tray. She looked at her shoes, then at the smears of mud on the floor.

"Oops. Sorry," she said.

It had been almost too easy, I thought, as I watched Dryden sitting in the dirt beside my dead body. She had slid into my life as if she had grown there. She fell in love; with the pigs, the dog, the cabbages and corn, the dirt, the oily chunks of metal in the repair shop, and her own sweating muscles, and like most people whose love finds a happy return, she was impervious to minor irritations.

Even when she went to the university, she did not really leave. She lived with a hermit-like detachment in a rented room during the week and came back to the farm every weekend, quick to tend animals, take apart lawnmowers, muck up her boots. Her close ties were my ties, to Noah, and to Otis, the neighbor with whom I shared farming tasks and equipment. Her high school friends, the socially awkward handful of brass players who labored through marches and fight songs at ball games, had all moved away from Gilham as soon as they could.

Now, too late, I worried. Her muscles were fit, her hands were skilled, but her emotions, it seemed to me, were barely tried. Although she and her saxophone teacher had been drifting along for years, using their lessons as cover for coupling, I was baffled by the persistence of her interest in him. Once a small-time club musician, now a store clerk, Jonathan was a self-described Taoist who mistook inertia for serenity and outgassed a dispiriting cloud of boredom and disappointment. Fortunately, he showed no inclination to leave his marriage.

She's too young, I thought. Too young to have settled into such a meager habit. Too young not to want something more.

Chapter 2

I felt wracked by a shiver and briefly hoped I wasn't dead after all. I could see my body, though, and it had not moved. The spasm of chill was in Dryden.

Coyotes, she thought. "Fay wanted me to give her body to the coyotes."

Her gaze wandered to the pigs, their jaws smacking as they chewed, and I felt her recoil.

"Did she really want…?"

Her muscles tensed, resisting details. She looked away, toward the pale daylight at the open end of the shed.

"Fay always said she did. She liked wild critters."

Avoiding the pigs, Dryden's eyes stayed on the patch of wooded hillside just visible beyond my fields.

"Can't let people find her, though. They'd bring her back and put her in a casket. She'd hate that."

Her mind started running through fragments of maps—dirt roads, trails, untraveled forest.

"I'd better get moving. Daylight's short…"

Was she really going to take me into the woods?

I tried to protest, no, I didn't mean it, not for real! It was a dream, a tale from the book of Fay, the philosophy of life you reveal late in the evening after good wine. You can't actually do it. People will misunderstand.

She couldn't hear me. Her mind was on all those funerals when I came home grousing, "I'm too old for such a fuss. Just leave me for the scavengers."

She put my cap back on and gently lowered my head to the ground. When she stood, her legs prickled and she walked to free the circulation. Then she bent, put an arm around my shoulders, and lifted me into a sitting position. My head flopped sideways like a newborn's. Scollay whined and licked my face, but I couldn't feel it.

Dryden slid her other arm under my knees and gave a heave. Halfway up, a leg slithered loose. She staggered forward and my body landed on the ground with a thump. She was a big strong woman, but not strong enough.

She frowned, contemplating the obstacle. *Could somebody help me? Noah...?*

Along with the thought came an image of Noah in my kitchen, pouring cups of tea. He moved with birdlike bursts of energy, eager to provide small pleasures for people. Then, with a shock, I saw myself, too, in profile, the sharp ridge of my nose, the bristling white hair, the deep wrinkles around my smile as I took a cup from his hand.

This was outrageous! It was bad enough to be a miasma hovering in Dryden's vicinity, hearing her present thoughts. Now I was snooping into her memory, too. Just how far would it go, this business of being dead?

Dryden tried to picture Noah hoisting my body like a bag of grain and put the idea aside. He'd be miserable and he probably wouldn't be much help.

Her mind raced through other options. No snow for a sled yet, though it was supposed to storm that night. A four-wheeler would be too noisy. But she needed wheels somehow.

Her next words were spoken out loud. "I've got an idea, Fay. I hope you don't mind."

She jogged to the house and rummaged in a spare-room closet where she found a sleeping bag dating from my own youth, stiff green canvas with plaid wool lining. In the shed, she found tension straps, bungee cords, and a couple of boards. Finally, from the workshop, she collected our dolly. She proceeded to truss me up, wrapped in the sleeping bag, with the boards along my back for rigidity. When I was a manageable bundle, she rolled me onto the dolly and cinched me down with the tension straps.

Don't do this, Dryden, I said, over and over, but my words could not get through. She heard only my living words, still echoing in her ear. "I don't want to be toxic waste! I want to be food!"

Soon I was loaded onto the back of the truck and covered with a tarp.

Coming out of the driveway, she turned north. A moment later, she hit the brake.

"Noah..." she murmured.

She looked at her watch, debating. She hadn't much daylight to spare. Then she looked at Scollay, who was pressed against her, watching every move as if he feared a betrayal.

"Yeah, you're right," she said. "Anyway, I've got a headlamp."

When Noah opened the door to her, his smile instantly gave way to worry. Dryden looked dreadful, so dreadful that I wondered how I had failed to notice. Her eyes were sunk into hollows and her warm tan skin, bloodless, had turned dun-colored.

"Dryden, what's wrong?"

"It's Fay..."

Her throat constricted and she couldn't form the words. As Noah drew her indoors, she started to tremble.

When he finally understood her meaning, he put his arms around her and wept and I marveled at the ordinariness of it. If there was reason to cry, he cried, an act of clear emotional logic unthinkable in my family.

After a while, Dryden eased herself free.

"I can't stay," she said. "Fay wanted me to take her into the woods."

"I know. To feed the varmints."

He tried to smile but couldn't.

"She's out in the truck. In case you want to see her."

Noah hesitated. "I suppose I should. She hates it when people try to avoid reality. It wouldn't be enough, that I can imagine..."

A picture snapped into focus, our bed, his hands turning down the covers on his side while my side lay empty, untouched, with my clock on the side table and the book I'd been reading, *Beak of the Finch*, still bookmarked halfway.

His thoughts jerked away and he reached for his coat.

You don't have to do this! I shouted. You understand all you need to.

"I don't know," he murmured and paused from buttoning. "Maybe she wouldn't mind if I didn't look..."

Of course I wouldn't mind, I shouted. Don't be cruel to yourself for my sake!

He shook his head. "No, I'm rationalizing. She'd be annoyed."

He pulled his boots on and went out the door.

Damn! For a moment I thought I'd gotten through to him. What a ridiculous indignity, this infantile helplessness, people guessing you'd like a diaper change when you'd really like a cracker, guessing you'd like a nap when you'd really like the radio on.

As Noah approached the truck, I found myself braced, almost nervous. It wasn't that I had any beauty for death to steal. Almost from infancy, my face had looked as though the obstetrician had hauled too vigorously on the forceps and stretched every feature along the vertical axis—long nose, long jaw, long front teeth, high forehead, thick eyebrows, eyes set deep under a jutting brow, and hair that sprang upward from my scalp like a scrub brush, once dullish blonde, now dullish white. When I was alive, I hadn't minded the way I looked. How could I dislike my face when Noah liked it? It was a good sound Yankee face, suggestive of the prow of an icebreaker.

Still, if you want a full appreciation of your cosmetic defects, there's nothing like seeing yourself dead. Dryden had nestled my head in a pillow and closed my eyes, but that was as much as she could do. My muscles still sagged into slack folds; my mouth still hung open; my complexion had drained to a grayish pallor. By any standard except a hungry scavenger's, I looked a horror.

Seeing me, Noah let out a little cry. He stood still, gazing, adjusting himself to the reality. When he reached to stroke my cheek, the skin was dry and cool to the touch, like a snakeskin. My cheek felt nothing.

He kissed his fingertips and pressed them to my lips, then turned and gave Dryden a hug.

"I should go," Dryden said. "While I still have daylight."

Quick, Noah, it's our last chance! Tell her not to do this! Surely you can imagine the trouble it will be! Tell her it's a crazy idea. Say I was joking.

"It is what she wanted, isn't it?" he said slowly.

"It's what she always said to me."

"Yes, to me, too. But it feels so... peculiar..."

"Yeah, I know. But when did peculiar ever bother Fay?"

They both began to laugh, shakily, and that was the end of it. They had decided.

Dryden spread the tarp over me, weighted it down, and got into the truck. Noah returned to his stoop. As she drove out of the driveway, she could see him in the mirror, his hand lifted to wave good-bye.

Even in disaster, inevitability can be calming, and now that my folly was launched, I was open to more temperate reflections. If there was one small thing for which I felt thankful, it was Noah's serene lack of either interest in, or competence with, inanimate objects.

Many people, seeing someone with a heavy load and a dolly, would be prompted to ask if more help was needed. In Noah's case, it never entered his head to consider how much my body weighed or what was a reasonable load for a human to carry. It was the sort of job that Dryden and I had always handled, without troubling him.

His mind was tuned to the beauties of abstract reasoning and the nuances of human interaction. His body was delicate and rather clumsy. In the 1800s, he would have been the tubercular poet who eked out a living as a tutor to a clutch of beefy aristocrats. In the present century, he was a high school teacher.

He taught physics and mathematics, the subjects that most nearly approximated the disembodied life of the mind. Governed by a gently immoveable atheism, he assumed that somewhere in the depths of every human lay the beautiful mathematical logic of physical laws and he treated people accordingly, as if they could be expected to be reasonable. Unlike Dryden, he would find no solace in the exertion of wrestling with my carcass. For him the task would be punishment and I wanted to thank someone, although I didn't know who, that he'd been spared.

Dryden drove for more than an hour to an old logging road in a remote area we'd once explored, unintentionally, after taking a wrong turn on the way to look at a log splitter for sale. When the logging road ended in a small clearing, she parked, unloaded the dolly, took a compass heading, and set off through the woods. Scollay followed close at her heels. The ground was still bare but the sky had a leaden look that promised snow.

Her progress was slow and exhausting. She needed all her strength to muscle the dolly around or over the rocks and fallen trees. She dragged me for most of another hour before looking for a place to leave me. When she spotted an ancient hemlock, gnarly and twisted, she stopped. Her shirt was soaked in sweat and her muscles were shaking.

The light was beginning to fade and a few flakes of snow were falling. Scollay circled her, whining. She quickly scratched together a pile of dead leaves and needles to make a nest at the base of the hemlock. Then she rolled me off the dolly, slid me out of the sleeping bag, and laid me in the nest with my head resting in a hollow between two roots.

Looking at me laid out in coveralls, she shook her head. I looked ready for a funeral parlor, and nothing like food. She thought my clothes should be off, but the thought of removing them made her shrink.

Don't bother, I said. The scavengers will take care of me, regardless. It's getting dark.

Suddenly, like someone diving into cold water, she knelt, pulled my boots off and started unfastening my clothes. When I was naked, she stuffed the clothes into the sleeping bag and strapped it onto the dolly.

My body was laid out neatly, arms at my sides, and there was nothing more to be done, but still she lingered, wanting to make some gesture. The snow was beginning to fall more thickly. Finally she knelt, took one of my hands in hers and lightly squeezed my chilled palm. Then, instead of returning my arm to lie with military neatness along my side, she curved it to rest casually across my torso.

"That's the best I can do, Fay," she said. "I hope you're happy, wherever you are."

She grabbed the dolly and set off at a jog through the woods. When Scollay realized I wasn't with her, he ran back, anxiously. She called to him to come but he stayed near me, trying to make us all stay together in one place. He and Dryden stared at each other, testing wills, until finally she came back.

Until this moment, she'd simply felt numb, but now, as she bent to loop a bungee cord through his collar, to pull him away from me, tears streamed from her eyes and her body shook with sobs.

"I'm sorry, fella," she said.

Chapter 3

On the way home, the new snow was falling so thickly she could barely make out the edges of the pavement. She kept her speed at a steady twenty-five and turned on the radio to counter the mesmerizing effect of the whirling flakes. Beside her, Scollay finally relaxed and went to sleep.

When she drove into the farm, I felt a shock of strangeness. My place had never been dark, not like this. Winters were too long and cold to be fought with self-denial; it made you mean. Darkness was fine outdoors; but I liked my house warm and bright.

With the truck headlights off, there was no light anywhere. The moon and stars were hidden by the cloudbank overhead. All sound was muffled by the falling snow. Dryden shivered and felt in her pocket for the headlamp.

She crossed the yard and went into the barn, switching on lights as she went. She dumped feed into the trough for the young pigs, filled their water and went into the chicken coop to collect the eggs. She had hoped the lights and the animals would make the place feel alive again, but they only reminded her I wasn't there.

In the house, Scollay rushed from room to room, whining, and then rushed back to where she was, in the kitchen. She knelt and hugged him, letting him lick her face. His whining was the only sound. The rooms beyond the kitchen were dark and the air smelled of emptiness when it should have smelled of food.

Suddenly, any kind of decision felt like a lot of work. For hours she had been running on adrenaline, occupied by physical tasks. Even dead, I had been there as an awkward object she had to deal with. Now, I wasn't there and time stretched away into vacancy. She had no task to occupy her except her own dinner, which did not seem important. She tried turning on the radio, but the voice of a newscaster was worse than silence and she switched it off. Even the thought of calling Noah felt more like pain than consolation.

Although she had not eaten since breakfast, she felt no hunger for food. The appetite she did begin to feel, with growing urgency, was for another human body, anyone's body, naked skin against hers, warmth surrounding her, weight on top of her, fullness inside her, and above all else, the forgetfulness of sexual arousal.

I'd have put my head into a bag, if I could. Did I really have to witness every single thing in her mind?

Dryden, too, recoiled.

"I shouldn't be thinking about that. I shouldn't want it. It's too weird..."

But she did want it, overwhelmingly. The more she tried to push the sexual thoughts away, the more they pressed at her, a positive onslaught of hot swellings.

She picked up the phone. It was crazy, she knew. The roads were treacherous and Jonathan's wife would be there. But she couldn't think about anything else.

"I need to see you," she said, the moment his wife gave him the phone.

"What do you mean? When?"

His tone was cold, but she ignored it and rushed onward, pleading with him.

"Right now. Please, Jonathan. I've never asked you for anything, but I really need this. Can't you meet me at the practice room? You only have to go a few blocks. You have four-wheel-drive. You'll be fine."

"OK, calm down, I'll come," he said.

Perhaps he really cared about her, but I wouldn't have bet on it. More likely, her unthinking implication that he was helpless had pricked his pride.

Although she had to drive several miles, Dryden reached the store first and was waiting in the shelter of the door overhang when he arrived. He let her into the building and followed her upstairs to the practice room, where he locked the door and switched on a recording of solo saxophone.

"I don't have much time," he said. "I told Gloria you were stuck and needed a ride."

Dryden's flinch was too subtle for him to notice. She'd intended to tell him about my death, but now she drew inward. Without saying anything, she began to take off his clothes.

"I thought you understood how things are," he said. "With Gloria, I mean."

"I do."

She unbuckled his belt and opened his zipper.

"I can't ever leave her. She'd be devastated."

"I know."

She shoved his pants down and took his penis into her mouth, speed dialing him to an erection. When he was hard enough to be operative, she shifted him to lie on the couch and fitted herself onto him. She accomplished this maneuver with such workmanlike briskness, I found myself thinking about Otis, attaching milking machines to a long line of udders, or Dryden herself, clicking together the hydraulic hose couplings on the tractor.

I wished I could stay there, in the far-off memory of barn chores. The last place I wanted to be was in this room with Dryden, looking down at Jonathan's bony chest and wispy gray goatee, smelling his stale sweat and a hint of cabbage on his breath from dinner.

Please, god, let me be somewhere else. I've never been much on prayer, but I'm praying now. If I have to look through someone's eyes, let it be someone else's eyes. Not Dryden's. Not right now. Spare me this, I'm begging you.

And yes, it turns out, sometimes prayers do get answered.

It was the first time I'd uttered a prayer of that kind, abandoning myself to a desperate wishfulness unhedged by skepticism. It was the last time I would utter a prayer of any kind without first making a careful analysis of what I was asking.

In my mind, I spoke the words, with fervor. The next thing I knew, I felt the heat of sexual craving turn inside out, like a sock, propelling itself outward. I felt pelvic muscles thrusting upward into the weight on top of them. Jonathan's beard vanished from my sight and I was plunged into an eyes-closed fantasy of melon breasts and pillowy buttocks, floating like seraphim around a centerpiece of phallic athleticism.

No! I bellowed. *Jesus Christ! No! No! No! Not this! Get me out of this!*

Jonathan jerked up onto his elbows and his penis popped loose.

"What the fuck!" he said. "What's wrong with you? What do you mean,

No?"

For an instant, the whole universe seemed to pause. Dryden gaped, I gaped, Jonathan waited for an explanation. Even the saxophone on the CD player seemed to take a breath.

"What?" she said.

"Why did you keep saying 'No,' just then? Did something hurt?"

She shook her head, mystified. "I didn't say no. I didn't say anything at all."

"But I heard you."

He slid out from under her and switched off the CD. "Do you think somebody's here?"

"It's snowing. The store's closed. Who would be here?"

"I don't know. Someone could have seen our cars."

Chilled by worry, his penis had drained to half-mast.

"I parked three blocks away," she said. "I knew you'd be worried."

She switched the CD back on and he let himself be led back to the couch. His mind got busy with the breasts and buttocks, some scanty undergarments, and two muscular bodyguards, and before long his erection was serviceable again.

My mind, meanwhile, was transfixed by the prospect of an indefinite future in the company of Jonathan Drummond. Please, if it should be the will of the inquisitor, might I be granted the liberty to die?

Jonathan was not much happier than I was. The residue of worry created gaps in his fantasies and allowed distracting thoughts to slip in. He remembered a dental appointment the next day, and then, much worse, the look of skepticism on Gloria's face as he headed out the door tonight. He felt his arousal start to slacken and opened his eyes to obliterate the image of his wife. Seeing Dryden, he winced. Had he ever thought that strong-boned face was pretty?

He clamped his eyes shut again. His mind seized the breasts and the bodyguards in a death grip, piling on inviting postures, bigger organs, rounder bulges, anything to keep at bay the thought of his wife and the dread that his arousal might dribble away.

If there was ever a thought that would become the deed, it was the thought that one's arousal might fail. However tightly he clung to other thoughts, he felt his blood seeping backwards, back into his chilling core, until finally his penis slithered out of Dryden and hung limp between her thighs.

"It doesn't matter," she said. Her hand stroked his back. "This is what I needed, more than anything."

He barely heard her. He was thinking about his own life, which at this moment looked like a lurching series of failures and retreats, leading with inexorable logic to this, that even his adulterous trysts had become a timid mule-track routine and he couldn't function outside of it.

His past was laid out in front of me, in fragments of memory that felt as real as if I had lived them myself. The years of second-rate nightclub gigs that he hoped would lead to a big break but never did. Mornings on the road, waking up next to whatever woman had been willing in the bar the night before. Gloria's methodical rise into management and prosperity. His own slow slide into resignation, as bookings dropped away and his days were spent tending a cash register or teaching lackadaisical kids who made the same mistake eight times running and didn't care.

But Dryden did care, passionately, and from the first moment, she had been a hit of joy. She craved challenge and every word he said to her came back to him transformed into music. When they played together, he could forget reality and lose himself in his old dreams.

He began to imagine the same connection for their bodies, an ecstatic union altogether different from the women in bars. At their lessons, he found occasions to slide his arm around her, to massage her shoulders and stroke her hair and tell her how pretty she was. She did not seem to notice these gestures, though, and he was puzzled how to take the next step. He could not shrug off a refusal the way he could in a bar.

His answer came by chance, one day when she had just raced through a hard stretch of Gershwin. "Your technique is brilliant," he said and then added, seemingly as an afterthought, "The expressiveness will come when you've had more experience with lovers."

The next time they met, she had changed. When he stroked her hair, she leaned into his hand. When he hugged her goodbye, she pressed herself against his pelvis. She was bent on musical expressiveness, and if sex was what it took, then she wanted sex, posthaste.

Her eagerness caught him off guard; he had expected the wooing to take some time. He had imagined a romantic pursuit akin to the long exhilarating tightrope dance of musical improvisation, not the cymbal crash and bass drum thud of his usual encounters.

He tried to invent reasons to slow down, pleading lack of time, lack of condoms. Her impatience always had an answer. She'd brought some condoms. They could skip her lesson. Why work on technical skills if the result would be deadened by her virginity?

He couldn't bring himself to confess to his daydreams, but he did, hesitantly, suggest that a little romantic anticipation might heighten the experience and make it more musically relevant.

She looked at him with skepticism.

"It's just humping," she said. "Pigs can get it done in five minutes, if the sow's ready."

The seduction proceeded, but the event did not live up to his fantasies, which had been woven around maidenly reluctance yielding to manly insistence. He had not imagined them assuaging their appetite in couplings as routine as a fast food hamburger, so that they could have more time for music. But that, apparently, was what Dryden wanted.

Did I want to know all this? How much easier it had been to despise Jonathan without reservation. Now to wish him miserable felt too much like wanting to squash some pathetic little bug. I couldn't bring any enthusiasm to my contempt. He despised himself enough for both of us.

But Dryden, oh my beloved Dryden, why are you still here? Why, why, why?

Jonathan became aware that her hand had stopped stroking his back. He opened his eyes and saw that she was weeping. Oh, brother. Was she about to make a scene?

Her arms tightened around him and he stiffened. He had no time for emotional turmoil. Already he was approaching the limit that Gloria would accept as plausible for a ride home.

"I thought you understood how things are," he said. "You know I care about you, but I'm not free. Gloria would never recover…"

Her arms released their hold and he slid off her and stood up. As he put his clothing in order, she lay without moving, watching him.

When he bent to kiss her goodbye, his lips shaped themselves for affectionate familiarity and at first she responded in kind. Then, quite suddenly, she slid her hand behind his neck and put fifteen years of muscle conditioning on the saxophone into a slow, nakedly sexual, full-tongue penetration. She released him and relaxed back on the couch. Her face looked calm.

Jonathan's guardedness changed to relief. *She isn't going to make a scene*, he thought.

A moment ago, I'd have been glad to strangle him. Now hope bubbled up like laughter and I didn't care what became of him, good or ill. He was too wrapped up in his own worries to see beyond the obvious, but my leisure was infinite and I could recognize sarcasm when I met it, even in a kiss. Feeling the silent derision with which she had seized and released his mouth, I remembered the moment so many years ago when she had made similar use of her mother's irreproachably correct beige business suit.

Here's hope indeed, I thought.

And please, Dryden, keep me with you when he goes. Don't abandon me to a life inside this spineless, prevaricating sack of neediness. If anyone wonders what hell is really like, I can tell them, this is it, and whatever I've done to bring myself here, I repent.

The door closed behind him, and now it was I who felt relief. I was still here. Dryden still lay on the couch, before my eyes. Whatever evasion Jonathan was formulating as he drove home to his wife, I did not have to witness it. Thanks be.

On the way back to the farm, snow was still falling, but it didn't bother her. The streaks of whiteness flying at her windshield seemed to align themselves like flights of arrows, marking a path through the darkness. The speed of the streaks should have been a warning, but she was not in a mood to heed warnings. Her thoughts were fixed on a single purpose, the call she meant to make when she got home.

Gloria would answer, she was sure, and the rest would be simple. No, she did not need to speak with Jonathan, just tell him thanks for the music, thanks for the sex, time to move on.

God would that feel good!

She was drunk with pain, oblivious to consequences, but I was sober and filled with dismay. Not that way, Dryden. It's not worth it. If he lies to his wife, that's between them. Get on with your own life and forget him.

How reasonable I could be, now that I had no blood to carry fevered chemicals through my brain. But I couldn't make my wisdom audible.

Suddenly, our mailbox appeared through the whirl of snow and she put on the brake to turn into the farm. Only then did she realize how fast she was going. Her wheels turned left but everything else kept going straight and the truck went into a sweeping skid, which she corrected and re-corrected, carving desperation S-curves through the snow. When the truck finally stopped, it was still on the road, but had traveled a chastening distance past the driveway.

She sat shaking in reaction and then she began to laugh. "What a goddamned lucky idiot I am," she murmured. She backed up, carefully, and drove into the farm.

In the kitchen, she added wood to the stove before picking up the phone. As she had anticipated, Gloria answered.

"Shall I get Jonathan?" she asked. "He's watching television in the other room."

"No, don't bother. Could you give him a message?"

"Of course."

"Tell him I think he's right, that I don't need any more lessons. I'm sure he'll have no trouble filling my slot."

"I'm sure he won't," Gloria said drily. "There are plenty of women in the world."

Her tone made her message obvious. She knew the truth and the knowledge was not as devastating as Jonathan had always suggested it would be.

Dryden sat still, digesting this understanding. To the extent that she had thought about her place in Jonathan's life, she thought of herself as a safety valve, an occasional secret thrill who wanted nothing more from him and hence was no threat to his marriage. It had not occurred to her that she might be neither a secret nor a thrill, merely one of many meaningless screws that his wife chose to overlook.

Before she could think what to say, Gloria spoke again.

"Dryden, there's something else. I've wanted to say this for years, but—"

She paused and Dryden braced herself for a blast of scorn.

"You're much better than Jonathan," Gloria said. "As a musician, I mean. You should play with people who will push you harder."

"You really think that?" Dryden was dumfounded. "But Jonathan never said..."

"I know he didn't. And it was wrong of him—" Gloria's voice stumbled. "He loved playing with you. So he let you mark time…"

She went on talking but Dryden had stopped listening. She remembered herself, years ago, hesitantly broaching the idea that she should branch out, maybe look for other people to jam with, maybe find a band and start playing some gigs. Jonathan had sighed, with an air of world-weariness.

"That life sucks the soul out of you," he said. "It kills off the reason you want to play."

"Then why do people do it?"

"Because they've been sold a fairy tale. Believe me, if you want to enjoy playing, don't go down that road. Just play for yourself and don't imagine other people want to hear you, or you'll wreck the music."

For a time, the disappointment had been crushing. Obviously, people liked listening to music. If he was warning her not to have hopes, he meant she wasn't good enough to play for other people. He was her teacher; he was as old as her parents; he said he loved her. If he thought she was not good enough, then she must not be. Taking him at his word, she abandoned the idea of moving beyond their small world of private pleasure.

Now I really did wish I had hands to do him bodily harm. It was an ancient story that someone aging and jaded should lust after youth and freshness. It was an equally ancient story that someone young and uncertain should lust after experience and skill. I could, almost, forgive Jonathan that he had succumbed to his sexual fascination. But for a teacher to become a drag on his student's superior talent was not forgivable. For that, he should be flayed to the bone, trussed up and hitched between wild horses, hauled over white-hot shards of steel, smothered in clammy wet cement and sunk to the bottommost circle of hell.

Except that I would have to be sunk there with him.

When had I ever said to Dryden, "You play beautifully; maybe you should widen your horizons beyond Jonathan?"

I had thought it often enough, but I had stayed silent. I had told myself I was leaving her free to make her own choices.

Leaving her free, hah! The truth was, I didn't want her to leave.

Dryden was shaking her head like a stunned creature. "Why didn't anybody ever say anything?" she murmured.

When she put down the phone, she realized she was ravenously hungry. She rummaged in the refrigerator and found a container of leftover stew, which she wolfed down cold along with half a quart of apple cider.

She thought again about calling Noah, but couldn't do it, even though it was undoubtedly the decent thing. Her nerves felt battered and to say ten more words to a human being was a task beyond her strength. Instead, she unpacked her saxophone.

She began casually, noodling among fragments of Cole Porter tunes. As her fingers warmed up, she spun out more and more elaborate improvisations, weaving one tune into another, occasionally making a playful leap into a different style, an Irish jig or a Bach partita, then sliding smoothly back to her home base in jazz.

I was riveted. I'd heard her play, of course, many hundreds of times, and I knew she was good, but my knowledge had come to me through the medium of my own ears. I had no complaints about my ears. They'd been functional middle-of-the-road equipment, good enough that I could notice an off noise in the tractor engine and identify the more obvious bird calls. Useful as they were, however, they were not the ears of a musician.

Now I understood the difference. It was like putting on lenses to correct nearsightedness. Every detail snapped into focus, clearly, brilliantly, without effort. The slightest flatness of pitch or thinness of tone was gratingly apparent. Potential harmonies and modulations stood forth in bold face type. Melodic improvisations leapt to mind and hand, like collies leaping to their task. I was still the person listening, but the ears hearing and the hands and lips playing were hers and I felt myself swept along, as in a dream where one can fly.

Neither I nor Charlie and Anita had taught her this. We liked music, our ears were not tin, but this was different. This was an urge and an understanding that ran in the blood. Surely it was an inborn gift from one of her birth parents, whoever they might be.

Did our incomprehension ever make her think about those other parents? Did she wonder, as I was wondering now, if they had played? What instrument? Or did they sing? Or had their gift been crimped by circumstance and never grown beyond a tune dreamed in the mind?

As long as I was alive, my experience and Dryden's had lain on opposite sides of an unbridgeable gap. I could neither hear what she heard nor imagine what she imagined.

Now, at last, I had crossed the gap. I knew what it felt like to fly and I understood how, having once flown, she would never want to stop. For the first time since my death, I wanted to kneel down and give thanks that I had not slipped off into oblivion, that I was still right here, awake and on earth, feeling music flow from thought to breath and fingers, through air to ears and back again to thought, in a quicksilver current of power and joy. Whatever else I might yet suffer in the way of remorse, frustration or grief, it would be worth it, just for this hour.

Chapter 4

Halfway through a phrase, the music was cut short. I heard the sound of my own name, spoken in tones of mockery.

"If this new project goes the way of the others, maybe Aunt Fay will hire you to run the pig farm."

In place of my living room, I saw the turquoise water of a swimming pool, lit by underwater lights. Beside the pool, my nephew Spenser lounged in a deck chair, holding a cocktail.

"Dryden seems to like it there," he added. "Maybe you would, too."

I felt muscles clench. For an instant I saw an image of myself, in green coveralls, even homelier than the reality. The image vanished and I felt sweat trickling from armpits across a ribcage. Sidney, it would seem. His sweat came from nerves, not heat. Even in Arizona, the evenings were cool and he was wearing a light jacket.

"It's not my fault the sales are slow," Sidney said. "People need time to adjust."

"Of course they do," said his brother. "On your projects, people always need time."

Anita slid into the chair between her sons.

"Sidney's had some setbacks, that's all. He'll hit his stride soon enough."

Spenser guffawed. "His stride isn't the problem. He just has a knack for catastrophe. I mean, look at what he did with our plastic clogs way back when. He decides the logical customer is an old lady who can't bend down and doesn't care how she looks. So he names them Ortho-clogs and starts hammering on old ladies to buy this logical footwear for their ugly feet. As if shoppers are logical. Thanks to him, our plastic shoe sinks without a trace and Croc grabs the market, selling to all the people who want to save two seconds putting on their shoes. Which is just about everybody except the little old ladies."

"Don't be so negative, Spenser. He was barely out of college. And I seem to recall you lost your first election."

"I won my second one."

"Not everyone can be as quick out of the gate as you were, Mr. Congressman."

She smiled fondly. Spenser leaned back and spread his arms, projecting magnanimity.

"I'm sure you're right," he said. "Sidney will make his mark."

Then he grinned and added, "Even if it's on the pig farm."

Anita's smile faded. "Seriously, Spense, you should watch that tone. It could kill you with the public. Voters don't like sourness."

"Except in New England," Charlie murmured, but I was the only one who heard him.

Easy for Spenser to be upbeat, Sidney was thinking. Spenser's whole life is perfect. Through the screen door came the sound of electronic pings and explosions, Spenser's two clever children engaged in video combat. Spenser's wife, slender and pretty, was sitting at his elbow, sipping a glass of wine and remaining becomingly quiet.

Sidney's own wife was an ex, departed before children were in question, and since remarried to a bariatric surgeon in Santa Barbara.

"Why is it always me who's the disappointment?" he said. "Dryden's done squat but nobody says a word about that. Poor dear, she's adopted, she's unfortunate, can't expect her to do much…"

As he was speaking, the screen door slid open and Anita's maid stepped through, carrying a tray of hors d'oeuvres.

"…and look at Aunt Fay," Sidney went on. "She's a mechanic for God's sake. Wish I could be so lucky, to do whatever-nothing job I feel like and have people keep their traps shut."

He took a gulp of his drink.

The maid had stopped midway between the door and pool deck. She stood awkwardly, holding the tray, waiting for someone to say something that would lead more naturally to an offer of stuffed mushrooms.

For a moment, everyone else was likewise suspended. Then Anita rose and took the tray, saying, "Thank you, Rosa, these look lovely."

The maid retreated to the house and Anita held out the tray to her husband, who was sitting off to one side, only peripherally part of the conversation.

"Charlie, why don't you have the first sample? It's your evening, after all."

Charlie's evening. Until this moment, it had slipped my mind that tomorrow was his birthday. My mind did quick math. It was 1999, so he would be 69 years old. Back in my kitchen, beside the telephone, a card was waiting for a message and a stamp. I had chosen it from the supply I kept in a desk drawer and intermittently remembered to send.

So this family gathering was for him.

Charlie took a mushroom and Anita moved on to offer them to the others.

Taking a small bite, Spenser's wife sighed and said, "This is delicious. I don't know how you do it, Anita." Her phrasing, ever tactful, bestowed credit on Anita whether she had invented the recipe or merely hired the cook.

Others echoed her enthusiasm and the conversation ambled on to the subject of favorite finger foods. When Rosa appeared with another tray, Anita remained seated and allowed her to pass it around.

In the midst of conversation, Sidney remained silent, brooding on familial injustice and his sister's blissful escape from expectations. Gradually, though, the minced shrimp, butter and bacon began to have an effect on his system. His thoughts left Dryden and my farm behind and moved in a happier direction, toward the prospect of dinner.

When the maid announced that the meal was ready, he stood up to go indoors and the last thread that held me there parted.

I found myself untethered, floating in darkness. Although I was still awake and seemingly had lost the ability to sleep, I saw and heard nothing. For the moment, no other eyes and ears replaced my own. I simply floated, in blind silence, feeling a small regret that the birthday card was still lying on my desk and Charlie would never know I had meant to send it.

Then, slowly, shapes began to emerge from the darkness. Around me were trees, thick masses of evergreen and forked black silhouettes of leafless hardwoods. Overhead, the clouds were breaking up, swept eastward by a fair-weather wind. Now and then, the crescent moon appeared in a gap and a ripple of light passed across the new snow.

For a long time, nothing moved except the shadows and the branches of the trees. Then, against one of the black tree trunks I saw an undulating slither of motion. A fisher cat.

Her sinuous weasel shape darted down the trunk and paused, just above the ground, with head cocked to assess the scent of my dead body. She dropped to the snow and crept closer, pausing again to sniff, poised for flight. She investigated my feet and apparently found their chill rigidity reassuring. She proceeded along the length of me, poking here and there, until she reached my face. Choosing the softest skin, she settled in to eat.

After the fisher left, all was quiet. The work of her teeth had released the scent of blood, to be carried on the air, but for tonight no other creature had caught the signal.

Thank goodness.

By herself, the fisher cat would do no harm. My body was many times greater than her appetite. But there were other creatures, larger ones, who were strong enough to pull my joints apart and carry chunks away to be cached. I could remember coming upon a coyote's deer kill, new since the previous day and already a scattering of oddments, a leg or two, the head, a few ribs and vertebrae, lying in a trampled patch of bloodstained snow. I was no larger than a deer; I could easily be taken apart and carried off.

This was what I had thought I wanted, to be devoured and scattered to feed the soil that had fed me, but now my philosophy yielded to reality. The modern world was not governed by soil and weather and coyotes. The world was governed by pieces of paper that people must type and sign and put into files. I had a bad feeling that Dryden would need such a piece of paper, and in order to get it, she would need my body, still identifiable, to show that I was really dead and that no, she had not split my skull with an axe.

Chapter 5

When morning came, Dryden set about doing the farm chores as if nothing more needed to be done about my death. There were people who would expect to be informed, Charlie and Anita, for instance, but she did not call them. Nor did she call Otis, whose concerns were more immediate. He and I had been trading farm help and machinery for more than thirty years, and while he might or might not feel tender sentiments about my death, he did need to know if he could still use our tractor.

Dryden was not stupid. She knew people would have to be told, eventually. She just wasn't ready to talk to people who felt less than she did and that included almost everyone except Noah.

People were busy with their own lives. My death was an incidental detail. If Dryden had needed any reminder of this reality, she had gotten it from Jonathan, who had never paused to wonder why she had made such an uncharacteristic plea for his help. For her to make polite acknowledgment of casually polite condolences would grate on nerves already raw. There was more comfort to be found in feeding the pigs.

When she had finished the barn chores, she attached the plow to the truck, cleared the snow out of the driveway, and then drove to Noah's house. As she was clearing his dooryard, he came to the stoop and waved for her to come inside when she was done.

They greeted each other with a wordless hug. Noah looked as if he had not slept at all. His eyes were sunken, with purplish shadows under them. The age lines in his face, usually very faint, had grown deep and distinct.

He poured two cups of coffee and mixed some scrambled eggs. He knew she wouldn't have eaten breakfast until after the chores were done.

"Have you called Charlie and Anita?" Noah asked.

Dryden winced and shook her head.

"Would you like me to do it?"

Noah's tone was gentle but definite. Being older, he was more aware of the price one could pay for offending people.

Dryden shook her head again. "No, I'll get to it."

"They'd be hurt, not to be told," Noah said.

How like Noah, to put it kindly rather than accurately. The truth was, only Charlie would be hurt. Anita would be furious and possibly spiteful.

I'd always wondered, did Noah really think that way or did he filter his thoughts so that only what was generous made it into speech? I'd rarely heard a barbed remark come out of his mouth. Faced with appalling behavior, he voiced only a baffled dismay that human beings should fall so short of our potential.

Noah was gazing at the family photos on the sideboard. One particular photo jumped out at me, a shot of Charlie, Anita and the three children in front of their house. Dryden was about four years old and looked like an intruder, her straight black hair and dark skin anomalous in the midst of pink curly blondness. She hovered at one edge of the group, holding Charlie's pant leg. On the other side of Charlie, Anita stood with her arms on the shoulders of the two boys.

"More fool them, that they let go of you," Noah said suddenly. "But I'm glad they did. Losers weepers, finders keepers."

"I don't think there was much weeping," Dryden said.

They began to eat, though neither seemed to have much appetite. Even the table was a reminder of my absence. Like everything in Noah's house, it was small and it was pushed against the wall to save space, leaving room for just three chairs. Their eyes avoided the one that had been mine.

After a few bites, Noah gave up and put down his fork.

"I feel like the guts are gone," he said. "I was always so lost in ideas… the math, the poetry… And then I met Fay, and it was as if the ideas came to life and had color and texture. Everything I found, I wanted to rush and show her, to make it more real. I had to hold myself back sometimes. I was so afraid I'd spoil things by grabbing on too much. I always wanted us to live in the same house, but I never pushed her about it. She had to have some distance…"

What?! I yelped. That was you as much as me! You always said we should keep our own houses. You said you didn't want to make the neighbors uncomfortable!

"It was a darned nuisance," Noah said. "This place has mice and ants and dry rot, and I'm hopeless at fixing things. But it was worth it. I'd have done whatever it took to keep her. I'd have raised goats and worn a kilt, if that was what kept us loving each other."

My nonexistent jaw had dropped to my collarbones and I started laughing. You canny, calculating little fox! My whole life you had me believing the devil himself couldn't sweet-talk you out of your own house.

Dryden was quiet for a while, turning the saltshaker in her fingers, studying it as if it held the answer to a mystery.

"Is that what it's like, then…? To love a person…?" she murmured.

Noah waved aside the idea that he was any kind of pattern.

"That was just me," he said. "Who knows what it's like for other people? I don't think you can say, until you're in the middle of it."

There's no instruction manual, I thought.

"So don't expect an instruction manual?" she said.

I jumped as if I'd been bitten. Was it coincidence? Was it years of familiarity, molding our thinking along the same lines?

Or had my thought become hers?

All this time, I'd been fuming at my inability to make myself heard. Now, when I wasn't even trying to be heard, when I was idly musing, she had spoken my thought aloud. This could be worse than anything. If my thoughts could float into other people's minds like dandelion seeds, I'd have to be careful what I let myself think.

And what if only a fragment of an idea came through? What if I thought to myself, "Dryden, don't marry him, he's a prize jerk," and she heard a voice, seemingly from the heavens, say, "Marry him, he's a prize?"

"But how did you know?" Dryden asked. "About Fay, I mean."

"Know what?"

"How you felt…that you loved her…" She was stumbling. "Did you know early on…?"

Was Dryden really asking these questions? If I'd had breath, I'd have been holding it, waiting to hear where the conversation would lead. For her to start talking about love was a sea change. She could talk freely about sex, but love was a word she had avoided as carefully as my Bostonian relatives avoided the word money.

Was it possible that the first small crack was opening up?

Chapter 6

If Noah answered with a useful insight, I didn't hear it. Without my having the slightest power to object, I was yanked away from Dryden and Noah and into the company of someone who was forcefully demanding my presence.

"Where the hell are you, Fay?" Otis bellowed, tramping manure-scented snow into my kitchen.

I'd been wincing at this habit for thirty odd years, but there was no getting him to remember to take off his barn boots. His own wood floors were worn to ripples by use and so thoroughly impregnated with boot drippings, he had little to gain by fastidiousness now.

Finding only silence and no dog in the kitchen, he rushed off to the barn, still shouting for my attention.

"Goddamn it, where's the truck? You said you'd be over to plow..."

Damn. Until this moment, I'd completely forgotten. He'd called me yesterday morning to say there was snow in the forecast and the hydraulic pump on his plow truck had blown a seal. I'd told him we'd plow him out, but I hadn't told Dryden, because I'd figured on doing it myself.

After grumbling his way through my barns and sheds, Otis concluded I'd gone to Noah's and headed back to his other truck, the "good" one, which was only eight years old and did not have a plow hookup. When he drove into Noah's yard and saw our truck there, parked and idle, he was ready to bite my head off. He bounced out of his rig, made a couple of heraldic bangs on the door, and without pausing for an answer came charging into the house.

"Where the hell is Fay?" he said. "She said she was going to plow my place."

Otis had never been a patient man and he was the reason Noah and I had developed the habit of locking the door if we intended to linger in bed past seven o'clock.

Dryden stared at him mutely. She was still sitting at the table with Noah, and seemingly couldn't make herself speak the answer to his question.

"I'm afraid Fay died," Noah said finally.

His voice caught on the word, and suddenly Dryden burst out, "And take off your boots, could you! This is Noah's house."

It took a lot to deflect Otis, once he had a head of steam, but that did it. He stood a moment, looking down at the ooze of brownish snowmelt spreading from his boot soles. At first, the matter of his boots was the only thing he could take in. He bent down and took them off, revealing two wide bunioned feet in rag wool socks.

"But how'd she—? Was it in the paper? I didn't see nothing."

"It wasn't anything that would be in the paper," Dryden said.

She assumed he meant a newsworthy accident. She was still well short of the age that automatically scans the obituaries, looking for familiar names, or failing that, rare diseases or complicated familial relationships.

"Everybody's in the paper," Otis said.

"It was a stroke, probably," Noah said, answering the original question.

Noah poured a cup of coffee and handed it to Otis, who accepted it without seeming to register what it was. He wrapped his hands around its warmth but didn't drink.

"Sit down, if you'd like," Noah said.

Otis hesitated, staring at the empty chair. Without saying anything, Dryden shifted to the chair I'd always used and gestured to Otis to take hers. He sat down, gingerly, as if Dryden's chair, too, might hold some lingering shadow of my presence.

"Is she over to the other house, then?" he asked.

"No, she's been—" Noah began.

He stopped abruptly. It seemed the question had finally alerted him to a problem I'd been trying to call to his attention for hours, that some people in official positions might have an interest in my corpse. Otis could not be relied on for discretion, if there was a story to be told.

"Had to go into the hospital, did she?" Otis persisted.

"No, she was at the farm."

"Well, that's something anyhow." He pondered his untouched cup. "You having the Nesby's do the funeral?"

"I don't know yet. I haven't thought."

"If you want, I got some boards I could knock together into a casket."

"We won't need a casket," Dryden said. "I took her out—"

Noah cut her off. "I've heard people say that Nesby's are good," he said.

"You could ask Joe Fiske about it," Otis said. "They did his dad last spring. I know some folks drive over to Shepping to use Corwin's, like it's a sign of respect to pay more money, but I can't see how making the undertaker rich is a sign of respect. More likely it's guilt money, trying to make up for what you didn't do before they died. Like it was with Ned Wilkie. Kids leave him alone in his house, living on doughnuts and peeing all over the furniture whenever his insulin got out of whack, but you never saw so many damned flowers at a funeral..."

Otis could go for days without talking to anybody, but once he got rolling, he was liable to keep rolling until something stopped him. He had quite a lot to say about the cost of funerals before Dryden finally burst out, "What does it matter who's cheapest? Fay's already had the funeral she wanted. She doesn't want some ghoul putting makeup on her."

"You already had the funeral?" Otis said. "But how—? You never told me or I'da come."

"It wasn't that kind of funeral, Otis. There wasn't anybody there except me. I took her out into the woods for the coyotes and ravens. It's what she asked me to do."

"You dumped her in the woods? Holy..." He gaped at her. "So where'd you put her? Right out back here?"

"I'm not telling you where," she said. "You'd probably shoot one of the coyotes."

"No, I wouldn't, not if Fay wanted them to—"

He stopped. He wasn't squeamish, but this wasn't a line of thought he wanted to pursue. Instead he said, "So the docs thought it was a stroke, did they?"

"The docs never made it," she said. "Fay was already dead when I found her."

"Oh." Otis paused. "But what about after? You musta had somebody come take a look, to say she's dead."

"Her body's cold and I need a doctor to tell me she's dead?"

"But you gotta get a certificate or something. I think you better bring her back and have somebody look at her, or you could be up to your neck in shit."

"I'm not bringing her back. They'll put her in a fridge and pump her full of chemicals. Why should they care whether it was a stroke or a heart attack? It's nobody else's business."

"Everything's somebody's business nowadays. And you always gotta have the right piece of paper."

"Especially in the outhouse," Dryden muttered.

"Do you think you could find her again... if we needed to?" Noah asked mildly.

"Of course I could," Dryden said. "But I won't."

There was a silence until finally Otis stirred himself and said he'd best go take Fay's truck and get his plowing done.

In the doorway, he paused, shuffling his feet. He thanked Noah for the coffee. He said Dryden would find the keys in the ignition of his truck, as if that wasn't obvious. He said if he could do anything, they should say so. After that he was silent, neither staying nor going, hovering in the doorway with the cold air pouring in.

Finally, in a rush, he said, "I'm awful sorry about Fay," and ducked out the door.

At my truck, he paused and ran his hand along the weathered boards of the bed. When the original metal bed rusted out, he and Dryden and I had built a new bed out of lumber, with low stake sides and quantities of eyebolts for attaching ropes. At the time, he had teased me about the eyebolts, saying it was just like a woman to want everything good and tied down. More than once after that, though, I'd caught him telling someone it was smart to have plenty of places for attaching ropes to your truck.

His finger traced slow circles around one of the eyebolts.

"It's no wonder the kid's so goddamned stubborn..." he was thinking. "She's been watching you all these years..."

Instead of scarred gray boards, I saw raw blond lumber and smelled the tang of fresh sawdust. Someone sunburned and bony was drilling holes in the new boards. Me, I realized, not so many years ago. Dryden was beside me, screwing the eyebolts into the holes.

"You planning on hauling an elephant?" Otis asked. "How many more of them tie-downs you gonna screw onto this thing?"

I looked up from the drill and grinned. "Can't ever have too many tie-downs or too much screwing, either one."

Had I really said that? Dryden was laughing as if I had.

"You got that half right, anyhow," he said.

Then he pointed at the boards behind the truck cab, where Dryden had painted a cartoon bull's head snorting steam from its nostrils, over the words, "Don't nobody mess with Bruno."

"You really call this thing Bruno?" he asked me.

"Yup. Or Old Bones, sometimes."

"If she starts calling it Brunhilde, look out," Dryden said. "She's really mad."

Otis shook his head. "Women! If I live to be a hundred, I'll never understand 'em."

"Women, nothing," I said. "It's just easier to talk to something if it has a name."

"Why would I talk to a truck?"

"To tell it what you want. How else is it supposed to know?"

"You two are downright crazy, you know that?"

"It's no wonder you're always in town buying parts," I said. "Maybe if you talked more, you'd save some money. That should please your skinflint soul."

Otis's eyes came into focus on the bull's head, now faded by the years. He ran his hand along the boards, feeling how time had smoothed their edges.

"How the hell we gonna get along without her?" he murmured. "Huh, Bruno?"

His diaphragm tightened painfully. He jerked open the door and climbed into the cab.

"Old fool. Get yourself out of here, before somebody sees you and starts fussing."

He was so bent on getting away, he forgot to lift the snowplow until he heard the grinding scrape of metal on gravel. He yanked the handle, distractedly, and raised the plow so high he nearly smashed the headlights.

"Christ, Otis, you're turning into an old woman." He lowered the plow a notch and let out a choked laugh. "And she'd kill you for saying that."

He turned the truck around and roared out onto the highway, heading for his farm.

"Goddamn you Fay. I thought we had a deal that I was goin' first."

Tears filled his eyes, blindingly. He felt his wheels bump onto the shoulder and slowed to a stop on the side of the road. He slumped forward and leaned on the steering wheel, not sobbing, not howling, just unable to stop the tears that oozed and oozed, like a seep hose, trickling down his cheeks.

A car drove past, then abruptly braked and pulled off the road in front of him. I knew the car. It was an old Ford sedan, plastered with bumper stickers about trusting Jesus. Its owner, Belinda Boyle, used a tube from a bike tire to tie the trunk lid down when she brought her lawnmower into my repair shop. She was a large, uncomplaining young woman, a nurse's aide whose Christianity was tangible. Even though she and her husband had no money to spare, she was forever baking cookies for town events and running errands for housebound neighbors.

She came over and peered into the truck. Otis wiped his sleeve across his face and rolled down the window.

"Are you all right?" she asked.

"I'm OK."

"You don't look OK. You look like you just lost your best friend."

He made a noise that was almost a guffaw.

"I guess I did, kind of."

"Somebody passed away?" she asked, with equal parts concern and curiosity.

"Fay Kirkwood. She had a stroke."

"Fay. Oh, my. I'm so sorry." After a moment of respectful silence, she added, "But at least we can be glad she's up in heaven with Jesus. She's one of the angels now."

No, on the contrary, I said, she's a cranky human being and she's still right here in Gilham with you and Otis.

Otis shook his head. "Can't see Fay as an angel, somehow," he muttered.

"Everybody is an angel, once they're in heaven. That's what happens. Because of Jesus."

"What if she ain't in heaven?"

"But she must be!" Belinda looked stricken.

For a moment, I heard a small, thin voice, whimpering in fear and shame. Then her mind flicked away and fixed on a memory of me loading her lawnmower into her car.

"Fay did accept Jesus, didn't she?" she cried. "She must have, somewhere in her heart. He'd have come to her, at the end."

"I dunno if he did," Otis said. "I wasn't there at the end."

"I'm sure he came to her. And he's so beautiful, nobody could turn away from him."

Her mind filled with the Sunday school image, a gentle bearded man with lambs nestled in his arms.

"She must have accepted him. Don't you think?"

Out of nowhere, I was engulfed by dread. I saw an elegant living room, with embroidered pillows on the couches and shelves of hand-crafted travel souvenirs. The people in the room stood motionless. Two children, mute with fright. A woman as neat and pretty as the pillows. Belinda herself, half child, half woman, disgusted by a body that bulged with fat. Faintly, from another part of the house, I heard the murmur of a man's voice and, at intervals, a sob.

"Your father caught her using my sewing box. She hadn't asked permission," the woman said.

The dread spilled over in tears. Belinda bolted down the hallway and pounded on the door.

"Daddy, stop! Please! Stop! She couldn't help it! She's too little—"

The door opened. Her father's gaze was quelling. "It's for her own good. You should know that. You've been bad often enough."

The door clicked shut and Belinda crept away.

For years she had been the one he took into his study to be disciplined. She couldn't have explained the dread she had felt, at the time and in memory. She wasn't spanked. Her father could say, truthfully, that he had never laid a hand on his children. He hadn't needed to.

She remembered how, after the door had closed, he would grow still and cool and instruct her to come and stand in front of his desk. From the shelf beside his chair, he would pick up a smooth leather baton, a British officer's swagger stick he had found in his travels. He would lean back in his chair and explain to her, calmly, how she had failed, how she had been weak, how she was unworthy of her family. As he talked, his fingers stroked the leather of the swagger stick. He said that in a cruder sort of family, she would feel the burn of that leather on her bare skin, but that he expected better of his children.

After the talk, he would simply act as if she did not exist. She never knew how long this invisibility would last. Usually it was a day or two, sometimes longer. When he did speak to her again, the remark would be offhand, perhaps a request to pass the salt. He said the discipline would make her a stronger person. It was proof he cared about her.

When she reached seventh grade, her body ballooned to two hundred pounds and his attention shifted to the younger ones. She was beyond redemption, he said.

Is there nothing I can do to trouble her father's sleep at night?

Payson Satterthwaite. I first encountered him twenty odd years ago as the signature on a form letter, inquiring if I was in need of financial advice. Although I never replied to his inquiry, I continued to receive solicitations.

He and his wife belonged to the fashionable set and lived in the high-rent corner of Gilham, adjacent to the resort town to the north. For their landscape work, they hired high school boys, but Payson always brought their lawn tractor to the shop himself, so that he could give me a long list of instructions as to its care. I didn't try to cut him off. I thought debating with him would only slow things down. I let him talk and occupied myself wondering what product kept every track of the comb still visible in his thinning black hair.

Now, too late, I wished my instincts had been as true as Dryden's. She loathed Payson's condescension and served it right back to him. Like an aikido master, she met his drive for control and deflected it onto his lawn tractor. When she was the one in the shop, she did exactly what he told her to do and his lawn tractor ran exactly as badly as his own ignorance dictated.

I, on the other hand, had chosen to tune out the human being and focus on the tractor, which was such a sweet machine I could not bring myself to treat it badly. I ignored what Payson said and did whatever was needed. To avoid discussion, I printed a non-itemized bill. Two entries. Parts. Labor. If he demanded more details, I would recite his list of instructions. The lie was not explicit. I never said I had followed the list. My goal was to sidestep trouble. I wanted to mind my own business and have him mind his. Our only point of connection was the tractor.

He had come to Gilham from Pennsylvania, apparently looking for a place small enough for his opinions to have an impact. Every year at town meeting, he stood up to speak about the work the town employees had failed to do and the ways they were wasting money. His political agenda was simple. Lower taxes. More spending on police and highways. Over the years, his efforts had transformed town meeting from an occasionally petty but generally amiable discussion of small items in the budget—too much on office supplies, too little on gravel, could we get by with a half-time music teacher—into a vitriolic and violently partisan shouting match.

In contrast to his political style, his private life was rather quiet. His house was handsome and well kept. His wife won prizes for needlework at the fair. He went to the Caribbean every March to go scuba diving. His children were known as polite and cooperative, no trouble to their teachers. When his son Curt ran his car into a tree at high speed, most of the town turned out for the funeral.

He tries not to remind people that Belinda is his daughter. The one time I mentioned that I had fixed her lawnmower, he embarked on a scornful recital of the ways she has let herself go. She married a nobody; she lives in a mobile home; she abandoned her parents' respectable brand of Christianity and took up with a crowd of Jesus people over in Leonardston who meet in a converted hardware store and talk about love.

"I'm going to pray for Fay Kirkwood," Belinda said to Otis. "Maybe Jesus can come to her, even after she's dead. He can do anything."

A car went by and she looked at her watch.

"Goodness, it's time for my hairdo," she said. "Do you happen to know about Fay's funeral, when it is?"

Uh-oh. Such an ordinary question, but not this time. Could I hope he'd dodge?

"I don't know as they're having a funeral," he said. "Fay wasn't much on preachers."

"But how can they not have a funeral? She has a soul. She needs our prayers. And besides, the whole town knew her. She was, like, the lawnmower lady..."

"Yup, I know, and if it were up to me I'd have the darned funeral, just to keep people from clacking about it, but it ain't up to me. Dryden and Noah are her family and if they want to feed her body to the coyotes, I can't see that it's anybody else's business."

Oh, no, Otis. I wish you hadn't said that. Belinda Boyle on her way to the beauty parlor. You'd just as well have driven through town with a bullhorn.

"Feed her to the coyotes?" Belinda gaped. "Did they really—? But that's awful!"

She was shaking her head in horror, but another part of her was gloating over the possession of news that would make her interesting to everyone she met. Most of the time she was not interesting at all. She made her way in the world by being obliging, generous, forever willing to put the needs of others ahead of her own. But today, for a few shining hours, she would be welcomed even if she did nothing to be useful. For today, everyone would want to hear what she had to say.

She drove to town as fast as she dared, but fast as she drove, her news gestated faster and by the time she reached the beauty parlor, she was bursting with it. She knew she should drop tantalizing hints and let the tale be teased out of her, but she was too hungry. Instead of holding back, she walked straight in and blurted out the facts.

"Fay Kirkwood died and instead of giving her a proper burial, they fed her body to animals."

Even as she spoke, she was conscious of squandering a prospective pleasure, like a child who crams a whole candy bar into her mouth and swallows it barely chewed.

As she had anticipated, all eyes turned to look at her, all ears wanted to hear what she said, but she had only a moment to revel in her importance before she was swept up in a chattering confusion of questions she couldn't answer and comments that ignored her.

"How'd Fay die? Did she go to the hospital? Who found her? Did the FAST squad come? What animals? Did they give her to the pigs? They'll eat anything, is what I hear. Who's going to get the farm? You think it'll get sold? Has her family come? Does Noah know? Are they going to bury what's left, after the animals get done? Is it part of some religion? Religion or not, it's disgusting. It's not disgusting, it's natural.

Strange idea of natural, getting eaten by animals. Whose idea was it, do you think? Had to be Dryden's, she's strange enough. And what about the lawnmower shop? Be a nuisance if we have to go to Leonardston. Who's gonna get Fay's money? I heard she's got quite a bit, from her family. I don't believe that. Why would she work on lawnmowers if she's rich? Who knows why rich people do what they do?"

All too quickly, Belinda had told them what she knew and the conversation progressed to speculation, very little of which concerned the state of my immortal soul. No one except Belinda was worried about my soul and her attempts to talk about it were swept aside by topics of more immediate interest, such as the possibility of a family quarrel over my money, the likelihood that my farm would get subdivided into house lots, and the question whether Dryden had broken the law when she disposed of my body. Since no one in the room had any certain knowledge about any of these topics, the conversation was lively.

In the middle of it, there was a change of shift, as one group of appointments departed and a new group settled into the chairs. By then, the story was barely recognizable. The animals had morphed from pigs to wolves and back to pigs again and the likely contents of my bank account had been increasing with each successive round of speculation. My sly coyotes were long gone from the tale and so too was Belinda's Christian concern for my spiritual welfare.

Such was the state of discussion when it was joined by Millicent Gray, a woman I found irritating even as a secondhand story from Noah. He had served on several committees with her and, as his gentle style put it, she "perhaps overestimated her importance a bit." My translation, based on more limited acquaintance, was that she was a sniffish gossip who did very little of the real work, but liked to think of her efforts as the small central gear without which the whole system would grind to a halt.

Initially, she showed only casual interest in my death. I was neither a social connection nor a client of her insurance agency and my acquaintance with her ex-husband would be a positive reason for disdain. Then someone remarked that Dryden might be in trouble for dumping my body and Millicent's attention focused sharply.

"So Dryden is involved," she said. "How very interesting."

The other women heard the tone of insinuation and turned in her direction.

"In what way is it interesting?" someone asked. "Do you know something about her?"

"No, no, not something in particular. What I meant was, the way she is."

I could feel that she was lying and her interest was very particular indeed. The mere mention of Dryden's name had sent bile pouring into her system.

But why? The two of them had no reason to know each other. Dryden did not join committees. Millicent did not use implements with small gas-powered engines. Although Harold Gray had once been our veterinarian, Millicent was not involved in his practice and they had divorced several years ago, when Dryden was still in college.

Millicent was staring at the row of hair dryers, barely aware of the stylist working on her hair or the other women in the salon, who were still talking about my death. Her thoughts were fixed on a memory of her own, from the time of her divorce.

She was at the town clerk's office. She was surrounded by a different cluster of women, all middle-aged, all furious at the husband who had abruptly closed his veterinary practice and moved across the state to live with someone else. The women assumed he had been lured away by younger and firmer flesh and, with sociable outrage, they lamented the male midlife crisis and the manipulative young females who took advantage of this period of vulnerability.

"Isn't that just like a man," they said, "to dump his wife and go off with some brainless bimbo with hot pants?"

Then, from outside this congenially indignant circle, a voice said, "Professor Hobbs is not a brainless bimbo."

The conversation halted. Everyone turned to look. Dryden was standing at the counter with the form for a dog license, waiting for the town clerk to be done talking.

Most of the group did not react. The name meant nothing to them. Millicent stayed very still. If she did not react, either, perhaps the moment would pass. Dryden was a peculiar kid. Maybe the others would take her remark as a random oddity.

The women's silence invited Dryden to join them and elaborate, but she did not respond. She had corrected a factual mistake about a professor she knew. Beyond that, the subject did not concern her.

The silence was broken by the postmistress Rosemary Dodson, who let out a squawk of amazement. "It's Agnes Hobbs he's gone off with? Well, that's a kick in the butt!"

"Who is Agnes Hobbs?" asked Dulcie Sullivan. "Do you know her?"

"I don't, but Larry met her a couple of years ago, on that BGH committee."

Rosemary's husband was a shy, soft-spoken dairy farmer who had become an activist against growth hormones.

"He said she's pretty memorable. Built like a bulldozer, but funnier than heck. She's a professor of animal science, been at the university for years." Rosemary shook her head in wonderment. "And here we've been thinking it was some pretty young thing."

There was an awkward pause and the women avoided looking at Millicent. Before long, though, the questions came tumbling out. How old was Agnes? Was she married? In what way was she like a bulldozer…?

Millicent longed to flee, but she could not bear to leave the field clear for her neighbors to pick over her life, as she knew they would. So she stayed and pretended to be as surprised as the others, pretended her husband had originated the fiction of the gorgeous young blonde, pretended to be as interested as they were in every detail Rosemary could dredge up about Agnes Hobbs.

Beneath the pretense, she was seething and the focus of her rage was Dryden. If that strange, thoughtless girl had just kept her mouth shut!

Now, from out of the chatter in the beauty salon, a phrase caught Millicent's ear. "There's a lot of money and Dryden's the nearest family…"

Family and money. The conclusion was obvious.

"Why would someone hide a body unless there was something wrong about the death?" she said.

The salon went silent. The women there knew me, knew Dryden and Noah, too, and the ordinariness of the acquaintance had kept them from considering a possibility as exotic as murder.

"Is it written down anywhere, this request Fay is supposed to have made?" Millicent went on. "As a religion, it's ridiculous, but as an excuse to get rid of a dead body, it's brilliant. If Dryden inherits the property, it would be awfully convenient that she and Noah were the only ones who saw the body."

Dulcie erupted in outrage. "That's nuts. I've known Noah for years. He taught all my kids. He'd no more be part of something like that than…"

Words failed her and she stopped.

"I don't think her religion is ridiculous," said Tempest Poole. "It's like energy, you know? We can't see it but it's, like, all around us, like auras, tree spirits, all that stuff."

Her hand made a circle in the air, pointing out the energy.

"Fay Kirkwood was hardly the type to beat drums and chant to the full moon," Millicent said. "Is there any evidence that she belonged to a hippie sect of that sort?"

Again the room was silenced. The others weren't yet ready to agree with her, but they were no longer sure they disagreed. Finally Lee Ann Saunders remarked that there was no knowing what I'd believed because I hadn't talked about it.

Having cut my hair for the last twenty years, Lee Ann knew as much or as little about me as most of my neighbors did, which is to say, whatever she could glean from general conversation. My lawnmower customers included some people, mostly new in town, who would tell me all about how they had been switched from Prozac to Paxil as they struggled to cope with the stress of their spouse's addiction to gambling, but I had never been inclined to reciprocate. Why would I tell people things about me that I didn't want to know about them?

"Maybe it wasn't religion," someone joked. "Maybe she didn't want to pay for a funeral."

"Yeah, her clothes were, like, ratty," said Tempest.

"No sense wearing good clothes to fix lawnmowers," said Dulcie.

"You know what I think? I think if anybody was going to have notions, it would be Dryden," said Lee Ann. "She's always been a little… different."

Around the room, there was a murmur of agreement.

"Nobody's different when it comes to money," Millicent said. "Everybody would like to have more of it."

People laughed, nervously. The mood had changed and the others were listening.

"Look at this situation logically," Millicent went on. "You have a rich old lady who will soon need a lot of care. You have a young person who will inherit her money if she dies. That young person hides her dead body in the woods, so that the cause of death can't be known. Doesn't that seem a little... dubious?"

She paused, to let her point sink in.

"And it could be more than money," she said. "Don't you think it's odd, how Dryden has stayed around that place and never struck out on her own? Maybe she has her eye on Noah. It wouldn't be the first time she went after an older man."

She paused again, to let the small known facts cement the speculation. Then she lowered her voice and her words oozed out like gear oil, viscous and insinuating.

"Do any of us really know what might have gone on in that household all these years?"

She left the question dangling and I heard the thoughts spring up all over the room. "Is it possible? It is awfully convenient about the body... and Dryden does go for older men. Noah's always talked about her like she's the cat's meow. Plus, he's so much younger than Fay... But there's no way he helped kill anybody. If she did do it, it was all on her own..."

In the midst of the babble, Tempest's thoughts were a separate track. "Wow. Like weird. An old lady and a young chick hooked up with the same guy and then the old lady gets, like, bumped off..."

I was aghast. God, if you are there, do something! How can that woman blithely declare that down is up and have no one challenge her?

But where were the means to challenge her? My will, so carefully crafted for Dryden's future, would damn her. Her stubbornness about my body, born of loyalty, would become evidence of guilt. If Noah defended her, he'd be suspected of connivance. The more lovingly they behaved, the more sinister they would look through Millicent's fractured funhouse lens.

Yes, I was old and likely to grow infirm. And who would point out that it was I, as much as Noah and Dryden, who had been liberated from the dread of my infirmity?

Chapter 7

Was this my fate, to be aware but useless for all eternity?

I never asked for this. Even when I was alive and could talk, I didn't probe into other people's minds. It would be futile, never mind exhausting, to ask people to translate all their private chatter. Their thoughts were their own business and speech was only an approximation anyway. Why chase after shadows when I could plunge a shovel into the dirt and pull forth crisp red potatoes whose meaning was self-explanatory?

Now I was hearing the chatter, whether I liked it or not, and a lot of good it did me, since I couldn't *do* anything. I'd have been glad to comfort my friends and smite my enemies, but I might just as well wish for the ability to call down lightning and floods. My knowledge gave me no power. I did not possess it; it possessed me. I couldn't even control what I saw and heard.

I had hoped that when the clientele at the beauty parlor got done with me, I would find my way back to someone I loved. Instead I was bounced from person to person, seized by whoever was curious about my affairs or eager to spread the news of scandal. I felt like a dollar bill being passed from hand to hand, a unit of currency in the gossip market.

Did I really need to know that when Doke Winslow, a longtime bachelor who ran bulldozers and lived with his sister's family, spent an inordinate length of time in the bathroom, he was not, as he publicly implied, lingering over a bowel movement, but in fact was using a pair of scissors to trim the hair from his nostrils? Was there a purpose in my feeling how his pulse raced in the presence of Sharon Kovalevsky, the round, cheerful waitress at the Butternut Diner?

Having shed a shiftless husband five years ago, Sharon still said she didn't need another, and most of the time Doke could not think of a way to start a conversation with her. Today, though, as she was pouring his coffee, he happened to hear someone say I might have been murdered and reflexively exclaimed, "That's nuts!" The next thing he knew, Sharon was laughing and saying she agreed with him. To his amazement, she put down the coffee pot and launched into companionable talk about people making more of things than was really there.

His half of the conversation mostly consisted of "Yup," but they talked longer than his most daring hopes and when he left the diner to go home to his sister's, his thoughts traveled in a direction they had not gone for years, toward the idea that his appearance could matter. At the first opportunity, he picked up a *Sports Illustrated*, remarked that he might be sitting for a bit and headed for the bathroom, where he could be alone with a mirror and a pair of scissors.

A lot of people besides Doke had had a reaction to my death, for all manner of reasons. For the two associates at the local real estate agency, the question was how best to approach my heirs to find out if they meant to list my property for sale. If they moved too soon, they risked offending. If they waited too long, another agency might get in ahead of them. What did they know about Dryden Kirkwood? Was she a tree hugger? Or could she be enticed by money? Would a fuss about my body delay settlement of the estate? More than anything, they hoped the issue would die down quickly. A controversy would not help business.

The Reverend Walter Inchkeep, on the other hand, did not care what my death might do for business. For him, the issue was sacrilege, pure and simple.

Inchkeep was the minister at the more literal-minded of the two churches in Gilham. He was by all accounts an impeccably upright, if cheerless, man. There had been no hint of impropriety, financial, sexual or otherwise, in his leadership of his flock. If he had a passion, it was for order. He seemed to see existence as a struggle between divinity who had set forth a perfectly clear set of rules and principles and a human race that refused to follow them.

Having sat through a number of his funeral services, I was acquainted with his view that humans are a sorry lot, in need of a tight leash to control their multitude of base impulses. His first instinct was to assume the worst, a habit he shared with a large segment of the local population, who found his gloomy predictions of eternal damnation to be comfortably familiar because they were so similar to what they heard every day from the weatherman.

When Millicent came into his office, which was in the rectory, and related her account of the recent events, he expressed no surprise. He merely offered the remark that sinfulness was infinite in its variety. Unlike Millicent, he did not leap to believe that a murder had been committed. The desecration of a dead body was sin enough and might even be worse than murder, because its damage was spiritual rather than material. Murder was a crime against God's commandments, but it was also a common law crime, with worldly motives and consequences. Murder could arise from anger or greed and a believer might later repent and be restored to grace. But to desecrate a dead body? That was a sin with no worldly motive, a defiant declaration of non-belief for which no repentance could suffice.

As Millicent came to the end of her tale, he leaned back in his chair, pondering.

"It is so very difficult to rouse people to the necessary vigilance," he said. "They are much too inclined to take their neighbors on trust."

"My own view, exactly," said Millicent, "and if there's anyone in this town who should not be trusted, it's Dryden Kirkwood."

"Ah." Inchkeep pondered some more. "So this is not the first time she's shown herself to be of doubtful character? I'm only slightly acquainted with her..."

"Doubtful! She is far beyond doubtful! It doesn't surprise me in the least that she would do something frightful. The only question is how the decent, right-thinking people in this town intend to respond."

She rose to her feet grandly, as if to add an exclamation point. In fact, the gesture was a first step in the direction of the door. Millicent did not have time to join Inchkeep in a meditation on the nature of evil. Her mission was to tell as many people as possible about the threat.

Her next target was Doke's sister Eloise, the town clerk. The walk from Inchkeep's house was not long, but it was halted twice by encounters with neighbors of lesser importance to whom she gave a quick synopsis before hurrying on. When she finally reached the town hall, she found Eloise going over a permit application with Bud Coutermarsh, a man you'd be glad to have on the scene if you were trying to solve a drainage problem, but one likely to be a lead weight of non-interest in a discussion of who might have done what to whom and why.

Rather than dampen the effect of her story by including him, Millicent stayed apart, gazing at a framed copy of an 1820 town survey map until he had finished his permit and left. When she approached the desk, her air of significance was so obvious, Eloise did not bother to ask if she had business with the town. She just said, "What's up?" and waited.

"You haven't heard then?" Millicent said.

Eloise shook her head. "I was at the dentist. I just got back to the office."

"About Fay Kirkwood?"

Eloise started violently. To cover the reaction, she shuffled a few papers. "I haven't heard anything. What about her?"

As far as I knew, I meant nothing to Eloise Ware. So why did my name make her jump?

"She's dead," Millicent said.

Ordinarily, someone like Eloise would have caught the scent of scandal in that one word, "dead." In Millicent's universe, pleasant, respectable people did not die; they passed away. But in this case, Eloise was deaf to nuance. She was gaping, thunderstruck, as if she'd just been told the sky had fallen.

Mute astonishment was not the reaction Millicent was looking for. She had expected to be begged for more details, which she could dole out with teasing reluctance, one by one.

"It was very sudden," she added. "And there's some question about exactly what—"

"Fay's dead," Eloise repeated, more to herself than to Millicent. She seemed fully occupied by that one fact. She started pacing circles around the office.

"Yes, she's dead," said Millicent, "but the point is, people are saying there might be something odd about the death. That it might not have been from natural causes..."

Her voice sounded peevish. She was playing all her high cards and getting nowhere.

"So Fay is dead," Eloise repeated.

And Noah is free, she was thinking.

Within seconds she was lost in a dream of herself and Noah in some soft-focus location beside a crackling fire. Her arms were around him, offering consolation. His body was pressed close to her. Her hand stroked his skin, which was scented with cologne. Musk, perhaps...

You dream, all right, I thought. Noah has never in his life used cologne.

"But don't you see, it's more than just an ordinary death from old age," Millicent said irritably, trying to get Eloise to show some interest in the dramatic part of the tale. "Why would Dryden hide the body, unless there was something wrong about the death?"

"I wouldn't ever try to predict what Dryden would do," Eloise said absently.

She was not thinking about Dryden. She was remembering her own life, decades earlier, when she was a student in one of Noah Macauley's classes. That class had given rise to the first and only passion of her life, a passion inspired in equal parts by Mr. Macauley himself—his face, his voice, his dreaminess—and by the beauty of the mathematical formulas he was explaining. Eloise had seen her whole future laid out before her. She would pursue a career in something mathematical and she would marry Mr. Macauley.

She had taken every course he offered, pursued extra credit, anything to spend time with him, but for all his praise and encouragement, he had kept a clear distance from anything personal. Of course he must, she told herself. She was his student and there were rules.

When she went away to college, she wrote him letters every week, pouring out her thoughts and feelings. His answers were sporadic, full of encouragement about the mathematics and news about the school, but silent about his own thoughts or feelings.

By the time she came home for the summer, Eloise was desperate. How could she make him understand the depth of her feelings?

On the 7th of June, a lucky number, she resolved to speak. The sky was blue; the air was fragrant with mown hay. As evening approached, she drank some wine, trying to calm her nerves. When the warm tingle reached her toes, she drove to his house. The moment he opened the door, she launched into her speech. Her words tumbled over each other—he was wonderful, beautiful, she'd always loved him, from the first moment, more than anything, she wanted them to be together, always.

Mr. Macauley did not interrupt. He stood in the doorway, listening, until Eloise came to a stop. Her body was trembling, but she felt glorious. She'd done it. She'd risked everything and there was no going back.

"Maybe we should sit down," he said.

He sat on his porch steps and gestured for Eloise to sit beside him. Then he said, "That's very generous. You have a generous heart."

Eloise still remembered exactly how she had felt, hearing that reply. A horrible dropping away in her stomach, as if she knew she was about to be pushed off a cliff.

Mr. Macauley was kind, of course. He said many nice things about Eloise, that she was a superb student and a lovely person and he felt the highest regard for her. But...

She already knew there was a "but." She could feel it looming behind the kindness.

But...

...the regrettable fact was—well, not regrettable, precisely, but unavoidable—the unavoidable fact was, his affections were already engaged elsewhere.

This answer was worse than anything she had imagined. Success had been too much to expect, perhaps, but she had thought she would be left with some hope. She had felt so strong, so lucky. She might fail today, but she could come back tomorrow and keep coming back, until he was won over. It had not occurred to her that he had already been won by someone else.

Fleeing in her car, she met a pickup truck turning into his driveway. She jerked the wheel and the bumpers just missed. She was about to drive on when a realization hit her.

Was that Mr. Macauley's "beloved" driving the truck?

In a flash, she was out of her car and creeping back through the woods. Crouching in the underbrush, she peered at his house, but couldn't see inside. She didn't dare go closer until it was darker. When the light faded and a lamp came on, she crept to the nearest window.

Across the room, two people were lying on a couch, kissing. She couldn't see the woman's face, only a head of short, bristly hair, and a naked back, ghostly white beside the tan of neck and arms. Watching the tableau of twined limbs and strewn clothing, Eloise was swamped in misery and yet she couldn't pull herself away. She felt like someone holding her hand to a flame, testing how much she could endure.

When the bodies shifted and she could see the woman's face, she recoiled. It was the hatchet-faced lawnmower lady, the one who raised pigs and wore coveralls like a janitor. Not only was she ugly and coarse, but she was also old! Her clever, poetic Mr. Macauley had rejected her in favor of a bony, homely old harpy who fixed lawnmowers. How was that possible?

How was it indeed? I was as mystified as she was. Eloise had been a smart, eager, pretty girl, full of possibilities. Even now, more than thirty years later, she was still quite lovely. So why had Noah chosen me, the homely old harpy? He'd never told me about her girlish adoration. If he still had her letters, they were filed away somewhere.

That night, she had turned from the window and ran, not caring if she made noise. She had driven aimlessly, she didn't know how long, until finally she felt hungry and pulled into an all-night truck stop two towns away from Gilham. There, working the evening shift, was Gerald Ware, a boy from her high school who was known as religious and doggedly studious. Although he was built like a football tackle, he wasn't an athlete. He played the organ in the church.

The cafe was quiet and he lingered to talk. They barely knew each other. She had been pretty and popular; he was considered a loser. She almost asked him to leave her alone, but his manner was gentle and every part of her was hurting. After a while, emboldened by her willingness to have him there, he said his shift ended soon and would she like to go for a walk?

They found a small dirt road along a river, where the sound of rushing water covered the lulls in conversation. At some point, he said she was the prettiest girl he'd ever seen. A little later he took her hand. From that point it was she who led him, first to a standstill so that they could kiss, then into a meadow so that they could lie down. There was no moon. She could not see his face and they didn't talk. He offered warmth, which she welcomed first inside her clothes and then inside her body, trying to annihilate one sensation with another.

There was little pleasure for her, but it was a distraction, to feel the friction and fullness of sex, to feel the occasional sensation that hinted at pleasure. She observed Gerald with interest, as if he were a specimen in an experiment. She watched his attempts at control yield to moaning urgency. When he climaxed, he seemed as vulnerable as a creature giving birth, and she felt something she had not expected to feel: tenderness. She also felt powerful, that she could bring him to such a state of enslavement to his own nerves while she remained cool and aloof. The encounter left her surprisingly happy. She was going to be fine.

But soon the feeling of power dissipated and grief came rushing back. She sought him out again the next night and then the night after, all summer long.

Gerald never asked why she wanted him. He said, many times, that she must be a gift sent to him by God and he began urging her to marry him. At first she said no, but she was also neglecting birth control, perhaps willfully. By August, she was pregnant and this seemed sufficient reason to accept him.

All in all, it had not been a bad life. She loved her children. She was fond of Gerald, in a friendly way, and they jogged along comfortably enough. She figured out early on that if they had sex regularly, he would assume the marriage was a success and ask very little else. She had briefly considered teaching him how to pleasure her, but realized she did not want to. There was only one person to whom she wanted to abandon herself in that way and it was not her husband. It felt like chastity to keep her nerves cool and Gerald seemed peacefully unaware that anything was missing between them.

Eloise had never allowed herself to imagine my eventual demise and what might follow. She knew if she permitted herself any hope, the life she had built for herself would crumble. In any case, her practical side told her there was no hope. The same eye that had looked at Gerald Ware and judged that he would make a comfortably undemanding husband had looked at Fay Kirkwood and seen the kind of gnarly New England rootstock that would still be grumbling about the present and predicting the worst for the future on its hundredth birthday.

But I hadn't made it to one hundred after all.

I was dead, Noah was free, and Eloise was just fifty-one, an age that yesterday had been starting to feel old, but today seemed young, far too young to write off forever the possibility of passionate love.

She felt as if she might faint and realized she was barely breathing.

She felt like Rip Van Winkle, waking up to find the world rearranged. All the skills that had served her in her life were useless. She could run a household, manage children, do her job, and chair a committee meeting. But to pursue a dream of her own, to court the person she loved? She could just as well be stepping onstage to sing an opera. She had no idea what to do.

She could begin with condolences, of course. As town clerk, she had long since learned how to express suitable sentiments on these occasions, regardless of her true opinion of the deceased. But once the formulas of sympathy had been spoken and she was face to face with Noah without a script, with all the words in the English language available to speak for her heart, what was she going to say then?

Did I have to be a witness to this particular dilemma? Wasn't I supposed to be a collection of subatomic particles bouncing randomly among forces with no larger meaning? Did the continuing movement of the planets depend on my awareness that my neighbor's wife was coveting my beloved?

Millicent, meanwhile, was still looking for an angle that would provoke a reaction more interesting than stupefied silence. Even though she and Eloise were alone in the room, she leaned closer and lowered her voice. "There's another thing," she said. "Maybe I shouldn't... except it's already being talked about... that Noah might have something going on with Dryden..."

"With Dryden!"

The name came out in a gust, as if expelled by a blow. Eloise inhaled a string of saliva and started coughing.

"I know. It's terribly shocking," Millicent said. "But you know how it is with men, as they get older. They can be so susceptible. And Dryden's right there, she's young, she's a very physical type of girl..."

"She's dumb as an ox!" Eloise almost shouted. Noah and Dryden. The idea was too grotesque to be borne.

Millicent rocked backwards in astonishment.

"I suppose Dryden may not be quick," she said. "But men don't always care about that."

She was staring at Eloise with obvious curiosity.

Eloise forced herself to an appearance of calm. "Do you really think it's true?" she asked. "Dryden's practically a kid, compared to..."

She couldn't say the name.

"...him," she finished.

"She does have a taste for older men."

"Yes, exactly!" Eloise said eagerly. "And Jonathan is just the type. But Noah's never done that sort of thing."

"Not as far as we know..."

Millicent left the words hanging, hinting at the infinity of what one couldn't know.

Eloise did not reply. Her mind was possessed by the image of Noah and Dryden as lovers. The idea was grotesque, but the more she thought about it, the more that grotesqueness became an argument that the story must be true. It was too outlandish to be an invention.

As Eloise continued to brood, Millicent edged toward the door. She wanted a signal booster to relay her news around town and Eloise seemed unaccountably reluctant to play the role. Then, just as Millicent reached for the doorknob, Eloise emerged from her daze.

"Is it true, what you said?" she asked. "That Dryden might have done something to Fay?"

Chapter 8

I was thinking along the lines of murder myself, but happily, or unhappily, I had no access to lethal weaponry. I could only dream of the accidents that might befall the neighbors who were spinning such myths about my death. Could I hope that Millicent Gray, Walter Inchkeep, and Eloise Ware would find themselves in a carpool and drive off a bridge together? People die in car wrecks every day. Couldn't some of the victims be people whose departure would be a positive contribution to humankind?

Ordinarily, I would not have put Eloise into this category. When not in the grip of thwarted lust, she was a perfectly decent human being and it would be a limp and watery personality that could go through life without falling into some kind of hormonal foolishness at least once. Even I could recognize that most of my irritation arose from envy that she still had flesh with which to lust after my beloved.

The hour had grown later and most of my neighbors had been picking up books, turning on the television, preparing for bed, and in the process, thankfully, forgetting about me. Not so with Eloise. Far into the night, she was on a house-cleaning tear, burning off nervous energy while she dreamed about Noah. Although I was a minor player in this drama and had already made my exit, I was dragged through scene after scene of fireside snuggles and trembling confessions, a relentless theme and variations that made me ponder, seriously, whether it was possible to be driven insane after you were dead.

At long last, Eloise slipped into bed beside her sleeping husband. As she dozed, fitfully, her daydreams began to drift and fragment, and I was granted a space of quiet.

After a time, I began to feel that I was moving, like a floating object, and gradually, without my having articulated a specific hope, I found that mine had been fulfilled. I had drifted out into the woods where my body lay. I did not need sleep, but what a relief to find the chatter of humanity silenced and hear nothing except the creaking of a branch in the wind and the trickle of a brook.

After a while, a large round shape separated itself from the shapes of the trees. A raccoon. In cautious stops and starts, it approached to investigate my body. Like the fisher, it started at my feet, sniffing and working its way toward my face. When it began to eat, three smaller raccoons emerged from the underbrush to join in. They ate their fill and wandered off, one by one, until only a small one remained.

Suddenly, the small raccoon leapt away from my body and scurried after the others. In the same moment, three lithe gray shapes seemed to materialize out of the air. Coyotes.

Although I knew their arrival might mean trouble later, I still felt a leap of delight at the sight of them. Coyotes were the playful shadow creatures, the sly dodgers, the midnight singers, the hunters of woodchucks, and thus the lifelong defenders of my vegetables and flowers. They were clever and beautiful and had never caused me any trouble, as long as I kept my chicken coop well fenced.

Lean and silent, these three circled me warily, as if they mistrusted their good fortune. It was a hungry season and my carcass was a hundred pounds of fresh meat that seemingly had fallen from the sky. Before long, like the other wild creatures, they closed in to eat.

As they pulled strips of meat from my bones, I could feel contentment spreading through their bellies. When they had eaten enough, they began to play, tumbling in the snow, growling, pouncing, and nipping in an overflow of well-being. Finally, like drunken revelers, they threw their heads back and sang, their voices rising and falling in eerie undulations, floating toward the moon.

My heart wanted to float upward with the sound, but my mind was earthbound by worry. What did this mean for Dryden? Would they tear my body into pieces and carry it away with them when they left?

I've given you a good meal, I murmured. I'm asking you to return the favor and leave the rest. To protect the child of my heart.

Fortunately, the coyotes had reasons of their own to do as I hoped. Under cover of darkness, their late autumn hunger had overcome their aversion to my human scent, but now their hunger was gone and soon it would be dawn. They gave my body a parting nudge and slipped away into the trees.

Chapter 9

I was yanked back to humankind by the ringing of a phone. It was still dark and the ring had the peculiar insistence belonging to any summons that disturbs one's sleep.

A body sat upright in bed. A hand groped on the nightstand, searching for the phone.

"H'lo?"

I didn't recognize the voice. It was male and sounded youngish.

"Terp, it's Randall. There's a story up your way." Another male voice I didn't know. Older. "Some old lady is dead and her body's missing. I want you to check it out. You got a way to write?"

The man named Terp found the light switch and a notebook. Still in bed, he scribbled the bits of information coming over the phone. Fay Kirkwood. Mechanic. Niece. Heirloom pigs. Schoolteacher. Macauley?

"You got all that?"

"Yup."

He hung up and looked at his watch. It was six a.m. Not a thing he could do at this hour. He pulled the covers up and drifted back into sleep. A moment later he was awake again, thinking, "Background. I'll need some background."

He rolled onto his side and started scribbling queries. What is the family like? Is there money? Who inherits? Who was screwing whom? (Literally.) Was the old lady religious? Was she nuts?

Who the hell are you? I thought.

He was skinny. That was as much as I knew. I could see the boniness of his hand and arm.

The writing paused. His thought was as clear as if he had spoken. "Gotta get to Dryden Kirkwood before she clams up."

You creep. I don't even know you and already I don't like you.

As he dressed, I caught mirror glimpses of a pale, narrow chest, wire-rimmed glasses, and curly hair. Fully awake, he was humming cheerfully, thinking about the day ahead.

A rich old lady was dead and her niece had hidden her body in the woods. This story sounded a lot better than his usual diet—the selectboard meetings and school budgets, the argument about four-wheelers on a hiking trail, the blocked culvert that flooded the church basement, the driver who was cruising radio stations and mowed down a row of mailboxes on the way to smashing his Suburban and his femur against the stone foundation of a long-gone barn.

He wasn't going to get his hopes up, though, not until he had more facts. Very possibly, the tale was a concoction of rumors and in reality the old lady had been as poor as a church mouse, the body had been found in the woods, not hidden there, and she was lying anticlimactically at the funeral parlor, certified as dead of a heart attack. A six a.m. phone call from his editor did not necessarily indicate urgency. It was a habit with Randall to make a phone call the moment a thought occurred to him, whether he was comparing prices on a new washing machine or arranging an interview with the governor.

As yet, Randall said, there was no police investigation. There was only speculation, which his wife had heard about at her community theater rehearsal. As long as the police stayed out of it, Terp would have to tread lightly.

"There's no way we can claim she was a public citizen," Randall had said grumpily. "She was so goddamned private, her own family had barely heard of her."

Although Randall didn't say so, he must have shared Terp's suspicion that the facts were mundane and people had talked them up into a mystery. If Randall thought the rumors were true, he wouldn't give the assignment to the new guy.

Terp looked at his notes, trying to recall if he had met either the old lady or the niece. He'd met a lot of people and Gilham was not very big. He couldn't remember a Kirkwood, though.

Strange name, Dryden. Had she been named for the poet? He was sure he'd never met her. That name would have stuck.

So how could he get the niece to talk to him? Might be best to ask her straight, but until he saw how the land lay, he wanted options.

Fifteen minutes later, his chattiness had gained him the loan of his landlord's snowblower and he was on his way to Hart's store to buy breakfast and a bag of marshmallows. He planned to try a trick he'd learned from a high school buddy, a dedicated slacker who occasionally liked to disable his family's lawnmower by plugging the exhaust. It caused no damage but the machine wouldn't run. He'd use a marshmallow, to make it look like a kid did it.

At the checkout counter, he made a couple of remarks about the recent snowfall and then asked if there might be someone in town who could fix a snowblower. He hoped to get Fay's name into the conversation casually, to get a feel for what people were saying. For now, he didn't want quotes to print. He'd ask for those later, if there was a story.

"There's, like, some lady out on Baker Road," said the clerk, one of the continuous series of teenagers who manned the cash register at Hart's. "But I think she might be dead."

The kid called across the store to Judy Hart, who was checking inventory. "Is there somebody around here who fixes snowblowers? Somebody who isn't, like, dead, I mean."

"There's Dryden," Judy said, "but I don't know as she'll be working right now. Or what it'll be like to deal with her, now that she's on her own."

Terp strolled over to where Judy was working.

"What, is she not such a great mechanic? I'm clueless about engines, so I'd never know."

Judy smiled and the note of caution in her voice eased a little.

"Far as I know, she's OK fixing things. She's just... different."

"Different? Like, what, she might slip a few extra parts onto the bill...?"

"No, no. She's not dishonest. She's just hard to figure. Like this thing about the body."

"The body? Is she one of those exercise nuts who struts around in Spandex?"

Judy exploded in laughter. "Dryden? Oh my word, what a thought!"

The joke was too good not to share and soon she had a cluster of people gathered around, relishing the absurdity of what he had said and filling in details of the story. Facts and embellishments were freely mixed and there were fresh bursts of hilarity at the image of Dryden in Spandex, but by the time he left, Terp had heard a lot about our family peculiarities and what might have happened.

I, meanwhile, couldn't decide whether to laugh or swear. The last thing Dryden needed was her name all over the newspaper but I couldn't see him killing a good story out of regard for her feelings. Why would he? He was a journalist. He couldn't enjoy his work unless he felt a cheerfully clinical interest in the misfortunes of other people.

Even as I cursed him, I had to admire the way he had disarmed any reticence in Judy Hart. She must have known he worked for the *Herald*, but he had acted his part with such conviction, playing the urbanite who is at once naïve and cynical, and outsmarts himself into stupidity, that she never stopped to wonder if he was working on a story. For purposes of duplicity, it didn't hurt that he looked like everybody's kid brother, outgrowing his shirtsleeves. He was tall and gangly with curly brown hair, a pug nose, and wide blue eyes. He even had freckles. Looking at him, no one would ever think, "Here's a fellow to be reckoned with."

Could he work the same trick on Dryden? Judy had been easy. Her reserve was the ordinary native form in New England, a sort of cold-induced resistance to movement that could be swept away by the first warm breeze in April. Dryden, on the other hand, was reticent all the way to her marrow. She spoke when she chose to. Period.

Terp headed straight for the farm, gulping his coffee as he drove. From his speed, one would have thought he was hot on the heels of a mobster or adulterous movie star, but probably it was just habit. At the entrance to the farm, he overshot the turn and had to back up. He then came bouncing into the dooryard with such an insouciant disregard for potholes, I wondered if his origins were in fact rural.

Once out of the car, he stopped rushing and stood for a while, studying the place where I had lived. I still remembered my own first reaction—the enthusiasm for well-drained hayfields and wooded hillsides that overlooked the peeling paint, missing shingles, and sagging corner posts of the buildings. Much has changed since then. Buildings had been demolished and others built. Fences, trees, paint colors, even the location of the driveway, had changed. It had been a long time. More than forty years.

It was unsettling to see something so familiar through a stranger's eyes. Details I seldom noticed—the animal smells, the juxtaposition of a red building and an orange farm implement—hit my senses with the force of novelty. Details that would have bothered me—a gate hinge pulling loose, a door ajar when it should be closed—Terp did not notice.

His eyes made a slow circle of the farmstead. A white clapboard house, the classic rambling collection of ells and dormers. A vegetable garden with snow melting down to patches of brown dirt. A meandering collection of farm buildings around two sides of the gravel dooryard.

Closest to the house was a machinery shed, tin roof, dirt floor. Economical. Board and batten siding painted red. Next to it was the lawnmower repair shop, a slightly different shade of red. Then the barn, two story post and beam, as old as the house probably. Steep-pitch shingle roof and unpainted board siding, weathered splotchy brown. Then a tiny shoebox chicken coop with red paint matching the machinery shed. Behind the coop was a low modern barn with plywood siding and red paint that matched the repair shop. All around the barns were pens and small pastures, some fenced with boards, some with wire. The chickens were patrolling the fence of their pen, clucking in the hope of table scraps.

Terp's eye returned to the two shades of red and lingered. Not a violent clash. Just not a match. Had the old lady gotten a good deal on some paint and figured she could live with it?

Chalk up one for Terp, I thought. The paint on the shed and chicken coop had come from a farm auction, dirt cheap.

Terp walked over to the repair shop, which had a sign in the window, "Closed." Without expectation, he put his hand on the doorknob. When the door opened, his first reflex, an urban reflex, was to jump away from it, as if alarms might go off.

Nothing moved. He opened the door wider and leaned in. Just inside the door was a snowblower with a handwritten note taped to its handle, "Won't start, please fix if you can." At the far end of the shop, more machines were lined up, with repair tags dangling from their handles.

The work areas looked like a running debate on housekeeping. Half the parts and tools were neatly ordered on racks and shelves. The other half were scattered about in seemingly random piles. On the counter near the phone, he saw a couple of completed repair tags along with checks made out to "Kirkwood's." Evidently the pick-up hours were flexible.

Terp backed out of the shop and headed for the house. The only shoveled path went to the side door. He could hear music somewhere inside, a jazz ensemble. Piano, bass, and a saxophone. No, two saxophones. The group sounded familiar, but he couldn't name it.

He knocked and waited. A dog started to bark, but no one came to the door. He considered opening the door and shouting a "Hello," but decided against it. If she was there, she must know she had a visitor.

Gradually the dog quieted, but the music continued. The identity of the group hovered on the fringe of his mind and it annoyed him that he couldn't place it. Maybe a lesser-known album by a big name.

Without much expectation, he flipped open his phone to see if he had enough signal to try a call.

Not a chance, I said. Try Massachusetts.

He left the porch and wandered around the barns, hoping she might see him and wonder who was snooping. Like the buildings, the animals were a hodgepodge. In the modern barn, the pens of pigs were neat and systematic, but the chicken flock was a motley mix of colors and the pasture out back held an ancient gray horse, two fat red and white steers, and a pygmy goat. When he approached the fence, the goat and the horse came to check him out, but the steers stayed lying down, lazily chewing their cuds in the pale winter sunshine.

After a while, Terp gave up and went to his car. Except for the music, there was no hint of a human presence. In most families, a death was an occasion for commotion, either outright wailing or a bustle of logistical arrangements to forestall wailing. Here, the stillness was eerie. There was a story here, he was sure, and somehow he had to talk to Dryden Kirkwood.

In the meantime, he had a list of other contacts, headed by the names Walter Inchkeep and Noah Macauley. He called Inchkeep first, figuring that a minister in a state of indignation would probably have something to say. Inchkeep said he was welcome to drop by his office.

Terp knew the minister by sight, from town meetings and other public events, but as he drove into the village, he realized he did not remember which church was Inchkeep's. He parked near the first one, an austere white building, and squinted to read the small sign by the door: "First Parish Church, the Reverend Timothy Eames." He crossed the road and walked the short block to the other one.

Both churches belonged to Protestant denominations, but in all the time I'd lived in the town, I hadn't found much they agreed on, beyond the calendar dates of Christmas and Easter. The one north of the post office, which most people called the Old Church, was a tall, colonial building with white clapboards, steep gables and plain rectangular windows. The one south of the post office, known as the Brick Church, was a later building with a bulldoggish profile, stained glass windows, and a clock in its steeple. A block apart, the two buildings faced each other obliquely, like cats watching each other out of the corner of their eyes.

The white one, the Old Church, I thought of as the Church of the Rummage Sale. Its pastors always seemed to be balding, mild-mannered men who were reluctant to say that any idea was actually wrong, although if pressed they might concede that they thought a bit differently themselves. It catered to a segment of the population who saw church as a community activity rather than a spiritual one and who preferred that the sermons mention God and Jesus as little as possible and confine themselves to urging people toward more neighborly behavior. A subset of its congregation stayed busy organizing rummage sales, bake sales, a food shelf for the poor, the summer craft fair, visits to shut-ins, rides to town meetings for the elderly, a non-stop round of community cheerfulness and service to those in need.

The parishioners rendered these services without any explicit belief that their good works would win a reward in heaven. They did good works because, well, because they were a good thing to do. If there was a human-shaped god, which was open to debate, they were inclined to think he was benevolent, mostly because it would be too depressing to think otherwise. Their god was not very active in his benevolence, however. To judge by earthly events, he was a sort of absent-minded inventor who spent most of his time puttering in his laboratory and only turned his attention to human affairs when the mayhem became too noisy to ignore. On the whole, the First Parish people felt it was better not to think too hard about God, just as it was better not to analyze the Bible too closely, for fear of running afoul of logic and, worse yet, common sense.

In the Brick Church, on the other hand, God was as present and vigilant as a Dickensian beadle. I thought of it as the Church of the Wrathful Father and it served the segment of the community who wanted a sterner Christianity, people who saw the human race as a rabble of slouching recruits in need of a tough drill sergeant.

Of the various styles of discipline that had governed the church, Walter Inchkeep's tended in the direction of abstinence and legalism. Rather than being urged to useful activity, his parishioners were exhorted to restrain their baser urges and follow God's laws down to the last letter. He could not be accused of hypocrisy in his beliefs. As far as anyone knew, he lived what he preached, devoting himself to prayer and spiritual improvement, and avoiding such trifling pleasures as dancing, movies, and sports. He also avoided my repair shop, possibly because of the same objections to my living arrangements that had prompted him, early in his tenure in Gilham, to try to get Noah fired from his job at the school.

He did own a lawnmower, though, a nice new Toro that he took to the dealer in Leonardston for service. If the neatness of one's lawn was any measure of one's standing in heaven, then Inchkeep had a place waiting at the head table. He trimmed his grass every five days, whether it needed it or not, and his sod had the uniformity achievable only by the religious application of broad-leaf herbicides.

When Terp knocked on the rectory door, the speed with which it opened gave him the unsettling sensation that the minister must have been lying in wait on the other side. When he was shown into the office, he discovered a more innocent explanation. The office window looked out at the approach to the house so visitors announced themselves the moment they turned into the yard.

Inchkeep was a tall man, fiftyish, almost skeletally thin, with a pale complexion, pale blue eyes and hair of an indeterminate brown. His build and coloring were rather like Terp's but their demeanor was so unlike, they would never be described as resembling each other. In contrast to Terp's ragdoll slouchiness and propensity for smiling, Inchkeep carried himself with rigid dignity at all times. He rarely laughed and his body had a habitual forward lean, as if his fervor was like a gale at his back, urging him onward. As the two men shook hands with each other, they called to mind the two-sided Halloween mask, clown and ghoul.

Terp sat down and propped an arm on the back of his chair. Although his posture was casual, he was soaking up impressions. The room itself was a handsome space, with oak wainscoting, built-in bookshelves and patterned moldings. Late 1800s, he guessed. Inchkeep had added no adornments to the ones built into the house. A simple cross hung on one wall. The other walls were bare. The furniture was massive and square, insistently lacking in beauty.

Terp's eye made a quick scan of the bookshelves. The books resembled the furniture, massive, bound in sober blues and browns, dense with edification. No slight and saucy paperbacks to tempt a man to idleness, Terp thought. He took out his notebook and pencil.

"I understand you've been involved in the debate about this matter of Fay Kirkwood…" he began, but before he could ask for comment, Inchkeep cut him off.

"There's nothing to debate," Inchkeep said. "One doesn't debate the word of God."

Terp was tempted to ask if God would be willing to offer a quote for publication. Instead he murmured a noncommittal "Hmm," and waited for Inchkeep to elaborate. He made a private bet with himself that little prompting would be necessary. People who were paid to air their views—ministers, professors, politicians—usually had to be shunted or stoppered, not prodded.

"Truth is truth," Inchkeep said. "Righteousness is not a matter for negotiation. God has blessed us with His Word so that we can know the truth and not be led astray. Doubt and debate are wedges that open the path for wickedness."

Inchkeep's eyes were fixed on Terp but not focused, as if he were looking past the physical man to a vision of Terp's soul, or perhaps everyman's soul, slipping downward into a dark pit of uncertainty.

"God's truth is unmistakable," Inchkeep said. "His justice is certain and terrible."

As he spoke, the books and wainscoting were gone and I saw a different room where everything looked bigger. The room was crammed with objects, a mélange in which expensive antiques mingled with plastic knickknacks, cheap housewares and stacks of magazines, toys and clothing, scattered helter-skelter as if the whole house had been tipped over and shaken. A nervous, wispy-haired woman was shuffling piles from one place to another.

"I'm sure he didn't mean to break it, dear," she said.

A child's voice protested, "He did too mean to. He threw it on the floor." The child's hands held out broken pieces of a toy sailboat. "Dad, why don't you do something!"

A man looked up from reading a magazine. He was tall and thin with pale blue eyes. Inchkeep's eyes.

"For pity's sake, Walter, stop whining," he said. "Maybe he meant to or maybe he didn't. This is an issue for you boys to work out between yourselves."

Across the room, an older boy with broad muscular shoulders was watching. His look of smug impregnability made the younger boy writhe. Crossing his fingers behind his back, the boy begged that someday he would be big enough to smash his brother's face in.

Inchkeep fought off the memory, muttering silently, "Thy will be done." As suddenly as it had opened, his mind snapped shut, closing me out.

I saw Terp with his pencil poised, waiting for more comment, but Inchkeep had paused. Having declared that God's truth was beyond debate, he had nothing more to say.

"Would you care to comment more specifically?" Terp asked. "About how the truth applies to Fay Kirkwood?"

Inchkeep waved his hand dismissively. "From dust were ye made and to dust ye shall return," he said. "The Word is clear."

"But won't Fay Kirkwood's body return to dust, after the coyotes are done with it?"

"That idea is an abomination!" Inchkeep spat the words. "We were made in God's image, to have dominion over His creation. It is an abomination for our flesh to become part of the flesh of a beast."

Terp made a note. In a tone of careful neutrality, he asked, "Is it your belief that burial is the only proper way to dispose of a body? Or is cremation acceptable?"

"This is not a question of my belief. God's will is clear. In the earth, we return to dust. In a fire, we return to dust. Only a beast with no soul can be left on the ground to be eaten by other beasts."

"But once the body is buried, is it okay that it will be eaten by the beasts of the earth, the worms and microbes and such...?"

"Our bodies are not made to be eaten by anything! It is God who returns us to dust and who will make us new again on the last day. We are not meant to pry into His mysteries. What that young woman has done is an act of disobedience, for which she will suffer eternal damnation."

"What do you think should be done here and now, on this earth?" Terp asked.

"Dryden Kirkwood must be punished, so that others will not be corrupted by her example."

"Put in prison, you mean?"

"Yes. Absolutely. Society must be protected from evil."

No such clarity guided the Reverend Timothy Eames. When Terp, on impulse, decided to drop by the other church to ask his views, Eames spent the first few minutes scuttling about, making tea, offering vanilla wafers, asking if the chair Terp had chosen was comfortable, before finally venturing the remark that while he personally found the idea of being eaten by animals distasteful, he appreciated that there could be many different points of view on the subject.

He was Terp's age, short, prematurely bald, nervous and self-effacing, with a soft voice and the look of someone who carried spiders outdoors rather than stepping on them.

"Do you think it goes against the Bible, to do what she's done?" Terp asked.

"The Bible?" The minister's face wrinkled in perplexity. "Well, as I'm sure you know, the Bible says a great many different things. I'd hesitate to make any absolute pronouncements about how it should be interpreted on this subject. It does speak about a natural ordering of creatures, which might imply that this act was sacrilegious, but on the other hand, it is in the nature of many wild animals to eat flesh and so there is nothing unnatural in this. And even Christ offers his body, symbolically, to be eaten. But on the other hand, there is the reference to the burial of an ass, which would argue in the other direction. So you see the difficulty..."

"Yes, I think I do. Would you say it is an issue that should be left to the civil authorities?"

"On the whole, yes, I think it belongs under their jurisdiction. Which is not to say that there is no spiritual dimension to the issue. It has many dimensions and people are bound to disagree about them. I only hope that in the end our legal system will come to a reasonable balance among all the various aspects."

Balance would be nice, Terp thought. He was starting to feel dizzy, trying to follow Eames' shifts of logic, or at least catch hold of one of them long enough to write it down.

"Do you think she should be arrested?" he asked.

"I'm not in a position to know," Eames said. "I would have to see all the evidence first, and learn the law, and even then, I'm not sure I could say... Not without knowing what was in her heart. By the way, if you don't care for vanilla wafers, I think we have some pecan cookies..."

Chapter 10

Before Terp could express a preference about cookies, he and Eames were swept aside and I found myself whirling downward, like some helpless soul in Dante, spiraling through visions of torment and remorse.

"It must be the devil, tempting me," someone was thinking. "It has the look of righteousness, but how can it be? Righteousness is firm and steady. This feels like a torrent, raging through my soul…"

A woman's voice interrupted. "Do you have any books of Christmas music for trombone and French horn? For my grandsons?"

Eyes focused, taking in a counter display of toys and maple candy and beyond it, Dulcie Sullivan, who was studying a rack of music books.

"Duets, you mean?" The mind struggled to think about music. "I might have something."

It was Gerald Ware, Eloise's husband, who owned the Strings 'n Things store and played the organ in Walter Inchkeep's church.

As he thumbed through the music, Dulcie chatted on about her grandsons, but Gerald barely listened. He was intent on finding a book for her, so that she would leave.

When she'd bought a book and gone, Gerald retreated to his office, leaving his three temporary clerks and Jonathan to handle the rush of shoppers. He was desperate for a quiet moment to think.

Last night at dinner, Eloise and Doke had been talking about the rumors going around, but he had felt only mild curiosity. Although he knew Dryden, as he knew most of Jonathan's students, he had avoided knowing too much, because he didn't want to feel he should fire a man whose general lack of competence might make it hard for him to find another job. As long as Jonathan's wife chose to overlook his activities, Gerald did the same.

Then, at breakfast, Eloise mentioned a fact that did interest him. She said the police didn't know about the rumors yet.

"How can they not know?" he said. "Hasn't someone told them?"

"I suppose it's a little too third-hand to go reporting to the police," she said.

He asked who had knowledge that was better than third-hand and she said probably nobody except Dryden herself. When he ventured to question whether Dryden would take her knowledge to the police, Eloise said not to worry, they were bound to hear about it soon enough.

Gerald thought "soon enough" might not be all that soon. Of the two officers in the police department, one was on medical leave after back surgery and the other was too new in town to be fully integrated into the loop of town gossip. Gerald was about to point this out when another idea struck him, so forcefully it seemed like a message direct from the almighty. He should not pass this idea on to his wife. He should go to the police himself.

They had been using the word "police" as a collective noun, but right now, the police in Gilham consisted of one man, a crew-cut blond named Jim Jorgensen, whose light-footed athleticism made him look much younger than his age. He was in his forties, soft-spoken, quick to smile and slow to take offense. The only complaint about him, as a police officer, was that the kids weren't scared of him.

Until now, Gerald had never had occasion to call the police and he probably wouldn't know Jim at all, except that he happened to be the conductor for a small community chorus and Jim happened to have a fine tenor voice. The choral group was ecumenical, for the simple reason that neither of Gilham's churches had enough good voices to make a performance ensemble, but even with the addition of some Catholics and evangelicals who worshipped in Leonardston and some people who did not go to church at all, the group was still chronically short of male voices. When Jim's hymn-singing caught the attention of the parishioners in the Old Church, he was persuaded to join the chorus, and even I, with my layman's understanding of music, had been able to hear the change from quavering hopefulness to sturdy resonance in the tenor section after he came on board.

So Gerald did know Jim, slightly, but only from rehearsals, where he had thirty people to direct and no extra time. Now he had a reason to seek him out for a conversation. He could go to Jim's office and say he had a serious matter to discuss and they would sit down, just the two of them, to talk.

The idea had taken possession of his imagination. He could see Jim in his dark blue uniform, clean and pressed. He could see the holster resting against his hip, the sinewy shoulders and flat stomach, and the sunny handsomeness of his face. If there was ever a creature the Lord could look at and think was good, Jim was such a creature. For months, Gerald had longed to talk to him, but the thought of walking up after a rehearsal and offering some idle pleasantry made his throat close up in panic and all idly pleasant words vanish from his brain.

This was not the first time Gerald had been paralyzed by admiration. A few years ago, there was the UPS driver who always wore shorts, even in midwinter. Before that there had been the bearded carpenter who replaced the clapboards on the Wares' house, and before that others, all the way back to the Ivy League athlete who taught swimming at his first summer camp.

From adolescence onward, he'd always had a hero who floated in his thoughts like an image of perfection. He had worshipped from a distance, torn between the yearning to move closer and disgust at the foulness of his own being. He hated that he could not summon the image of his hero without also feeling the heat of his animal organ and he lived in fear that his furtive nighttime satisfactions would end in eternal damnation.

When Eloise appeared in his life, like a gift, he thought he had been saved. Counseling him for marriage, his pastor had said she was a sacred vessel, waiting to receive his seed, and Gerald had seized the idea, gratefully. With a wife by his side, he was free to dream about his heroes, because the urges that resulted had an outlet sanctified by God. The act that had been foul was now holy.

To his relief, Eloise had wanted nothing more than to be the receptacle into which he poured himself. He understood, vaguely, that some women were afflicted by the same animal urges as men and he was glad she was not one of them. He did not object to her body, exactly, but he felt no wish to explore it more intimately. They seemed perfectly suited. She took an undemanding view of the duties of the marriage bed, and in all other things, they enjoyed a detached and amiable companionship.

Lately, though, he wondered if his heroes were turning into devils. He couldn't stop thinking about them and physical gratification no longer satisfied his hunger. He wanted to talk to them. He wanted to go fishing or go for a walk in the woods. He began to imagine that Jim Jorgensen liked to sing arias and that he, Gerald, could accompany him on the piano.

Now, his earlier struggles looked simple. When the allure was physical beauty, only his body had been tempted into sin. From that temptation, the bulwark of marriage had protected him. Now his heroes were calling to his spirit and he felt defenseless. If thirty years of marriage had not made Eloise into a soul mate, there was nothing that would make her one now.

In mid-afternoon, the crowd of shoppers thinned and Gerald told his employees he had an errand to run. Alone, out in the crisp winter air, he felt as if he had escaped a net. His pulse began to race and he set off briskly towards the police department, which lay at the other end of the village. As the distance shortened, he walked more and more quickly. He could feel the danger in his eagerness and considered turning around, but the stronger voice said he was meant to do this. Whatever came of it, he would have his hour of conversation.

As he came abreast of the Old Church, the police parking lot came into view, beyond the town hall. The lot was empty. Jim's cruiser wasn't there.

He stopped and stared. He hadn't considered this possibility, though it was obvious. Jim was often out of his office, on patrol. If Gerald had been sensible, he would have phoned before coming.

Except that he wasn't being sensible and he knew it.

For a long time he couldn't move. He stared at the empty parking lot, feeling no impulse either to go forward or to go back the way he had come. He could not postpone the errand. This had been the moment. If Jim was gone, it must be a sign from God that the conversation was not meant to be. But he could not bear to let go of the idea. Not yet.

He was still staring when a car approached from the far end of the village and turned into the parking lot. The cruiser. He saw Jim get out and walk with loose easy strides toward the building. The winter sun shone on his hair and his face was ruddy with cold. As he disappeared into the building, Gerald sprang forward to follow. His heart was pounding again, but now it felt strong, like a soldier or hunter. He bounded up the steps and into Jim's office.

Jim turned from hanging up his coat and his face lit with pleasure.

"Hey there, Coach," he said. "How are you?"

Coach. The joking title had originated with some of the younger chamber singers, caught between "Gerald" and "Mr. Ware" and comfortable with neither. Now all his singers used it, even those older than he was.

Jim scrambled around the desk to proffer a chair. The office was small and their bodies bumped as he passed. The touch, slight as it was, set every nerve in Gerald's body buzzing. His face grew warm and he sat down hastily, because he no longer trusted his legs. He pulled off his winter gloves and fingered them like a set of worry beads.

"I'm fine, thanks," he managed to say.

"What brings you here—no trouble, I hope? Would you like some coffee?"

Strangely, Jim seemed nervous, too, as if his choral conductor was a personage to be treated with deferential awe. He darted in the direction of the drip pot.

"It's been sitting a while. I could make some fresh..."

"No, no, don't bother," Gerald said. "I don't really want any—"

"Are you sure?" Jim's hand paused in the air, already holding the pot,

Gerald realized he did want coffee. It might distract his wayward nerves. "Maybe I will have some," he said. "But this pot's fine. Don't throw it out."

As Jim turned to fill a cup, Gerald gazed at his back, at the straw-blond hair clipped short and the small hollow between the muscles of his neck. His thoughts bucked and reared, threatening to yank free of his control and gallop rioting through images of... what?

He looked away and fixed his eyes on the desk. Along with a computer, it held a neat pile of papers, a cup of black ballpoint pens, and two photos, one of a yellow Labrador, and the other of a gray-haired couple outside a summer cottage on a lake. Jim's parents, perhaps?

Jim started to offer the coffee cup and then his hand pulled back a little. "Oops, I forgot. Do you take sugar? There's no cream... sorry..."

"No, no, black is fine."

Normally Gerald took cream, but he'd never admit it now. As he took the cup, his gloves dropped to the floor and Jim's fingers, sliding free of the cup handle, brushed the back of his fingers. Gerald's hand jerked at the touch and coffee splashed onto his skin.

He winced. He felt clumsy and old.

Before he could protest, Jim pulled out a handkerchief to wipe away the spilled coffee. He took Gerald's hand in one of his own, as if to steady it, and with the handkerchief he patted the coffee off Gerald's skin.

The incident lasted only a few seconds, but every detail was fired into Gerald's brain. The exact place where each of Jim's fingers had touched his hand. The masculine roughness of Jim's skin. The soft cotton of the handkerchief.

He felt like Jacob with the angel, battling the urge to seize Jim's hands in his own and pull his body into a fierce embrace. He thought about how in the past a woman in labor would bite down on a rag to stop herself from screaming and he wished he had something to bite or twist, something against which he could batter himself, until yearning gave way to exhaustion.

Why had he come here? He must have been mad.

But now he was pinned, sitting in a chair with a cup of coffee in his hand and Jim's look of inquiry facing him across the desk. He struggled to think what to say.

"Sorry about your handkerchief," he began. "I hope it's not—"

He stopped. He needed to say something, but this was ridiculous.

"It's no problem," Jim said. "It'll wash right out."

"I can get you a new one."

"No, no, I'm happy to be, you know, helpful." He smiled. "It's my job."

OK, Gerald wasn't altogether wrong, I conceded. Seen objectively, Jim had a beaked nose and large front teeth, but looking the way he did right now, with his head cocked sideways and that self-deprecating smile, he was downright winning and not far from handsome.

"So, what brings you here?" Jim asked.

The question was inevitable, but it made Gerald freeze. He'd almost forgotten his reason for coming and now that he remembered, the excuse seemed flimsy.

"There are some rumors going around," he began. "But maybe you'd rather not be bothered... It could be all talk..."

The apology awoke his conscience and he suddenly saw clearly what he was proposing to do. Without having any definite knowledge of wrongdoing, he was about to bring trouble down on the head of one of his neighbors. Dryden had never harmed him. He had no real information, only speculations. It would be wrong compounding wrong for him to instigate official action against her.

So what was he supposed to say? Here he was and Jim was waiting. If he said it was a mistake, he would look ridiculous, the addle-pate who came running to the police and then said oh silly me, it was all in my head. But what else could he do?

He stood up abruptly. "I'm sorry. I was wrong to come. All I know is what people are saying and that's not enough. It would be false witness for me to speak. I'm sorry..."

He spun around and headed for the door, then realized he still had the coffee cup in his hand. As he turned to put it down, the cup tipped and the remnants of coffee sloshed across the counter and he thought, how much clumsier is it possible for me to be? How much more humiliation am I meant to suffer, in punishment for the lust that brought me here?

Yes, lust. He spoke the word to himself, scornfully, and fumbled for paper towels to sop up the mess he had made. In the next moment, he found that Jim was beside him, tearing off sheets of paper towel also, and together they mopped the counter, with bodies not touching but close enough to feel each other's warmth. Their hands tumbled over each other, awkwardly bumping, and gradually he realized that it was not just his own hands that lingered and melted towards Jim's, like an insinuating cat, but that Jim's were seeking his as well, and he felt a shock, first of joy, then of terror, facing the most perilous temptation of his life.

He turned to flee and in the same instant, the outside door opened. Millicent Gray came gliding into the office, carrying herself with a diplomat's air of conspicuous discreetness.

The two men froze where they stood. Gerald felt as exposed in his guilt as if they had been caught in a naked embrace. In his mind, he was that guilty and he could not possibly recognize how innocent he looked to a person whose mind was bent on other business. To the uninquiring eye, he and Jim were two ordinary middle-aged men making the usual hash of domesticity, mopping up spilled coffee.

Millicent made a nod of automatic civility toward Gerald before fixing a pointed gaze on the man in uniform. "As soon as you're free, I have a matter of some urgency to discuss with you," she said.

Chapter 11

Somehow Gerald muddled his way out the door, with apologies and assurances that he had been about to leave anyway. Only after the door had closed did the others notice that his gloves were still lying where he had dropped them, beside the chair.

Jim picked up the gloves and stood in a daze, looking at the door.

"If those belong to Gerald Ware, I could easily drop them off," Millicent said.

"What?" Jim shook his head, trying to focus. "No, no, I can take them."

"Really, I'd be glad to," she repeated. "My office isn't far from his store."

Jim's grip on the gloves tightened.

"But I'd really rather... That is, I need..." He stumbled, casting about for a reason to deliver the gloves himself. "I have to ask him more questions."

Millicent looked curious but was obliged to yield the point.

Jim arranged the gloves neatly, palm to palm, and laid them on a corner of his desk. Then he turned to Millicent and asked what he could do.

"Has anyone spoken to you about Fay Kirkwood?" she said.

"Not specifically. I heard she passed away. That's all."

"But it's not all," she said. She leaned forward, lowered her voice, and proceeded to recount what "that girl" had done with my body.

Jim let her talk without interruption. Even when she conjured up images of my body split to pieces by wild animals, his expression remained non-committal.

"That girl has always been strange," she concluded. "But this goes beyond..."

Failing to find strong enough words, she stopped. Jim waited, but she didn't elaborate.

"And you have reason to think the situation should concern the police?"

"Reason to think! It's awfully convenient that Fay should turn out to have some bizarre religious belief. That girl is about to inherit a pile of money and no one else knows how Fay died. How much more do you need, to consider it a matter of concern?"

"Mmm."

"It was very sudden, you know. I saw Fay in town just a few days earlier and she looked healthy as a horse."

Healthy as a horse, all right, I muttered. Horses are as finicky as opera singers. Horses can colic and drop dead on a moment's notice.

"Do you have some particular connection to the family?" Jim asked.

"Not as a relative, no. But I believe that neighbors should look out for one another."

"Yes, it's good when they do," Jim murmured.

The words were a reflex. His eyes had wandered to the gloves. *Hang Fay Kirkwood and all her helpful neighbors*, he thought. If there was one thing he did not want right now, it was a homicide investigation. He wouldn't be in charge—homicide would go to the state police—but just providing local support would swallow every spare minute.

Why did this have to come along now, of all times? At any other moment, he would have thrilled to the challenge. Even yesterday, when he thought his longing was hopeless, he would have been glad of the distraction. Just yesterday, Gerald Ware had looked out of reach. He was straight; he was married; he respected the conventions. His regard for Jim was undoubtedly the same mentoring benevolence he felt for all the singers in his ensemble. So Jim had thought.

Today, everything has changed. Jim had seen a flash of possibility, and having seen it, he wanted to pursue it to its source. Their conversation hovered in his mind, awaiting completion.

But now, instead of speaking the next phrase, he had to go haring off after a rumor that would very likely turn out to be false. His private opinion was that bizarre religious beliefs were far more common than homicides, but his opinion didn't matter. If the rumors were running wild, he'd have to do something. He'd lived in small towns most of his life and he knew the issue wouldn't go away.

"So what do you intend to do about it?" Millicent's voice was sharp.

"I'll look into it, of course," Jim said. With smiling blandness, he added, "Do you by any chance have information that could have a bearing on the case?"

Millicent was impervious to embarrassment.

"Why would *I* have information?" she said. "That's your job."

Half an hour later, Jim was knocking on the door of our farmhouse, but the only response was the barking of a dog. There were no other sounds in the house, not even music. If Dryden was at home, she wasn't answering the door.

The setback didn't bother him. He will try again tomorrow. Perhaps she would answer or perhaps not. If she did not want to open the door, he could not force it open without going to a judge first and he saw no reason to rush to a judge. No one was in danger. The girl was not about to take flight, not if her motive was to get her hands on an inheritance. He could wait a bit and see what developed. He would prefer an informal conversation with her willing participation.

In the meantime, he had an item of lost property to return to its owner.

Touching the gloves in his pocket, his mind flew to an image of Gerald in front of the chorus, his hands shaping the mood, his eyes holding the eyes of his singers. How could a man so unassuming become so magnificently imperious when he stood up to lead a chorus? Perhaps today Jim would begin to find out…

Or not, I thought. Gerald's store was a holiday madhouse and even though his wife might burn the pot roast because she was thinking about Noah, she still would expect her husband to come home for dinner after the store closed.

For me, it didn't matter. Whether or not Jim's hopes had foundation, they had driven all thought of me out of his mind. Before his cruiser had even left my dooryard, I was snared by someone else for whom I was still a topic of interest.

In the split-second gap of transition, it occurred to me to be glad I no longer needed to use the toilet or change clothes or floss my teeth, because I would never have a private opportunity for any of these things. Then my eyes came into focus on a narrow gravel driveway and a shifting tracery of leafless shrubs and trees lit by moving headlights. The lights flashed across the front of a tiny house and stopped.

Noah's house. Terp had saved this interview for last, thinking it would be at once the hardest and the most interesting.

When Noah opened the door, Terp had to stop himself from staring.

He was not given to describing men as beautiful, but this was a face that must have been beautiful when it was young. Even now, with deep lines around the eyes and mouth, it still had the delicacy of a line drawing.

"I appreciate your willingness to talk with me," he said. "I'm sorry for your loss."

"Thank you," Noah said. "Could I make you some tea or coffee?"

"No thanks. I'm fine. Reverend Eames gave me all the tea I can manage for now."

Noah smiled. "He has a generous hand with the tea and cookies."

"You're a parishioner, then?"

"No, but we're on some committees together."

As they sat down in the pair of easy chairs near the woodstove, Terp glanced around at the room, which served as kitchen, dining and living all in one. It's like a boat, he thought. Compact and orderly, the opposite of Fay Kirkwood's place. Possibly a wise decision, not to live together, but what had drawn them to each other in the first place?

Why does an orchid take root in the muck, I thought.

Terp hesitated, wondering where to begin. With the actual man in front of him, it felt awkward to intrude on his bereavement. Did the public indeed have a right to know?

"As I said on the phone, the *Herald* might like to do a story about Fay Kirkwood."

Noah nodded, waiting for specifics.

"I gather you were the person closest to her."

Noah nodded again. "Or perhaps Dryden, in recent years," he said. "A child goes very deep."

"Yes. I suppose so."

The gentleness of Noah's manner was making Terp feel like a voyeur.

"Look, you don't actually have to talk to me," he said. "I can imagine it's not what you'd choose, right now, to be in the public eye."

Noah lifted his shoulders slightly, absolving Terp of rudeness. "I'm not altogether surprised. If one does something unorthodox, it gets noticed."

"Would you rather stay out of it?"

"Yes, but I don't think that's an option. People are bound to have questions. Perhaps if you answer some of them, then I won't have to."

"I hope that's true."

Hope, but don't expect, Terp thought. People will never run out of questions.

Noah's expectation was unsettling. How much less equivocal it felt, to tease answers out of a reluctant subject. If they resisted, he felt less obligation. As it was, the bar looked very high. On one side of him was Randall, wanting a juicy story, and on the other side was Noah, looking to have his life simplified. How could he possibly do both things at the same time?

"So, you and Fay Kirkwood had known each other…how long?"

"Thirty-five years."

"How did you meet?"

A smile flashed across Noah's face, even now.

"Through a classified ad."

Terp gaped. It was too improbable. "A personal?"

"No, no. Fay had homegrown pork for sale. I love pork."

"Pork…?"

In spite of himself, Terp was staring again, taking in Noah's delicate bone structure and slight, scholarly physique. He did not look like a man who loved pork.

"It sounds foolish but it was true. It made a bond. Fay is… was… quite passionate on the subject of pigs. She loved them. And she loved good pork. It was an obsession really. She thought the modern breeds had ruined the meat, making it so lean. So she started collecting heirloom pigs and breeding them. Fat ones. The meat was extraordinary. She gave me a free sample and as soon as I tasted it, I came back and bought half a pig. It got us talking, first just about pigs, but then, before long, about everything under the sun, and she was so…"

He paused, searching for a word.

"Vigorous. And full of substance. I felt like such a wisp, myself. Lost in abstractions. There was nothing abstract about Fay. She was…"

He paused again. Terp waited, giving him time.

"Grounded, somehow. Everything in her life was so concrete and immediate. If she was hammering a nail, you felt like the nail and the hammer and the wood were all that mattered right then. It felt so rich to me and I just gravitated, wanting to be where she was. She was so not like me. She was blunt and she didn't worry what people thought. I was always trying to make things smooth. I felt silly at first, like a puppy, wanting to hang around her. Why on earth would she have any interest in me? But I kept gravitating and she didn't seem to mind. And then one day, I still remember the exact words, she said, 'I hope you won't think it's grotesque,' and then she said she wanted to be my lover...."

His eyes filled with tears and he stopped. He looked away from Terp, across the room, collecting himself.

"Grotesque, of all things. She didn't have a very high opinion of herself. But I suppose we were a pair, that way. Each of us thinking the other was so far above..." He smiled. "Thank goodness we got that sorted out."

And thank goodness he was talking, I thought. Until now, he'd been out of my sight, out of my reach. Whatever his thoughts, they did not draw me into his presence. Perhaps we'd known each other too well and his mind had no space for new impressions. Or perhaps his thoughts held no yearning because in his universe I was peacefully at rest. How often we had debated between his sweet-tempered certainty that this tangible world is sufficient and there is no other and my cranky insistence that we can't know for sure, either way.

But at least he'd spoken, and Terp, one of the innumerable people who meant nothing to me, had brought me there to hear.

"Did you agree with Dryden?" Terp asked. "About leaving her in the woods?"

Noah hesitated. "In theory, I did. Fay wasn't much on funeral parlors. But I could see it might upset people. Fay's family especially. But Dryden was determined, and I thought, if it's that important to her, we can figure out a way to deal with the family later."

"What about people here in town? Were you worried about them?"

"I suppose I didn't think about them. It's not really their concern, is it?"

"If what she did was illegal?"

"It can't be that huge a crime, can it?"

"I don't actually know. One wouldn't think so. Not if the death was natural."

Noah looked startled.

"Of course it was natural. What do you mean?"

"I don't mean anything, myself. But sometimes people gossip and, without a death certificate, there's nothing to stop people from imagining things."

"Imagining..."

Noah was silent, absorbing this idea.

"She'll never change her mind," he murmured.

"Change her mind?" Terp asked.

"You can't possibly understand, without knowing Dryden. She goes her own way. She won't be swayed by what would make life easier."

Later that night, when Terp sat down at his computer, he was thinking, is there any chance it was murder? Not by Noah, he was convinced. But what about Dryden, the one bent on taking the body into the woods? He'd already noticed the pause that so often accompanied Dryden's name in conversation, a suggestion of something strange or uncomfortable or hard to describe. Even with Noah, her close connection, the pause had been there.

Clearly Terp had to talk to her, but the problem was finding her. He had driven out to the farm a second time and there was no sign of her, not even the music on the stereo. He had telephoned and gotten no answer. Now he was close to deadline and would have to use what he had. Tomorrow would be spent on her doorstep, if need be.

Before starting to compose, he opened his internet browser to see if could discover anything related to the name Kirkwood. He didn't expect much, but one had to check.

To his surprise, Kirkwood.com did exist. Its owner was Spenser Kirkwood, a congressman from Arizona. Could he be related? From Arizona, not likely. Except for the name. Spenser. Another long-dead British poet, like Dryden.

Terp scanned the information. The congressman was young, only thirty-seven, in his second term. Parents were Charles and Anita Kirkwood. They were said to belong to a "distinguished New England family." Could they be Fay's cousins? Not out of the question. Fay was thought to have family money.

So who could tell him? Dryden, obviously, if he could ever find her. Or Noah.

Terp felt an unaccustomed reluctance as he picked up the phone. Noah was so decent and this inquiry about a congressman was so patently a hunt for scandal. But he had to find out.

Probably the congressman was no relation. Noah had not mentioned him. No one in town had mentioned him. And even if there was a connection, Terp didn't have to use the information. Not unless it was relevant. But Randall would not be happy, if it turned out later that a congressman was part of the story and Terp had not known about it.

Noah was surprised by the phone call, but not for the reason Terp expected.

"Spenser?" he said. "I'm sorry, I assumed you must know that. Public information and so forth. He's Fay's nephew."

"Her nephew. So he's Dryden's cousin?"

"Not cousin. Brother."

Brother. Holy Pete. No wonder Noah thought the family might be upset.

"Do people know, generally, around town I mean, that Fay's nephew is in Congress?"

"I don't think so. He hasn't been back here for a visit in years. And the local paper doesn't give much coverage to Arizona politics."

Quick, name a congressman from Oregon. Or Nebraska. No can do.

"So I gather Fay was not the sort to brag about him."

"No, that's a safe statement."

"And Dryden wouldn't either?"

"No. She and Spenser aren't exactly—" Noah hesitated. "They haven't much in common."

"Ah."

If it wasn't murder, could it be a family feud? Had she hidden the body out of spite, to make trouble for her brother? Not likely but who knew. He jumped up and started pacing. He had to talk to her. Whatever it took.

Should he go out there again now? He glanced at his watch. He had to file his story first. By the time he was done, it would be too late. She probably went to bed early, like most people in this night-is-for-sleeping slough of tranquility. Better to go first thing in the morning. Surely she had to feed the pigs. Or something. She couldn't ignore him forever.

In the meantime, he would hedge his bets. Start with a story that mentioned a possible controversy, possible legal questions, but don't take it too far. Stay with basic facts. Unexpected death. Unorthodox burial.

Expressions of concern from the religious community. A dead body hidden in the woods would get people interested. He need only hint at larger possibilities, the lack of a medical exam, the family money. If nothing came of the murder angle, he could ramp up the theological debate. He thought he could count on Inchkeep to stay outraged.

You scumbag, I thought. People's lives are just material, to be shaped into something amusing. Why did Noah talk to you?

I wished I did have the power to summon wind and lightning, blast a transformer, cause a blackout, shut down his computer. Instead I could only hover and shout fruitless appeals to his better nature, to consider who might be harmed by what he wrote.

And he did seem troubled. He stopped several times, rethinking his wording, removing a reference to "unexplained death," replacing a particularly vituperative quote from Inchkeep with a slightly more temperate one. The trouble was anything he wrote would make trouble. As he'd already observed, putting a death in the news rather than in the obituaries gave rise to speculation.

You don't have to print it! I shouted. You could tell your blinking editor that it's personal, private, there's no story. You could save us all a lot of grief—

Chapter 12

I felt something akin to a bounce, as if I'd been spat out.
 Terp and his computer vanished and I felt eyes squint against the glare of the setting sun. Chair backs threw long shadows across a polished dining room table.

The eyes closed, and I felt a gut, numb and clenched. I saw images, jumbled together. A girl in a plaid parka pulled a sled up a hill through deep snow. She turned and shouted, "Come on, Grampaw!" and I recognized myself, a teenager, shouting to my little brother. Then I saw myself gray-haired, braced to stretch new fence wire around my chicken yard while Charlie hammered staples into the posts. The air was brisk; the work was cheerful. He joked about his hammer technique and I groused about the skunk who had found a weak spot in the old wire and killed three hens.

Then I was twenty-four, hunched awkwardly into a white wedding dress, standing in a receiving line next to Tyrone, the poor fellow on whom I inflicted my brief attempt at marriage. As I greeted guests, my smile looked like it was held in place by thumbtacks. Charlie, who was in high school and still idealistic, watched me with fondness mixed with dread. The thought flashed past, "Oh, Crabster, why him? He's dull as oatmeal. You'll be bored out of your mind." Crabster. Crabcake. Crabbag. Crablegs. I could be any of those, depending on his mood.

Charlie was right, although boredom was only a small part of Tyrone's and my troubles. But Charlie never voiced his doubts to me. We were a family that minded our own business.

Then we were at the farm, some years later. Charlie and I were chatting and chopping vegetables. When the kitchen door opened, my face lit up and Charlie turned to look. It was Noah.

As I introduced them, Charlie wondered, *Who is he, exactly? Is he helping on the farm? He doesn't look very stout. She adores him, that's clear, but he's so young. Is it possible she's serious?*

He felt as he had at my wedding, fond but worried. "Can this really make you happy?"

Yes, it can. It has. It always will, as long as I have being.

"Are you all right, Charlie?" It was Noah's voice, now, on the phone.

"Yeah. I'm just…" Charlie's throat was tight. "So it was quick, anyhow."

"Yes. It was quick."

Whatever Charlie felt was obliterated by a white-hot arc of rage and grief. The word shot back like a spear. *Quick! What good is quick? I wanted her here forever.*

For one blazing instant, Noah was there with me and then he was gone again and only my brother remained.

"She'd have wanted it that way," Charlie said.

They were quiet for a while and then Charlie asked, "Is Dryden OK?"

"I'm not sure. You can't ever tell with her."

"No, you can't."

Even as a child, Charlie thought, Dryden had looked out at the world from behind a hedge. She had stopped crying at a much younger age than either of the boys, probably before she turned two. At the time, he had been too weary to be anything but grateful. Only later did he look back on her precocious stoicism and find it worrisome.

Was it the product of her history? He had tried, conscientiously, to treat her exactly as he treated his own boys. If anything he loved her more. But perhaps it had felt false to her. Perhaps, in trying to make up for Anita's indifference, he had exaggerated his demeanor and made even his honest feelings seem forced.

For Anita, it was different, more complicated. Still, he wished she had found it in herself to be loving. Or, failing that, at least willing to maintain a pretense of affection. How could she not love the child? How could she look at those velvet brown eyes, so hopeful and so wary, and not feel wracked by love?

Charlie gazed absently at the calendar hanging on the wall. He was still sitting where he'd picked up the phone, in Anita's neatly organized phone space adjacent to the dining room.

"Is there any way I can be helpful?" Charlie asked.

Noah hesitated. "I don't think so."

"What about the memorial service? Could we help with arrangements?"

The pause was longer this time.

"I don't think we'll be having a memorial service."

"Not having one! But how will—?" He stopped.

Poor Charlie. How will all the relatives know where to go and what to do?

For pity's sake, go ahead and have a funeral, I said. Don't worry about what I'd want. I'm not the one who has to find suitable clothes and think of something to say. It won't kill me to listen to a minister's speculations about my current spiritual condition.

A service might make Dryden's life simpler. That's what counts. At a funeral, everyone will know how to behave and everyone can go home afterwards and close the book on me.

"It's your decision, I suppose," Charlie said. "But what about burial? Will she be in the family plot? Or do you have a place up there...?"

"We have a place up here."

"Ah."

Behind that brief syllable, I felt an ache of disappointment. Charlie loved our long family history. For generations, the Kirkwoods had been as tenacious as a horseradish plant, impossible to uproot. Now we were scattering and there was nothing he could do. He could see the fact of my death, and someday his, recorded by an indifferent clerk in a place where no one cared who we were. He could see the space beside our parents' graves forever empty grass, as if they had been the last of the line.

For myself, I didn't care. What did it matter if my existence was forgotten? It's not as if our name was notable. We were just a family that happened to stay in one place for a long time, prospering modestly, contributing to the ranks of businessmen, lawyers, engineers, teachers, and social workers in our chosen county.

But it did matter to Charlie. Apparently it would be a balm of sorts, to have my name carved on a stone and added to the line of other family names, and to know that it would be many, many decades before the edges of the letters were worn away by rain and the hardness of granite yielded to the gently insistent encroachments of lichen and moss.

If this small thing could soothe his sorrow, I said, then where is the harm?

And strangely enough, although Charlie had said nothing and my voice, speaking for him, could not be heard, I heard Noah speak for both of us.

"If you like, we could have a marker near your parents," he said. "Even if she isn't buried there."

"Could we? I'll gladly make all the arrangements."

Charlie reached for the message pad to make a note.

"Fay would want it simple," he said. "No flowers and cherubs. Is there a stone she particularly liked?"

"I haven't thought. Granite probably. But not pink. She never had white pigs, because of their pink noses."

"Pink noses?" Charlie began to laugh and his eyes filled with tears. "OK, no pink. What about polishing? Would she want it rough or shiny?"

"Rough, I think. And not too big."

"Unobtrusive, then."

Exactly, I said. Like a toad.

Charlie was struck by a horrifying thought. "She wouldn't want it flush with the ground, would she?" he said. "Like those awful cemeteries that look like golf courses?"

"No, I think she'd say a gravestone should look like a gravestone."

Yes, and if you can persuade a raven to perch on it, all the better.

This was going to be a very fussed-over lump of granite. Charlie needed a task, and if he couldn't plan hymns and readings, then he would plan one heck of a gravestone.

"I'd like a line or two of poetry to put on it…" he said. His brow furrowed, mulling over quotations.

Enough already. I wanted to respect his feelings, but please save me from verse. I started to sing, loudly, the funerary jingle from our youth: "The worms crawl in, the worms crawl out, the ants play pinochle in my snout…"

He shook his head. "Maybe I should stick to name and dates. So the date would be…?"

"It was the thirtieth. When she died."

Charlie wrote the date on the message pad.

"Is that a message for me?" said Anita, from the doorway.

Charlie jumped. He quickly said his goodbyes to Noah and turned to his wife.

"You're back," he said, conscious that he was stating the obvious. His hands, which had been still, resumed their habit of pill rolling.

"I only went to the post office," she said. "Who was on the phone?"

"It was Noah. About Fay. She's..." He stopped.

"Is she ill?"

He shook his head. He could joke about my gravestone, but his tongue couldn't pronounce the final word.

"She passed away? When?"

He glanced at the notepad. "On the thirtieth."

"The thirtieth! She passed away two days ago and he didn't call us? That's outrageous."

"Perhaps he needed some time..."

"Needed some time! You're Fay's brother. You should be told immediately. Not whenever Noah happens to feel like it."

As if to emphasize her point, she opened a drawer and put away the stamps she'd bought.

"It doesn't matter that much," he said. "I'm not—"

"I know. You'd lie down in a puddle so that other people could keep their feet dry. And I suppose he's gone ahead and planned the memorial service without consulting us, either."

"No, he hasn't," he said. "They aren't having a service."

"Not having one? This is beyond anything! He doesn't tell the family. He doesn't bother with a service. What is he going to do with the body, wrap it in a plastic bag and put it out with the trash?"

"I'm not sure...I think they have a place up there. But Noah did suggest putting a marker with our family, too."

"That's absurd. One doesn't scatter headstones all over the countryside. She should have one grave, period, and the proper place is with your parents, since she has no family of her own."

"She does have... And anyway, it's not really my decision..."

"Of course it's your decision. You're her closest relative."

"Well, not exactly... There's Noah, too..."

"Noah is not her husband," she said. "Their whole attitude was frivolous."

Suddenly, as present as life, I saw Dryden's face, laughing and handsome, with its straight definite eyebrows and angular bones. Except that it wasn't exactly Dryden. It was the way Dryden would have looked as a boy.

I felt a flinch and the image vanished.

"It did last a long time," Charlie pointed out.

"Years don't mean anything, if it isn't serious to begin with." She picked up the phone. "I'm going to deal with this business of burial right now."

The conversation with Noah was brief and civil but failed to calm her irritation. When she put the phone down, she was frowning.

"Something isn't right," she said. "Noah said the body has been taken care of, but he wouldn't say how. I asked if it had been cremated or donated for research and he wouldn't say. He just said that Dryden had handled everything." She shook her head. "Since when has Dryden ever handled anything?"

Anita picked up the phone again.

"There's only one way to sort this out," she said.

"Don't be rough with her," Charlie murmured.

"Of course I won't."

In any event, she couldn't be rough, because Dryden didn't answer the phone. Anita left a message, irritably, asking her to call.

"This is such a nuisance," she said. "I can't plan flights until I talk to her. I have two important meetings and there's Spenser's fundraiser. I can't believe she's so thoughtless..."

Charlie did not say anything. He was across the room, gazing out the window. His body looked small and hunched, as if he had folded himself inward. He couldn't think about plane schedules. He felt like an amputee, as if he had just lost the first fifteen years of his life, because there was no one else still alive who remembered them.

It occurred to him that he needed to choose a font for the lettering on the marker. Something classic, like the older churches in New England. Should it be a serif font? Usually he liked them, but for this they might be too fussy. The stone should be a medium gray, he thought. Dark charcoal was too modern and anything close to white would feel sterile.

His thoughts drifted off into visions of granite, in all its varieties of color and speckling, and soon he was gone altogether.

Chapter 13

People should sleep more. That was one conclusion drawn from my brief experience of death. If only they were more like dogs, snoozing away half the day.

Someday, presumably, I will be forgotten. In the meantime, the intervals of tranquility were scarce. Only when every thought that clung to me had slid into sleep or found distraction could I have time to myself. Only then did I find silence and solitude. Blessed solitude. How unthinkingly I had enjoyed it while I was alive.

With the first unfolding of the morning paper, the chatter that assaulted me was almost unendurable. A great number of people were reading about my death, forming opinions, making remarks to their spouses, but I ricocheted from one mind to another so rapidly that no single thought could be heard in its entirety. Reactions to Terp's news article ran together into a roiling gabble from which occasional small fragments of intelligibility came popping to the surface.

"Seventy-nine isn't so... Dryden... no death certificate... alone in the barn... denial of the miracle... Dryden found... says many different things... suits Fay... beliefs... no warning... Dryden... heirloom pigs..."

Along with the thoughts and comments, I was barraged by sensations—bright kitchen lights, smells of coffee and bacon and cat pee, arthritic aching of joints, gas pains, squeaking chairs, the taste of cocoa puffs and grapefruit juice, too-tight blue jeans, rooms that were stuffy one moment and drafty the next, a chaotic blare of input that reminded me of an orchestra warming up, fifty musicians making a last quick run-through of fifty different bits of the score.

Finally, with gratitude, I heard a single voice take the lead, the oboe sounding its A, and the cacophony died away. I was in the car with Terp, on a road I recognized as the approach to the farm driveway. Once again, he was drinking coffee and eating a bagel, but he had moderated his speed.

In the cold overnight, the wet ground had exhaled a fog that reduced his surroundings to a milky blur and coated every wisp of vegetation in hoarfrost.

Driving into the dooryard, he saw lights in the repair shop. Although he no longer planned to use the snowblower as an introduction, the lights were promising.

As he stepped out of his car, the shop door opened and a woman came out, followed by a small tri-color collie. When she saw Terp, she stopped. He had a quick impression of dark coloring, broad shoulders and work clothes, and then his focus shifted to the dog, who approached at a trot and circled him, keeping a few feet of distance. Its demeanor was neither friendly nor aggressive, just businesslike, scouting the visitor. Terp bent and dangled a hand, letting the dog decide whether to greet him. He liked dogs, but at this moment, the gesture was pure calculation. A reporter needed to get along with people's pets.

The dog sniffed his hand and then allowed Terp to scratch its ears. Terp could feel that the woman was watching. When she came forward to meet him, he put out his hand, ready to introduce himself.

With only a glance at the hand and no greeting, she walked past him to the back of the car and opened the tailgate. He scrambled after her, telling her not to bother with the snowblower, but she had hoisted it out of the car and was wheeling it into the shop before he could make clear that his protest was not just a chivalrous offer to unload it himself.

"Is this here for an annual tune-up?" she asked.

"No, that's actually not why I'm here," he said. "That's what I was—"

"Good thing," she said.

She choked and primed the snowblower and pulled the starter cord. The engine fired and immediately died. She opened the choke and tried again and it did the same.

"So... what's bugging you?" she murmured.

She gazed at it, frowning.

Terp, meanwhile, had decided to take what was offered and keep his mouth shut. He was content to be ignored, if it gave him the chance to study her.

What struck him most strongly was her self-containment, a kind of force field that didn't so much repulse overtures as absorb them without recoil. He didn't think she was cold. He knew people whose emotions were deadened and they were enervating companions. This was different. Her emotions felt powerful but inaccessible, which only heightened his curiosity.

As he tried to gauge her personality, part of his mind was making reporter's notes about the visible—age mid or late twenties; tall, strong build, strong facial bones; looks distinctly Hispanic, but has no accent; striking features, not beautiful, exactly, but they hold the eye; wears men's clothes but most women would if they worked on engines; and how did someone named Dryden Kirkwood come by those Latin looks? Either her father's Yankee pallor had been submerged in a cross-cultural marriage, or else she had been adopted.

Focused on the snowblower, Dryden was oblivious to his scrutiny. She bent and sniffed the carburetor. Then she picked up a screwdriver and probed into the exhaust pipe.

"Huh. No wonder."

With a pair of needle-nose pliers, she worked the obstruction free and laid it on the workbench. The marshmallow was squashed and smeared with soot.

"That's weird," he said.

He squelched an impulse to start babbling about the weirdness. Social chat would not be welcome, he was sure. She was looking at the marshmallow the way she had looked at the snowblower, as if waiting for it to communicate what she needed to know.

After a while, she slid her hands into her pockets and leaned back against the workbench.

"So, what do you want me to tell you?" she said.

"Tell me?"

The echo was a delaying action, while he re-calibrated. She'd seen right through to his real purpose, but she didn't seem angry. She just looked tired and sad.

"OK. That was a bonehead thing to do," he said. "But how did you figure it out so quick? It could have been some kid, messing around."

"It's Jerry Blakeney's machine. His kids aren't kids anymore."

"Right. I should have thought of that. I didn't realize you'd be on a first-name basis with a snowblower."

"It's a small town. You find friends where you can."

The joke surprised him; her mood had seemed somber.

"You might as well ask your questions," she added. "You've gone to such trouble."

"Why are you so sure I have questions? I could be trying to hit on you."

"Sure," she said. "By being a goofball."

"Goofball! That's better than I hoped. I was afraid you'd think I'm a weasel."

"A weasel would have been smarter."

"Ouch. She bites."

"No, you put yourself in the path of teeth. Just as well say Scollay bites the kibble in his dog dish."

Terp laughed and his insides felt tipsy. He was onto a story all right. *She* was a story, all by herself, if he could pin it down. The neighbors called her "different" but that was too mild a word. Just being a Methodist in a town of Baptists could earn you that title. She was odd by any standard, but anyone who thought she was stupid wasn't paying attention.

It almost didn't matter what she had done. Perhaps it was murder. Perhaps it was a bizarre death ritual. Either way, readers would lap it up.

But would she let him print what she told him?

Most people who shied away from publicity were afraid they'd be shown in a bad light and he usually could talk them around. His argument was simple: some version of their story would get printed, with or without their cooperation. If they talked to him, he would make sure their side of the story got told. He would tell it fairly; he wouldn't quote out of context; he wouldn't give it a misleading slant. His assurances were as true as he could make them, within the constraints of space and time at a daily newspaper. He avoided mentioning the reality that a crucial explanatory paragraph might get cut from his story if a few column inches were needed for a car wreck.

With Dryden, his usual argument seemed irrelevant. He couldn't see that she cared how he would make her look. At any moment, she might decide she'd had enough of him and pick up a wrench to go back to work.

But what was the nature of her unconcern? Was she a sociopath? A saint? A fanatic? A misanthrope? What *did* she care about, if not other people's good opinion?

"Sorry about the marshmallow," he said.

"Doesn't matter. But it would have been simpler to ask for a tune-up."

"That was a miscalculation. I thought it must bug you, people waiting until it snows to get a tune-up."

A flicker of something—was it surprise?—crossed her face.

"That's never stopped anyone else," she said. "Better not ask for a rush job, though. Fay would put you on her shit list and you'd get done when she darn well felt like it."

She shrugged toward a sign on the wall behind the cash register, a yellow placard in the style of an ad from the phone company: "In a hurry? Try the Yellow Pages." I had made it as a joke, years ago, after a run-in with some suburban transplant who thought one-hour dry cleaning and 24-7 espresso were constitutional rights.

"I take it you're not listed," Terp said.

"Don't need to be. There's already more work than we want..." Her voice caught and she corrected herself. "More than I want."

Her fingers fiddled with a screwdriver, one of mine. The whole time we worked together, we'd had differing views about screwdrivers. My fingers were stiff-jointed and liked a coarse grip, hard plastic with big indentations; her fingers were subtle and deft and liked springy rubber with small grooves. Sometime after she finished college and settled in to work with me, I noticed she always used one particular screwdriver, a beat-up rubber-handled one that I'd found on the side of the road and used on tasks that might damage my good ones. She never said a word about it, though.

I never said a word either, but the next time I went to Leonardston, I bought a set of rubber-handled screwdrivers and hung them on the tool rack and she started using them.

I wondered what she was thinking now, holding my screwdriver, but all I could hear was the chatter in Terp's brain: *So the old lady had a shit list, wonder how often her niece was on it? Sounds like she was a dragon; can I get Dryden to say as much? Or will she be loyal to the dead, no matter what? But murder? The kid's too calm, but she couldn't knock somebody off and not be jumpy. Could she? And what made you call her a kid? She's as old as you are, maybe older; kid or no, she doesn't give much away; maybe she really could be that cool; she's strong enough; wonder how big the old lady was? Still, it seems too extreme, murder; better start on the weird religion angle, see where that gets you; and take it easy, Terp, don't push too hard...*

Instead of asking a question, he picked up a carburetor from the workbench and ran his fingers over its shape.

"That's off Doke Winslow's roto-tiller," she said. "He was putting his garden to bed and it quit on him. Machine's older than I am."

"Can you fix it?"

"Don't know yet. I expect Fay could have. People were always bringing her some precious old hunk of iron, hoping she could breathe a few more years of life into it."

"So she knew her stuff."

"Yup." The word was clipped, as if she didn't trust her voice.

He put the carburetor carefully back on the workbench.

"Did she know things you don't?"

"She had a touch," Dryden said. "She'd take something you'd swear was dead and start sweet-talking it and pretty soon she'd have it running again."

"But a machine can't hear," he protested. "What does it matter if you sweet-talk it?"

"I don't know, but it does."

He stared. She wasn't being facetious.

"You don't really think machines are alive?"

She shrugged. "Is the calcium in your bones alive?"

"Not by itself, it's not."

"But it's part of something that's alive."

"True. But so what?"

"So Fay thought the whole cosmos was alive."

Did I really think that? I know darn well I never said such a thing to Dryden, because I'd never in my life said anything whatsoever about "the cosmos." But she was right about one thing. I did talk to machines and they did seem to listen, a lot of the time.

"But the machine is just metal," Terp said. "A person can think and move around and reproduce. Are you saying she thought atoms and molecules are the whole of existence, and notions like spirit are wishful thinking?"

"Just the opposite. I'm saying, maybe atoms and molecules are the spirit made flesh. Fay thought it was egomania, the way religions treat the earth as if it's just a backdrop for the human drama. She'd have said the universe is an organism and people are part of it. On bad days, she thought humankind is like a cancer that is growing out of control and will end up killing its host. On good days, she thought we're just gonads going through a raging adolescence and we'll outgrow it."

She picked up the marshmallow and rolled it between her fingers

"You know how Jesus said, 'This bread is my body, take of it and eat?'"

Terp nodded, bemused. Where was she going next?

"So the Church invented stuff like transubstantiation, trying to explain how the body of Jesus could become bread. People wanted their god to look like a person, so they twisted their thinking into a pretzel. Think about it. What if Jesus meant exactly what he said? That the whole universe *is* the body of god? No mystical transformations required. Just think of god as the unifying spirit. Not some dried-up old schoolmaster who dictated his thoughts into a book two thousand years ago and hasn't had a new idea since. Something that's alive and changing, and everything is part of it. Dirt, dandelions, skunks, clouds, people, nuclear waste dumps—we're all part of the organism and whatever you do to any of those things, you're doing to god. That's another good Jesus quote, by the way. 'What you do to the least of mine, you do to me.'"

Terp stared. This was not what he'd heard from the neighbors at Hart's, who had portrayed her as a plodding ox and her aunt as an atheistic curmudgeon.

"Do you follow Christian teachings? You and your aunt?" He tried not to betray his amazement, lest that turn out to be offensive.

"Only the ones that make sense," she said.

Terp laughed. "But you do seem to think about them."

"I think about all sorts of things. Changing spark plugs doesn't exactly occupy your mind."

"I thought you said lawnmowers have a spirit."

"Payson Satterthwaite has a spirit, too, but he's still tedious."

Terp's antennae shot up. Satterthwaite was an inescapable personality in Gilham politics, but what was he to Dryden?

"How do you know Satterthwaite?" he asked.

"I can't not know him," she said. "He has a lawnmower and he always tells me exactly how to take care of it. 'Just clean the spark plug, don't change it.' 'Forget the air filter. Mechanics put in new filters when they aren't needed.' On and on, for twenty minutes."

"Why do you put up with it?"

"It gives me a chuckle. I do what he tells me and since he doesn't know shit, his machine runs like shit. But he'd rather be able to say I'm an idiot than have his lawnmower work."

"Don't you care? That he's telling people you're an idiot?"

She shrugged. "Why would I care what his pals think about me?"

"If we're all one organism, maybe their opinion affects your life. Maybe it tweaks some cosmic thread that will come around and yank on you."

"And maybe it will yank in a good way. If a creep doesn't like you, maybe that's a plus."

"But..."

She had a point. You'd need a good stout spine to live that way, though.

As a reporter, he thought of himself as a chameleon—alert and flexible, ready to adapt to his surroundings. The more he fitted in, the more people would open up and talk to him. Or so he thought. Was it a failure of courage, not to assert his own opinions? Was he in fact a golden retriever, so eager to be liked that he was afraid to have a mind of his own?

He realized he was staring at her, and worse, that his mouth was open. He clamped it shut and looked at the Yellow Pages sign. He still had not asked her anything about the story he was supposed to be writing. The trouble was, he wanted to ask her about everything. He wanted to ask what she thought about Brussels sprouts because it seemed possible her answer would surprise him.

Get a grip, he thought. *You've got a job to do.*

"I'm a reporter," he said. "I expect you've already gathered that."

"I figured you were here about Fay. But I thought it would be somebody official, wanting forms filled out. I wouldn't have thought this mattered enough to be in the paper."

"My editor thinks it might. My name is Terp Jones, by the way."

He stuck out his hand for her to shake. As he expected, her grip was strong.

"Terp?" she said.

"It's a corruption of Turnip, which is what I looked like, at the time. At school I became Twerp or Drip, take your pick. My real name is Lionel Turnbull Jones, from my grandfather, and that might have been worse. But what about you? Were you named for the poet?"

She nodded. "My brothers' names are Spenser and Sidney. My dad was halfway to a PhD in literature when he got married and went to work in business. Our names are like the flowers you plant where you buried your cat."

They were starting to wander again. Terp pulled out his notebook. When he could, he waited to make notes, because often people whose talk had been colorful and memorable would become stilted and trite if they saw their words being written down. Today, though, he needed something to make him focus.

"Had your aunt's health been failing at all?" he asked.

"Not that you'd notice. She crabbed about being old and creaky, but she sure wouldn't let anybody lighten her load. She was lugging five-gallon slop buckets the day she died."

"What happened, exactly?"

"I don't know, exactly. I wasn't there. I was working in the shop while she fed the hogs, and then I had a question, so I went to look for her. She was lying on the ground outside the hog pens." She hesitated. "Her skin was already starting to cool."

"So you didn't call a doctor."

She shook her head. "Fay used to say she'd like to wander off in the woods to die, when the time came. I couldn't do that for her, but at least I could keep things simple."

"It's not going to be simple, having no death certificate. It's going to be a can of worms."

"Not for her, it won't. She's off in the woods and nobody can bother her."

No, on the contrary, I'm not off in the woods. I'm right here and people can bother me quite a lot. Beloved Dryden, you should go get my body and save yourself.

"But it must be illegal, what you've done," he said. "Would she want you to get in trouble for the sake of some—?"

He stopped. He'd been about to say, "wacko spiritual belief."

"For the sake of her dead body?" he finished.

"That part's not her decision anymore. And I like that her body may come back around as a beetle's egg or a coyote's toenail."

He stared at her. "Do you have any idea what kind of a mess you could be in?" he said. "People are going to think—who knows what they'll think, but it won't be good."

He heard himself with astonishment. Since when did he become Sir Galahad? Here he is, on the trail of a great story and instead of nailing it down, he's worrying about how to save her from all the vultures waiting to feed on her life. Forget her aunt's body. She's the one who will get picked apart.

It's as obvious as the law of gravity that she didn't kill the old lady. If she has weird beliefs, they're hardly satanic. But so what? Winter's coming and people need things to talk about. He could try to sit on the story, tell his editor it's no big deal, but the news is already out and Randall may insist he pursue it. And the solution is so simple..

"Couldn't you just have somebody check her over…a doctor…?"

"You think they'd let me leave her in the woods after that? You said yourself, it's got to be illegal."

"You might not be able to settle her estate. Without proof she's dead."

She shrugged.

"Does she have a will?"

"I don't know. I'll have to ask her lawyer. She always said she was going to divide things between Noah and me."

Terp winced. "You might not want to say that to everybody, about her dividing things. You might want to say you don't know."

"Why?"

"Because…" How do you tell someone that some of her neighbors think she's a murderer?

"Because people may think that you wanted her property for yourself and…"

"I already had her property," she said.

"You did? I thought you said…"

"I don't mean legally. But I live here. The only difference if I own it is more worries. I'd be crazy to want that."

"But…" The usual arguments for ownership—control, independence, security and so forth—sounded like neurotic anxieties. Had he ever trusted another person as much as she apparently had trusted her aunt?

"Not everyone thinks that way," he said. "Some people might be eager… to have control. To have the other person…"

"Dead?" Her tone was biting. "Anyone who thinks I could wish for Fay's death has the brain of an aphid."

So much for giving advice. He'd only made her dig in harder.

"If your aunt didn't write a will, who will get her property?" he asked.

"My father, I suppose. He's her closest relative."

"What would he do with it?"

"He'll do whatever Anita—that's my adopted mother—tells him to do."

"Ah." Another can of worms, it seemed. "You didn't say 'adopted' with your dad. Is he your biological parent?"

"No, but he feels like he could be. For what it's worth. He's very sweet but he hardly changes a light bulb without Anita's say-so. As for Anita… Let's just say, if you could return a baby for a refund, she'd have done it."

"Then why on earth did she adopt you?"

The question leapt out before he thought. It was nosy beyond any reasonable standard of journalistic inquiry but she didn't tell him to buzz off.

"I've wondered that myself," she said slowly. "It's a hassle to adopt, so she must have thought she wanted another baby…"

Her brow furrowed and she looked much younger, almost like a child puzzling over some secret of adulthood.

"Is she upset about what you did? About your aunt, I mean."

"I haven't told her yet. But she will be."

Anita would be annoyed no matter what Dryden did, I thought. The whole setup here bugged her. Me, Noah, the farm, the hogs, the shop, even the town of Gilham, all of it bugged her. If I'd had a nice country estate, with a Kubota mini-tractor in the shed and bark mulch around the shrubbery, that would be OK. That would fit her image of what it means to be an old New England family. She thought she was marrying an aristocrat when she married Charlie. She didn't understand that in New England, belonging to the aristocracy means having the freedom to raise pigs and use a tire repair kit to patch your barn boots and in general do whatever you want, as long as you leave the same money to your kids that you got from your parents.

"Do your parents live near here?" Terp asked.

"They live outside Phoenix. In a gated community."

Phoenix. A chicken on every grill, a pool in every yard. Terp had flown there once, on the way to a Grand Canyon raft trip. He remembered the approach to the airport, mile after mile of neat stucco houses, each with its sparkling turquoise swimming pool. There were no people in any of the pools; perhaps it was too hot, or everyone was busy elsewhere. Not like a hot day on Cape Cod, where every strip of beach would be thronged with people too eager for sun and ocean air to care that the sand was strewn with pebbles and the water teemed with hermit crabs, seaweed and jellyfish.

"Will it upset them that you're talking to me?"

"I expect so."

"So why are you, then?" he asked. "You could have said no comment."

She didn't answer right away. She was looking out the window, where the sun had started a drip of snowmelt from the eaves. When she turned back to face him, he almost took a step backward. He didn't often meet such a direct gaze.

"I guess I liked your vibe," she said.

Her tone was matter-of-fact, not flirtatious, but even so, it sent a current rippling down his spine and belly to his sexual organs. He looked away from her, toward the rows of machines.

There was no blocking awareness, though. Everything he looked at was part of her life. The dog curled on a rug in the corner. The plaid wool jacket hung on a nail. The racks of tools. A pair of leather gloves with holes worn in the thumb and index finger of the right hand. The questions were piling up in his mind, but one was uppermost. What would she be like in bed?

Fast, reliable, and businesslike, I told him. Rather like a man, in fact. Two days ago, I didn't know that. Now I know more than I want to. Just don't go messing with her life because you're curious.

Leave it alone, Terp thought. Find a new line of questioning, fast.

He noticed that her fingers were moving, tapping patterns along her leg.

"Do you play an instrument?" he asked, pointing at her fingers.

She slid her hands into her pockets.

"Saxophone."

"I play bass. Both kinds, but I love the stand-up, it's such a comical beast."

He paused to see if she would respond with something about her horn. A lot of musicians could talk music all night, once they got started, but she wasn't started.

"What kind of stuff do you play?" he asked.

"Various things. Jazz and such."

Again he waited. She'd been almost garrulous about religion so why was this seemingly harmless topic so sticky?

"I'll try most things," he said. "Jazz, blues, classical, folk. I go to the jam session over in Leonardston, at the Blue Heron pub. Do you play anywhere?"

"Not really. Just for myself."

"That sucks. Sorry, I shouldn't say that. But how much can you do without other players?"

"I did jam some..." she said reluctantly. "With Jonathan Drummond."

"You play with Jonathan? Then why didn't he bring you to the Blue Heron?"

"He plays there?"

"Sure. Now and then."

"That prick."

The word was muttered under her breath, but it was unmistakable.

"So, what, are you such hot stuff on the horn, he didn't want to share?" he said, jokingly.

She recoiled and he cursed himself. Whatever the story was here, it was too close to the bone for joking. Death, god, sex, family, all were fair game, but not her saxophone, apparently.

"Seriously, how good are you?" he asked.

For the first time in their talk, she ducked his gaze. "I don't know for sure," she said.

"Jam with me sometime and I'll tell you," he said. "But be warned, I'm a ruthless critic. People who play badly usually are."

He smiled and spread his hands, as if to say he was willing to admit his failings. She didn't smile back.

"Will you be honest?" she asked.

Damn her anyway. Not a word he had just spoken was honest. He was not a ruthless critic and he did not play badly. It had become second nature to say what he thought would get the response he wanted. Did he have it in him to be honest?

His answer, if he had one, was cut short by the phone ringing.

Dryden didn't move. The phone was three feet from her elbow, but she stayed still, frowning at it. Before she made up her mind to answer, I was somewhere else.

Instead of the clutter of my workshop, I saw the gleaming stone countertops and hand-painted tile of Anita's kitchen. At the far end of the room, Anita paced back and forth with a phone to her ear. Outside the windows, the sky was still dark.

I felt Charlie's tension, watching her. He was sitting at the breakfast table with a cup of coffee but the thought of drinking it made him queasy.

"I'm glad you finally answered the phone," Anita greeted her daughter. She gestured toward a second phone and Charlie picked it up, even though he knew she did not expect him to say anything.

After a perfunctory phrase of sympathy and an equally brief reply, Anita proceeded to the subject on her mind. "What is going on back there? Noah said you're not putting Fay in the family plot."

Dryden's voice was flat, explaining the bare facts.

"You did WHAT?!" Anita's voice sounded like a power saw hitting an unexpected nail. "You can NOT be serious!"

Having already said plainly what she had done with my body, Dryden replied that yes, she was serious and it was what I had wanted.

"That cannot be what she wanted. Not even Fay would want something that outlandish."

Dryden was silent, not bothering to argue.

"You must have misunderstood her," Anita said. "You'll have to go get the body and bring it back. That's all there is to it."

"I can't do that."

"Can't or won't?"

"Whichever you like. Won't."

"I see," Anita said, in a tone meaning that what has been seen is unacceptable. "We'll discuss this when we get there, but I have to say, this is the most bizarre and thoughtless thing you could have done. Did you even consider how this could affect Spenser?"

When she punched the phone off, Charlie braced himself.

"That girl is impossible," she said. "She's made our family look like crackpots, but does she care? No. It's not her problem. She's not in a position like Spenser, with the media."

"You know, if you think about it," Charlie ventured, "it *is* the kind of thing Fay might —"

"No, it is not the 'kind of thing,'" Anita said sharply. "I'll grant you, Fay's style was earthy and she might have joked about it, but joking isn't the same as doing. Nobody but Dryden would actually do such a thing."

She picked up the phone book. "I'm calling the airlines this minute. We have to straighten this out." She found the number and punched it in. "I just hope they will give us something reasonable in the way of a bereavement fare..."

Crows and beetles, preserve me! Which circle of hell was it, to be trapped listening to Anita haggle with the airlines about getting a bereavement fare on two first class seats while Dryden's life was going forward elsewhere?

In the midst of my complaint, I felt a lurch and Anita's discussion of prices was cut short. As swiftly as I'd left, I was home again, in my workshop.

Dryden was standing near the phone desk, hunched and glaring. Her body shook, visibly, but she didn't make a sound. Scollay hovered near her legs.

Her eyes shifted to a particular object, a crescent wrench lying on the near end of the workbench. Her hand grabbed it and hurled it across the room. It bounced off a wooden beam, skittered across the concrete floor and banged into a can of WD-40. Can and wrench together clanged off the augur of a snowblower and the can went on rolling in a slow curve that brought it almost full circle before it stopped. She stared at the can. Its spray nozzle had been knocked loose and was lying on the concrete.

She slowly walked over to retrieve the nozzle and slide it back into place on the can. The task seemed to calm her.

Terp was watching, not saying anything.

I wasn't surprised to find him there. He had the tenacity of a tick. What did surprise me was that she had lost control of herself in front of him. I'd lived with her for years and never seen her emotions out of control. I'd seen her on the night of my death, her flesh wide open to her lover as she tried to drown her grief with lust, and even then, she had not lost control of herself. Not while Jonathan could see her.

The hymen was just meat. Orgasm was just the drive motor on a hydraulic pump. Her affair with Jonathan had breached only the outermost layer of her virginity. Was Terp the person with whom she would eventually shed the rest?

Could he be trusted?

I found myself thinking in gangster talk. You treat her right or I'll break your knees. Except that I was powerless to break anything. Unless it was his mind. By yapping at him.

"Can I do anything?" he asked.

The sound of his voice unstoppered hers.

"The fucking public!" she said. "That's all she cares about. She doesn't give a flying fuck about Fay! Or Noah..."

Or you, I thought, but you won't say that. It might smack of self-pity.

"Your mother?" he asked.

Her head jerked in an affirmative. "Technically she is."

"I take it she's not happy...?"

Before the words were out, he was irritated with himself. It was a reflex, that facetious understatement. Wrap yourself in a feather boa so that people will laugh and look no further. Would he ever speak plain words when it counted?

"Not happy, no." She laughed, harshly. "More like ice-cold furious. I've made a scandal for the family and that is unforgivable. That's all she could talk about. She barely pretended to care that Fay is dead."

"You're very strong, you know that?" he said.

"Yeah. I can smash a wrench. What good is that?"

"Most of us would have caved," he said. "Your mom gives you the chill treatment, do what I say or you're out of my heart, and you don't even flinch. That takes courage."

"That's not courage," she said. "I was never in her heart."

Her tone was flat, stating one of Newton's laws.

"That can't be true," he protested. "You're so—How can she not—?"

He stopped. He had been about to make himself ridiculous, spouting phrases of flowery chivalric bravado. *You're so fine! How can she not leap to do battle with those who would cause you harm? How can she not love you 'til the mountains are worn to sand and the seas gang dry?*

"...not care about you?" he finished.

"Very easily," she said. "When you meet her, you'll understand."

"Am I going to meet her?"

She smiled faintly. "I expect you'll find a way. She's part of the story you're after."

The story. He'd asked what he could do for her. Was this the answer? Did he want his brave phrases to mean something?

"Would you like me to drop the story? Would it simplify things?"

"Can you do that?"

"I don't know. I'd have to convince my editor there's no story."

"Don't do that for my sake. It won't help and it doesn't matter anyway."

"If it kept her off your back...?"

"She isn't on my back. She doesn't actually care what I do, except when it makes a fuss. Just write the truth, OK? I'll take my chances."

Just write the truth. Sure. A reporter couldn't even write about a town's budget for road salt without the risk that someone would say he was biased or had the facts wrong. This story involved money, religion, civil disobedience, a possible love triangle and a corpse, and he was supposed to write nothing but the objective truth?

Forget objectivity. He needed an angle. One that would cover the facts but make them look harmless. One that would fit the story into some comfortably familiar pigeonhole of oddness, like Jehovah's Witnesses or ultra-marathoners.

"What does your mother care about?" he asked. "Does she have religious beliefs?"

Dryden shook her head. "She sometimes goes to church, but it's like the Rotary. You make contacts."

"So it's the notoriety she's worried about. Not your aunt's immortal soul."

"No, the soul wouldn't come into it. Mostly she'll be worried about Spenser's career."

"Which is...?"

He knew the answer. He just wanted to hear her tone.

"He's in Congress."

No inflection. She could have been saying he worked in a shoe store.

"And you and Fay never, like, told people about him?"

"No, why would we? Nobody around here knows him."

This reticence still puzzled him. Why be secretive about something people might admire?

Secretive like hell, I said. Just as well say a bull's being secretive if he isn't bellowing. If anyone had asked, I'd have answered, but you don't go around grabbing people to brag about a nephew they don't even know. Not in our family, you don't. Besides which, I was actively repelled by some of Spenser's political views. Why would I go out of my way to tell people that one of my relatives was having a successful career as a parasitic insect?

It occurred to Terp that the reticence probably went both ways. Unless he was campaigning at the Farm Bureau, Spenser Kirkwood probably did not mention that his aunt was a pig farmer. So what else did the Kirkwoods not bother to tell people?

"Just out of curiosity, what's the name of your mother's family?" he asked.

"DeWitt."

"As in DeWitt plastics?"

She nodded.

Oh great. He needn't have wasted their time, asking if she wanted the story killed. He couldn't kill it if he wanted to. It was turning into a hydra.

Somehow he had to shift the focus away from individual personalities. The story must not be seen as a bizarre act by a bizarre person; it must be seen as an expression of the values and traditions of a cultural group. An odd group, perhaps. A group so small it might be approaching extinction. But a group nonetheless. If one person claims that his view of God is the only proper view, he's called a lunatic. If a group of people claims the same thing, it's called a church.

What he needed was an authority. Someone who could put the story into a larger cultural context. Someone quotable. Preferably at great length.

Chapter 14

"I think it's perfectly beautiful, what she's done," said Coral Hoskins. "Of course, Singing Wolf prefers the purity of fire, but he has complete respect for every native tradition and one of those is to offer oneself to one's fellow creatures after death."

Coral's silvery blond hair was worn in a braid to her waist. Her clothes were earth-colored cotton, but their plainness was backdrop to her jewelry and accessories, a dazzling array of silver, turquoise, beads, shells, feathers, and bright hand-woven scarves and belts.

I was not surprised to see her. When Terp decided to look for an authority on alternative spirituality, he was bound to wind up where he was, sitting in Coral's teepee-shaped living room, hearing her describe how the room and the jewelry had come into her life, and trying not to grimace as he sipped the tea she had brewed from plants she found in the woods near her house.

No reportorial skills were needed to draw forth her tale. It poured out of her, unprompted, to anyone who crossed her path. Even I, who tried to steer clear of soul-baring conversations, had heard pieces of her story, usually when I was delivering a box of my pork to her house.

Apart from the pork, our acquaintance was sporadic because Coral did not own a lawnmower. She believed that plants and animals should be left free of human control, with the result that the opportunistic patches of burdock, ragweed, and honeysuckle that had sprung up after the construction of her house had grown into an impenetrable thicket outside her windows and her small flock of chickens, unconstrained but also unprotected by a fence, was regularly and freely dined upon by the local population of raccoons, skunks, weasels and foxes. The only creature happier than the foxes was Otis, who counted it dumb luck that the woman he called the "tooth and feather lady" kept showing up in his dooryard looking to pay him six dollars a bird for some aging and unproductive hens to replace her flock that had been slaughtered by predators.

Terp's visit had put Coral into a state of earthly bliss. Instead of hurrying through her tale as her audience edged toward the door, she could linger over details and bask in the pleasure of being asked for more.

Some years ago, she said, after her youngest son left for boarding school, she had begun to feel that her life was sterile. Her husband was an insurance executive in Hartford; they had a nice house and an active social life; she was healthy, safe, and prosperous; nothing in her life could be described as bleak. And yet bleak was how she felt. Was there any purpose to her life, really?

Christianity offered no comfort. She could not see that her distress arose from any failing of her own, so she had no need for forgiveness or redemption. What she craved was the feeling that her life had large and beautiful meaning.

For months she had drifted, deep in melancholy. Then one day, she fell into conversation with a stranger in the lift line at Stratton Mountain, a young man who said he had once been where she was, sunk in despair. The change had come, he said, when he discovered the teachings of Singing Wolf.

As the chairlift carried them to the summit of the mountain, he told her how this prophet of the Great Spirit had made him understand that his own existence was as necessary as the existence of the sun or the oceans or Mozart or Thomas Edison. By the time they skied off the lift, Coral felt electrified. Hope had been restored.

After her first sojourn at the Singing Wolf Training Center in New Mexico, Coral knew she had found her spiritual home. The prophet was just as the young man had described, a magnetic presence, bold and eloquent. Although Singing Wolf was not himself Native American—his ancestry was Irish and Norwegian—he said he had been chosen as a prophet precisely because of his lack of native heritage. His soul was an expanse of untouched sand on which the principles of native spirituality could be written in a new and purer form.

From the moment Coral dedicated herself to his Fourteen Pathways, she had felt the most extraordinary lightness of spirit. The smallest details of her life had meaning. What she ate. What she wore. Her furniture. Her artwork. In time, she persuaded her husband to buy land in the northern woods and build a house that embodied Singing Wolf's teaching. The center living room was modeled after a teepee with slanting fir beams and triangular expanses of glass; the two wings were built from adobe with rooms opening onto long glassed-in arcades. She only regretted that the climate did not allow the arcades to be open to the outdoors, as they would have been in New Mexico, and that after bringing a roofer from Albuquerque to install an authentic red tile roof, the ice and snow had proven so damaging to the clay tiles, she'd been forced to replace them with standing seam metal, a material so hideous and unnatural, it wounded her to think about it.

Then she flicked her hand outward, shedding the negativity. The roof was a small thing, she said. She had taught herself not to look at it. In all other ways, the house felt like a temple, surrounding her with objects that enriched her spirit. With a giggle, she confessed that she did love to buy things and she had worried this might be contrary to teaching, but Singing Wolf had assured her that shopping could be spiritual, if she followed the guidelines in his book.

She paused from her recital and took a drink of the herbal tea.

"He has guidelines for shopping?" Terp said.

Don't stop now, he was thinking. Never mind that he was miles away from his story. This he wanted to hear, for the pleasure of hearing it. Was there anything more delicious than a truly virtuoso display of effrontery in the dog-eat-dog world of faith-based business enterprise?

If Coral had been a trailer mom with five kids, mailing her rent money to a televangelist who promised riches to the believers in his God, then Terp would have been itching to write an exposé. As it was, he could relish every detail she told him. Coral was happy. She had money to spare. If she wanted to build a desert-style house in the ice and mildew climate of New England, it would be a minor footnote in the catalog of human oddity. If her contentment made Singing Wolf a richer man, it was a fair bargain in the world of free enterprise.

"What sort of guidelines?" he prompted.

Given that nudge of encouragement, Coral leapt up, seized a book from her shelves, and pressed it into Terp's hand, exclaiming that this was now her personal Bible. All of Singing Wolf's books were glorious, she said, but this was the one she could not live without. Its cover design of zigzags and spirals suggested Anasazi pictographs. Its title was self-explanatory: *Spiritual Shopping: A Complete Guide to the Spiritual Properties of the Products You Buy*.

Terp flipped it open and saw that it catalogued a mega-mall array of consumer goods, rating them on a scale from nurturing to toxic. Coral said it had been her life goal to replace all of her toxic possessions with their nurturing alternative. It had taken time, she said, but every object she owned now came from the highest category of spiritual nourishment and a houseful of toxicity had been safely removed to the thrift store or the dump.

As she described the more noteworthy of her acquisitions, such as her new Volvo SUV, Terp leafed through the book to see if any pattern governed the ratings. Some patterns were obvious. Everything for sale at the Singing Wolf Center was nurturing. Most junk foods were poisonous. No surprises there. But why were the electronics made by Onkyo nurturing while Panasonic was neutral and JVC and Sony were somewhat toxic? Why was Coral's prized Volvo singled out for a gold star as the most nurturing SUV?

Don't even ask, he thought. This is not the realm of reason. People want magic, not reality. He'd just as well ask why a Christian believer chooses the elaborate idea of the immaculate conception when the same story could arise from ordinary human events: a young girl gets married to an old man; for reasons known only to them, the marriage is not consummated; the girl encounters another man and conceives a child; to save herself from being stoned to death, she says that an angel told her she is carrying the child of god.

That human story had profound miracles, all right, but they weren't the conception or the angel. The miracles were the resourcefulness of Mary, finding a way to survive, and the kindness and generosity of the cuckold Joseph, who kept his mouth shut, backed up her story and accepted her child, instead of calling down the law to have her put to death. Making amends. Forgiving. Moving on. Those were the miracles.

Trouble is, Terp thought, people don't like the idea that the angel of god might be some pudgy bald working stiff who coaches T-ball, builds stage sets for the school play, and gives his wife foot rubs when they're watching TV in the evening. They want their angel to be a gorgeous creature who arrives in a blaze of glory, preferably bringing wealth and happiness when he comes. The miracle people really want is for god to make a bigger needle, so that not just a camel, but a Volvo SUV, can pass through the eye of it.

Terp handed the book back to Coral.

"It's very comprehensive."

"Yes, isn't it? And it's such a waste, all the people still dragged down by negative energy." She pointed at Terp's jacket. "That jacket, for instance. You should find one without Velcro."

"Velcro?"

"Yes. Velcro is very toxic. Zippers are bad, too, especially metal ones. The best things to use are buttons and drawstrings. You should think about these things. It will change your life."

She spread her arms as if to invite the whole world into her embrace.

"Speaking of changing one's life," he said, "what can you tell me about how a person is supposed to die? In the Native American tradition."

"Ah yes, death. It is nothing to be afraid of."

She shifted her legs into a new position.

"It's the most beautiful moment of one's life, when the spirit moves on to another realm. It's the summit of one's journey, one's union with the Great Spirit."

She was speaking more and more quickly. Her fingers turned her tea mug in circles.

"It's natural. It's joyful. It's an event to be celebrated, not mourned."

Whistling in the dark, Terp thought. She's scared out of her wits by the thought of death.

He remembered his grandmother, emaciated and racked by the pain of cancer, needing every ounce of will just to brush her teeth. Tell her a joke, though, and her eyes would sparkle, her mouth would twist into a smile. Holding on to that last squeezed-dry rind of life.

"How do they celebrate?" Terp asked. "Are there ceremonies?"

"Oh, yes, beautiful ceremonies. First you say goodbye and feel sad. The way you do whenever someone leaves on a journey. And then you rejoice. Because the person isn't gone at all. They're right here with you. In the wind and the grass. In the music of a flute. In everything."

Everything, hah! I interjected. Everything nice is what she really means.

I'd been keeping my trap shut a long time, but I finally had to say something. Why do people think they can dump all the bad stuff and keep all the good, just because they're dead? If they want to stick around in the wind and the grass, then they're going to be here in the ocean-going barges full of garbage, too, and the child prostitutes and tin-roof shacks, and the traffic jams of cars with seven cup-holders and one occupant. A person can't pick and choose, any more than the law of gravity could hold onto Ghandi while letting Hitler fly off into space. We're all in one boat. Doesn't matter if the world is a complex of wave-particle probabilities or the deliberate creation of a supreme intelligence. There's a thread that ties the Starbucks mug in Coral's cup-holder to the tin rice bowl of a beggar in Asia and the day we're not all tied to that beggar is the day there aren't any beggars.

"They're here in everything?" Terp said. "Really?"

"Everything," she repeated, with fervor.

"Even in the toxic things? Like Velcro?"

I jumped. Had he heard me? It was the same teasing poke I'd have wanted to give her.

Coral blinked. "I don't know... That isn't how..."

She shook her head in bafflement.

"I'm sure it isn't like that," she said, in a tone of distress. "It can't be. I'm sure Singing Wolf could explain it better..."

Terp smiled, letting go of the point.

"Maybe it's only the people who use Velcro that turn into Velcro after they die," he said.

"That must be it. Exactly," she cried. "That's why it's so important to get rid of toxins."

Her face was radiant with relief.

"Would you like a little more tea?" she asked. "It's an energizing blend."

"No thank you," he said hastily. "I'm fully energized from the first cup. But I do hope you can tell me more about the traditions surrounding the bodies of the dead..."

As they plunged into a discussion of tribal methods of corpse disposal, I felt a most peculiar sensation. I wanted to hug him.

Chapter 15

"It's pablum," Terp muttered. "So why is it so difficult?"

He paced the square of floor beside his desk. What was wrong with him? Usually he could knock off a story in one uninterrupted rush of typing, no second drafts. But this story. It was like trying to make thin gruel hold a shape. He'd been deleting, retyping, cutting and pasting for two hours. He looked at his watch. He didn't have another two hours.

He knew what the problem was. He wasn't writing the story. He was writing a smokescreen of verbiage to divert attention from the story and every journalistic instinct was screaming in protest.

He could see the real headline, floating before his eyes in blocky tabloid typeface: "Where's the Body?" He looked at the first sentence on his screen. "**The cultural traditions associated with death and funerals are as widely varied as the traditions surrounding weddings, cuisine, clothing, and religious worship.**" He wanted to gag.

With reflexive speed, he typed a different sentence. "**Three days after the sudden death of Fay Kirkwood, 79, of Gilham, Kirkwood's niece Dryden still refuses to tell authorities what she has done with the body of the deceased.**" That story would write itself.

Then he thought about Dryden. How she had raged after talking to her mother. The set of her jaw as she said, "Write the truth. I'll take my chances." He could still see her fingers dancing saxophone riffs and her eyes ducking away when he asked about it.

Forget what she'd said about writing the truth. Probably she'd be in trouble, no matter what he wrote, and probably she was strong enough to take it, but he would not be the one to call in the hounds. He highlighted the attention-grabbing sentence and hit the delete key. The sentence vanished and cultural traditions hopped upward to the top of his story.

She'll be annoyed, I said. She meant what she said, about writing the truth.

Terp stared at the innocuous phrases on his screen.

"What if she despises me for this?" he thought.

The simple facts were doubly tempting. He could write a piece worth reading and the controversy would give him a reason to talk to her again. So what was stopping him?

Such a small thing, really. That crescent wrench, flying across the shop and spinning to a stop on the concrete. The rage and pain that had sent it flying.

It didn't matter what she could endure. He would do what he could to shield her. He would write his diversionary pablum and maybe it would work. Maybe she would be left in peace. Let her damn him as a deceitful coward, but he would obfuscate to the best of his ability.

He looked again at the paragraphs on his screen, the respectfully bland discourse on the subject of funerals. It was too bland, he realized, even for his own purpose. He quickly retyped his opening: **"One of the many funeral traditions in cultures worldwide is the practice of offering the body as a gift to wild creatures. Before her unexpected death three days ago, Fay Kirkwood, 79, of Gilham, had expressed a wish to follow this tradition..."**

He had to lead with the dead body. If he didn't, Randall might rewrite the piece and possibly would yank him off the story as well. Ten minutes before deadline, he turned it in. He'd written worse pieces, but not by much. It was innocuous, irrelevant, and deadliest of all, boring.

In other words, it was perfect.

Moral indignation would never be calmed by a reasoned argument, but possibly it could be lulled into a stupor by a blend of smarmy reverence and minute technical detail. He had included more information than anyone was likely to want about the construction of funerary scaffolds by certain tribal groups and he had managed to make Dryden and her aunt sound like sweet, unworldly nature lovers, as huggable as bunny rabbits.

When he finally crawled into bed, he couldn't sleep. He lay awake in the darkness, wondering how he had gotten sucked into such an uncharacteristic wrestling match between lust and nobility. He was attracted to Dryden and she would never see him as a white knight. So why couldn't he slide into his usual mode with her?

He'd always liked to keep things light. Sex should be a pleasant diversion, not grand opera. Conversation should be a dance, not an excavation of the psyche. The goal was pleasure. If affection happened to follow, that would be a serendipitous event.

But with Dryden, perversely, he wanted her to demand feeling. He wanted her to hold back and ask him to be splendid. He wanted to *be* splendid. He wanted to make her smile at the thought of her saxophone. He wanted a bed to come at the end of the day, after hours together eating good food, talking, making music, reading comics.

This is completely nuts, he thought. I don't even know her.

Chapter 16

"This L.T. Jones fella must be a granola-head," Otis said. He swatted the news article with the back of his hand. "He's made up so much fool stuff about Fay, you'd never know he was talking about the same person. What's she got to do with some tribe in Montana or wherever?"

He and Noah were sitting at my kitchen table, both of them seemingly drawn there by an impulse to look in on Dryden. The morning milking was done and Otis was content to settle in with coffee and our copy of the newspaper and wait for Dryden to show up. Noah had made a cup of tea, but he was on his way to work and had a perched look.

"Where do they get this stuff?" Otis said. "Fay never would have said animals are just like people."

"Not unless she was pissed off at the animal," Dryden said from the doorway.

They were startled by her voice and so was I. None of us had heard her come.

"Did you really talk to this guy?" Otis asked. "He says you did."

Dryden nodded. She poured herself coffee and Otis slid the paper across the table to her. As she read, her lips twitched in a hint of a smile. When she finished, her eye lingered on the headline "**Local Woman Honors Native Traditions.**"

"Was he as goofy as he sounds?" Otis asked.

"Goofy like a fox," she murmured. Then, more loudly, she said, "It's drivel. The guy should be fired for bad writing."

"That's just what I said to Noah," Otis complained. "He makes you and Fay sound like a couple of birdbrains. You ought to write a letter to the paper and straighten him out."

"I don't think so."

"People are gonna think she was a fruitcake. Reporters can twist things around till they mean the opposite and people are so dumb nowadays, they're liable to believe it. They got no common sense any more…"

Otis was launched on a familiar theme, about the ignoramuses from the city who move out to the country and wreck everything, and he was soon far afield from his concern about my reputation. Dryden slid the paper across for Noah to read and sat drinking her coffee.

For a time, the scene felt surreal, because it was so familiar. If I'd been sitting in the fourth chair, nothing would have changed. Otis would have gone on grumbling, Noah would have gone on reading the newspaper, Dryden would still be gazing into her coffee cup.

Then I saw that Noah was not reading any more. His eyes rested on the newspaper, unfocused, and slow tears were sliding down his cheeks. He didn't ask for comfort and neither of the others moved to offer any. His tears were a private matter. After a while, as silently as they'd started, the tears stopped. He folded the paper and got up to leave.

His movement stirred the others. They swallowed the last of their coffee and got up, also.

As Otis was putting on his jacket, he said, "Do you remember that time Fay went headfirst after that runaway pig and actually caught the darned thing?"

The moment he spoke, I saw what he was seeing, clear as life. Myself, in coveralls and barn boots, rolling in the dirt, struggling to keep my grip on a furiously protesting shoat.

Some details were hazy, but I remembered the pig making a bolt to escape the herd and me making a reflex dive to stop it. My grab had snagged its hind legs, one in each fist, and the two of us had landed on the ground together, thrashing. Otis and Dryden were watching and laughing, but neither could come to my aid without letting the other pigs escape. Almost certainly I was swearing, but nothing I said could be heard over the screeches of the captive pig.

It was a stalemate. The pig couldn't get away. I couldn't get up. Dryden and Otis couldn't move until the herd was safely penned. The herd couldn't be penned until someone opened the next gate. Finally, after what seemed a very long time, Noah heard the noise and came to help.

"I dunno what she was thinking, making that tackle," Otis said. "That pig woulda come back on his own if she hadn't riled him up."

"I don't think she expected to catch it," Dryden said.

"And I think she rather regretted her success," Noah added.

They were still chuckling together, putting on boots and gloves, when the phone rang.

Dryden went to answer, and in a matter of seconds, her whole body tensed.

"Yes…That's fine… No, I know that; I… I was busy last night… Of course I'll be here… No, it's not a problem. The guest bed has some papers on it, but I can sort those out…"

From the doorway, Noah made a gesture of inquiry, could he do anything? Dryden signaled not to wait; she'd be OK.

Two hours later, Anita faced her daughter with Terp's article gripped in her fist.

"Can you possibly give me a reason why you talked to the newspapers?" she said.

"The reporter was amusing," Dryden said.

"Are you out of your mind?"

"It's the *Leonardston Herald*. The people you worry about won't even see it."

"You don't know that. Things get picked up by wire services. People come here to ski. No place is far away anymore, not for a man in public life."

Anita threw the paper onto the table and shifted her glare to Charlie, as if to say that his silence was as bad as collusion. Rather than tangle with her, he decided it would be a good moment to take luggage upstairs. When he picked up the two bags, his shoulders sagged.

In three long steps Dryden crossed the kitchen, snatched the larger bag out of his hand and hoisted it to her shoulder.

"I got it, Dad."

As she spoke, I saw a young man lift a bale of garden mulch and flash a grin as he asked, "Where do you want this?" He wore a t-shirt and sneakers. His frame was wiry and he could almost have been Dryden's twin. I felt a flinch and the image vanished.

He was the boy I'd seen before, but who was he? Was he one of the parents who had given Dryden up? Or did she have a whole other family somewhere and this was a brother?

No answers were forthcoming. All I heard was Anita's voice as she followed Dryden and Charlie up the stairs to the guest bedroom and then back down again.

"If I live forever, I'll never understand you," Anita said. "It ought to be a no-brainer, to stay away from the media. Reporters love a sensation. They don't care what trouble they cause."

"Actually, I think he's trying to save us trouble."

"Oh, so that's the line he used, is it? He makes us sound like crackpots."

"He could have done worse."

"Worse how? What could possibly be worse than this?"

"Well, there are the people who think I clocked Fay with a hammer to get her money."

Anita was momentarily halted. This was a new idea and she needed to factor it into her calculations. She looked again at the earnestly broadminded headline, then back at Dryden.

"Are people really saying that?"

"How would I know? I'm not the one they'd say it to. You could go for coffee in town and maybe you'll find out. Or you could ask Otis. He generally knows what's going on."

"I'm certainly not going to talk to Otis about our business."

"Then I guess we'll have to live with the suspense."

Anita's irritation hit the boiling point. "Why are you acting this way? If you really did want Fay's money, at least that would be an intelligible reason. But this!"

She stabbed the newspaper with her forefinger.

"Do you get some malicious pleasure out of this? And it could all be so simple! Just get a death certificate and have her buried."

"It's not what Fay wanted."

"Fay's dead! She won't even know! Charlie, can you make her see sense?"

"It's not really our business..." he muttered. "Since Noah's the executor... and we'll have to see how she left things..."

"How she left things! We know how she left things. Half to Noah and half to our kids. She told you that, back when she wrote her will. You're the successor executor."

"I know, but... that was twenty years ago. She could have, you know... changed her thinking... And she did know Dryden better..."

"Know Dryden! When has that ever...? That's not how..."

Anita was livid and she didn't have to finish her sentences for me to know why. In the matter of inheritance, my forebears had operated on a principle of mathematical fairness as measured by degrees of kinship. All relatives with an equal degree of shared blood were to be treated equally, regardless of feelings. No black sheep and no favorite nephews. My money was a blip, compared to the DeWitt conglomerate, but as a symbol, it was as potent as a cobwebbed bottle of Bordeaux.

For what had she married Charlie, if not for his family's aristocratic tone, that serene high-mindedness about material possessions that was possible only after several generations of having plenty of them? Her own family supplied all the vigor and ambition she needed. Her husband's family was supposed to rise above such things. We were meant to shun favoritism as instinctively as we would shun loud talk and excessive hugging and all the other distasteful behaviors of the rambunctious and overpopulated races of the world.

Too late now, Anita, I said. There's a spot of rot in our twig of the family tree, as you'll soon discover. I have indeed done the unthinkable and followed my heart.

My nephews would receive a token of familial regard, enough to pay for a week in Europe, perhaps, or a down payment on a car. A few charities would receive similarly modest gestures of support. With the rest, I had pleased myself, giving it to the two people I loved most. If I had chosen fondness over fairness, I felt not the slightest twinge of regret.

If my choice had unleashed the furies, however, that I might well come to regret.

Within minutes, Anita was on the phone with my lawyer demanding a meeting at the earliest possible moment. He quickly intuited that it would be more trouble than it was worth to put her off. He offered four o'clock that afternoon, saying he had some research he could postpone and the delay might even be a good thing, if it let some folks cool down about taking their next-door neighbors to court.

In his way, Joe Lambeth was as old school as my own family. He grew up in Leonardston and except for his time in the military and law school, had never lived anywhere else. His weathered skin and broad callused hands suggested he worked as a logger or farmer, but in fact were the result of two seasonal passions, for wintertime hiking and summertime cultivation of a nursery of rare peonies. He'd been my lawyer for decades and our outlooks were similar enough that we didn't have to waste time explaining ourselves to each other. Given the dizzying price of every sentence a lawyer uttered, his succinctness was a double virtue.

At the meeting, he kept the preamble to a minimum and went straight to content.

"Fay's will is very simple," he said. "All the real estate and tangibles go to Dryden. The residue in cash and investments is divided into specific percentages..."

With a few neat numbers, he conveyed the essential fact. Sidney and Spenser were getting nothing of significance.

"I see," said Anita. The tightness of her jaw was the only sign of her mood. Her glance flicked toward Dryden and then away again.

"When did Fay make this will?" Anita asked.

"Five years ago."

"Why wasn't Charlie sent a copy?"

"That would have been up to Fay. Charlie already knew he was the successor."

"And of course he'd never ask for a copy..." Anita muttered.

She stood up and put out her hand.

"Thank you, Mr. Lambeth, you've given us a very clear picture of the situation. I don't think we need to take up any more of your time."

Dinner that evening was a strained affair. Dryden had invited Noah to come and although no one at the table seemed inclined to talk, Anita was determined that they must. To eat in silence would grant Noah the status of a family member rather than a guest and this she had never been willing to do. Instead, seizing on the homegrown pork chops Dryden had cooked, she started asking questions, with exaggerated interest, about pigs and pig breeds. Noah was too polite and Charlie too cowed not to respond to her, so the three of them labored along, finding things to say about pigs. Only Dryden, the person with the most knowledge on the subject, said nothing. From pigs, the conversation moved on to pork and pork recipes, then on to diet fads, then on to fads in general, popular culture, any topic that could generate sound and create the appearance of a dinner party. Except in reference to pigs, my name did not come up.

By nine o'clock, Noah had gone and Anita and Charlie had retired to the guestroom. Lying in bed with his book, Charlie could hear Dryden prowling around the house, too restless to go to bed. When he heard the kitchen door open, he got up to look out the window. The moon was bright and he could see her in her work jacket, hatless in the wind, heading toward the hayfields with the dog.

He'd read most of a chapter when he heard the phone ring in the kitchen. He lay still, vaguely thinking that he ought to get up and answer. Then he heard the kitchen door bang open and settled back under the covers, letting Dryden take the call.

Chapter 17

Terp was pacing, wondering how Dryden would react to his voice on the phone. Would she hang up on him immediately?

Answering her hello, he tried to assume the best. "Hey, it's Terp Jones. Any chance you'd like to come over and jam a little?"

"Right now?" She paused. "It's almost ten o'clock. Don't you have neighbors?"

So far so good. She hadn't instantly said no.

"Not close enough to hear," he said.

There was another pause, much longer. He wanted to urge her, but some instinct said to keep his mouth shut and wait. Smart man, I thought.

"How do I get to your place?" she asked.

Coming into his house, she looked as if she had been blown there by a gale. She burst in, breathless, dropped her saxophone case on the floor and yanked off her boots. Her hair was in a tangle and her face glowed with color, from cold and from excitement. She was still wearing the wool jacket she used for chores, her prized two-dollar discovery at the thrift store. Although it was warm and durable, it was also remarkably ugly, a sickly yellowish-brown plaid to which farm work had added splotches of iodine, smudges of engine grease, and a tweed-like thatch of pig bristles and dog hair.

She tossed the jacket in a heap near her boots and looked for a flat place to lay her instrument. Under the jacket, she was still wearing town clothes from visiting the lawyer. Her blouse was the kind of color she chose when she thought about it, a vivid blue-green.

Terp watched her, lost in admiration, but she was busy unpacking her horn and didn't notice. Her reed was already in her mouth, soaking up spit. He saw that she'd brought the tenor, the voice he liked best. The friendly, laidback member of the family.

Laidback like a mule, I thought. She had persuaded me to try it once and all I'd gotten out of it were some ill-tempered squawks and a lot of spit-laden air.

Terp shook himself out of his daze and asked if she'd like anything to drink. "Coffee? Tea? Wine?"

"Uh ah-er," she said through the reed.

Translating the garble, Terp fetched a glass of water and set it near her. She was playing slow notes, testing the reed. A piece of him felt mildly bruised, that she seemed so unaware of him, but mostly he was enchanted by her absorption in her horn.

He also was hoping she could play. He wanted to tell her she was good, but what if she wasn't? Would he give her the honesty she had asked for?

She paused from warming up and smiled.

"I can't believe we're doing this," she said.

The radiance in her face sent a rush through his gut. Having always thought "weak in the knees" was an empty figure of speech, he found he was gripping the neck of the bass to steady himself. He plucked a couple of scales, experimentally. His fingers felt like sausages.

"Should we tune?" she asked.

They played matching notes and he adjusted his tuning a little, with head cocked to focus on the sound. The routine calmed his nerves.

"I haven't done that since high school band," she said. "Tuned with a different instrument, not just another saxophone."

"Your music teacher should find another line of work," he said.

"Yeah, well, it's too late for that now," she said. The light had left her face.

"I'm sorry. That was presumptuous...."

"Don't worry about it," she said harshly. "He's not worth thinking about."

"But you're worth thinking about!" he protested.

The words were trite, but he meant them, for all the good it did. He could feel her retreating, as if she'd been groped by a stranger.

"You sound like a shrink," she said.

Worse than groped. Probed. Was there any way to retrieve the mood?

"Two cents, please," he said jokingly and held out his hand.

When she didn't react, he blundered on, "OK, I know, my advice is overpriced. But I can't help it, the payments on the Porsche are..."

Enough already! I yelled. If you want to see her happy, shut your yap and start playing your stupid fiddle. You almost lost your chance back there.

He didn't finish the sentence. He had had some further witticism in mind, but it had slipped away. To fill the gap, he plucked a phrase from Cole Porter.

In a flash, Dryden echoed the theme, matching the breezy mood. He played a few more bars, and again she echoed him, with embellishments. He grinned and launched into the tune for real, not pausing. She stayed right with him, easily, and her eyes were sparkling. When he changed key and upped the tempo, she didn't waver. Her eyebrows wagged and he felt his body relax. She could play, all right. He would not have to steel himself to be honest.

As they bounced improvisations back and forth, he quickly realized that she wasn't just good enough; she was far beyond him. The bass was an unwieldy beast and he'd never play note for note with a saxophone, but even playing bare bones, he was already at his limit and she was not even breaking a sweat. He decided to shift to rhythm, which he could do on autopilot.

His hands settled into their groove and he gave her a wink. "Let her rip," he said.

She winked in return and he sat back to enjoy the show. He didn't have to think about his hands. They could keep up their steady thm-thm-thm-thm on the strings through anything, fire drill, blow job, or political debate, and that was all she needed from him. The weight of the bass was now an engine rather than a drag.

With nothing to hold her back, she fired up the afterburners and played the way she did when she was alone. I'd heard her play this way for years and so had Noah, but we may have been the only people who had. The few times I'd heard her play with Jonathan, she had reined herself in to stay at his level. I had wondered then and still wondered whether she'd been making a musical choice to subordinate individual virtuosity to the good of the whole, or whether it had been an unconscious feminine reflex, not to show off at his expense.

If it was a reflex, it was not in operation now. She was showing off plenty and did not appear to be thinking about Terp at all, except as a reliable rhythm on the bass.

Terp, for his part, was so awash in pleasure he had almost forgotten his own hands, which were still moving up and down the strings with the steadiness of a heartbeat. His thoughts, to the degree that he had any, were a lazy rotation around the core of amazement. *She's stunning. She's breathtaking. I hope we go on playing together until I'm a wizened old geezer who can hardly keep a grip on his fiddle. But how can she be this good and not have played with other people? Doesn't she realize it's the best thing going? Her teacher must be a jerk...*

As the thoughts went round, his hands began to give them voice. One minute, the thrum of his strings was a cheerful chuckle; then it became abrupt and irritable, with leaps and dissonances. With every shift, Dryden's playing mirrored his, moving from flow and sparkle to edge and jumpiness and soon I couldn't tell who was leading and who was following.

Then, midway through a phrase, she caught his eye, grabbed a fragment of the melody, changed key and tempo, and slid seamlessly into a different tune that began with the fragment. The new tune was as lazy as the other one was breathless and she played it like a drawl, squeezing the flavor out of each languorous slide.

With a head gesture, she invited him back into a melodic give and take. He leapt in, happily, but by now he knew she was beyond him in more than just agility. She could make the reed sing with whatever voice she wanted, melted caramel, cigarette smoke, tap dance, dark alley, freight train, or hopeful tomcat. He replied with the best voice he could manage on the bass, the guy humming to himself in the shower.

After a while, she signaled "going out." They closed with a flourish and looked at each other, grinning like fools.

"You are something else, you know that?" he said.

She laughed and played a phrase, goofily, part of a trumpet fanfare.

"That was the best!" she said.

He shook his head, still grinning. "Not even close," he said. "You've got to play with some serious musicians. I'm just a dubber, compared to you. You've got a real gift."

"You don't have to say nice things, you know."

"It's true. You're better than a lot of people who get paid."

She shrugged, almost frowning. Did she think he was lying to make her feel good?

"I'm not exaggerating," he said. "There are some very cool bands that would be glad to have you play with them."

Now she did frown, unmistakably. Her fingers fiddled with the keys of her horn.

"Why would I want to?" she said.

"Why would you–?" He stared at her. "Because it's fun!"

"That's not what I've heard."

"Heard from whom?"

"Someone who's been there."

"Someone who's full of shit!" he exploded.

Or someone who can't play for shit, he thought, but he bit back the words.

"Of course it's fun!" he said. "Playing with musicians who are really hot. Getting a crowd totally juiced. There's nothing like it."

Her frown relaxed a little. "You really think that?"

"I don't just think it, I know it. It's the most fun you'll have in your life, ever."

He grinned.

"Or maybe I should say, the most you can have with your clothes on."

She stiffened again and he cursed himself. How was it that yesterday every word he spoke seemed exactly right and today every word was exactly wrong? She turned and looked straight at him. When she spoke, her voice was flat.

"Should we just fuck and be done with it?"

"What?"

For a moment he felt as if he couldn't breathe, as if he had crashed into a brick wall and all the air had been driven from his lungs. How could he possibly answer that question? If he said yes, let's do, she would hate him and if he said, no, let's not, she would hate him, and it was what he wanted, more than anything, sometime, somewhere, but not like this. Was there any way to get back to how he did want it?

Help me out here, please, somebody, he thought. What was he supposed to do?

Stop pushing her, for god's sake, I screeched. You're like a goddamned bulldozer!

It drove me wild, that he might ruin everything, but what did it matter how I felt? I was dead. The point was to get through to the living.

I forced myself to calm down and said, OK, I shouldn't have yelled. It's not your fault you don't know about Jonathan and her life on the farm and why she's never played the way she could. But please, please, please, whatever else you do, don't take her up on her offer of a fuck. Not right now. Or she may never believe another word you say.

Stick with the music, I said. The music is key.

He ignored my advice, of course. Not that he actually took her up on her offer. It was more that he fell into a kind of paralysis and did nothing. I certainly couldn't fault him for being a bulldozer. If anything, he became the mud in front of the blade.

After that reflex exclamation of dismay, his wits seemed to freeze. As he stood there, searching for words to explain what he felt, Dryden put aside her saxophone, leaned his bass against the wall, and started methodically unbuttoning his shirt. Every nerve in him was crying out in protest, but he did not stop her.

How many times in the last twenty-four hours had he imagined how it might be? Always with conversation and laughter and a long, loving approach. Not this businesslike disrobing, as if she were a nurse preparing a patient for a medical procedure.

He could feel the sarcasm and self-loathing in every gesture she made. The care she devoted to each button of his shirt was a parody of passion. There was neither joy nor lust in her face. Only grim sadness. He didn't know what was driving her, but something was, and he was racked by the dread that this was the end, that they were deliberately, almost wantonly, destroying what might have been and the moment of actual copulation would be absurdly symbolic, the spectacular smash followed by implosion into rubble.

As it turned out, he was saved from the catastrophe, but not because he shook free of his paralysis and found the power to act. Just the opposite, in fact. He did absolutely nothing. The event rushed toward him and he made no move to stop it. Their clothes were shed. Their naked bodies met. They were approaching the moment when judgment would yield to animal urgency.

Except that it didn't.

Because instead, for the first time in his life, Terp found himself in the grip of erectile dysfunction.

He had pictured all manner of potential disasters, but this possibility had never entered his head. His penis had always been a workhorse, sturdy, eager, and, as such things go, biddable. It was incomprehensible that its enthusiasm could fail him now, but so it was. The organ that should have been electric to the touch was curled up like a caterpillar that is trying not to be noticed.

His first impulse was to do the same with the rest of himself, curl up in a ball, emotions inward, and not expose himself to further humiliation. So much for being splendid, he thought. He had just failed at a physical function that was within the capacities of a gerbil.

What must she think of him? Was she angry? Contemptuous? Or worst of all, would she go all tender and solicitous, as if he were an invalid?

He pulled away a little, muttering an apology. Beside him, he felt her body grow still. Not angry or disappointed. Not hastening to reassure. Just still. Like someone schooling herself to feel nothing at all.

You bloody idiot, I shouted. OK, so you can't copulate in gerbil fashion right now, but you're not a goddamned gerbil. You've got hands. You've got a mouth. You've got eyes and ears and a voice and most of all, a brain. You've got all those things and you're going to let a recalcitrant penis be the spokesman for who you are?

Snap out of it, for pity's sake.

The thought was like a starburst in his brain. Maybe she thought he didn't want her. Maybe she thought his feelings were as limp as his body.

With frantic eagerness, he rolled so that he could reach her with his hands and his mouth and began to touch her skin and hair, every inch of her, stroking, kissing, trying to pour what he felt through his lips and fingertips so that she would feel it, too. When at last her body arched and the cry of animal pleasure burst from her throat, he felt another starburst, under his breastbone, happiness flooding his veins.

Chapter 18

Later, when Terp had fallen into a deep sleep, Dryden slipped out of his bed and put on her clothes. In the living room, she paused beside his string bass and ran her hand along the varnished curve of wood, then silently departed. She did not leave a note.

When the door closed behind her, I was alone. Except for Terp's steady breathing, no sound or thought disturbed the nighttime quiet.

Might this be a moment to try for autonomy? There were so many experiences I had missed when I was alive. Sailing on the open ocean. Seeing a wolf in the wild. Prague. The Sahara Desert. A demolition derby. The Metropolitan Opera. Mardi Gras. The prospect of eternity would look more palatable if some small bit of it was mine to choose.

Was it possible for my thoughts to propel me in a particular direction? In the vacuum of outer space, the pressure from a stream of subatomic particles could change the path of an object. Could my path be changed by a stream of ideas?

I fixed my mind on the wolf. Of the possibilities that had come to mind, he interested me the most. I imagined him, lithe and watchful, padding among the scrubby trees of the far northern woods. I imagined myself launching a spider filament to catch in his fur and reeling myself, hand over hand, to wherever he was. My being had no weight. The filament could be weightless, too. It was only the arrow's path, not the arrow. I bent my whole will toward the wolf, hoping to catch some hint of his presence and let that hint draw me closer.

I heard a muffled yelp and for one astonished moment, I thought I'd succeeded.

Then the yelp subsided to soft, intermittent whimpers and I heard small scratches and the brush of fur against a surface. Wherever I was, it was very dark, but gradually I made out two shapes of lighter gray, windows, and then I saw the faint glow of an electric clock face.

I was back in my own kitchen. The sounds were coming from Scollay, whimpering and twitching as he dreamed, his claws scratching on the linoleum floor.

Suddenly his feet twitched so violently that he awoke and I was blasted by sensations. Not light. The room was as dim as before. But the noises were jarring. The refrigerator motor sounded like a jet engine. The electric hum of the clock was a mosquito whine. And the smells were overwhelming. The boot tray smelled like a feedlot. The pork from dinner was as present as if it were still in the pan. The lingering scent of Anita's perfume was chokingly sweet.

Along with all the ordinary smells, magnified, were microscopic smells I had never noticed before, slight chemical odors from the linoleum and the paint on the cupboards, metallic smells from the table legs and doorknobs, the plastic smell of the waste basket, the paper and ink of the newspaper, and infusing everything, the overpowering smell of different human beings, each one as potent and distinct as the most private and immediate smell of a lover.

With a shock, I realized that two of the smells were recognizable. Noah's. Of course. And my own.

Scollay crossed the room and rummaged among the pile of shoes near the door. He found a shoe that smelled powerfully of me, picked it up in his teeth and carried it over to his bed. When he lay down again, the shoe was close to his head. His attention was fixed on the door.

Gradually I realized that a pattern of sounds was repeating itself, over and over, like a tune you can't get out of your head. First the sound of an engine, faint in the distance. The engine got steadily louder and then tires crunched on gravel. The engine stopped. A truck door thunked shut. Feet crunched on gravel, surprisingly loud.

As the footsteps reached the front porch, Scollay's belly fluttered with anticipation. The boards of the porch reverberated with each tread. There was a metallic click as the doorknob turned, then a squeak from the hinges as the door opened. A gust of new smells filled the room, plants, rain, outdoor air and, most of all, my own rank human odor.

Except that there was no truck and the door had not in fact opened. The room was still dark and my smell was there only in the empty shoe. The flutter of hope in his belly subsided into gloom.

Then, after a while, in the distance, the truck's engine could be heard again.

There was no chatter of thoughts for me to hear. No analysis. No calculations. Only concrete sensations. The pain was like nothing I had ever experienced, wordless and all-encompassing.

Did he understand that I was dead? Or had he felt this way every time he had been left alone, not knowing if I would return in an hour, in a week, or never?

Do those prophets of self-help who urge us to live only in the present moment ever consider that the present moment might be rotten?

Eventually, Scollay moved on to a different moment. His muscles relaxed, the sound of my approach faded from his hearing, and he went back to sleep, leaving me to ponder whether my attempt at autonomy could be considered a success. Although I hadn't seen a wolf, I had moved in the general direction of "wolfness." Was this a coincidence or was it the first fruit of a skill that could be perfected?

And suppose I did perfect this skill. Suppose I learned to free myself from the ties of my own history and could travel the world, rootless, sampling its infinite splendors. Would my quest for freedom close the doors now open to me? Would I find myself permanently a spectator to abstract marvels, a tourist wandering from the Grand Canyon to the opera in Vienna making polite conversation with a population of strangers?

Perhaps the laws that governed my death deserved more credit than I had given them. I had asked for a wolf and I'd been given Scollay. On the whole, it was the choice I'd have made myself.

Chapter 19

In the morning, I discovered that my corpse had become trivia on a national scale. Somehow, the story in the *Leonardston Herald* had found its way onto the news wires. From there it had been seized as an item of colorful but inconsequential scandal to spice up the inner pages of world news, which otherwise held a grim repetition of budgetary difficulties, violent unrest, ecological degradation and political corruption.

For me, the effect was akin to bedlam. It was bad enough, being bounced from house to house in Gilham. Now my life was scattered coast to coast, a moment's accompaniment to breakfasts and bus rides in all parts of the country, from Baltimore to Tampa to Minneapolis. I felt like a tidbit tossed into the chicken coop, being snatched by one hen after another in such rapid succession that no hen can get a good solid bite. I caught fleeting impressions of palm trees, Formica with sparkles, graffiti on concrete, kids bickering, perky blondes on a TV talk show, eggs frying, the metallic shriek of subway wheels, sleet, sun, fog and the smell of fabric softener in the dryer, but nothing stuck, not until I heard a voice say, "Jeezum crow, would you look at that?" and the whirligig spun to a stop.

Sharon Kovalevsky was staring at a middle page story in *USA Today*, dateline Gilham.

Although she wouldn't have said so to her neighbors, Sharon liked *USA Today* more than she liked the *Leonardston Herald*. She liked the bright colors and the way the news was packaged into single-serving instant meals, with lots of borders and bold type. To her way of thinking, the Herald's expanses of sober black and white text made the news seem too gloomy.

To my way of thinking, the problem with the *Herald* was its prose, not its layout. It was owned by a former New Yorker who mowed his lawn with an old and lovingly tended walk-behind Lawn Boy and considered the *Times* and *Wall Street Journal* of his youth to be the divinely ordained models of newspaper layout. Not being a journalist himself, he didn't quite grasp that a plain, densely-packed page of newsprint could be a vehicle for rubbish as well as brilliance. His own paper survived, neither by prose nor by layout, but by its church calendars, school bus routes, town election results, weddings, obituaries, and other mundane utilities.

Despite her opinion, Sharon did buy the *Herald* every day, as a matter of course. It was necessary to know who had died and who had been elected to the school board. But for real news, for "news" news, she turned to the color-coded sections of the national paper. Finding the town of Gilham mentioned in the real news was news in itself, an event to be announced to everyone who walked into the diner for breakfast. In all her years reading *USA Today*, she had never encountered a story about Gilham.

At first she kept the paper closed between showings, so that she could open it to the relevant page with dramatic effect. After a while, the sheets began to wrinkle and tear, so she took the section apart and refolded it neatly, middle out, with the Gilham story front and center.

Although none of the morning's customers had a compelling interest in my death, almost all of them were idly curious, and together, their filaments of thought kept me trussed as thoroughly as a fly in a spider's web. Whenever the discussion showed signs of flagging, a new person would come through the door, Sharon would proffer the paragraphs of national fame, and a fresh thread of opinion and speculation would be added to the web that was holding me.

Then I felt a hard yank and the threads yielded to a definite thought.

The door to Jim Jorgensen's office swung open and Anita marched through it, with a click of leather heels. Charlie shuffled in after her, looking apologetic.

"We have a problem that requires your attention," Anita said.

She moved the available chair a few inches to the left and sat down. Charlie glanced toward an extra chair in the corner, but could not make up his mind either to sit in it or move it closer. Instead he remained standing, a little behind Anita.

After a moment, Jim got up to move the chair and invited Charlie to sit. He murmured an automatic question, how could he help, but his gaze kept straying to Gerald's gloves, which were still on his desk.

I felt a thought, griping like an acid stomach. *What is it with this guy? He acts like we don't exist. Look at him, counting his ballpoint pens. Typical small-town bureaucrat, dumb as a post and full of self-importance about his little fiefdom.*

Anita, without a doubt. Heaven help me.

"Excuse me," she said, with an edge of sarcasm. "Have we come at a bad time, perhaps?"

Jim started. "Sorry. No, it's a fine time. What's the problem?"

Anita introduced herself and Charlie, which prompted a polite exchange of condolences and thanks. Then, after a suitable pause, Anita proceeded to her purpose.

"The problem is that the whole situation is unacceptable."

"It's unusual, certainly," Jim said.

"Unusual! It's an outrage!"

"So the family wasn't—?"

"Family! The family would never have done what she did. My son is a US Representative. He can't have people thinking he had any part in this mess."

"Excuse me a moment. When you say 'she,' you're referring to…?"

"Dryden, of course. Who else would I mean?"

She pronounced each word distinctly. Did she need flash cards with this guy? He looked like a third grader faced with long division.

"What exactly would you like to see happen?" he asked.

"A proper burial, obviously. To get this thing out of the papers. We need Fay's remains."

"So you'd like me to organize a search?"

"No, of course not. That would be another public spectacle. I want you to speak to Dryden. Perhaps, as a law enforcement officer, you can persuade her to say where she took Fay."

"And if she won't?"

"Then you could remind her that it looks very bad. That she will inherit a considerable amount of money and no one else saw the body."

"Noah saw it," Charlie said.

"Noah is an interested party. I meant, no one in an official capacity."

Jim was silent, his expression noncommittal. It could be good training for this job, I thought, to be a homosexual from North Dakota. It would be second nature, not to reveal oneself.

"Do you have any reason to think this was a homicide?" he said finally.

"At least that would make sense," Anita said irritably. "To want Fay's money. Dryden's story makes no sense whatsoever. But the way she is, that probably means it's true. It would be exactly like her, to do the thing that causes the most trouble."

For the first time, Jim looked surprised. "More trouble than a homicide?"

"A homicide would be dreadful, of course, but at least it's not abnormal. We have murders every day in this country, so the newspapers move on. And it's not unprecedented for a public figure to have a relative in jail. But this thing! It's utterly perverse! It's just the sort of thing the media will make into a sensation.

"I've said all this to Dryden, but it was wasted breath," Anita added. "I hope that an official inquiry might encourage her to cooperate."

Hope, but don't expect, she thought. It'll be a cold day in hell when that girl decides to cooperate with anybody. She could still see Dryden's shrug of refusal, so cool and indifferent, as if to say she'd done what she'd done and no one else counted.

Then the image dissolved into another, far in the past but as clear as the present moment. Dryden was seven years old and already she could look straight at her parents and set her jaw in defiance.

"You said I could choose," she said.

"I meant the instruments in the orchestra," Anita explained. "What about the violin? Or the flute? Those are good instruments for a girl."

"I don't like them. I want to play jazz."

"Jazz!" Even now, decades later, Anita recoiled. "You are not going to play jazz."

"You and Dad listen to it."

"It's one thing to listen to it. Playing it is different. We're not that sort of people."

"What sort of people?"

"The wrong sort. If you don't want to be in an orchestra, you can learn piano. But we will not buy you a saxophone and that's final."

Anita was appalled by this confrontation. All her efforts to give Dryden a good start in life had made no impression at all. The child's nature is still inclined toward coarseness.

Dryden had settled on the piano, and for a time, she seemed to be moving in a better direction. She practiced with surprising diligence and progress came easily. Her teacher said she had a gift. Then, just when Anita began to feel more hopeful and even a little proud, she learned that Dryden's diligence was a front for cunning. One day, she walked into the house after work and faintly, from the basement, she heard the bleating reed notes of a saxophone, playing scales.

She called her daughter upstairs and asked where she'd gotten the instrument.

"From Sidney's friend Brian."

"He gave it to you?"

Dryden shook her head. "I paid for it."

"How much did it cost?"

"Not much. He said he's done with the school band, now that he's gotten into college."

"How much?"

"He wanted a hundred dollars but he said I could have it for fifty if I would play with his weenie. And I only had fifty-two dollars saved up, so I said OK. And then he started—"

"That's filthy. You are a filthy little girl. You are taking that instrument back right now."

Dryden clutched the horn to her chest and glared. "I won't. I earned it. It's mine."

Anita was about to yank the instrument out of her arms when Charlie, her spineless, aimless husband, stepped in and undermined her authority.

"What's done is done," he said. "It won't take away what happened to take away the instrument. You can see how much she wants it. And it's really Brian who's—"

"She's disgusting. I can't believe you want to let her get away with this."

"But she's serious about it. I think we should let her try."

"Well, she's not giving up the piano to do it. If she wants to play that thing, I suppose she can, but she has to keep up the piano, too. And I hope we don't regret this later."

She turned to Dryden. "You do understand, don't you, that what you did with Brian is filthy? Do you want people to think you're a slut?"

Dryden glared and clutched her saxophone.

"Do you? Answer me."

She slowly shook her head, no. Apparently, despite her stubbornness, she understood that her mother could still take away the instrument.

She was stubborn, all right, I thought now.

She could have ended the argument right there, if she'd told them the whole story. She was starting to tell it, when her mother cut her off and called her filth. After that, there was no way she was going to tell her mother about the true deliciousness of her triumph.

She'd never told me the whole story, either. She only told me the other half, the part she didn't tell Anita. She said that she and Brian had agreed on a price, but before she could pay him, he started teasing her, saying she was a girl and too little for the saxophone and she wouldn't be strong enough to make a sound, the first time she blew into it. And she said, yes she would, and he said, want to bet, and she said, yes, double or nothing.

At that point, telling me the story, Dryden started laughing and said she'd had a fool's luck, because she had never actually touched a saxophone before and she had no idea what to do. When it came time to try it, to win her bet, she'd nearly blown the top of her head off.

But she'd done it. She made the reed play a note, first time out. Several notes, in fact. And Brian honored the bet and she got her saxophone without paying him anything at all.

At the time she told me the story, I had assumed the price was just money.

Chapter 20

She'd be strong enough to kill an old lady.

Such was Jim's first thought, seeing Dryden. She used her pants as a grease rag. Her hand looked comfortable on a wrench. He had never met her before, which was not a bad thing. The people he did meet in his job were mostly not the ones you'd invite to dinner.

She came to greet him with the engines-forward attitude of someone accepting a dare. Maybe because of the uniform. He was about to extend his hand and smile when some instinct said she'd find the gesture phony. It wasn't a social call.

"I'm Jim Jorgensen," he said matter-of-factly.

"You're here about Fay's body," she said. "Otis said I'd need a piece of paper."

"Otis...?"

"Friend of ours," she said. "What's the penalty for not having one?"

"I'm not sure, off the top of my head. I've never encountered this before. Why didn't you get one?"

His inquiry was launched, it seemed, whether he was ready or not.

"I didn't want an argument," she said.

"You'll have one anyway, won't you?"

"Yeah, but Fay won't. She's out of reach."

"We'll have to organize a search."

"Don't bother. You won't find her."

His body tensed. What a waste of time this was. Today of all days, he longed for the usual lazy jog of existence in Gilham, where demands on his attention were rarely too urgent to be postponed for an hour or two. There hadn't been a homicide in Gilham in recent memory.

"You do realize that without a body there will be some awkward questions," he warned.

"For god's sake!" she burst out. "Why can't anybody talk straight? If you've got awkward questions, just ask them. Why fool around with a search?"

Because there are protocols to be followed, he thought, but he was reluctant to say so.

"Well, the obvious question is whether your aunt died of natural causes. Or was there an accident, say...?"

"What on earth kind of accident? I found her lying on flat ground with an empty slop bucket beside her. There wasn't even a pebble she could have tripped over. And even if she tripped and broke her neck, what does it matter? Dead is dead. Or do you have some piece of paper with a box you have to check?"

"OK, forget the accident. The real question is how do we know you didn't kill her?"

As soon as the words were out, he was kicking himself. He'd let her get to him. He'd let her play on his own frustrations with paperwork, red tape, and general institutional clumsiness. For that brief moment, she'd made it seem natural to ask that question. It was what he wanted to know, after all.

Had his brain gone soft? Protocols were there for a reason. If she now said, "On November thirtieth I split my aunt's skull with a double-bladed axe," it would not be admissible evidence.

How do we know you didn't kill her? Gut-straight question. And gut-stupid, if there actually had been a murder.

"You don't, but I didn't," she said.

Was it possible to cover more ground with fewer words? He studied her expression. She looked him straight in the eye, but that didn't mean she was telling the truth, any more than shifty eyes would mean she was lying. His credit rating had been wrecked by a lover who looked him straight in the eye. His mother, on the other hand, never looked straight at anyone. Harried by shyness, her gaze would flit from collarbone to chin to collarbone as she conversed, but she was also the only person he knew who reported her barter transactions on her income tax.

His question had been premature, but he couldn't retract it so he'd just as well follow up.

"What did happen then?" he asked.

With a sigh, she began to recite the facts one more time.

Jim didn't look at her while she talked. He had found he heard more clearly that way. People could use body language to deceive as well as reveal. He remembered Oliver North, testifying to Congress. Watching him, watching that ramrod-stiff military posture, you'd swear he was speaking straight. Listen to his testimony on the radio, though, and you could hear how his answers slithered and dodged.

Dryden's account plodded forward like a bored mule. Neither hurry nor hesitation, just here we go again.

"What you've done is illegal, you know," he said when she finished.

"Which part?"

"Several things. Failure to obtain a death certificate. Failure to get a permit for private burial. Failure to comply with standards for burial."

She shrugged. "So put me in jail."

"I hope it won't come to that. You could simplify things greatly if you would retrieve the remains and comply with the statutes."

"Comply with the statutes means what?"

"You could get a permit and bury her here on the farm."

"She didn't want that. She wanted her body to be eaten by varmints."

To be eaten by varmints. Wild beasts. Scavengers. Until she spoke the words, he had been able to blur the details of a body being left in the woods. To think of it, fuzzily, as something akin to going on a nature walk or camping out.

Now the blunt fact had been shoved in his face. She wanted to be eaten.

Surely this was blasphemy. The body was meant to be lifted up on the last day. How could that happen, if it had been torn apart by animals and scattered?

But why not? As a boy, he'd seen old people who were withered and tottering and the preacher said their bodies would be made perfect again after death. So why did it matter what became of the body? What about the soldiers, blown to bits, or the bomb victims, nothing left but teeth?

Christ cared for everyone; that was the whole point. Jim had felt the truth of this in his own life. In school, he had been teased for the neatness of his clothes, for being soft. He had kept his head down, kept his mouth shut, but the other boys had sensed he was not like them and had closed in like jackals, taunting him. He had called out to Christ, begged for his help, and Christ had come and stood by him and said this happened to me, too, this is what the worst in humankind does, it torments those who are different, but I'm here with you and we will outlast their hate, because kindness is stronger than cruelty and goodness is stronger than evil.

Jim did outlast his tormentors and his strength grew, until one day he felt called to become a warrior for the meek and despised. To wear the uniform of the powerful and use that power for good. He had done his best to embrace the mission, but sometimes the call frightened him, because he was not always sure where goodness lay.

When he was a teenager and his dog died, the preacher said it had no soul and therefore no afterlife. Jim had prayed that the preacher might turn out to be fallible, like all humans. Surely dogs were among the lowest and least and thus deserving of Christ's care. Perhaps the preacher had made a human error. But how did one know when one had made such an error?

Was it wrong, what Dryden had done? It was not a sin for a man to gnaw on the bones of a chicken. So why was it wrong for a coyote to gnaw on the bones of a man?

Yet the thought of it made him queasy. The idea that his body was meat, no different from the drumsticks he'd eaten for dinner last night. He glanced at his hands. He thought about small busy teeth chewing on them, as the flesh grew soft and putrid. His stomach turned over.

"Your aunt really said she wanted that?" he asked.

"Yes."

"But it's..." He grimaced.

"No it's not. It's clean. Fay used to joke about it. She said just give her bones a year in the woods and they'll be cleaner than Martha Stewart's toilet."

As she spoke, her eyes filled with tears. She scowled and turned her head away from him.

Watching her weep and fight not to, he felt little doubt about where truth lay. If you hate a person enough to kill her, you don't weep when you repeat her jokes. But he couldn't put intuitions into a case file. What he needed was the body.

It could be so simple. With an autopsy, he could give Anita Kirkwood her peace of mind and close the case. With the case closed, he could turn his attention to other things.

"It's considered a public health risk," he said. "To leave a person's body unburied."

"That's only because there are too damned many of us, and not enough varmints."

"But what if everyone did the same thing?"

"They won't. They all think it's..." She mimicked his grimace, tweaking him.

Despite his frustration, he couldn't help smiling. He recognized that lip curl of repugnance. He'd seen it on the faces of his schoolmates, directed at him. The primal 'yuk.'

"Is it true, what you said? That the bones end up clean?"

"A lot cleaner than they would be after a year in a casket," she said. "Now there's a truly revolting prospect."

Cleaner. Who would have thought.

Not as clean as cremation, of course. But cremation makes smoke. Jim couldn't tolerate smoke. The lung and throat irritation had become unbearable the one time he tried to live in a large city. This was a problem, for a homosexual. Out here in the woods, there were plenty of men, single men, muscular, capable, weathered, and completely unaware how gorgeous they looked in their faded jeans and guy-toy logo baseball caps—Jonsered, Makita, Caterpillar. They were an inexhaustible source of yearning, but none of them wanted him.

Until now. Maybe.

Not that Gerald Ware had ever driven a backhoe. He was gentle and orderly. He liked music, children, home life, and church suppers. He was exactly the kind of man Jim might have met, if he could have tolerated the air in a city.

But he couldn't tolerate it so here he was in Gilham, and now God had brought him such a man anyway. Maybe. If only he could get on with it.

Half of him admired Dryden's loyalty and would have liked to tell Anita Kirkwood, politely, to take a hike. The other part, the rational part, thought defiance would be far more trouble than it was worth. Fay Kirkwood was dead. She was in the company of Christ and together they would forgive Dryden for retreating from a battle whose cost was greater than its purpose.

"When your aunt asked you to do this, did she know that it's against the law?" he asked.

"I doubt she thought about that, because she didn't think it would actually happen. She figured she'd get sick and go to a hospital, just like everybody else."

"Do you think she cared about your well-being?"

"Of course she did. Duh."

"So why not go along with that?"

Dryden didn't answer right away. The toe of her boot kicked at a lump of dried mud stuck to the concrete floor.

"This feels like my well-being," she said. "To do this for her."

"Even if you go to jail?"

"It would be a stupid system that would put me in jail for this. You can't organize your life to fit a stupid system."

I couldn't contain myself any longer. What you're doing is stupid, I yelled. What's the good to anybody, you stubborn, ornery, damn-the-world child!

I was ready to burst, I was so full up with love for her and rage at everything, at her, at myself, at this tedious and inescapable companion death, who held me here like a child holding a fly by the wing. Just squash me and be done with it, if you really are a god!

It was I who had taught her this stubbornness, no doubt. I and the regal Anita. Between the two of us, we'd taught her self-reliance, to a fault. Don't look to the world for reason or kindness. Look to yourself for what you need.

Ok. I'm sorry. I goofed. You can look to other people now and then. They might help you. You've got a *policeman* on your side, for pity's sake.

You're like the guy in the flood who insists on trusting God. The water reaches his porch, his neighbors come by in a boat and he sends them away, saying he's always been a faithful believer and God will take care of him. The water reaches the second story, the police come by in a boat, and he sends them away, too, saying God will protect him. The water reaches the roof, the National Guard comes with a helicopter and he sends them away likewise. The water keeps rising and he drowns.

When he gets to heaven and meets God, he is indignant. "I trusted you and you let the waters rise and drown me," he complains. And God replies, "Don't complain to *me*. I sent two boats and a helicopter."

So here she was, sending the boat away. And for what? My dead body, a piece of meat.

The thought had barely completed itself when I found myself there. In the woods. With the piece of meat.

A fox was circling my body, warily. Even when perfumed by the beginnings of rot, my human scent made him cautious. His belly was tight with hunger, though. The smell of decay, to me repellent, made his saliva run.

The air was full of other smells, too, musky and rank. His rivals. Their scents, like mine, made him wary. His nose darted here and there, making sure the news was old.

In his hip was a shooting pain and he put no weight on that leg. A bullet was lodged near the bone. His gait was awkward. Probably the hunting had been hard. The ache in his stomach was almost as sharp as the pain in his leg, but stronger than either pain was the chill of fear, that he was weak and clumsy and he was seeing the mice he once caught with ease now dart away, just beyond his reach, and he could no longer trust the speed of his feet to keep him out of reach of the teeth that might catch him.

Finally, his hunger overcame his caution and he sidled forward to eat. The flavor of my flesh was as rank as its smell and slightly sweet.

Once begun, the fox set to with famished haste, gulping down chunks only half-chewed. Gradually, the tightness in his belly relaxed, his fear calmed, and warmth spread through his limbs. Contentment filled him like the swell of rising sap, until finally it pressed upward through his throat and emerged in a whimper of relief.

Chapter 21

Regardless of Jim's personal opinion, it had become impossible to let things slide. One could not ignore an event that had been mentioned in *USA Today*.

Until the situation received this stamp of national significance, most people's opinions had been fairly vague. If pressed, they'd have said something like, "It's not what I would have done, but it's their own business." Only a small minority had worked up any fervor.

Now the debate divided itself into two distinct camps. On the outraged side was an uneasy alliance of secular suburbanites who thought what Dryden had done was variously icky, primitive, unhealthy, or frightening to their children, and religious conservatives who thought it was sacrilege. On the supportive side was an equally uneasy alliance of back-to-the-land, grow-your-own-quinoa progressives, who thought it was a fine example of living in harmony with nature, and old school Yankee conservatives, who thought the government should keep its nose out of people's private business. There was also a small group of people who weren't concerned about funerary rituals because they thought the police should be investigating a murder.

When Jim Jorgensen made his customary lunch stop at the Butternut, he was accosted by three of the outraged parties, all wanting to know what he intended to do. Talking into one ear was Payson Satterthwaite, who had undertaken to unite the secular and religious objections by propounding the view that an action could be both sacrilegious and icky at the same time. The real problem, Payson declared, was the underlying social decay, a condition he would strive to eradicate if he won election to the state legislature.

Talking into Jim's other ear was Millicent Gray, who insisted the issue was murder and were the police making any progress on that front?

Behind them was Walter Inchkeep, looking sepulchral and interjecting the opinion that sacrilege outweighed all other considerations and could not even be placed in the same scale with worldly concerns such as elections and murders.

When Jim, with foolish frankness, allowed that he had talked to Dryden and did not plan to investigate further unless the family made a formal report of a missing person, the three streams of opinion merged into a single geyser of indignation.

"Wait for the family!" said Inchkeep. "The family is mocking our sacred institutions!"

"They could be protecting her!" cried Millicent. "They all stand to gain from this!"

"This is dereliction of duty!" said Satterthwaite. "Ever since I came to this town, I've been saying we need more police and this proves it."

A murmur arose among the people listening. Finally a voice said, "What does Royce think?"

Royce Palmer. Our senior police officer. He'd been on sick leave for two months, recuperating from an operation on his back. He was a gruff, thickset man, unimaginative but hard-working. He didn't own a lawnmower. His whole dooryard was graveled, a staging area for his collection of old cars, machinery and the equipment for his oldest son's firewood business. He did own several snow machines, however, and I saw him occasionally when he needed a part. His youngest son had suffered severe brain damage from a snowmobile accident years ago and still lived at home, where his parents took care of him. Royce's response to this event had been to collect more snow machines than before, in the manner of a religious man refusing to let disaster shake his faith in providence.

"At the very least, we must ask his opinion," said Millicent. "As an officer with such long experience in this town."

Her emphasis on the word 'long' dismissed Jorgensen as a whippersnapper with no understanding of the community. This view was a product of the moment. At other times, she'd been heard to question whether Royce had the necessary sophistication for modern police work.

Asked for his opinion about my body, Royce had no doubts about his answer. A search must be launched. He thought homicide was unlikely, but it reflected badly on his profession to have a stray body lying around. As it happened, he had just been cleared to go back to work and could take charge himself. He said he'd put out word for a few volunteers to meet first thing in the morning at the town garage and he'd ask his wife to lay in coffee and doughnuts.

When morning came, he faced a crowd several times larger than the ten or twelve he expected. Fortunately, his wife had made her own prediction, taking into account the news media and the general level of talk around town. She had provided two large urns of coffee and four dozen doughnuts and these were generating an atmosphere of good-fellowship despite the cavernous dankness of the cinder block building in which the group was gathering.

As more and more people streamed into the building, Royce's scowl deepened. He thought he'd be working with a small group of old-timers who hunted every year and knew the woods, not this motley herd of eagerness whose level of experience he could not estimate. Worse yet, Jim Jorgensen was missing and he didn't know why.

Scanning the crowd, Royce saw that some people had equipped themselves with things that might be useful—binoculars, daypacks, water bottles, a dog who might or might not have a good nose—but others had no more than a jacket and sneakers. His eye came to rest on a brand new red daypack, slung awkwardly over the shoulder of Gerald Ware, and his whole body sagged. What sort of a search party included the church organist?

The church organist was thinking much the same thought. What was he doing here?

Gerald had packed everything he could think of—map, compass, GPS, two flashlights, a whistle, some power bars and an array of extra clothing—but the abundance of gear was small comfort. He was not an outdoorsman. Two days ago, he would not have been here. He was here now because, in his present mood, he would be willing to scale a peak or swim a river, if he could do it in Jim's company.

But Jim was not there. Gerald had searched every corner of the crowd and he was nowhere to be seen. The fact was incomprehensible. The search was police business. How could Jim not be part of it?

Gerald stared blankly at the only uniform in the room, Royce's. When a couple of his singers greeted him with pleased exclamations, it took an effort to mutter an acknowledgment. What a fool he was, standing there with coffee in hand, dressed for the Arctic, with no idea what would come next. A pet parakeet knew as much about the woods as he did.

It occurred to him, with a feeling of irrelevance, that at least his effort would be pleasing to his wife. Ever since Eloise heard about Fay's death, she'd been unaccountably eager for the body to be found. Right in the middle of an unrelated conversation, she would suddenly start talking about how unexpected the death had been and how the police needed to clear away any suspicion that might attach to Noah Macauley. When he asked why Noah might be suspected, she said of course there was no real reason but this was not a time for ambiguity. The dead should be good and dead, she said, so that the living could know where they stood.

While Eloise had contributed cheering words to Gerald's preparations, her brother Doke had contributed more tangible support in the form of gear. In declining to join the search himself, Doke repeated the same stolidly earthbound view he'd been expressing all along: he had been in Fay's shop two days before her death; she and Dryden had been as cozy together as a couple of old littermate hound dogs and there was no way it was murder. Especially because they were women and women mostly didn't kill people, not unless they were hysterical types, which Fay and Dryden weren't. Also, he'd seen how fast Dryden could take apart a carburetor and he thought if she'd set her mind on keeping the body hidden, it would stay hidden, at least until some deer hunter stumbled on it who-knows-when in the future. The net result of his reasoning was that Gerald was welcome to borrow compasses, knives and anything else he wanted from Doke's hunting gear because it was every man's privilege to waste his own time.

Conversations swirled around him but Gerald barely noticed. His eye was turned inward, painfully, imagining what might have been. He could see himself with Jim, tramping together through the woods. He could see them wandering away from the search party until the other voices faded and they heard only the sound of their own footsteps, crunching on frosted leaves. Perhaps they would come upon a sheltered grove and pause. The air would be cold and still, just the creak of branches and the sound of their own breathing.

Here his thoughts halted, not daring to continue. To be alone together, among sheltering trees, was enough. He did not want to imagine what lay beyond that moment. Beyond the grove of trees lay wife, children, church, business, neighbors—a tangle from which his thoughts shrank.

Someone spoke to him, a remark about how cold it was, and he replied, automatically, that yes, it was a nice morning. The neighbor looked at him oddly and only then did Gerald register what had been said. He told himself to get it together.

Then he looked up, past his neighbor's retreating back, and there was Jim, standing with Royce.

Gerald had meant to be discreet but now he felt as if his heart had launched itself upward, hitting the top with a clang like the sledgehammer challenge at the carnival. An "Oh!" yelped from his throat and a grin spread across his face. Again and again, he caught himself staring, smiling foolishly, and hastily looked down at his feet or took another gulp of coffee, but it was no good. In a matter of seconds, he'd be looking again.

I wanted to whisper to him, go ahead and gaze. I'd gazed at Noah for years before anyone noticed. People aren't so quick to see something that isn't what they already expect.

Jim had brought a sheaf of maps and he and Royce were studying them. After a while, Royce announced that everyone should organize into small groups and pick a group leader.

As the crowd sorted itself, Gerald hovered at a neutral midpoint, hoping not to commit himself until he saw which group was Jim's. His plan was foiled when three of his singers caught sight of him and called out, "Gerald, come be part of our group. We need someone to take charge."

He couldn't talk his way out of it. The more he protested that he knew nothing about woodcraft, the more eagerly his singers professed their faith in his leadership. He was stuck there, without a shred of expertise, in charge of three people as helpless as he was: a retired dentist from Philadelphia, a pale twenty-something computer geek with a surprising bass voice, and his church's Sunday school teacher, who worked as a bookkeeper. Their only qualification for a search party was their shared horror at the idea of a body not receiving proper burial.

The three singers were giddy with delight that he was their leader, and they could just as well have been lambs, so trustingly were they giving themselves into his keeping. He wished he could do likewise with the divine shepherd Jesus, but faced with an expanse of trackless woods and three lives depending on his judgment, he could not summon faith that the right path would be shown to him in a manner he would be able to discern. He pulled out Doke's compass, as if it might somehow point him towards an answer, but he had never actually used one to find his way somewhere and he wasn't even sure he was holding it the right way. He stared at it, puzzling.

Then, miraculously, Jim appeared at his elbow, slipped the compass out of his hand, and laid it next to a map, saying, "This will be very useful."

As Jim pointed out features on the map, his arm lightly brushed Gerald's sleeve. Gerald's face grew warm and he barely heard the explanation of the map. His universe had narrowed to a spot just above his elbow where he could feel small movements of cloth as Jim talked. The midwestern cadence of Jim's speech reminded him of Mozart. No guarded local diphthongs. No urban edginess. Just genial grace. He looked at the hand tracing features on the map. It matched Jim's physique, all sinews and bones.

He heard Jim say, "The five of us will cover as far north as Terry Hill Road, right here..." and Jim's finger tapped a line on the map. Gerald thought probably the line was important and he should remember it, but he knew he wouldn't because his whole mind was fixed on the words "The five of us..." His gaze traveled a swift arc, looking for any other "five of us" Jim could mean, but he and the three singers were the whole of Jim's audience.

He suddenly felt very calm. Jim had sought him out. They had the whole day ahead of them. It was enough for now. This is the day the lord hath made. He would not look beyond it.

He felt an overwhelming need to say a prayer of thanksgiving, and not just silently. Out loud. But he was a native son and it was not in his nature to drop to his knees in public and cry out adoration of God. When he spoke, the words were awkwardly abrupt. "I'd like to offer a prayer, if that's all right with everybody."

From the crowd, there were murmurs, a few of approbation, but mostly dismay. Darkness came early this time of year. Was he going to waste precious daylight droning on?

You couldn't really argue, though, so people crossed their fingers and quieted. When the room was silent, Gerald bowed his head. His words were not remarkable, but his voice shook with emotion. Give us your blessing. Guide our path. Bring us home safely. And thank you for this beautiful day.

Around the room, the amens were fervent. He had taken less than half a minute.

Chapter 22

The two men never found a quiet, sheltered grove, but even in the midst of a chattering flock, they had managed to arrive at a happy understanding. What to do with that understanding was a separate problem, which the day in the woods had not resolved.

For both of them, the solution lay in prayer. Although they could not yet give prayer their full attention, I began to overhear fragments hinting what they meant to say when the time came, a warm-up conversation in which Gerald asked for guidance and Jim offered the divinity some suggestions as to what sort of guidance should be given and both men debated whether it was proper to hope that Eloise might run off with the mailman or feel called to become a nun.

As for my corpse, the object of the day's activities, it was not found and the search ended with no one's opinion changed. Those who thought I had been murdered still thought so and likewise those who considered it natural for me to be returned to the cycles of the earth. If anything, the day's exertions had only reinforced people's views. Depending on one's prior cast of mind, the thoroughness with which I had been hidden strengthened the belief that I had been murdered or the beauty of the forest strengthened the belief that I had wished to return there.

When the searchers reconvened at the town garage, few people seemed to care that the day's efforts had not found the body. Royce's wife had organized crockpots of canned chili and fresh urns of coffee; the road commissioner had turned up the thermostat in the garage, and with everyone warm and fed, the morning's murmur of a crowd still stuporous from sleep had turned into a roar of competing voices all eager to describe their adventures.

Terp wandered through the crowd with a notebook, collecting quotes for a story. "Didn't see so much as a track," was the summary of the search itself, but he met plenty of people who wanted to tell him how their clothes got soaked when they sank into a boggy patch, or how they got so twisted around, they came back across their own footprints, or how they'd seen coyote scat or the remnants of an owl's kill, or how they'd spotted a nice eight-point buck but didn't care to say where, because they might come back and look for it next hunting season.

Only Royce Palmer voiced frustration at the failure. "We covered that ground like we were combing fleas and there was nothing there," he said.

"What do you plan to do next?" Terp asked.

Royce scratched his chin. "We can't search the whole darned state this way. But we've got to find the thing. You can't just leave dead people lying around and forget about them."

"Will the state police get involved?"

"I can't say yet. There's money to think about. There's people. It all takes organizing. We haven't decided anything."

About the answer Terp expected. Could he get more from Jim Jorgensen?

He saw Jim across the room, surrounded by a cluster of people who had the look of admiring cockleburs. Three of Jim's companions were spooning up chili and chatting together. The fourth was standing in a daze, holding a forgotten bowl in his hand and smiling into space. The first three were strangers, but the daydreamer Terp knew. He was Gerald Ware, the store proprietor who had gone to some trouble to order the right replacement strings for Terp's bass.

When Terp's circling approach brought him a view of Jim's face, he paused to digest an impression. Under other circumstances, he might have thought Gerald and Jim were stoned. They were standing together, not touching, but less than a foot apart. They were smiling, seemingly part of the larger group, but neither was talking and their expressions did not shift to match the conversation. If their gazes happened to meet, they quickly looked elsewhere.

Poor fellows. If they weren't on drugs, they must be in love, but not without impediment, since Gerald was still married to the impressively efficient town clerk. For the two men, this was a predicament, but for Terp, it might be an opening.

He strolled over and greeted Gerald with a friendly remark about the strings he'd bought. Then he turned to include Jorgensen and added, "I didn't know the two of you were such good friends. Do you play music together, too?"

Gerald's face turned pale. His mouth opened to answer but no words came out.

"We've never played..." Jim began, then stumbled. "That is, I used to play the flute, but I'm not much good. Not like Ger— like Coach. He plays beautifully."

"Perhaps you could play duets," Terp said smiling.

Neither man answered and their gazes dodged one another. The three singers took their discomfort for modesty and seconded Terp's suggestion with enthusiasm.

"Oh, yes, that would be so wonderful if you played together!"

"You could give a concert at the church!"

The moment could hardly get riper. Terp turned to Jorgensen and said, "By the way, what can you tell me about this matter of Fay Kirkwood? Are there plans for a wider search?"

As he hoped, Jorgensen grabbed the new subject and ran with it. In his eagerness to relieve Gerald's distress, he became garrulous on the subject of Fay Kirkwood, answering any question Terp asked, so long as it made no reference to music or masculine friendship.

No, in his opinion, it was probably not a homicide. No, he personally would not recommend a large expenditure of tax money to pursue a violation of the laws on burial. The family could always organize a search using private means, but without more information, a search would be an expensive long shot. On the whole, he thought the situation was far less dramatic than people feared.

As the subject of duets was left behind, the color returned to Gerald's face and Jim remembered the need for care in speaking to a reporter. He hurried to point out that nothing he had said should be taken as an official statement. Chief Palmer was in charge of the case.

"Nevertheless, I appreciate your openness," Terp said. "I can always make use of information, one way or another."

"Make use of information?" Jim's glance flicked sideways towards Gerald.

"For the Kirkwood story," Terp said. "I'm not concerned with anything except my story."

He held Jim's gaze, like a handshake to confirm his meaning.

Driving away from the town garage, Terp started to laugh—at the absurdity of love, at the thought of two middle-aged men acting as euphoric and terrified as a pair of teenagers—and above all, at himself. Who was he to mock romantic excess? Did he measure the usefulness of information by any standard apart from Dryden?

He too was caught on a seesaw between euphoria and panic. One minute, he and Dryden were curled up in bed, laughing together, talking about pizza and Duke Ellington. The next minute she was dressed and gone, saying she had wood to split or a yen to walk in the woods with the dog, not saying when he'd see her again.

It had taken some effort to understand that the music meant more to her than the sex. In his experience, one could jam with any competent player and have no regrets the next morning, while sex was likely to create complications. For her, the music was the complication.

Her logic was agricultural. Pigs can have sex. Toads can have sex. Slugs and potato beetles can have sex. Only humans get together to create music. Compared to the shared humanness of making music, the animal pleasure of rubbing sensitive skin together is prosaic. Not sinful or dirty. Just limited. Like scratching an itch.

He thought it scared her a little, that he knew this about her.

What he didn't know was how she felt. She liked talking to him, but then she would have to leave. She would not fall asleep with him. She always had reasons why she had to go. Her chores. Her dog. Her visiting parents.

He believed her reasons. What bothered him was how readily she remembered them. If he'd had chores, parents, a dog, he would be neglecting them, just as he was neglecting the journalistic opportunity of a missing body in a small town. He wanted to think she was drawn to him, and not just to his string bass, but often he thought the opposite, that without the bass he would be nothing to her.

Which led to another question. If she loved the music so much, then why hadn't she gone further with it? Was it the influence of this fabled aunt, now rotting in the woods?

Hah! I scoffed. Would that I had some influence now.

Yes, I failed her. Mea culpa. Come and flay me, if you can find a way to do it, but what good will that do? What matters is what comes next, here on earth.

You're wrong, that she only cares about the music. It's so obvious, why can't you see it? You saw it instantly, with a pair of strangers, and now here you are, dithering.

It's not as if you're some genius on the bass. Musically, there's not much to choose between you and Jonathan. But as men? No comparison. There aren't enough circles in hell to describe how I'd feel about an indefinite future in Jonathan's company, but with you, the prospect is at least tolerable. Unfortunately, you never knew me so you can't appreciate how highly I must think of you to say that.

Then I laughed. Easy for me to urge him on. In truth, I knew as little of Dryden's heart as he did. If I'd had to take action, I'd have dithered, too. My boldness was a measure of my helplessness. Like some church-anointed charlatan who claims superior knowledge of the unseen, I could proclaim certainty where in reality I only had hope.

As soon as he got home, Terp sat down to write his story. He knew exactly the angle he meant to use. He would lead with an amusing anecdote about falling into a swamp. He would play down the possibility of murder and instead focus on burial regulations. He would talk a lot about the small-town spirit of volunteerism and not at all about religion.

The story took him less than forty minutes to finish. He typed almost without a pause, barely glancing at his notes. As he attached it to an email, he knew he ought to be clicking Trash rather than Send but he didn't care. The moment he'd sent it in, he picked up his phone. With amazement he realized he felt sure Dryden would want to see him.

An hour ago, he had been bedeviled by questions. Does she or doesn't she? Now he felt carried by the flow of events. He didn't believe in a god with any certainty, but he had the sensation that an invisible intelligence was nudging him toward Dryden and cheering him on.

It's true, I said, there is someone cheering you on, but don't get an inflated idea that you have a divinity on your side. What you've got is a dead old woman with opinions. If you ever need actual help, there's not a thing I can do.

My warning didn't dent his conviction. He was in synch, in a zone, following his bliss. As he punched the final digit, his ear was already tuned to the deep, gruff cadence of Dryden's "H'lo." His own greeting, "Hey, it's Terp," was already half-formed on his tongue.

Then the phone picked up and a bell-like soprano trilled "Hello?"

Terp was too flummoxed to speak. He knew that Dryden's parents were staying at the farm but he had been so fixed on the idea of talking to her, he had forgotten about them.

"Hello, who is this?" Anita repeated, less melodically.

"Sorry. This is Terp Jones. May I speak with Dryden?"

"You're the man from the newspaper."

"Yes, among other—"

He stopped. He'd been about to say cheerfully that this was a social call when it occurred to him that he didn't know what Dryden had told her parents.

"Yes, from the newspaper," he said noncommittally. "Is she at home by any chance?"

"You've got a remarkable nerve," said Anita. "My sister-in-law's passing is of no concern to the public. One expects to see this sort of snooping and muckraking in a supermarket tabloid, but not in a serious newspaper."

Terp took a deep breath. He could see how Dryden had been driven to hurl a wrench.

He didn't mind the insults. It was a hazard of his profession to be accused of muckraking by people whose questionable behavior one reported. If the insults had come in a snarl of rage, he could have shrugged them off. What infuriated him was the tone of condescension, the implication that he was an inferior creature who ought to be beneath her notice.

"I have no wish to intrude where I'm not welcome," he said carefully. "If you'll just tell her I'm on the phone, she can decide whether she wants to speak to me."

"Her willingness is not the issue," said Anita. "These stories affect the whole family."

So much for being aligned with the flow of the universe. He couldn't even get through on the phone.

"Have we printed facts that aren't accurate?" he asked. "If you tell me which details I've gotten wrong, I'll do my best to correct them."

"Details! This isn't a question of details. My husband's family has a very distinguished history. The idea that we would engage in a pagan funeral ritual is insulting."

"Are you saying your daughter is lying? You must realize what that would imply..."

He let the sentence hang. For a while, the only sound was the hum of the phone.

"You really are a snake, aren't you?" she said. "Do you have any scruples whatsoever?"

As many or as few as will help Dryden, he thought.

"I won't knowingly write a falsehood," he said.

"You shouldn't have written anything at all."

"That wasn't one of the choices I was given. And I'm sorry if the story troubles you. That was not my intention."

Hearing his own words, he wanted to kick himself. He didn't even like the woman and here he was, sliding into his habitual puppy-dog mode, trying to get along with everybody.

"You're not just a snake, you're a spineless snake," she said.

Touché. For the first time, he recognized a family resemblance between Dryden and Anita. Like them or hate them, you knew who they were.

"A spineless snake who would like to speak to your daughter," he said. "If you would be so good as to tell her I'm on the phone."

"I'm afraid I can't. She's out in the barn."

"Then perhaps you could tell her when she comes in?"

"But of course."

He hung up. She'd put it on the list, no doubt, somewhere below cleaning the garage.

Along with irritation, he felt an urge to laugh. Did that woman ever take her eye off the ball? As a journalist, he had a soft spot for people he didn't like. So often they made great material. The more Anita insisted he keep the Kirkwood name out of the newspaper, the more he wanted to put it there. Except for Dryden.

The phone rang and his heart jumped. Was it possible he had misjudged Anita? He grabbed the phone before the second ring.

"What the hell is this?"

Randall. Evidently he had looked at the story.

"The search didn't find anything," Terp said.

"Yes, I gathered that, but what the hell difference does that make?

That's a story, too. Where's the body? Why did she hide it so thoroughly? Hell, there was more blood and suspense in two paragraphs in *USA Today*. A person would think you were reporting a church supper."

"Do you want me to report gossip? The police are not calling it a homicide."

"OK, forget the homicide. Maybe we can't go there. But what about the religion thing? For Pete's sake, Terp, the national press got months of copy out of a brain-dead woman on a feeding tube. Can't you give me something better than a yawn out of an old lady being fed to wild animals? I thought there's some preacher who's on a tear about it."

"The family doesn't want this in the paper."

"Of course they don't want it in the paper. The nephew's a damned congressman for crying out loud. It might be embarrassing. But the day we stop printing stuff because somebody in government thinks it might be embarrassing, we'd just as well turn out the lights and go home. You know that."

"Yes, I know. But…"

But what? He could be as fierce as anyone, defending the right of a free press to make public officials squirm. Dryden herself had said, go ahead and publish. So why was he reluctant?

"You've got a couple more hours," Randall said. "I want you to get hold of that pissed off preacher, see if you can prod him into a quote. Better yet, get two preachers."

"It's a little late in the day to bother people…"

"Oh cripes, Terp, don't even apologize. A guy can't set himself up as a spokesman for God and then say he's only in business from nine to five."

Chapter 23

Driving to Inchkeep's, Terp switched on the radio. He felt edgy and the news had always been a reliable diversion from his more immediate worries.

The first two items were grim but familiar. A car-bombing in the Middle East. A factory closing in Ohio. In the third item, I heard my own name. Terp heard it too, and reached to turn up the volume.

The story was brief, a filler. The highlight was my nephew, Spenser. Terp's stories had not mentioned him, but someone else had traced the connection and my identity had been collapsed into a pair of attributes. Dead, I was the body that had been fed to wild animals. Alive, I had been the close relative of a congressman.

The reporter was trying to make the story sound exotic. He didn't mention that I was old enough for my death to be unsurprising. Nor did he say that my town was next door to one of the richest ski resorts in the state. For the purposes of radio, I lived in the "remote northern mountains," my death was "sudden" and "unexplained," and my corpse was the object of "a pagan death ritual" which had aroused "bitter controversy" in an "isolated rural community."

Isolated, hah. It's getting darned hard to find any place that deserves to be called isolated. Even in Gilham, you could call an 800 number and get sushi overnighted to your doorstep, if you were willing to pay. These days, isolation means going around with your ear wired into your Walkman.

But true isolation? A place free from the influence of humankind? Those were as rare as the California condor.

Not even death had found me such a place.

The news soon moved on, which was good for me personally, but less good for humankind. The next story had to do with tropical deforestation, global climate change and species extinction, and its soberly analytical tone was more chilling than any flight of alarmist rhetoric would have been. Listening to it, Terp and I slid companionably into a state of cosmic gloom, which reached swamp bottom just as Inchkeep's church came into sight.

Inchkeep's welcome was more an enlistment than a greeting.

"I've been praying and God has answered by bringing you here," he said.

He gestured Terp to a chair. His office was lit by a single lamp, which gave him the look of an El Greco martyr, gaunt pallor starkly outlined and eyes sunk deep in shadowy sockets.

"All day I prayed that Dryden Kirkwood would renounce her evil, but it is clear that she has hardened her heart against God. Now God has issued a call to action and he has made you His instrument to help me. This young woman is speaking the devil's message and we must answer."

Terp raced to write notes. "Answer in what way?"

"If she continues to defy God's truth, then she belongs in prison. This is a Christian country, governed by Christian principles."

"Isn't it possible the court and the statutes will only require a fine—?"

"Then the court and the statutes are flawed! There is a law higher than the laws of men. Our courts must follow God's laws."

"What do you personally intend to do?"

"I shall summon the faithful to action! My words in your newspaper will be the beginning. Tomorrow, my sermon will make the walls shake!"

"You do understand that my story will cover the other side of the question, also."

"So much the better. If you lay evil out in plain sight, it will be seen more clearly!"

From what he knew of the Reverend Eames, Terp did not expect his views to add clarity to the debate. Eames was so hopefully convinced that everyone, given a chance, would be generous and open-minded, he was unwilling to say either that Dryden was wrong to feed me to the scavengers or that Inchkeep was wrong to want her in jail.

"I'm sure if the Reverend Inchkeep could talk with Dryden and understand what is in her heart, this whole misunderstanding could get resolved," he said.

On the contrary, Terp was thinking. If the Reverend Inchkeep talked with Dryden, he might hear the Bible described as one of many utterances from a divinity far too large to be captured in a single volume. Her attitude would not endear her to a man who believed he was a miniature copy of God and who was perhaps more comforted than dismayed to think that God found writing as laborious as people did and had run out of energy and ideas after just one book.

By persistent questioning, Terp managed to push the Reverend Eames into one definite statement. Yes, Eames agreed that the police and the citizenry should stay within the bounds of the law in their response to Dryden's action.

He immediately added qualifications. "I don't mean to imply that anyone has ill intentions," he said. "It's quite natural that a person who feels the law is inadequate might want to follow his conscience…"

"Do you think the law is inadequate in this case?"

"No, no, I didn't mean to suggest… That is, I wouldn't be qualified to say… I merely meant that there might be occasions where it could be reasonable to think that a law didn't quite cover all the issues…"

"And in such a case would it be OK for the police to go outside the law?"

"No, no, that isn't… Oh dear, what do I mean?"

"Would it be a fair summary of your views to say that people in positions of authority, such as the police and the government, must obey the law even when they are dealing with a criminal who has not obeyed the law?"

"Yes, yes, that's it. Although there could be some question…"

"But I can quote what you said?" Terp said quickly.

"Yes, of course… that is, what exactly did I say?"

Terp looked at his notes and read Eames's original quote back to him. "I do think the police need to stay within the law, and other citizens, too, as we try to sort this out…"

"Yes… OK… I think that's not an unreasonable thing to have said…"

Chapter 24

Sunday morning was approaching. All over America, all morning long, people would drink coffee and read the newspaper. I needed a survival strategy, some way to fend off the disintegration of time into milliseconds of jarring connection with legions of strangers. What I wanted was a stack of firewood to split or a ditch to dig. What I had were my own thoughts.

Hearing the first fragments of what would soon become an unendurable din, I decided to try a technique I'd read about somewhere, the repetition of a simple syllable as a way to achieve tranquility. Achieving tranquility struck me as an oxymoron, but what did I have to lose?

The trouble was, I couldn't find a syllable to use. The traditional Om hit my ear as parody, "the syllable suitable for chanting," and when I tried other syllables, I discovered that my mind was remarkably quick to attach meanings to things. "Rur" reminded me of the river, "iv" sounded like "if" with a phony foreign accent, and "ul" morphed into a cockney "hull." I never found a syllable I liked, but for the time I was looking, the chaotic blare of input became a background of white noise, rather like the gabble of seagulls at the beach.

The first clear sensation to emerge from the cacophony was dread.

I saw the *Leonardston Herald* spread out on a table. My kitchen table. The hand holding the paper trembled. I saw age spots and a wide gold wedding band. Charlie.

Peripherally I saw a headline, "**Local Woman Still Missing, Minister Demands Action**," but the words were out of focus, because Charlie was listening, not reading. On the counter, the radio was on, tuned to the national news. The update from Arizona was brief, just the statement that Representative Kirkwood emphatically denied any connection to "this appalling situation with my poor, unfortunate aunt."

The words made Charlie shrink. Spenser had been driven to defend himself to the press and Anita would be livid. Charlie wasn't seriously worried about Spenser. His son would spin this in whatever way was necessary to protect his position. But Anita's fury would measure the idea of the threat, not its reality, and Dryden would be the one who paid.

Charlie was often troubled by a guilty feeling that he ought to love his sons more than he did. It seemed contrary to nature that Dryden had grabbed his deepest heart, while his blood children inspired only a measured fondness. Spenser, especially, was so blithely self-confident and dedicated to his own success that Charlie could easily summon respect and admiration for his accomplishments, but had difficulty feeling warmth. Was it biology that linked worry with tenderness? Or was it an expression of self-loathing that he was most drawn to the child with no genetic resemblance to himself?

An image flashed past, the boy I'd seen before, the dark-eyed one who could have been Dryden's brother. He had paused from lawn-mowing to move a soccer ball out of the way. In an impulse of youthful exuberance, he started to play with the ball, dancing in circles as he tossed it up and caught it on top of his sneaker. His body was lean, his movements graceful. He looked like everything Charlie was not—dashing, strong, agile, full of life.

Charlie blanked the boy from his mind and stared at the newspaper. Best not to mention the radio report to Anita. Perhaps there would be a blizzard or an airline crash and the press would have forgotten about Spenser by the next news cycle.

He looked at the headline, **"Minister Demands Action,"** and grimaced. Why couldn't people mind their own business? Terp had avoided the most inflammatory language, but even the most temperate of Inchkeep's remarks were a sharp condemnation.

Charlie's eye settled on a quote. "**... there is a law higher than the laws of men...**"

Indeed there is, he thought. In fact there are several. The law of gravity. The laws of motion and thermodynamics. Entropy. Conservation of energy and momentum. Laws whose rewards and punishments were even-handed and inexorable.

In Charlie's mind, law and worship were separate spheres. Laws belonged to science and government. Worship belonged to art, music and literature. Never the twain shall meet, except in metaphor. If Jesus turned water into wine or fed a multitude with a loaf of bread, he did not do it by overturning the laws of physics. He did it by making people believe that if food and drink are partaken in a spirit of sharing, the water tastes as sweet as wine and the bread feels like plenty.

Charlie thought it was incongruous, these churches quarreling over my dead body like two dogs at opposite ends of a bone. As if the technical details mattered more than the spirit in which Dryden had acted. It made him tired and irritable when he wanted simply to feel sad. Couldn't he be left to grieve in peace?

As if in response to his question, the phone rang. He waited a couple of rings to see if someone else would take the call, then pushed back his chair and went to the phone.

His hello was swept aside by a rush of furious speech.

"What the devil is going on back there? I got a call last night from a reporter wanting me to comment on my Satan-worshipping sister."

Spenser.

"It's all over the media back here. There's already some cretin saying this should be an issue in the primary. Where's Mom? I need to talk to her."

At that moment, Anita materialized at Charlie's elbow. If Dryden was Charlie's favorite, Spenser was hers and she seemed to know by telepathy when he needed her. Charlie didn't resent their affinity, but he did feel a prick of sorrow, remembering his early years with Anita when their feeling for their children and their feeling for each other had seemed part of a single stream.

He handed her the receiver. "It's Spense," he said.

"Hello, darling," she said. "Is this foolishness becoming a huge nuisance?"

She was silent for a while, listening, and Charlie could tell the news wasn't good. He could see each small muscle in her face grow tense.

His own gut began to churn. He could try to point out that Dryden hadn't intended harm, that the voters in Arizona shouldn't care about private religious beliefs, but he knew he would have no effect.

He felt a great longing to be elsewhere, to be holed up in a quiet room full of books, pondering the embalmed agony of people who had been dead for centuries. He could smell the books and hear the stillness. He could feel the dry pages under his fingers and his heart quivering like a tuning fork in response to a perfect quatrain of universal sorrow.

What a feeble, nerveless creature he was, alive to the sentiments of faraway poets, but paralyzed by present reality. What good was a heart that swelled with fondness at the thought of his daughter if it failed to energize his muscles and brain?

But it would fail. That was the one inalterable certainty of his existence.

He heard his wife's voice, speaking simple declaratives.

"We'll get this sorted out. I'll do whatever it takes."

She hung up the phone and turned to Charlie.

"Where's Dryden?"

"I think she's in the barn. What are you—?"

His voice trailed off as she brushed past him on the way to the door. She shrugged into her coat and headed out to find Dryden. Charlie hurried to put his coat on and follow.

They found Dryden in the barn, leaning on the fence rail watching the pigs.

Scollay was sitting pressed against Dryden's leg. Since my death, he'd been staying with her whenever he could and I was glad to see him there now. For me, dogs had been an antidote to neurosis, a reminder that contentment was mostly a matter of food, sleep, companionship and being able to go outdoors, and only as a luxury concerned itself with whether one had gotten more or less parental love than one's siblings.

"I am sick to death of this nonsense," Anita said. "Is there any chance you'll behave like an adult? Or do I have to act on my own to resolve this mess?"

Dryden didn't answer immediately. Only her hand moved, dropping to hang near her leg, near Scollay. He nudged her fingers with his nose.

"Act however you want," she said.

"Have you seen the papers? This could ruin your brother's career."

"If this can ruin his career, then he must be beholden to a lot of nitwits."

"Of course he is. So is anyone in his position. You can thumb your nose at the world, because no one cares. Spense has to pay attention to public opinion."

"And what does he do when public opinion has two sides? Castrate himself landing on the fence?"

"Spenser has never been afraid to stand up for his principles, but it's harder when he is betrayed by his own family."

Dryden's muscles tensed. Her hand curled into a fist and then, very deliberately, uncurled itself and reached to touch Scollay's fur.

"What principle is he standing up for here?"

"The highest possible principle. Our faith in God."

"Spenser's faith is just a credential on his resume."

"That's not true. He's become quite devout. In any case, this isn't about his faith. He's defending the beliefs of his constituents."

"What about Fay's beliefs?"

"Oh, please. Don't get all high-minded about freedom of religion. He can't go into a campaign saying his family has a constitutional right to be pagans."

"Depends whose votes he wants to win," Dryden muttered but Anita did not hear her. The remark was masked by the grunts of the pigs, who were gathered near the fence.

What Anita heard instead was silence, the same stubbornly resistant silence she had been meeting ever since Dryden acquired enough language to make silence a purposeful choice.

"You leave me no alternative," Anita said. "I have to do what I think is best."

This time around, Anita did not waste any time talking to subordinates. She went directly to Royce Palmer.

"I'm afraid I was mistaken in what I told your junior officer," she said. "I'm now convinced that my sister-in-law's death should be treated as a possible homicide."

Beside her, Charlie's mouth dropped open in shock. He had not known what she meant to say and he started to protest, but Anita stopped him with a look. She had a plan.

"Dryden's story simply isn't credible," she went on. "My husband's sister would never have made such a barbaric request. And Dryden does inherit a substantial amount of property..."

If she expected a reaction more dramatic than Jim Jorgensen's, then she was disappointed. For a while, Royce pondered the clutter on his desk and shifted a few objects, as if he were trying out strategies in checkers. Finally he said, "Hmmm. That's not so good."

Anita's call had interrupted his Sunday morning. Probably a part of his brain was calculating the number of hours it would take to get the right wheels in motion compared to the number of hours before the start of the Patriots game on TV.

"You're sure about that, are you?"

"Positive."

"Hmmm." He pondered a few more moves with the stapler and notepad. "Guess I'll be turning it over to the state police. And for sure we've got to find those remains."

"Yes, indeed. I should say we do." Her smile was complacent.

In the car, Charlie finally voiced his protest.

"I don't understand how—I mean, I know it's a nuisance for Spense—but to say Dryden might have... You don't seriously think..."

"Of course I don't 'seriously think.' But she's got to be made to see reason. And it's perfect, all the way around. For a homicide, they'll make a thorough search, and the media can drop this lurid stuff about paganism."

"But what if they put her in jail...?"

"Oh, for pity's sake. They can't convict her of murder. Not if she didn't actually commit one. It will be the best thing for everybody to find Fay's body. If she died of natural causes, the body would prove it. If she didn't, if Dryden really did something, then jail is where she belongs."

Chapter 25

The pews in Inchkeep's church made no concessions to the frailties of human flesh. Built from flat planes of varnished oak, their backs were nearly vertical and their seats several inches narrower than the corresponding dimension of the body. As if to compensate, the pews had been mounted too high, so that their cutting pressure on the back of the thigh could be relieved only by arching the feet upward on tiptoes.

My acquaintance with them was limited to a few funerals, but it was enough to make their discomforts recognizable, even when these came to me secondhand, by way of Terp's more youthful frame. He had not been sitting long before he began to shift from one position to another, relieving first his spine at the expense of his pelvic bones and then his pelvic bones at the expense of the circulation in his legs. Finally he folded his coat and sat on it. He felt a sidelong glance from the end of his pew, a white-haired couple silently taking note of his capitulation. Their coats were lying on the seat beside them.

As his legs grew numb, despite the coat, he eyed the fat hymnals in the rack in front of him. Could he stack a couple of them on the floor to make a footrest? Would he be booted out of the church if he did?

From the moment he woke up, he had been out of sorts. Dryden had not called and he didn't know if she had received his message. He'd sent an email but gotten no reply, which confirmed her warning that she rarely went online. He did not want to call again or go to the farm, lest he create awkwardness with her parents. So he was stuck and also unnerved by how much it bothered him to be stuck. Rather than spend the morning brooding, he had decided to check out Inchkeep's sermon, but he had arrived too early and the wait had not lightened his mood.

At last, the organ began to play. The instrument was a good one, rich and resonant, easily filling the space with sound. The music was Baroque, some chuckling, effervescent trifle of melody. Vivaldi probably. If Terp had been in high spirits, the music would have sent him floating. Instead, even as his ears were tickled by the sound, his brain was grumbling, "What makes you so all-fired happy?" He looked up at the organ loft to see who was blessing the congregation with such insistent joyfulness.

At the sight of Gerald Ware, Terp's annoyance evaporated. No wonder the man's happy. He's in love and he thinks he's loved back. How could anyone grudge him a bit of Vivaldi?

But what had brought a squelched homosexual into Inchkeep's church?

Terp's ears gave him the answer. The organ, of course.

It was perfect symbiosis between natural enemies. Gerald probably suffered soul torment from the strictures of Inchkeep's theology. Inchkeep probably suffered soul torment from the sensual pleasure of Gerald's music. But Gerald wanted to play the organ and Inchkeep wanted to put more rumps in the pews, so Vivaldi served them both and each man must have cut a deal with his own psyche to make the arrangement work.

Precisely on the hour, the organ prelude came to a close and Inchkeep stepped to the pulpit. He spoke a few words of greeting, offered an opening prayer and then invited the congregation to rise for the first hymn. Terp bounced to his feet, thankfully.

As the organ played a phrase of introduction, its massive authority gave reassurance that everyone, no matter how hesitant a singer, would be kept safely in the vicinity of the tune. The crowd responded, if not enthusiastically, at least with stoic determination. The singing was muddy but respectably loud, a broad wave of approximation that spread outward from the organ's certainty like the bow wave of a boat spreading outward from its prow.

From the first line of the hymn, Inchkeep's theme was clear. "Let all mortal flesh keep silent, and with fear and trembling stand; ponder nothing earthly minded..." His mind was on the fate of the flesh and my decaying flesh in particular.

After the hymn, he proceeded to a reading from Genesis, "...for dust thou art, and unto dust shalt thou return..." and then onward to Romans, "...the carnal mind is enmity against God... if ye live after the flesh ye shall die..."

Before beginning his sermon, Inchkeep stood for a long moment in silence. His hand rested on the open Bible. He looked like the incarnation of Paul's words, a man who would do without his body altogether if only he could. His eyes were a glint of paleness in shadowy hollows. His lips were two thin bloodless lines. His black clothes hung from his shoulders with the flat loose folds of a suit on a hanger.

He began to speak. "The word is clear. 'They that are in the flesh cannot please God.' We are commanded to leave behind all that belongs to sinful flesh and live only in things that belong to the Spirit. There is a great temptation to glorify the things of the earth. We see that they are beautiful and pleasant and think surely they must be good. But it is a measure of the power of the Spirit, that we can look at all this beauty and pleasure and say, 'All of this is nothing.' It is here to be despised and mortified, to the greater glory of God."

As Inchkeep developed this theme, at considerable length, I found myself thinking about his lawn, which he kept mortified to such geometric neatness. He must see a vision of Satan incarnate, watching his neighbors leave their grass uncut for a week or more, growing into a sweet succulent carpet whose stems greet every passing breeze with sensuous undulation. But at least he lived what he preached.

Approaching a finale, his hand swept downward, indicating the floor beneath his feet, and his voice vibrated with feeling. "When we elevate the things of the earth to a place of honor, we are turning away from the spirit. The earth is flesh, as our body is flesh, and it is made to die. Only the Spirit is eternal. Our immortal soul should be the whole and only object of our care!"

He paused, gazing out over his congregation. When he resumed, his voice had dropped to a silken purr.

"All of us know the story of the serpent in the garden, creeping into the minds of the unwary and turning them away from God. We have such a serpent here among us in this community. A serpent who denies that we were created by God in his own image. A serpent who glorifies carnality.

"Some people will point to the laws written by men and say that no law has been broken, or only a very small law. But our earthly laws are as transient as our flesh. It is by God's law that we must be governed and God's law declares that the serpent must be destroyed or its corruption will spread. If even one soul is persuaded to doubt, that is too high a cost.

Not one soul can we allow to be taken away from God!"

As he came to a close, his frame was stretched to its fullest height, taut and quivering, as if at any moment his flesh might turn to flame and vanish into the ether.

He bowed his head. "Let us pray."

Terp fixed his eyes on the hymnals in the rack. He felt tense and gloomy. Nothing in the sermon had surprised him, but he had not been able to maintain his customary detachment. The more Inchkeep vilified the life of the body, the more Terp became aware of the physical present, here in this church. What had been a congregation of human hopes, worries, humor and irritability became, in Inchkeep's vision, a steaming, gurgling mass of digestion and filtration, a collection of lumpish sacks of meat, blood and waste, exhaling the rankness of sexuality and the sweet stench of decay.

As the prayer ended, Terp glanced around at his neighbors. Whatever people thought of the sermon, they were keeping it to themselves. Perhaps they would simply swallow the message, like a familiar dose of tonic, and go about their business.

The closing hymn was announced and the congregation rose to its feet. Terp read the first line and grimaced. "Arm, soldiers of the lord..." Silence fell as the crowd waited for the opening chords from the organ.

Nearly a minute passed and no sound came. Feet began to shift, uneasily. Every small noise, every shuffle of pages and cough, sounded startlingly loud. Terp glanced up at the loft. On the organ bench, Gerald sat rigid, staring straight ahead.

From the pulpit, Inchkeep repeated the number of the hymn with loud emphasis. Gerald jumped and hastily moved to face the keyboard. His feet found the pedals; his hands hovered over the keys, poised to play. His fingers came down and a chord sounded, then the beginning of the tune. Halfway through the first phrase, the notes stumbled, corrected themselves, stumbled again, and then stopped altogether. Gerald paused and started over. The notes stumbled again, badly, but he didn't stop. He finished the introduction, soldiering on despite the ugly hash that was coming off the keyboard.

When the singers joined in, the stolid drone of the opening hymn was long gone. With every misstep by the organ, the voices faltered, backed off in volume, and began to seek notes by trial and error, until finally the singing disintegrated into a nervous agglomeration of guesses, hesitations and adjustments. Eventually the hymn staggered to a close and there was a palpable exhalation of relief. The congregation hurried to return their hymnals to the racks.

Ignoring the jangled nerves of his parishioners, Inchkeep used the benediction to punctuate his sermon, urging firmness in the face of doubt. After the final amen, there was another pause as people waited for the organ to begin the recessional. When it became clear that no recessional was forthcoming, people began leaving the pews in straggling clumps. In the absence of music, they refrained from conversation, also, and the silence began to take on the uncomfortable solemnity of mourners walking past a casket. To remark on Gerald's lapse would be unseemly, but people seemed reluctant to break the silence by speaking of something else.

When Terp emerged from the church, the clouds were spitting scattered flakes of snow. He glanced at his watch. Although he'd be a few minutes late, he could still attend the competing church service, to see what sort of vision it offered. He expected to hear plenty of kindness from Reverend Eames, but very little authority.

He jogged across the street and slipped into a pew of the Old Church just as the congregation rose to sing the first hymn. The hymn was familiar from his childhood, its words written by St. Francis. "All creatures of our God and King, Lift up your voice and with us sing, alleluia..."

Although the message was joyful, the singing was anemic. The church had no organ and the voices of the congregation were tentative, despite the simplicity of the tune. The plump, white-haired lady at the piano was making a valiant effort to bolster the sound but her instrument was a modest upright whose slender tone was swallowed by the vast high-beamed space around it. The one confident voice, a robust soprano in one of the front pews, was singing an octave higher than most voices could reach and her effect was to loosen other people's grip on the notes in their own range.

As the first verse wobbled to its end, Terp heard another latecomer slide into the pew behind him. A moment later, the second verse began and Terp felt as if he and everyone around him had been lifted by a wave. A new voice had joined the singing, a clear, resonant tenor whose range was comfortably in reach of all but the basso profundos and who soon began to carry a whole section of other voices with him, the sound swelling with newfound certainty. "...Thou rising morn, in praise rejoice, Ye lights of evening find a voice, alleluia..."

The certainty spread from the back of the church to the front, and then, as the third verse began, the stout soprano shifted to sing a descant harmony and a couple of weak-throated but bold-spirited neighbors followed her lead, their voices floating like a shimmering veil above the melody. With the tune now solidly planted in the middle range, a couple of deep basses gained the confidence to open their throats and add weight below, "...Thou fire so masterful and bright, that givest us both warmth and light, join the chorus..." until by the final alleluia the whole church was in full voice.

As the congregation sat down, Terp glanced back to see who owned the tenor voice.

The singer was Jim Jorgensen and it seemed his vocal ability did not depend on his mood. He was scowling, and when Terp nodded hello, he didn't notice. Terp filed the observation. Last night, Jim had been cheerfully inclined to shelve the Kirkwood case. Today, he'd come to church late, looking preoccupied. So what changed?

Like the opening hymn, the service was hopeful and also blessedly concise. A parishioner rose to read a Mary Oliver poem. Three teenagers came forward nervously to perform a short trio for flute, viola and piano. Eames prefaced his sermon with an announcement that volunteers were still needed for the Christmas crafts fair.

Curiously, the pulpit and the audience had a calming effect on Eames and he spoke clearly, without fidgeting. His public speaking voice had a soft conversational cadence that reminded Terp of Mr. Rogers. In fact the whole service had the same atmosphere. It felt like the childhood dream of a sweet small town where everyone is nice. He half expected to hear the toot of a toy train whistle. He doubted this crowd would rush to do battle with any issue more vexing than the poor drainage at the school soccer field. On the other hand, they also would not rush to pass judgment.

Reverend Eames took his text from the gospels. "In my father's house there are many mansions." His theme was simple. God appears in myriad ways. He comes to each person in his own way. He does not care what name he is given. He cares only what is in a person's heart. Whenever a person acts with loving kindness, that person is acting in the spirit of Christ. God is not a tax collector demanding tribute. God is not a rock star demanding applause. God is the power of goodness enabling us to be our best selves. Give thanks. Amen.

There was no fervor in his delivery, but there was more backbone than Terp had expected. For all the quietness with which Eames spoke, his message was as firm as Inchkeep's. It felt like water, a force that did not have to insist on its power. A force that occasionally burst forth in grandiose display, in a waterfall or a geyser, but for the most part worked its miracles subtly, carrying specks of rock from here to there, seeping life from cell to cell.

The thought might have been comforting, had Terp not also reflected that water takes its shape from the shape of its container and its patient miracles can be thousands of years in the making. To do any good for Dryden, he needed a force with less inevitability but more speed.

His first concern was to talk to Jim, to find out if there had been new developments, but he couldn't just leap in after the benediction to ask, "What's the latest word on the dead body?"

Instead, as people gathered their coats, he turned to Jim and said casually, "That was beautiful singing."

It took a moment for the remark to register. "What? Oh… yes, it's a pretty good group," Jim said.

"No, I meant you. The rest of us were a little lost before you joined in."

Jim murmured an awkward thank you and edged his way into the stream of people moving toward the doors. Terp slid in beside him.

Trying a different angle, Terp said. "You must have had a good teacher along the way."

Score. Jim smiled.

"Mrs. Bisby," he said. "For eight years of church choir. She was… well, you didn't mess with her. And you sure didn't say bad words about Bach."

"Would you have wanted to?"

"Not me. But Skip Harlow did. It got him a month staying late to help rebind hymnals."

"Did that improve his opinion of Bach?"

"No, but nothing would have. He was interested in the sopranos, not the music."

"I have some sympathy for your barbarian Skip. My high school orchestra had a wealth of gorgeousness in the violin section and I had a great view of it, playing bass."

They emerged into the foyer, where people were piling up like livestock at a ditch crossing, milling about, chatting, postponing departure. A squall had blown in and outside the windows the buildings and trees were faint shadows behind a curtain of wind-whipped snow.

Jim glanced at the window and shrugged.

"This isn't much," he murmured. "It'll be gone in a minute, I bet."

He edged through the crowd toward the doors. Terp stayed close behind, hoping to get a useful word with him outdoors. With anyone else, he'd expect the weather to put an end to conversation, but Jim's casual shrug might have been sincere. Presumably, his definition of "not much" came from North Dakota, where blizzard winds could tear across hundreds of miles of prairie without meeting a speed bump.

By the time they reached the sidewalk and started toward the town hall, the wind had slackened and the snow was thinning to flurries.

"You called that right," Terp said.

"The weatherman called it right. He said scattered squalls, but no accumulation."

"Nothing that would hinder a search, then," Terp ventured.

Jim's expression changed to irritation.

"Wouldn't matter if we got three feet. The chief's decided she's got to be found."

"Has something happened?"

"There's some new evidence," he said, "if you want to call it that."

"Physical evidence? Or a witness?"

Jim shook his head. "I really can't talk about it. You'll have to ask the state police."

"What about off the record?"

"Off the record…?"

Jim's walk slowed as he considered whether to answer.

"Is your family ever a pain in the neck?" he said finally.

"A couple of them are, sometimes. Typical, really."

"So, it's the same thing here. With the Kirkwoods."

"Which one's making the fuss?" Terp asked.

Jim shrugged, declining to elaborate.

"Check out the family, that's all," he said. "If they'll talk to you."

Right, Terp thought. If they'll talk to me. That's already the problem.

Still, Jim's comment was suggestive. Someone in the family was pushing the police to take action. Terp's money was on Mom. The adoptive Mom, as Dryden was so careful to point out. Estrangement tended to go both ways. But what, exactly, was Mom after?

At the town hall, he and Jim stood for a moment, awkwardly, needing to bring a polite end to the conversation but unable to ignore the freight of significance they couldn't discuss. They were underlings, with opinions, but no power to make things happen.

"Thanks for the tip," Terp said. It felt feeble. He wanted to return the favor, somehow.

On impulse, he gestured toward the Brick Church and asked, "Have you by chance seen Gerald Ware today?"

Jim tensed and shook his head. "Is there a reason I should have?"

His tone did not invite intimacy and Terp considered backing off. But he remembered that moment of frozen silence, and then worse, the hands stumbling across the keyboard and the hymn, the simplest of music, disintegrating into chaos.

"He seemed pretty upset, that's all," Terp said. "After the service."

"You talked to him?"

"No, he was at the organ. But there was definitely something wrong."

Jim's foot traced patterns in the dusting of snow left by the squall. Several times, he started to speak, but changed his mind.

Eventually he did ask a question. "What made you think—?"

Half a question, anyhow. Enough for Terp to presume further.

"It was the way he played," Terp said. "At the beginning of the service, he went whipping through this crazy fast Baroque piece, like he could do anything, fly if he wanted to. He sounded really happy. But then, after the sermon, he completely fell apart and couldn't play anything. The closing hymn was a mess and he didn't even try to play a recessional."

Jim stared, no longer trying to feign a lack of interest. "Did something happen?"

"The sermon was a little harsh. Pretty much anything to do with earthly pleasure was on the list for damnation. It made me depressed and I didn't even buy it. If I did buy it, I'd have to start praying for a nuclear war to vaporize humankind out of this snake pit as soon as possible. I sure wouldn't be in the mood for music."

"No, one wouldn't be..." Jim murmured. As he turned to go into the building, his steps dragged and he seemed to have forgotten Terp's existence.

Chapter 26

The earthly obstacle to Jim's happiness was baking a casserole and trying to quell an unsuitable urge to thank god for my death. Eloise Ware didn't worship a god, not with her gut, but she did go to church regularly and she did feel, superstitiously, that she shouldn't rejoice too much at a blessing that arose from another's misfortune, lest she provoke some unspecified retribution by whatever unspecified power had organized the universe.

Eloise didn't think in words like sin and salvation. Her cosmology was founded on the sort of abstract principles of order that found expression in mathematics and double-entry accounting, where every equation had to balance. If the payments in misfortunes and blessings failed to equal the receipts, an adjustment must be made. How the adjustment would happen was a mystery, but the need for balance was absolute. This she did accept in her gut.

That same gut was presently in a state of turmoil, waiting for her casserole to bake. She fidgeted around her kitchen, wiping counters that were already clean, rearranging the fruit in a bowl on the counter, straightening the magnetic notepad on the refrigerator. Every half minute or so, she glanced at the digital stove timer, as it marked its countdown from ten to nine to eight.

She had divided her casserole between two dishes, one for tonight's supper, the other to be offered as a neighborly gesture of condolence to Noah Macauley. She worried a bit that the appropriate moment for casseroles had already passed. A person who had suffered an untimely loss was entitled to extended prostration and could properly accept consoling sustenance for a period of months, but I had been rich enough in years that my loved ones were expected to do most of their grieving on their feet. Already a week had gone by since my death and it was possible the neighbors, or worse yet, Noah, might consider her gesture excessively solicitous.

She'd been sleeping poorly all week. Every night, she had lain awake, scrutinizing her memories for hints that, had circumstances been different, he might have felt more than neighborly good will. On the whole, she inclined toward hopefulness. She had often heard warmth in his voice and seen softness in his gaze. She could not expect more than that. He was a man of principle. He would respect both her married state and his own attachment. The most he could offer would be hints, and hints there had been, she was almost sure.

Maybe or maybe not, I said. Noah was so absurdly handsome and his manner so sweet, he probably left the dental hygienist feeling that their hour together had held special meaning.

I felt her confidence waver. Was she deceiving herself? She remembered the painful spectacle she had made of herself when she was nineteen. This time, she would proceed with caution, testing the waters.

And yet... and yet... Her heart was pounding with anticipation at the thought of an hour alone with Noah. Had they ever had such an hour, before now? There had always been committee work in the picture, some public purpose. There had been the implicit presence of her husband and Noah's... whatever the appropriate word would be. "Lover" seemed too glamorous a word for Fay Kirkwood. "Companion" would be more accurate.

As for Gerald's feelings, they were a factor to be argued into insignificance, like friction in a physics problem. Her marriage was a social contract, she told herself, not a spiritual tie. The only deep feeling she and Gerald shared was their fondness for their children.

She thought Gerald's music meant more to him than she did. Witness how unreasonably upset he had been by his slipup on the organ this morning. Having committed a minor faux pas, he had behaved like a man whose spirit is in torment. His affection for her could never cause him such agony, she was certain.

The content of the sermon did not factor into her analysis for the simple reason that she had not listened to it. She'd never had much use for Inchkeep's theology. It was dreary and his equations didn't add up. Years ago, after sitting through a few months of his sermons, she had developed the habit of bringing a paperback novel to church, as well as a method of holding it discreetly shielded by her purse. She felt no worry that her ignorance of the sermon would embarrass her in conversation later. There were those in the congregation who could debate indefinitely the pros and cons of putting nutmeg into an apple pie, but discussion of the preaching began and ended with "Fine sermon, wasn't it?"

Eloise attended church to maintain her place in the community, not to seek enlightenment. The Brick Church had been her family's church and it was Gerald's church now. She would not be driven out of it just because the current pastor was a bit tiresome.

When Inchkeep announced the closing hymn, she had been two centuries distant in the Napoleonic Wars and when the organ failed to spring into action, she assumed Gerald must have fallen asleep, exhausted from helping in the previous day's search. After the service, she had assured him that the incident would be forgotten in a week, but nothing she said helped and he did not want to talk about what was bothering him. While she had felt concern—how could she not—she also was quietly recording this evidence of how little she mattered to him.

At long last the stove timer dinged and Eloise pulled her lasagnas out of the oven. She glanced at her watch. She had most of the afternoon to herself. Gerald was at his chorus rehearsal and Doke was watching football and neither would expect dinner for several hours.

She laid the lasagna in a cardboard box, nestled in dishtowels to keep it warm. She considered whether to include a bottle of homemade raspberry cordial as part of the offering, but rejected the idea. Spirits would set the wrong tone. They suggested festivity when her purpose was supposed to be condolence. The future was long, she hoped. There would be other occasions for cordial, if she did not make a mess of this occasion. She made a quick pass over her clothes and hair, tucking and tidying, wishing her perm was fresher, and then she was out the door.

As her car came around the last curve and she caught sight of Noah's mailbox, I discovered that one does not need a body to hold one's breath. All my nerves were stretched tight, wondering how he would react to Eloise's overture. I felt the way I had decades ago when I was suspended, breathless, waiting for his response to the idea of our becoming lovers.

Back then, I had thrown out the idea in an offhand tone, ready for a swift backpedal. No big deal. Just a thought. Really it's the friendship that counts.

Hah.

And now here I was, appalled at the possibility that he might leap to embrace Eloise and yet strung up like a teenager on the way to the prom, waiting to see what would happen.

She turned into his driveway and drove through the short stretch of woods that shielded his house from the road. After a last clump of evergreens, the driveway opened out into his dooryard and there she was greeted by the one predictable source of dread that for some reason her imaginings had not considered. He had another visitor.

Beside his venerable Honda, whose every rust spot and bumper sticker she knew by heart, was another car, a large, well-waxed, nautical-blue Buick sedan.

Millicent Gray.

The jolt very nearly made Eloise drive through Noah's picket fence. At the last moment, her reflexes kicked in and she slammed on the brake and stopped, a foot short of the gatepost. She sat trembling, staring at Millicent's car.

Was it possible Millicent had already wormed her way into Noah's affections? She had no husband to keep her at home in the evenings. She could have been here every night this week, offering casseroles and cookies. She might already be at the point of offering cordials.

A dark wave rose into Eloise's throat, choking her breath. Had she just walked into a replay of the worst moment of her life? If she looked in the window, would she find Millicent and Noah grappling on the couch?

Her first impulse was to flee, except that now, at age fifty, a part of her brain warned her that she was not in a safe state to drive. She switched off the engine and sat still, trying to will herself calm. She might be imagining things. Perhaps Millicent had come as a disinterested neighbor. Perhaps she was offering condolences and nothing more.

Perhaps, but Eloise didn't believe it.

Ever since her divorce, Millicent had been consumed by bitterness at her single state. How often had Eloise heard her bemoan the lack of eligible men in town and complain that the few there were wanted younger women. Now here was Noah, available and demonstrably free of that Neanderthal prejudice in favor of youth. What could be more likely than that Millicent should make a play for him? All those sly hints about Dryden had been red herrings, designed to keep Eloise from recognizing her true intentions.

It was especially galling that Millicent had preempted her own strategy. One woman with a casserole could persuade herself she looked innocent, but a series of women with casseroles would begin to look ridiculous and Millicent had gotten to the head of the line.

How could Eloise possibly compete? Millicent had every advantage. Money, time, freedom, sophistication, not to mention some indefinable air of glamor. She socialized with prominent people like the Satterthwaites. She had traveled in Europe.

Eloise felt painfully aware of her own identity in Gilham. She was the town clerk, a position of infinite utility but one devoid of either sexiness or mystery. Even Fay, crude as she was, might have been thought colorful, but what did Eloise have that could entice a desirable man? She was hopelessly ordinary. Good-natured, reliable and dull. Except for one trip to Montreal, she'd never been out of the United States. She'd never been west of Ohio and only went that far because her son-in-law had taken a job in Cincinnati.

She stared at the Buick, its glossy metallic finish sparkling in the pale winter sun. Not a speck of dust marred its paste wax shine, even though it had just driven up a dirt road to Noah's driveway. Somehow its finish must repel the dirt.

She looked at the cardboard box on the seat beside her, the flowered dishtowels neatly tucked in place around the pan of lasagna. It looked pathetic. Probably Millicent had brought something made with exotic mushrooms and Brie.

Eloise couldn't face another contest for Noah's affections. She was bound to lose and it would be, if anything, worse than the first time. She should leave now, before she makes a fool of herself. She could turn and go home and no one would ever know she had been there. The lasagna could go into the freezer for some future evening when committee work kept her late.

She was fifty-one years old. She'd been married almost thirty-two years. It was time she accepted that she was never going to be the heroine in a romantic fairy tale.

As her hand moved to start the car, I let out a screech that would have shattered every wineglass in Gilham, if it had had substance. NO-O-O-O!!!

You can't leave now! You can't abandon him to Millicent! Hold your ground, for god's sake! Be bold, have faith! You could carry the day!

Eloise's hand hovered near the ignition, suspended by indecision. Yes, stay! I shouted. He loves Italian food! Your lasagna will be just the thing!

This was only partly a lie. Noah did like Italian food and although lasagna was not his favorite, I was sure he would be gracious and Eloise would not be embarrassed. I was regretting, bitterly, every one of my scornful thoughts about her. What folly, to beat my head against the inevitable. Someone would end up in Noah's bed, sooner or later, and at least Eloise was a decent human being.

But Millicent Gray! The thought that Millicent might somehow capture Noah's heart was enough to make a person long for the pure clean agony of hellfire.

A moment later it seemed that Eloise had come to the same conclusion. I can't bear it, she was thinking. Millicent will be insufferable and I won't be able to avoid her. At least Fay stayed on her farm and didn't join committees.

With sudden haste, hoping to outrun another failure of courage, she pulled the key from the ignition, jumped out of the car, seized her lasagna and headed for the house.

It was impossible to say which of us was more relieved to find that Millicent had not yet reached the point of grappling with Noah on the couch. When Eloise came in, Millicent was sitting decorously at the table holding a teacup. On the table was a china platter decorated with a gorgeous Asiatic lily blossom floating in a bowl of water. The bowl and flower were surrounded by spirals of cookies, which Eloise recognized as Millicent's famously delicate lace cookies and her meltingly rich shortbreads flavored with Cointreau.

Eloise felt a renewed urge to take flight, but it was too late. She had to allow herself to be ushered into the room. As Noah closed the door, she abruptly held out the cardboard box with the lasagna.

"It's just a casserole," she said. "I hoped maybe you could use it."

"That's very kind. Thank you."

He set the box on the kitchen counter. Eloise tried to think of some suitable words about my death, but every ordinary phrase of condolence sounded blatantly hypocritical, because she was not in fact sorrowful. In the end, she murmured a generic, "If there's anything else I can do to help, I hope you'll let me know."

Once again pathetic, she thought. No doubt Millicent had said exactly the right thing.

Likely she was right, I thought, since Millicent would not be stopped by any consciousness of hypocrisy. She could slide from insinuations that my niece was a murderer to expressions of deepest sympathy to all my family without any disturbance to her composure.

Noah asked if Eloise would like tea and she said yes, that would be nice. With a reflex move toward the kitchen, she added, "Can I do anything to help?"

She immediately chastised herself for repeating the same empty offer. Too much eagerness, too little wit. Meanwhile, Millicent looked perfectly self-possessed, her teacup balanced in one hand.

"Hello, Eloise," she said, in a tone impeccably civil and yet faintly mocking.

Eloise returned an awkward greeting. Poise was beyond her and she felt that every instant, every word spoken, every tiny detail down to the choice of neck scarf, was adding to Millicent's advantage. She stood wavering in a no-man's land between the table and the kitchen. Lame as it was, her offer of help made it impossible to feel right about sitting down.

She was rescued from indecision by Noah. "You can indeed help me," he said. "You can peruse the shelf of tea and tell me which you'd like."

He smiled and pointed at the relevant shelf.

In that split second, I began to think her hopes had a chance. With most people, Noah would have done the ordinary polite thing. He'd have hastened to say no help is needed, take it easy, have a chair. He delighted in providing small pleasures to other people. But Eloise was not in a state to enjoy sitting down. She needed a task, however trivial, and he had had the sense to give her one. Kind as he was, Noah was not always observant, but in this case, seemingly by instinct, he'd done the one perfect thing to make her feel better.

To my way of thinking, that kind of instinct went a lot further in a love affair than any calculated list of desirable attributes and areas of compatibility. He liked her; he had noticed what was needed. They might mesh.

With nothing to distract me from observation, I was aware of my own absurdity. In less than an hour I had swung like a weathervane from jealousy and revulsion at the sight of Eloise to partisanship in her favor, for the simple reason that she was not Millicent Gray.

But how could I be sure that Noah had not been equally alert to Millicent's mood? Millicent would not have wanted a task to keep her busy. She'd have wanted admiration, the reassurance that she was preeminent. She'd have wanted him to ooh and ah about the lily, the cookies, the perfection of it all. For all I knew, he had done just that.

Eloise opted for plain black tea, the choice I'd have made myself. Noah had topped up the kettle and he and Eloise stayed near the stove, waiting for it to boil. His posture was casual, leaning back against the counter. Only a few feet of linoleum floor separated them from the table where Millicent presided, but the span was enough to shift the balance of power. Nothing occurred that could be considered incivility. Noah took pains to include Millicent in the conversation. Yet somehow, as the kettle took its time coming to a boil and the three of them filled the air with banality suited to the occasion, her place looked more and more like that of a figurehead monarch, swathed in silks and jewels and trapped on a throne of ceremonial helplessness while the affairs of state are carried forward elsewhere.

The kettle boiled at last and the tea was poured. The interlude was over, I thought. When the others sat down at the table, Millicent would be back in charge.

Except that they didn't sit down. The tea steeped. The spent leaves were removed and dumped into the trash. The cream was poured. Yet still Noah lingered near the stove, leaning back against the counter, and the conversation ambled here and there, politely wearing away at Millicent's resolve. The awkwardness of her position was just subtle enough to leave her with no remedy. If she stood up and moved to the kitchen, she would only call attention to her loss of status. I saw no calculation in Noah's behavior, any more than there is calculation in a pebble rolling downhill rather than up. He found Eloise to be more congenial company, that's all.

Eloise, meanwhile, was maintaining an appearance of calm, but behind the façade, her mood pinballed between joy and self-doubt. Was she reading too much into Noah's proximity? Perhaps he wanted to stretch his legs. Perhaps he felt sorry for her and her homely casserole. Perhaps he was trying to conceal a romance with Millicent. She could think of an array of discouraging explanations, but again and again her body measured the relative distances and happiness came flooding back.

Millicent held her ground for a surprisingly long time, but in the end, she yielded. After taking a conspicuous last sip of tea, she rose to her feet and clattered her dishes into the sink in a declaration of disgust at their lack of manners. She told Noah he could keep her platter until the next convenient occasion for returning it and swept out the door.

And Eloise had her wish. She was alone with Noah.

Too late, she realized that Millicent's presence had made things easier. The three of them could talk about social nothings while Eloise floated on her awareness of Noah's proximity. Now, she could talk openly, but what did she actually want, or dare, to say?

They both shuffled their feet. She still had her tea so she took a swallow. Noah asked if she would like to sit down and have some cookies. She didn't want one of Millicent's cookies, but she said yes anyway, because she hoped that eating might ease the awkwardness. She sat in the third chair, avoiding the one Millicent had chosen.

They sat for a bit, nibbling the cookies, taking refuge in remarks about Millicent's baking skill. I was struck by how suitable they looked. Eloise was pretty and personable, a natural complement to Noah. Despite her rattled nerves, I could feel her core of common sense and competence, precisely the qualities most desirable in the spouses of mathematicians and poets. She would keep the bills paid and remember to call the plumber when the drain backed up.

But would it take?

She'd have no quiet interlude to find out. Few marriages were more publicly woven into the life of the town than hers. Few love affairs could be more delicious material for gossip than this one would be.

For now, though, the opinion of the neighbors was far from her thoughts.

Her gaze was on Noah's hand, resting near his teacup. She longed to touch his skin, and she was conscious of the amazement she felt just as she had at nineteen. For thirty years of an amicably businesslike marriage, she had accepted the idea that emotions mellow with age and people in their fifties do not feel things with the same intensity as the young. Now she faced the reality that euphoria and agony were still possible, but might be more hazardous, if mature emotions were as slow to heal as mature muscles and joints.

To keep her hand still, she looped a finger through the handle of her cup. She had changed from nineteen, not in the intensity of her feeling but in her ability to anticipate consequences. Instead of assuring her that pain would pass, her experience puzzled her with contradictory advice. Time was too precious to be squandered on needless suffering. Love was too precious to let any chance slip. So she sat still and stroked the handle of her teacup, trying to be purposeful but cautious.

I could see that Noah preferred Eloise to Millicent, but given the degree to which a person could reasonably loathe Millicent, his preference did not necessarily signal any feeling beyond polite liking. The tension in his manner might be pent-up passion, but it could equally well be embarrassment at the memory of their long-ago encounter or the ordinary social awkwardness of a conversation between deep grief and polite sympathy.

My intuition said his constraint was more than a social difficulty. Politeness would have kept him on the move, making gracious gestures. His stillness now held something stronger. Maybe simple sex. Maybe something more complicated. But not indifference.

They had run out of admiration for Millicent's cookies and the subsequent pause was approaching the limit after which no remark could sound casual. Something had to be said and Eloise seized the first safe topic that came to mind.

"This tea is very nice. What is it?" she said.

She berated herself for the dullness of the remark, but Noah's face lit up.

"It's an Assam," he said. "Fay was very fond of it. She liked her tea to be forceful, nothing flowery."

"So Earl Grey wouldn't have been her—"

At the last moment, Eloise bit back the phrase "cup of tea." Worse than dull, silly.

"First choice," she finished.

He smiled and shook his head. "She used to say Earl Grey was the reason people invented the phrase 'not my cup of tea.'"

Eloise started. She almost looked over her shoulder to be sure I wasn't there.

"It's funny, because in a general way, Fay wasn't fussy about tea," Noah went on. "For herself, she'd buy any old tea bag. But whenever I gave her a cup of something better, she'd look surprised and say, wow, this is really good!"

His voice was warm with emotion and Eloise battled an urge to say something disparaging about me. She told herself it was ridiculous to be jealous of the dead and she should be glad Noah was talking so personally, but it didn't help. Hearing the affection in his tone, she longed to find a crushing remark to prove how misguided his choice had been.

She reminded me of myself early on, when I had itched to make waspish remarks about all the women in Noah's vicinity. At the time, Gilham had seemed to me a hotbed of nubile maidenhood and my own hopes for the most improbable of midlife fantasies. How I had wanted to point to those beautiful girls and mock their shallowness, their perpetual giggling, their mangling of the English language, all the shortcomings of youth, to try to divert his attention from their glowing skin and soft curves, their agility and freshness.

No virtue of my own stopped me. I'd been saved by Noah and the impossibility of being a shrew in his company. He didn't mind my crabbing about the human race but the moment I shifted from curmudgeon to bitch, trying to wound or gain an advantage, his unhappiness would stop me. No reproof, just unhappiness. As if reality had fallen short of his hopes.

Noah was gazing at his teacup, smiling. "Thirty-odd years I knew Fay," he said, "and it always surprised her that good tea tastes better."

"But what about her pigs?" Eloise said. "I thought the meat was supposed to taste better."

She considered it a dig to mention my agricultural hobby, but Noah didn't notice.

"Her pigs, yes!" he cried. "She went to endless trouble, trying to breed them just so. But the tea she didn't think about. I don't know why not."

He shook his head, as if my inconsistency continued to surprise him as much as good tea had continued to surprise me. Then his attention shifted to Eloise.

"What about you?" he asked. "Do you pay attention to tea?"

From the intentness of his gaze, one would have thought her opinion was vital.

The blood rushed to her face. In a flash, her mood leapt from jealousy to elation and, disconcertingly, she felt a surge of sexual arousal. For a moment she couldn't remember his question. When she did remember it, she stumbled over her answer. She was longing to make herself interesting, to say yes, she had a passion for all sorts of exotic varieties of tea, but she couldn't. She had no gift for frothy conversational invention. She was hobbled by a steadfast regard for facts.

"I don't think my palate is very subtle," she said. "Mostly I drink coffee. For the jolt."

"I need a jolt myself, to face ninth grade algebra," he said. "I often have coffee."

"You do?" she said stupidly, then hurried on. "Of course you do. All those meetings, where you'd bring a travel mug..."

The thought trailed away. Just when she wanted to sparkle, her mind was a jumble.

"How were you to know? It might have been bourbon," he said.

The joke was tiny, but it made her laugh, giddily. She wondered if the deep flush she could feel on her skin was visible. She tried to think quelling thoughts, but no thought could quell her awareness of his eyes on her.

For a moment neither said anything. They just looked. Eventually the charge in the air became too palpable to ignore. Their mutual awareness demanded action, a conclusion they arrived at simultaneously. In a gesture of perfect sympathy, they extended their hands, picked up their cups and each took a swallow of lukewarm tea.

"How is Gerald?" Noah asked.

Words could quell where thoughts could not. Eloise's blood subsided, chilled by guilt. Damn his honor anyway. Just when she hoped he might encourage her to sin, he recalled her obligations. The message was clear. As long as she was married, she was off limits.

"He's fine," she said. Actually, she thought he wasn't fine, but she didn't want to talk about Gerald.

As her nerves calmed, she became conscious of a new anxiety. She needed to pee. She knew from experience that once she noticed it, the need would rapidly become urgent.

"When is the choral concert?" Noah asked. "Does he have a good group of singers?"

They chatted, desultorily, about the program for Gerald's concert. As the urge in her bladder became harder to ignore, her posture grew more rigid. Now and then she shifted position, trying to calm the sting of need.

She dreaded interrupting to ask about the bathroom, but she had almost steeled herself to the necessity when Noah suddenly cut short what he was saying and stood up.

"I'm going to put the kettle on to warm up my tea," he said. "And by the way, if you happen to need a bathroom any time, it's over there."

Heaven help me. As Eloise shut the door and sank gratefully onto the toilet, I tried to look out the window and hum a tune but even that much autonomy was out of reach. I was stuck to her like a passive burr, feeling the familiar shape of the toilet seat, seeing the familiar rack of books and magazines. The rack I'd helped build.

With urgency gone, she lingered a bit, relishing the chance to be alone with some of Noah's things. She idly opened one of the books on the rack, a history of jazz that Noah gave Dryden years ago and recently borrowed back. Her eye fell on the inscription inside the cover and the glow in her heart turned to ice.

To a disinterested eye, the note was a paragraph of harmless birthday wishes. To Eloise, the wishes were a scrawl between a glaring bracket of salutations, her worst imaginings written out in black ink. "To Dryden… Love, Noah."

Suddenly, Millicent's insinuations took on the inarguable force of logic. That Noah should fall for someone who came from the same mold as Fay. Someone crude, strong and brusque. Someone independent and difficult. Dryden was Fay's protégé. She was available. She was full of vigor and animal energy. She and Noah saw each other all the time. Everything added up. And as long as she was married, Eloise could only look on.

Where joy had been, she felt panic. She had to do something. The thought that she and Gerald would spend another thirty years in their present state of vegetative placidity was unendurable. This was her chance to make sense of her life. If she let it pass, she might never have another.

She felt terrified and yet sure she was right. Her whole stake was on a single number, but the alternative felt like choosing to live in a universe where everything was gray.

When she came out of the bathroom, Noah's face lit with a smile.

"Would you like some more tea?"

For a moment she wavered. Half of her wanted to stay, to drink tea and talk with him late into the night and forget about her husband and brother, at home expecting dinner, wondering where she was. But the other half wanted to bolt homeward as fast as possible and put the axe to her marriage before her courage failed, so that she could come back to Noah boldly and openly, free of encumbrances.

On the one side was her fear that it would take too long to free herself and she would be too late. On the other side was her gut belief that equations must balance and one could not bring good out of evil. This could be her whole life and she wanted it clean and clear.

But was clearness possible? And what if Noah didn't wait?

He was waiting now, the kettle suspended over her cup, invitingly.

"I have to go," she said.

She pulled on her coat and boots and fished in her pocket for her gloves. Now that she was committed to leaving, her reluctance was uppermost. She worried he would think, wrongly, that her haste to go home was an affirmation of love for her husband. She had to give him some small hint of the truth, within the bounds of the clearness she craved.

An embrace was impossible. Much too much.

Words were impossible, too. What could she say? I love you, I'm getting divorced?

Her hand was suspended in the air, with some vague idea of taking his hand or touching his cheek, but nothing felt right. Finally, she reached and touched his shirt, near his collarbone.

As her hand withdrew, he caught it in his. He started to bend, as if to give it a jokingly gallant kiss, but then changed his mind. He stood tilted awkwardly, unable to decide what to do with the hand he had taken. In the end he simply let it go.

They had touched, though, and as Eloise drove away, she carried with her the memory of how his hand had felt, lightly catching her fingers as if he was about to lead her into a dance.

Chapter 27

"Divorce?"

As she expected, Gerald was staggered by her declaration. He repeated the word, blankly, and then felt with his hand to find something on which to sit, the sofa as it happened.

They were in the living room, the usual site for their serious discussions. Gerald had once read that one shouldn't argue in the bedroom because the negative associations could lead to insomnia and the principle had gradually been extended to every room where a pleasure or necessary bodily function might be spoiled by bad associations, until only the living room and laundry were still available for disagreements. They favored the living room. It had places to sit and was used only for company, which was already a disruption. In any case, they rarely argued.

The moment she came home, she told Gerald they needed to talk and led the way to the living room. She had not wanted to postpone the conversation, not even for the hour it would take to eat dinner. She feared that creeping familiarity might overwhelm her resolve. Every minute in her house would remind her of the weight of inertia on the side of her marriage—the possessions to divide, the legal issues to untangle, the comforts of routine she would lose, the shock to her children, the distress to her husband.

She made her announcement almost without preamble. "I think we should get a divorce."

While she'd expected him to be surprised, she had not anticipated the intensity of his reaction. He looked thunderstruck, his power of speech overwhelmed by emotion as he took wavering steps backward and sank down onto the sofa.

She felt a rush of guilt. Did he love her more than she realized?

If he was truly distressed, her calculations would have to change. Debts and credits had to be fair. Her happiness could not come at too great a cost or it would be poisoned from the start. But short of retracting her words, she did not know how to make things easier for him.

He still had not said anything, after that first dumfounded echo. He kept giving his head little shakes, as if that could help clear his thoughts.

Finally she made a small nudge. "I really think it's the right thing," she said.

He lifted his head to look at her. He looked a wreck, red-eyed and haggard, as if he hadn't slept in a long time. It took visible effort for him to speak.

Eloise was braced, ready to express regrets, ready to answer protests, ready to offer explanations, ready to try to comfort. Ready for almost anything, except what he actually said.

"How did you find out?"

Huh?

"Find out?" she repeated. "Find out what?"

They stared at one another, in a perfectly balanced state of bafflement.

"You mean, that's not—?" He stopped.

"What's not... what?"

"But... if it isn't that, then... why do you—?"

"What do you mean, 'that'? Is there something going on?"

"No, there's nothing. I mean, not like that. It's just... I don't..."

He stumbled to a halt, not weeping, not howling, but looking as if he might do either.

Eloise was still at sea. Nothing in the conversation bore any resemblance to her expectations and Gerald in his current state of anguish and stupefaction bore very little resemblance to the man she thought she knew. She had never seen him in this state. He had never been in this state, not during their marriage. But despite his inability to speak a coherent sentence, he clearly had more on his mind than her wish for a divorce.

Her own nerves had been wrought up all day, but now the extremity of Gerald's distress began to have a calming effect. Someone needed to keep a clear head and it fell to her.

"Are you having an affair?" she asked.

At last, a sentence with specific meaning.

"No! Of course not!" he cried. "You're the only woman—person—I've even... been with..."

"Then, why are you so—? What did you mean, when you said, 'not that'?"

"Nothing. It was nothing."

"It was not nothing. You asked how I found out."

"I mean, it was nothing that matters. I just thought... that it must be part of all this... but it isn't. So it doesn't matter."

"WHAT might be part of all this?" she almost shouted. "I don't have any idea what you're talking about!"

"You don't?"

Again they stared at each other. Suddenly Gerald started to laugh and once started, he couldn't stop. He laughed and laughed, to the point of coughing, and then his body began to shake in nervous reaction. Eloise remembered his musical collapse in church this morning and wondered if she should call a doctor. Was he having some kind of mental breakdown?

Before she could make up her mind to take action, he managed to say something clear.

"Then why do you want a divorce?" he asked.

This was a question for which she had thought she was prepared. For the whole drive home, she had rehearsed explanations, phrasing them to be logical and irrefutable, but no more hurtful than necessary. Unfortunately, her phrases had been scripted for a different scene. She had imagined sorrow, dismay, shock, possibly anger. She was prepared for conflict, but had assumed it would be a calm sort of fight, proportional to the habits of their marriage.

Ungovernable hilarity had not been on the list of emotions she expected to encounter. All of her soothing words about "feeling she needed something more" and her discontent "not coming from anything he had done" sounded all wrong, not because they were platitudes, but because they seemed irrelevant.

She had no energy left for invention. If none of her kindly-meant generalities would serve, then the path of least resistance was the truth. But even the truth had two branches. That she wasn't in love with him. That she was in love with someone else. She chose the second. It seemed less of a personal insult.

When it came to the point, she couldn't speak the words "in love." Too dramatic. And too humiliating, if her hopes turned out to be misguided.

"I'm fond of someone," she said. "I don't know if it will come to anything, but..."

She trailed off to an apologetic shrug.

"You're fond of someone?" he repeated. "Really?"

He sounded like someone who thinks an offer looks too good to be true and he wants to get it nailed down fast.

Eloise nodded, but she felt unmoored. Nothing made sense. Her marriage may not have been exciting but she had thought he would feel some regret at ending it, just as she did.

Instead he was laughing again. His wife was in love with someone else. Wasn't that the funniest joke he'd ever heard?

Then, suddenly, he lifted his head and shouted, "I don't understand you! What do you want me to do?"

Eloise was about to answer when she realized he wasn't talking to her. He was looking at the ceiling and her brain briefly skipped to the idea that one of their kids must be upstairs. Then she returned to present reality and remembered that their kids were grown and gone. Unless he really had lost his mind, he must have been yelling at god.

This was as strange as everything else. He'd never been a breast beater about his faith. Apart from the collective recitations in church, the only audible devotion she'd ever heard from him was a muttered amen after a prayer.

"Gerald, what is going on with you?"

"Me? Nothing. Absolutely nothing. I'm perfectly fine and this is all too perfect and I don't have any idea what I'm doing."

With that, he burst into tears.

The lasagna had turned to dry layers of rubber by the time Gerald finally made his tongue form the syllable that described the natural direction of his affections. Fortunately, the football game went into overtime and their talk was not interrupted by any inquiries from Doke about the status of dinner. After a tortuous process of indirection, embarrassment, and euphemism, they came to an understanding on the main points. He was gay. They both loved other people. They felt nothing but friendly good wishes for one another's future happiness.

Neither had offered to reveal the name of their beloved. They were too shy, too uncertain of success. They could not bear to expose the absurd grandeur of their aspirations to the critical eye of another person, not even a spouse. Nor did either of them probe the other for a name.

Having been governed by civility rather than passion in their marriage, they had a high regard for fair play.

Most of ordinary reality had been postponed for the moment. How their children would react. How their possessions would be divided. What the neighbors would say. They were unaccustomed to being in love and their faculties were saturated by the sensation of it.

At dinner, they barely spoke and barely ate. At first Doke tried to tell them about the game, which had been dramatic, but he soon saw they weren't listening. Lapsing into silence, he methodically sawed his way through the desiccated noodles on his plate.

After dinner, Eloise busied herself cleaning up but Gerald was too restless to settle and went wandering from room to room. Finally, he retreated to the bedroom and knelt beside the bed. I heard fragments of prayerful thought trying to take shape in his mind, "Show me the right thing to do. Tell me if this is a sign of your will…"

He couldn't keep his mind on the prayer. Again and again, his memory intruded, recalling his tramp through the woods with Jim. Most of the time, their mutual gravitation had been limited by the presence of their fellow searchers, but once, for a few seconds, the others had moved out of sight beyond a rock outcrop and they were alone. They had stopped walking and looked at each other, and then, without saying a word, Jim had pulled him closer and kissed him.

The kiss was brief. They could hear the voices of their companions, who were nervous and would not like them being out of sight. In one motion, they kissed and separated, hurrying to join the others.

Gerald had hoped the act of kneeling would reconnect him to the habit of prayer. Instead, it reconnected him to his marriage bed and all the decades of soft-focus longings that were now fused with a moment of physical reality, a sensory memory as vivid as the feel of the rug under his knees. He could no longer pray in this bedroom.

As he rose to his feet, he felt guilty and a bit desperate. If he could not reach his god, how could he know if the dissolution of his marriage, which he had not caused, was an answer to his prayers or a temptation from the devil?

He went downstairs, told Eloise he needed to pray, put on his coat and headed across the village to the church. He unlocked a side door, turned on a single light, and made his way through the shadowy space to a front pew. There he fell to his knees and tried again to pray.

The church did not help. Instead of images of Jim, he was tormented by echoes of Inchkeep's sermon. "…if ye live after the flesh ye shall die…our immortal soul should be the whole and only object of our care…"

He could not form the words of a prayer, because he didn't know what to say. The words he wanted to speak—thank you for sending me love, thank you for sending love to my wife, show me the right path—were stopped in his throat, because he thought the god to whom he wanted to speak must despise him in every part.

He felt as he had in high school, the year his muscular build was recruited for the offensive line of the football team. He was forever doing the wrong thing, because he couldn't keep his mind on the game. He had been berated, repeatedly, for his failures. In front of the whole team, the coach told him he lacked character and was letting his teammates down.

These tongue-lashings had left him terrified and inarticulate. The coach was not a man to whom he could try to explain his treacherously wandering thoughts, whether their object had been the complexities of a fugue, the splendor of another boy's physique or simply the wondrous colors of the autumn foliage near the field. He had lived the whole season in a state of dread, knowing he would fail again, that he would go right when he should have gone left, because he was fundamentally not the player the coach wanted him to be.

Football he could leave behind and had, gratefully, after those three interminable months, but god he could not leave behind. His god and his music were inextricably woven together. Without god, his music would be a hollow shell and without music, he would be lost.

So he knelt in the semi-darkness, seeking a way to reach his god and feeling a terrible dread that his efforts would be fruitless, because nothing he said truthfully could be pleasing to his divinity and he did not believe that a god could be fooled by a falsehood. He struggled for words until he was nearly weeping, but the only message that emerged was a muddled plea for guidance.

In despair, he left the pew and made his way to the organ loft. If he could not put prayer into words, he could at least make an offering of music, to let his god know he was there and was seeking to be heard. As he sat down on the bench, he felt very strongly the echoing emptiness of the church and the evening quiet in the village outside. Although it was unlikely anyone would be abroad at this hour, his first motion was to stop the organ down as far as he could, to avoid calling attention to his presence in the church.

His hands paused over the keyboard, considering what to play. He settled on Bach, the master. His spirit craved calm and Bach gave voice to the most perfect faith, if not in god, then at least in the ordered beauty of existence. His hands dropped to the keys and he began to play.

He barely made it to the end of the first phrase. The organ's voice was too bold, too grandly self-proclaiming. Even stopped down, the instrument seemed to bellow his presence and he felt that he was making too much of himself, clamoring so loudly for god's ear.

He sat, helplessly, staring at the keyboard. He longed to immerse himself in music and forget everything else, but the organ was all wrong. He considered going home to the piano in his study, but immediately knew that that was wrong, too. He could not find forgetfulness in the house with his wife.

Then he remembered that the other church had a piano, one notable for the smallness of its sound. Would the door be unlocked? The Old Church was sparsely decorated, very little to steal. Perhaps it still upheld the ancient tradition of sanctuary. He put on his coat, locked the door behind him and headed across the street.

As he hoped, the Old Church was open. Inside, two wall sconces were lit, dimly, just enough for him to find his way across the room to the piano. He switched on a lamp over the keyboard and sat down to play.

The piano's tone was as modest as he'd remembered and for his mood it was exactly right. The sound seemed to fill his small pool of light and then melt away into the darkness beyond. If god wanted to hear, he would. No one else needed to. He chose pieces that demanded concentration and the effort was calming. As he played, the images of Jim and the words of Inchkeep's sermon receded from his mind, leaving only a meditative absence of thought.

For me, the interlude was brief. Jim was too good-natured to curse me outright, even in his mind, but his muted grumbling was enough to steer my drift, away from the sound of the piano and down the street into his office, where he was staring at a map of the state.

It's Sunday evening, I thought. Why are you at work?

His grumbling expressed much the same thought. If ever there was a wild goose chase, this was it. There was no evidence of homicide and even if there had been, where should they search? The body could be a hundred miles away.

He made a note to himself to get a sample of dirt from the truck. He'd read about a body that was found by analyzing dirt from the killer's vehicle. Or was the dirt from a shovel in the vehicle? He couldn't remember now. Perhaps he should wait and see if the state police would send a specialist to get samples. Jim wasn't a detective. His mind was on the case because the alternative was to fret about Gerald.

Yesterday he'd been on top of the world, thinking he was done with the Kirkwoods, thinking he and Gerald might have a happy future. Today the case had been resuscitated and by the time he finished the paperwork, he had missed half of the afternoon choral rehearsal. Then, when he finally got to the rehearsal, Gerald had avoided talking to him. Jim still didn't know what was wrong and now Gerald was at home with his wife.

No, he's not, I said. He's right down the street, in the church, playing the piano.

Alive, I hadn't spent much time speculating about what might make some random neighbors happy. Now, like it or not, I was stuck in their company and I couldn't help thinking it was better for them to be happy than sad. In the spirit of rooting for the home team, I began to chant, Church! Now! Church! Now! Church! Now!

Jim frowned at his computer. He'd meant to search for something, but the thought had slipped away. Try as he would to distract himself, he kept remembering details of the day in the woods—Gerald's unscuffed hiking gear, his efforts to hide his nervousness, his misplaced eagerness to prove himself tough and woodsman-like. As if the man who had just chosen to kiss the church organist would rather have been kissing a lumberjack.

Jim shut down the computer and grabbed his coat. Perhaps motion and cold air would improve his mood. Outdoors, the air was still and the ground barely dusted with snow. With hands in pockets, he walked along the edge of the town common, where the windows threw patches of yellow warmth across the frosty grass.

So far so good, I thought.

Then, as he neared the Old Church, I heard a car coming from behind, moving slowly. The pace of its approach and the pace of Jim's footsteps soon began to look like two converging lines, destined to meet at the church and then diverge, with the sound of the car holding his ear until he was out of range of the piano. The coincidence was maddening. The exactness of the timing. The unnaturally slow creep of the car. He and the car reached the church together, their paths still parallel. In a few more steps, the chance would be gone.

Stop, dammit! I yelled.

My shout was aimed at Jim, but it seemed there was a ricochet in the fabric of the universe, because the car turned into the next driveway and parked in the garage. Another cosmic coincidence. I didn't even know who the driver was.

The change made Jim pause, appreciating the quiet. When his ear caught the sound of the piano, he thought at first it must be far away. Then he realized the faintness of the music was due to walls, not distance.

Assuming that the pianist must be Mrs. Crane, the usual accompanist, Jim made no move to go into the church. He was not in the mood for pleasant chat. But neither did he leave. He stood, listening, and the longer he stood, the more his inclination tilted toward the music. If he slipped quietly into the back, the pianist need never know he was there. The church had two entrance doors and being prone to lateness, he knew which one did not squeak.

He slid through the door and eased it closed behind him. When he saw Gerald, he stopped still. He was not surprised, exactly—it seemed fitting that Gerald should be here—but he had to restrain an urge to rush forward and plead his case. I heard a murmur of thought, "Help me out here. Please," and then he began to walk, quietly, up the side aisle toward the piano.

He could not have asked for better help than that of Bach. The music was swift and intricate and Gerald was oblivious to anything else. When Jim glided out of the darkness into the pool of light around the piano, he must have seemed like an apparition, materializing out of the air. He was tall and graceful and his blond hair glowed in the lamplight. It wouldn't be altogether irrational if Gerald thought for a moment that the music had summoned an angel.

When he saw Jim, he stopped playing but his hands did not leave the keyboard. He sat, suspended, and he looked almost frightened, as if he knew the moment of decision had arrived, but he still was not sure if the beauty before him was the true beauty of god or the deceptive beauty of Satan. He stared and I could hear his thoughts, confusedly begging for some clear sign of god's will.

Oh for pity's sake, I growled. What do you think god's going to do, make the piano start playing "Some Enchanted Evening" without the help of human fingers? Do you really think J.S. Bach and your wife and this eminently decent cop are all in league with the devil, trying to lure you to damnation, and what god wants is for you and Eloise to spend another thirty years in a state of deceitfulness and mutual indifference as a model of holy matrimony for your grandchildren? Everybody deserves the chance at a soul mate. You, Eloise, Jim, everyone.

So do me a favor, Gerald. Make us all happy.

As for what god thinks, I can't help you there. I don't know his whereabouts any more than I did a week ago. If I were you, I'd ask Bach.

Neither man had spoken, but now Jim made a tiny nod toward the keyboard. "You don't have to stop," he said.

Gerald struggled to collect himself. He closed his eyes, listening for the phrase he'd been playing when he saw Jim. Going back to the start of the phrase, he began to play.

He continued all the way to the closing chord, giving Bach his due respect. Jim did not speak or move again until he finished. Only the music crossed the gap between them, but the music, it seemed, was enough. By the time he stopped playing, Gerald had decided. He could accept the idea that he or his wife or Jim or all three together might be sinfully mistaken, but it was not possible for him to exist in a universe in which Bach, too, could be the voice of the devil. If Bach could lead him to damnation, then hell was where god wanted him to be.

As the last chord died away, he leapt from the piano bench and Jim leapt forward to meet him and they flung themselves into an embrace.

A moment later, they sprang apart, wordlessly agreeing that the sort of embraces they had in mind did not belong in a church, no matter how liberal its denomination.

They looked at each other, asking now what, and such was their harmony of spirit that the decision was made in an instant. Hand in hand, like a pair of urgent teenagers, they rushed out of the church and headed down the street to Jim's office, which was the closest place they could think of that was both unsanctified and warm.

Chapter 28

The state police were not hindered by any private emotions or neighborly connections to the situation. They arrived on the scene in the morning, armed with warrants and investigative expertise and visible irritation that so much time had been allowed to pass before they were called in. They did not ask for any gut assessments of the case and Jim's gut assessment of their mood stopped him from volunteering any.

Initially, Dryden's behavior made them hope the whole business was a youthful gesture of unconventionality and not a serious crime. She was straightforward and polite and she made no objection to their searching the entire farmstead, including her private belongings. If anything, she was pointedly helpful, opening doors and gates and warning them of low beams and high thresholds. She showed them where she found my body, the clothes I was wearing and the dolly she had used to load me onto the truck. When they said these objects must be taken away for laboratory examination, she said fine.

Everything was going so smoothly, they began to think the difficulties in the case had been overstated and they would soon have the old lady's remains in the morgue. But they did not know Dryden. I recognized her mood, that gliding acquiescence combined with detachment. It was exactly the look with which she had once donned her mother's beige business suit for a cocktail party. The police were there at Anita's request and Dryden treated them as Anita's minions, with an air of civility that cloaked disdain, right down to her invitation to include the guestroom and her parents' suitcases in their search.

They met the limit of her obligingness exactly where everyone else had when they asked where she had taken my body. She replied, politely, that it was not possible for her to tell them. She didn't care that the officer had emphasized the "detective" in his title of "detective sergeant," that his civilian clothing marked his superior status and he was flanked by a pair of uniformed subordinates. She was not pugnacious in her refusal; she was just immoveable.

Having thought they were close to success, the police were doubly exasperated by failure and they rebounded into a belief in her guilt. If Dryden had shown signs of a chemical addiction or a delusional disorder, they might have seen a plausibly innocent explanation for her irrationality. Instead, her demeanor was a model of calm lucidity. She wasn't nuts and she wasn't a junkie, so she must be guilty, because no sane person would make this much trouble for herself unless she was trying to escape bigger trouble.

In the end, they decided to arrest her, which must have looked like a no-lose decision. There was no doubt she'd broken a law. If her crime turned out to be homicide, then she belonged in jail. If her offense was a misdemeanor, then they hoped the hard reality of a jail cell would bring her to her senses.

I wished the same myself, for all the good it did. From the moment the police showed up at the farm, I'd been yelling at her to forget my carcass and save herself, but the only person who showed any sign of paying attention to me was Charlie. He kept hovering on the fringes, muttering about how I wouldn't have liked all this commotion. Unfortunately, being Charlie, he did not try to make anyone listen to him.

The one voice that made Dryden waver, briefly, was Terp's. The morning after her arrest, he came to the lockup in Leonardston and asked to see her. The officer on duty was quick to assure Dryden that she didn't have to talk to reporters, but she assured him in return that Terp was there because she had called him. This response classed her as a new kind of troublemaker, the sort who would take her case to the newspapers and try to get public opinion on her side. The officer's manner was distinctly chilly as he showed Terp in to see her.

Sitting in the visitors' room, Terp kept thinking he ought to feel gloomier. He did feel some of the proper emotions, especially worry, but a part of him was simply happy to see her and even happier to know that he was the person she had chosen to call.

Only two days had passed since he'd seen her, but they felt like the days of a child or a dog, every hour stretching into the distance. For two days, he'd been balked by his conscience and the dragon mother standing guard, and his mood had alternated between wonder and irritation at this unfamiliar persona, a man with serious intentions. He'd been determined to put her welfare first and not make trouble with her parents, but all the while he'd been hoping his phone would ring and she would say, "Bother what my parents think, I want to see you." When his phone finally did ring, he was so glad to hear her voice, he had to remind himself she was calling from jail.

She didn't sound upset. If anything, she almost seemed relieved, as if she'd rather be watched by the police than by her mother.

For a while after he arrived, they didn't speak much. They just looked at each other, across the space that separated their chairs. In this situation, less was more. Nerves could be as electrified by the space that prevents touch as by a touch itself.

Eventually, though, Terp felt a need to talk about ordinary reality.

"Is this really worth it?" he asked.

He gestured at the surroundings, the pale green concrete walls, the gray vinyl floor, the flat fluorescent lighting, and the watching guard.

"I don't know," she said. "But you can't give up what you think just to get out of jail. Can you? You wouldn't be the same person."

He suspected this was why he loved her.

"I guess if you do then that's who you are," he said. "The sort of person who thinks whatever will keep him out of jail."

He'd be that, probably. A chameleon. Or maybe just a liberal thinker, always open to the possibility that the opposing point of view has merit.

"But there could be good reasons, too. For changing your mind," he said. "For instance, wouldn't your aunt be worried about her pigs?"

Dryden smiled faintly. "The pigs will cope, as long as someone shows up with the feed bucket. I've set that up with Otis. But I do worry about Scollay."

"I could take Scollay, if it came to that, but it won't. The whole situation is absurd."

"Lots of things are absurd. Getting a tattoo. Fly-fishing. This isn't anything remarkable."

Her calm was incomprehensible.

"But why aren't you pissed off?" he said. "At the outrageousness."

"Because I'm happy."

"Happy!" This was not what he'd expected.

His thoughts raced to the most hopeful interpretation, that her happiness matched his own, that she loved him and everything else seemed secondary. In the next instant, he mocked himself for conceit. He was the clown who briefly leavens the tragedy, not the hero to whom the diva's last breath sings passionate devotion. Obviously she meant something different.

"How can you be happy?" he asked doubtfully.

His skepticism made Dryden pause. When she answered, I felt something rare with her, that she was not speaking the truth.

"It's very restful to be stripped down to essentials," she said. "The fuss has been exhausting. This is simpler."

"As simplicity goes, this is pretty radical."

He tried to make it sound like he was joking, but disappointment put an edge in his voice. Despite his self-mockery, he'd been hoping to be part of her answer. His posture straightened into the stance of a reporter, his public purpose.

Her mirroring movement was barely perceptible, a ripple dying away into stillness, but I felt the change. She would rely on herself.

You fool, don't back away now! I yelled at him.

Terp came to the same thought, but the moment had passed. When he leaned toward her again, she straightened further, and the distance remained.

They took refuge in talk of practicalities—when was her first hearing, did she have a lawyer, did she need a toothbrush? Within a day or two, she said, she would find out about bail.

"You should have a lawyer," he said. "You don't want to get screwed just because you don't know the system."

"That *is* the system, isn't it?" she said. "Without a lawyer, you're screwed."

"It does work out nicely for the lawyers," he said.

The meaningless jokes put even more distance between them. Why couldn't he say, straight out, that he loved her? He wanted to make some bold gesture, but he was too aware of the concrete walls, the guard watching, all the practical concerns that were weighing on her.

"Can I be useful, at least?" he said. "There must be something I can do."

She stared at her hands, frowning. He waited, expecting to hear no, she needed nothing.

"There is one thing," she said finally.

"What is it? Just tell me and I'll do it, whatever it is."

"That's a large promise."

"I mean it."

She hesitated and glanced at the guard, who might hear what they said.

"Think jazz," he suggested. "Pick a theme for improv."

"I'd like to know... how the banquet's going."

"I could check on it," he said. "If I knew where."

She glanced at the guard, whose look of boredom had not changed.

"There are directions."

"There are!"

His voice was too loud, but the guard didn't look.

"I left them with your fiddle," she said. "A while ago."

Terp's mouth opened in amazement. "You expected this?"

"Not exactly. I just thought someone should have them."

"Do they cover... everything?"

"I think so. Can you recognize a hemlock tree?"

"Not offhand, but I can look it up."

She smiled. "I knew I'd got the right person."

Leaving the lockup, Terp was flying. He supposed he should be worried or angry, but he couldn't stop smiling. For the moment, he could do without the word love. She trusted him and that was enough.

Never in his life had he felt heroic, not even in small ways. He was jester to the core, the pratfall-taker who left the serious combat to people who wouldn't trip. Now he'd been given a mission and, to his surprise, he found the prospect exhilarating.

Halfway to the parking lot, lost in daydreams, he nearly collided with Anita and Charlie.

"I see the press has its nose into people's business," Anita greeted him.

"Always," he said cheerfully. "If a crime has been committed, the press has a duty to keep the public informed. Don't you agree?"

He eased past her and headed for his car.

Anita watched him, frowning. Coming to a swift decision, she turned to go back to the parking lot. "Dryden can wait," she said to Charlie. "That guy's up to something."

Following Terp's car, Anita tried to stay a discreet distance behind, but his speed forced her to close the gap, in order not to lose him.

"He's driving like he's gotten a tip," she said.

"Perhaps he has a deadline," Charlie said.

She shook her head. "He looked way too smug. I wonder if Dryden told him something, just to annoy us."

When Terp turned down a side road, parked his car and went into his house, Anita grumbled about how people could do everything on their computer nowadays, but she also stuck with her instincts. They would wait a while and watch. She found a parking spot down the road where she could still see the driveway and tuned the radio to a news program to pass the time. Charlie fished in his briefcase for a book.

Two chapters later, he was pulled from his reading by Anita's grip on his arm and her voice in his ear, "Would you look at that!"

Terp was walking across the yard to his car. He was dressed for the outdoors, with a jacket and hiking boots, and he was carrying a daypack.

"I think Dryden told him where she put the body. God knows why, but I bet she did."

Damn her intuitions, anyway. You'd think her heart had some affinity with Dryden, given how lucky her guesses seemed to be.

Terp turned onto the road and Anita fell in behind him. Abandoning skepticism, Charlie tossed his book aside to watch the car ahead.

They'd driven about ten miles, heading roughly north, when Anita suddenly swore and turned up the volume on the radio. Charlie had not been listening, but now he heard what she had heard, the name "Kirkwood" spoken in tones of journalistic salivation.

It seemed that one of the biggest televangelists in the country had decided my corpse was a matter of Christian concern and had added "pagan desecration of the dead" to a litany of satanic influences that already included stem cell research, homosexuality, evolution, sex education and the myth of global warming. The preacher had called the "dumping" of my mortal remains an act of aggression and was urging the faithful to fight back.

"Enough is enough," the preacher roared. "This is a Christian country. We will no longer allow the demon seeds of science and skepticism to tempt believers away from the truth of the Bible and the sweet promise of eternal life."

You can believe whatever sweet promises you want, I said to the preacher, but I'm betting it won't matter a particle whether your body is eaten by crows, or casketed in silk and mahogany. This question of eternity isn't any clearer now than it was when I was alive but as near as I can figure, the only difference between heaven and hell is what I left behind on earth. If you want my advice, which you don't, you won't spend your time bowing to altars or chanting prayers to the unseen; you'll plant daffodils and help your kids with their reading and kiss your wife at every opportunity.

The radio broadcast went on talking, heedless of any opinion of mine. It wasn't in real time anyway, it was tape, and the next stretch of tape held a bombshell that might have launched Anita into orbit if she hadn't been strapped down with a seatbelt.

"...I have learned that this outrage touches me personally," the televangelist intoned. "My own hometown, the town where my sainted mother still lives, is represented in Congress by a member of this very family, a spawn of the devil who has assumed a mask of righteousness..."

"What!" The word was a screech. Anita grabbed her purse and dug for her mobile phone.

"...I only hope that I am mistaken and that Mr. Kirkwood can prove, beyond a doubt, that he had no part in this blasphemous act..."

Anita flipped open the phone and punched buttons, trying to call Spenser, but like most places in the state, the road was surrounded by hills and she could not get reception.

"Hell and damnation! How much worse can things get!"

"That preacher can't be serious," Charlie said doubtfully. "Can he...?"

"Of course he's serious!" she exploded. "These people are always serious, the benighted idiots."

She punched the number again, but it still had no signal.

They're not really idiots, most of them, I murmured. They just don't want to die.

I wasn't normally a partisan on behalf of evangelical Christians, but any group Anita scorned I was bound to defend. A moment later, I heard an echoing murmur from Charlie.

"It's understandable, isn't it? To want eternal life?"

"Jesus Christ, how can you be defending those delusional dunderheads? Don't you realize what this means for Spenser? If he loses their vote, it's all over!"

She punched the phone one last time, uselessly, before flinging it back into her purse.

"This bloody backwater!"

She'd been driving on autopilot, too transfixed by the news to pay attention to the road or anything else. Now her eyes came into focus on the vehicle still visible in the distance ahead of her. It was a jacked-up black four-wheel-drive pickup with a large German shepherd pacing side to side behind the cab. Terp's aging Toyota station wagon was nowhere to be seen.

"Where'd he go? Did you see him turn?"

Charlie looked around vaguely and shook his head.

Anita floored the accelerator and tore past the pickup. The road ahead was empty. She accelerated more and kept going, for several miles, before conceding that the chase was pointless. There was no sign of Terp and they had passed several side roads he could have taken.

Chapter 29

I caught up with Terp in the woods. Or perhaps he caught up with me. The laws of causality still weren't clear.

He was on foot, about halfway between the logging road and my body, making a rabbit zigzag from compass check to compass check. As an orienteer, Terp was more determined than he was skillful. His compass headings were like the steering in one of my old trucks, several degrees of approximation, and he tended to stumble over rocks and branches every time he tried to check his reference points. On the other hand, he'd had the wit to bring a roll of orange surveyor's tape, which he strewed on branches to mark his path back out.

The hemlock tree was even more striking than I remembered. Terp passed other large evergreens, but none so massive and fantastically twisted, and none that were hemlocks. When he spotted mine, he stopped. He was still some distance away, but he was sure it was the one.

He stood a moment, preparing for what he might find. Perhaps the body would be intact, like a wax figure. Perhaps it would look like roadkill, mangled and bloody, or be stripped to a bare skeleton, like a science display. Or it might be gone altogether, dragged away by animals, except for one small bone to show it had been there, the jaw perhaps, or part of a rib.

When he undertook this task, he had thought only of Dryden. Now, seeing the huge, scarred trunk and twining limbs of the hemlock, he felt a sensation somewhere between spooked and reverent, as if he was entering a place of spirits where a person would be wise to observe the proper rituals. If only he knew what would be proper. The rituals of institutional Christianity were familiar enough, but in this place they seemed irrelevant. They had nothing to say to trees and coyotes except "Make yourselves useful to mankind."

Finally he murmured, "I hope you don't mind that I'm here. I won't bother you."

As he approached the tree, his pulse quickened, more from curiosity than fear. He remembered a museum exhibit he'd once seen, of plasticized human cadavers. Those cadavers had been sanitized and educational, but his fascination had been mixed with discomfort, because the exhibit had spiced its science with whimsy by posing the cadavers as skiers and acrobats. As if reality was insufficient and people had to be teased into absorbing knowledge. Terp had found the experience a little prurient, almost like a strip club, where the human body becomes material for showmanship. Surely the space inside a person's skin was as private as the sex act.

He worried he might feel the same way now, that he was intruding on something too private. Wasn't death the most secret, inward and solitary thing a person ever did?

Hah! I snorted. That's what you think. Just wait until you try it. I've hardly had a moment's privacy since I died. At least those dead people on display in the museum gave their permission to be gawked at. When did I ever say I wanted to stay at the party forever?

My head, the most obviously human piece of me, caught Terp's eye first. Braced as he was, the reality still made his stomach turn over. He stopped a few feet away, getting used to how thoroughly my physical being had become meat.

Most of the body was still there, including head, torso and pieces of limbs, but some parts had been chewed and others had been disjointed and rearranged. Although the snow was gone, the air was cold enough that there was no smell of decay. When he'd had time to adjust, he found the reality less disturbing than what he'd imagined. It was calming to know the worst.

Terp walked closer to study what was left of the face. He saw no resemblance to the photos he'd seen. Just anonymous muscle and bone, the food the old lady had wanted to be.

What struck him most was the absence of individual personality. He'd seen dead bodies before, his grandfather and his cat among others, and he knew there was no confusing death with sleep. Death was unmistakable. But even in death, his grandfather and his cat had looked like the beings he'd always known. Gazing at their stillness, Terp could imagine that every part of them was there in the room with him, body, mind, spirit, everything, and that all of it was equally still.

With this body, he saw nothing that could be called Fay Kirkwood and he couldn't feel the same completeness about her death. This body reminded him of a package of fryer parts in the grocery store. There was no suggestion of any spirit, alive or dead, in the dismembered legs and breasts of a chicken, and so it seemed to him with Fay Kirkwood's chewed flesh. If her body had ever housed a spirit, that spirit hadn't stayed with the body and died with it. Either no spirit had existed in the first place, or else it had cut itself loose and gone elsewhere, and the flesh still lying here couldn't tell him which was the case, any more than the chicken parts could.

He'd never believed in a personal afterlife, because it made no sense to him. What would happen to someone who had outlived three different spouses over the course of a lifetime? Would they all be together in heaven, one big happy polygamy?

You're not as far afield as you think, I said. For all I knew, Terp's grandfather and his cat were wandering around with him, too, watching what happened.

A question followed, inescapably. Would my fate have been different if my corpse had been buried? Was my present existence the ghost of a troubled death, stalking the corridors of a gothic mansion?

Terp left my skull and torso and walked a slow spiral outward, looking for other bones. He found part of one leg, but nothing else. He was careful not to touch anything. My remains could still become evidence and he did not want anyone to claim he had tampered with them.

Returning to the hemlock, he lingered a bit, taking in the surroundings. It's a nice quiet spot, he thought. Maybe the old lady wasn't crazy, wanting to rest here.

"What do you think, you old troublemaker?" he said. "Should I make a record of this tree, just in case?"

You're darned right, you should, I replied.

He reached into his pack, pulled out a camera and took a couple of photos of the hemlock. I noticed that he carefully did not include any of my bones in the shot. Then he put the camera away and headed back to his car, picking up his flags as he went.

At the highway, Terp slid a blues cassette into the player. Gradually, the sound of the guitar drew him away from the present time. His thoughts ambled along in a meditation on bass runs and cool chord progressions, which was unintelligible to me, but very restful.

Then, like the flip of a switch, the guitar and the chord progressions were gone and I heard the insistent sharpness of Anita's voice.

"If you're not the person I should speak to, then who is?" she asked.

"That'll be Detective Sergeant Mayhew," Royce Palmer said slowly. "But I don't know as he's got time for this… It sounds a little…"

He paused, looking for a word, but Anita spared him the trouble of finding it.

"If Sergeant Mayhew is the person with authority to decide what's important," she said, "then perhaps you should tell me how to reach him so that he can exercise that authority."

Royce thought a bit and apparently decided he'd rather deal with an irritated Sergeant Mayhew than an irritated Anita. He said the sergeant would be coming by the office in a while.

Knowing less of the history, Mayhew was more receptive to Anita's information.

"You say Mr. Jones equipped himself for hiking. Did you actually see where he went?"

"No, I'm afraid we didn't. He took steps to evade pursuit. He'd gone as far as Alcott when we lost sight of him."

"Alcott, huh." Mayhew sounded disappointed. Alcott was only fifteen miles from Gilham and still on a major road. It didn't narrow the possibilities much. "And what exactly is the relationship between Mr. Jones and the suspect in custody?"

"Relationship isn't quite the word. He's covering the story. He's a reporter."

"Reporter!" The sergeant's dismay was obvious. "That could be—"

He stopped abruptly, and then resumed in a more neutral tone. "Do you have reason to think he won't publish what he knows?"

"I think he'll publish enough to make a lurid story but not enough to help the investigation. She wouldn't have told him anything unless they'd agreed what he could print."

"Did he take a camera?"

"I don't know. He was carrying a daypack. He could have had anything."

"Hm." Mayhew considered the situation. Finally, he said, "I guess the morning paper will tell us where things stand…"

"You're not going to let him publish photos!"

"I can't say for sure how we'll choose to proceed," he said. "It's a delicate situation."

His unspoken thought was a shout in my ear. Blast the nosy bastards! You can't take two steps in this job without tripping over a reporter, but it's more trouble than it's worth to mess with them. People get all over you about freedom.

"But it's a homicide case!" Anita said. "Can't you make him tell you what he knows?"

"It's a little more complicated," Mayhew said. "I believe the issue of religious freedom has been raised…"

"That is hogwash, about religion. Our family is Christian and this thing about paganism is a complete fantasy. The point is to get after this reporter."

"Yes, well, we'll certainly speak with Mr. Jones. That's as much as I can promise…"

Chapter 30

Mr. Jones, at that moment, was holding his phone some distance from his ear as Randall vented hours of pent-up aggravation. "Where the hell have you been? I've been trying to reach you all day and you haven't even been checking messages, never mind answering your goddamned phone. There's a bunch of guys mad at me that I let you have this story and now you go AWOL. Do you still work for this paper or should I be putting somebody else on this?"

"I'm still on the story. But something came up. I had to deal with it."

"What something? It better be big, like you won a Pulitzer."

"It is big but I can't talk about it."

"Personal?"

"Yes and no."

"Look, I gotta have somebody on this who's gonna be where he needs to be. I can't have you disappearing every time your girlfriend's got the day off or your mom's pipes have burst."

"It wasn't like that. I got some good information. I just can't talk about it yet."

"Yeah, I already gathered you talked to the girl this morning. So, what, did she give you a scoop on where the body is?"

"Sure, and a blow job, too. Look, you'll have to trust me on this. I had good reasons."

"If I had all day, I'd tell you all the reasons I don't trust anybody who says, 'Trust me.' Right now, I need you to get your butt over to the church tonight, because some people are trying to organize a protest."

"Which side is organizing?"

"Believe it or not, it's the squishy liberals. Starting with that burdock-worshiper you interviewed about burial rites."

"Coral Hoskins!"

"Yeah, her. It seems she read about the arrest and got on the horn to people and then some of those people started sending out group emails and now there's a meeting in the parish hall."

Group emails. Hooray for the union of semi-conductors and spirit animals. If fundamentalists can use the products of science to broadcast their objections to the scientific method, then why shouldn't the disciples of Singing Wolf talk electronically about finding oneness with the natural world?

When Terp got to the parish hall, he found a crowd that was modest but still bigger than either he or I had expected, maybe twenty-five people. From the scraps of conversation I could hear, people were talking as much about the constitution and the trampling of civil liberties as they were about Dryden or me. I saw that Noah had come and was sitting with a cluster of committee regulars. Ordinarily he would have been chatting sociably, but tonight he was quiet, leaving the talk to others.

Terp took a seat at the outer end of a row and scanned the crowd, noting faces he knew. His eye halted at a figure hunched in the back corner. "That guy never goes to meetings," he thought.

I had no clear thought except astonishment. "That guy" was Otis and Terp's instinct was dead on. Otis would rather pluck and gut a hundred chickens than spend an hour at a meeting. For this event, he'd spruced up with a shave and town clothes, but the clothes sat awkwardly and he already looked like he wanted to leave. Yet there he was and I was inordinately pleased that he'd come, even if he never opened his mouth.

Serving as moderator, Coral began the meeting with an exercise designed to open everyone's thoughts to the larger energy of the universe. She asked people to close their eyes and visualize a clear mountain lake reflecting a cloudless blue sky. As they contemplated the lake, they were to see a majestic stag poised at the water's edge, perfectly attuned to the energy flowing into him from the water he was drinking, the moss under his feet, and the air coming into his lungs. Finally, she asked everyone to imagine themselves as the stag, taking in the power and beauty of the universe.

Half the crowd sat calmly, breathing deeply, at one with her message. The other half of the crowd shifted and squirmed, their energy absorbed in keeping their eyes closed and trying not to feel foolish. The meeting had attracted the same tenuous coalition that had defended Dryden at the diner. On the one side, aligned with the stag, were the New Age thinkers and back-to-the-land pioneers for whom compost was a symbol of eternity. On the other side was a congregation of old-school Yankees like Otis, governed by the granite principles that your religious beliefs were your own concern and the business of government was to make sure you were left in peace. This latter group was extremely resistant to the idea that Coral or anyone else should tell them what to daydream about, especially not as a group and in public.

When she brought the exercise to a close, a palpable shift in energy rippled through the room, as the half of the crowd that had relaxed into a meditative dream remembered their outrage and grew tense again, while the half that had been squirming grew calm and settled themselves in their seats, ready for the real discussion to begin.

As soon as she invited people to share their ideas, Lawrence Buell leapt to his feet. He was a short, vigorous man, an engineering consultant with a meticulously low-impact lifestyle and a ferment of convictions for which town meeting served as an annual safety release valve. No matter what articles were on the warning, from the new road grader to the wheelchair ramp at the community center, he invariably found a link to larger principles that compelled him to speak, usually at length.

For him, science was the only truth and any idea of spirituality was self-delusion. His fervor swept aside any suggestion that a human mind could encompass Darwin and a divinity both. He was the one person in the room who had neither visualized a stag nor squirmed with discomfort at the idea that he should. He had sat with his eyes wide open, making a silent public declaration that Coral was speaking gibberish and the only energy in existence was the energy described by the laws of physics.

"Do we want to live in a theocracy?" he demanded. "If we let the government start writing religion into our laws, where will it end? Will we have a law banning antibiotics because the Bible makes no reference to bacteria? Will we throw away our medicines and go back to prostrating ourselves in front of altars to beg God to save us from the plague?"

As his speech came to its climax, he punctuated it with a scornful sweep of the arm, encompassing any object with religious significance. The supply of targets was meager—the parish hall did not even have a crucifix—but he made do with what was there—a couple of paintings and a small, conscientiously ecumenical display of cultural artifacts from around the world.

Whether intentionally or not, the arc of his gesture ended with him pointing in the direction of Reverend Eames as he uttered his most biting remark about the stupidity of preachers. Buell did not value tact and he would never temper his words to avoid insulting someone, not even an ally. He thought people should know better than to take things personally when the future of civilization was at stake.

In fact Eames was too mild tempered to take offense, at least not visibly. When Buell sat down, Coral turned to him, to give him the chance to respond. Eames just shook his head and murmured, tangentially, that he very much agreed with Buell about the separation of church and state.

Others were less inclined to be forgiving. When it became clear that Eames did not mean to defend himself, Dulcie Sullivan stood up and said fiercely, "Tim may be too nice to get mad, but I'm not and I want an apology. You may have your opinions, Lawrence, but you're way out of line when you insult someone who does as much for this town as Timothy Eames."

Lawrence shot back that he was speaking generally, not personally, and the world would never make serious progress if everybody had to worry about who might get offended.

Before long the crowd was embroiled in debate about whether one had to consider private feelings when one was pursuing a large public good and nearly half an hour went by without any mention of Dryden. The bulk of the opinions came from the stag visualizers, who split along a fault line between devotion to political activism and devotion to self-realization. The long-time residents mostly stayed silent. Raised in the belief that it was rude to interrupt, they sat and waited, while the other group, raised in the belief that civil discourse depended on letting everyone's views be given ample hearing, talked on and on.

Finally Otis, who was unused to meetings and lacked stamina, decided he'd had enough. Without having said a word, he heaved himself to his feet and headed for the door. His action prompted panic. The stag visualizers turned as one, urging him to stay, apologizing for getting off topic. Every warm body counted, and his counted extra, because he was a native of the state and also a close friend of the corpse, whose existence they suddenly remembered.

"Please stay, Otis," Dulcie said. "We need to hear what you think."

"I don't think nothing about that stuff you've been talking about," he said grumpily. "I thought we were gonna do something about Dryden."

"We are," she said. "That's why I called you. To help do something."

So Dulcie had talked him into coming. Now it made sense. Dulcie was a cheerful, capable woman who would bust a gut finding common ground where you'd swear there wasn't any. Like a lot of the town, she wasn't a native. She'd come to Gilham from Minnesota more than twenty years ago as part of the wave of barefoot, tie-dyed college graduates eager to live on the land, but unlike many of her hopeful cohorts, she had a natural affinity for rural culture. From the beginning, she had been lending her efforts to the kitchen cleanup after community chicken pie suppers and the sorting and pricing of rummage sale contributions, earning her place in town. If she hadn't made local people forget she wasn't one of them, she'd certainly made them not care.

Otis had paused and was standing near the door. He looked a lot like he'd rather be at home in front of the television but wasn't sure he wanted to march out of the meeting, now that he couldn't slip away quietly.

Dulcie made one last push. "We really need you," she said. "You're vital to the proc—"

She stopped herself just in time. The word "process" would have tipped the balance to the side of his easy chair and the TV.

"...job we're doing," she amended.

She succeeded in keeping him hanging and Reverend Eames added the clincher. "We thought you and Noah would know what Fay Kirkwood would have wanted."

"She'da wanted Dryden out of jail, that's for goddamned sure," Otis said. "I can't see why you'd need me to tell you that."

Despite his disgust, Otis returned to his chair. Probably he'd come to his own conclusion about why he was needed.

The meeting finally did get down to business but even on the main topic, agreement was scarce. Some people wanted a noisy demonstration to attract the national media. Others wanted the opposite, to keep Gilham out of the news, to work through the local system, maybe raise money for a good lawyer. At the mention of money, there were murmurs about concerts and walk-a-thons, and then the discussion drifted elsewhere. One lively imagination suggested that Dryden's customers could take their snowblowers and march on the state capitol, which prompted a lot of uneasy throat-clearing until someone pointed out that the legislature was not in session.

After a while, Otis started shifting around in his chair again and Coral interrupted the discussion to ask him if he wanted to speak.

"I dunno if I do," he said. "But I don't see why we're running on about how to get folks' attention when we got this reporter fella sitting here. We oughta just decide on something and he can put it in the paper."

There was a pause, as people considered which of the various "somethings" they would choose to put in the paper. The discussion resumed and although the result was no one's first choice, the group came to a decision to organize three committees, each charged with "exploring possibilities" in a particular area. A fourth area, the internet, was assigned to Lawrence as a committee of one. With these agreements reached, the mood began to trend towards adjournment.

Then Dulcie popped out of her chair and said, "But aren't we going to *do* something?" Dulcie, the washer of dishes and sorter of rummage, the person everyone was glad to see when there was actual work to be done.

Fatigue had diminished people's eagerness to talk, so when Dulcie suggested a small protest at the town hall, people asked what she meant by "small" rather than leaping to object. A discussion clarified her meaning: small enough to stay below the radar of the national media but persistent enough to get the attention of the community. In other words, one person with a placard whenever the town hall was open for business.

She sealed the deal in her usual manner. "I can be there tomorrow afternoon, if someone else can take the morning," she said. Hands went up to volunteer and the group set about designing a placard.

Lawrence, meanwhile, had been scribbling on sheets of paper and he now rose to his feet to propose a resolution objecting to Dryden's arrest. He proceeded to read his document, which vehemently condemned the arrest as an example of misplaced zeal on the part of the police, an infringement of civil liberties, a waste of law enforcement resources, and a dangerous erosion of constitutional protections.

The meeting had taken on a mood of "can-do" and if anyone but

Lawrence had proposed the resolution, it would have been approved by acclaim. As it was, several people suggested changes and the meeting embroiled itself in a discussion of wording. After considerable debate, the group reached a compromise on all but two phrases, a negative reference to the police and a use of the word "absolute." Neither side would yield and the debate went in circles, until Coral had what she thought was an inspiration. She called for a pause and turned to Terp.

"If we get every word just right, can you print it verbatim? Or are we wasting our time on these last details?"

Terp didn't think hard about his answer. He wanted to go to bed. He'd already written his story and he just needed the actual vote to confirm what he'd written. If a dose of reality would prod the group along, he was willing to give it.

"It's too long to print all of it," he said. "If it were a third this length, I could make a case to print it, but as it is, I'll have to excerpt. So no, those details don't matter."

As soon as he'd spoken, he regretted his choice of words. Hearing was selective and this group was bound to hear the wrong thing.

"A third this length?" Lawrence said. "And then it could be printed verbatim?"

Terp recognized the crevasse and tried to backpedal. "I can't guarantee anything. I'm not the editor..."

It was too late. Everyone still awake enough to argue had fixed on the phrase "a third this length" and their zeal was united in pursuit of a single aim, to cut the resolution down to a size where every one of its perfectly chosen words could be immortalized in print. Unfortunately, they were as divided about means as they were united about ends.

As the talk went on and on, Terp thought about Solomon and the two mothers, wishing he could threaten to chop every sentence in half, brutally, mid-syllable, until someone volunteered to subordinate pride of authorship to the common purpose. The stupidest part was that it hardly mattered which phrases they kept. Nothing composed by a committee would be memorable anyway. All they needed was an intelligible statement that they objected to Dryden's arrest.

He'd have liked to tell them so, except that he was still clinging to the few remnants of journalistic principle that hadn't been dumped overboard when he fell for Dryden. In this case, the principle that reporters are supposed to write down what happens and should not try to reshape events. He was tempted, however, and finally he did permit himself one action aimed at influence. He quietly closed his notebook, got up from his chair and headed for the door.

The meeting came to halt even faster than it had for Otis.

"You're leaving?" Coral cried.

He tapped his watch regretfully. "Deadline."

In fact, he still had an hour to spare before he would be up against the deadline, but who at this meeting would question that he needed every minute of that hour to perfect his prose?

"Can you give us a few more minutes?" Coral pleaded. "I'm sure we can get to a vote."

Terp made himself into a picture of conflict, looking from his watch to the moderator to the doorway, before finally saying yes and waiting near the door.

The effect was better than he hoped, worthy of Solomon even. People were tripping over one another in their eagerness to let go of their pet principle, their brilliant phrase, whatever it took to come to agreement so that the resolution could make it into the morning paper. In something less than ten minutes, the paragraph was cleavered down to the requisite size and submitted to a vote, which was unanimous.

Terp kept his opinion to himself, that they'd have saved time and had a better result if they'd let him do the pruning. As it was, they had jettisoned everything with a hint of pungency or point and kept only the most innocuous generalities.

Chapter 31

"Freedom of religion! What a crock! Fay was about as religious as one of her hogs."

Anita took a swallow of coffee and glared at the *Leonardston Herald*, which was spread on the table beside her breakfast.

"But why would a reporter care about truth! He'd rather have a controversy."

"He wasn't the one who organized—" Charlie began.

"He'd just as well have been. Those people could have talked all night and it wouldn't have mattered a cent, if he hadn't splattered it all over the newspapers."

She shoved the paper across to her husband. The story started on a small bottom corner of the front page, headlined "Gilham Group Protests Arrest." To my ear, Terp's prose sounded scrupulously bland. "Twenty-six members of the Gilham community met last night at the First Parish Church to discuss their concerns about the arrest of Dryden Kirkwood…" Just the facts, ma'am, in a tone of measured calm that probably would leave both sides feeling shortchanged.

As promised, Terp had included the truncated resolution and he also mentioned the protest at the town hall, but the more colorful rhetoric had not made it into print. Lawrence Buell, in particular, was likely to be disgruntled, because the fullest quotes came from the Reverend Eames, whose rambling argument that a secular government was the key to religious freedom had, with the help of a few ellipses, become a marvel of concise eloquence.

In fact the story was an accurate representation of the meeting. Many opinions had been aired in an atmosphere of earnest open-mindedness, but very little had been agreed upon and even less had actually been done. Despite the vehemence of Anita's reaction, Charlie quickly realized that there was no impassioned brigade of citizens ready to storm the jail.

The meeting notwithstanding, Dryden's freedom presently depended on cash rather than vigils and placards. Either her bail was posted or it wasn't, and at first it wasn't, because Anita was dead set against paying it.

"Maybe a few days in jail will bring her to her senses," she said. "I can't see that anything else will."

Although she didn't testify at the bail hearing, Anita managed to convey to the relevant authorities her opinion that her adopted daughter was unpredictable and might be a flight risk. The resulting bail was much higher than might have been expected for dumping a dead body, high enough to stop an average person, such as Otis or Noah, from writing a check on the spot.

Rather than defy Anita openly, Charlie decided he would wait and come back later, by himself. Perhaps if Dryden had asked for his help, he'd have acted right then, but Dryden had stated, in her stiff-necked way, that she was content to stay in jail. So he gave her a hug and followed his wife out of the building.

Later that afternoon, when Terp came to visit, he said he couldn't see what good could come of her gesture.

Dryden shrugged. "I'm not a political martyr, suffering for the first amendment," she said. "I'm doing what Fay wanted, that's all."

"How does it help anyone for you not to be out on bail?"

A reasonable question, I thought.

"She's sure I'll change my mind. I'm showing her she's wrong."

The "she" who need not be named. Anita.

"You'll lose your chops in here," he pointed out.

She frowned but didn't waver.

"They'll come back when I start playing again. They get flabby in haying season, too."

He'd run out of arguments. The saxophone was his last shot and it had fallen short. If there was a way to persuade her, he couldn't see it because he'd never be where she was, sticking to a decision through a barrage of contradiction. He couldn't imagine feeling so sure he was right.

Nor could I, I thought. When I said I wanted to be eaten by varmints, I wasn't stating a fixed conviction. I was venting spleen at the destructive egoism of the human race. How typical of our self-absorption, to drench our carcasses in preservative chemicals and encase them in silk and rare tropical wood, as if heaven was one more gated community to which only well-dressed people were granted admission.

I still didn't know squat about god. Whatever any human said about a divinity was just party conversation, a roomful of dentists discussing the best way to throw a slider or build a submarine. It was mischance that Dryden had latched onto my idly chosen emblem of irritation and was treating it as a sacred wish. It made me think that if there was a god and he ever did seek to reveal himself to people, he'd better take care not to burp at the wrong moment, lest he find a million people building large round echo chambers in which to gather and chant "U-u-u-urp."

Having failed to persuade Dryden to leave, Terp settled himself to stay for as long as the authorities would allow. In tacit agreement that there was no point in talking about her situation, they talked about other things, some of consequence, mostly not. As before, they maintained an appearance of detachment, the reporter and his interview subject. For Terp, the space between them felt like a gesture in itself, a constant reminder of his longing to reach across it.

They were talking about a safely unimportant topic, movies, when an officer came to tell Dryden that her bail had been posted and she was free to go.

"Is it obligatory that I leave?" she asked.

The officer looked nonplused. Probably he'd never been asked that question and he didn't have a ready answer. He consulted the other guard, who shrugged and said something about needing to follow procedures. The first officer said he'd better check with a superior.

At that point Dryden said to forget it, she was joking. She wanted whatever would make the least fuss and the least fuss was to do the expected thing.

They found Charlie waiting in the reception area. He gave Dryden a hug, with the nervous, sidling affection of a dog who knows there's a mess in another part of the house.

"Does Anita know about this?" Dryden asked.

He hunched and shook his head. "She was talking on the phone when I left."

There was a long moment of foot-shuffling reluctance. As long as they were standing still, the clock had not yet started and the reaction Charlie was dreading lay in the indefinite future. Once they headed for the car, everything else would follow at predictable time intervals.

Recognizing Charlie's frame of mind, Terp ventured to offer him a back door.

"If Dryden can spare the time, I'd be glad to talk with her a little more, maybe get a cup of coffee," he said, "I can easily give her a lift, so you could go straight home."

"You mean, I could..."

The calculations were visible in Charlie's face. He could duck the immediate confrontation with his wife; he might even slide past the whole question of Dryden's bail. If Anita asked Dryden about it later, she wouldn't lie, but she might well answer with sarcasm of some kind, that it must have been the tooth fairy. Charlie just needed a plausible reason for his trip, some groceries maybe or a copy of today's *Wall Street Journal*.

He looked at Dryden doubtfully. "Would you want to do that?"

She shrugged. "I'm not in any rush. Maybe I'll hit him up for a hamburger, too."

"You're sure...? You don't have to..."

"I'm sure."

Charlie gave her another hug and scuttled out the door.

Chapter 32

In the morning, I was greeted by the smell of my woodstove. The weather had turned cold overnight and Charlie was arranging bits of kindling on the embers, nursing the fire back to life. The new wood had not yet caught completely and struggling wisps of smoke swirled into the room. He opened the drafts wide and tongues of flame appeared. He added a small log, balanced on the kindling. He was completely absorbed in the task, happy in the same way I would have been. We'd known woodstoves since childhood, from annual trips to our grandparents' vacation cabin in what then seemed like a remote mountain wilderness.

He knew as well as I did that the fire did not need his tending. The coals held enough heat that he could have dumped logs into the firebox, opened the drafts and left the fire to revive itself. He fussed over it for pleasure, not utility.

He had picked up another log and was studying how to place it when Anita's voice broke in on his absorption.

"What the bloody hell?" she said. She was standing beside the window, staring out at the driveway.

Charlie's heart lurched and the log slipped out of his hand and dropped onto the fire. The scaffold of burning kindling collapsed in a shower of sparks and as the fire retreated, smoke poured from the half-burning logs. He hastily shut the stove door and scooted across the room to the window.

Dryden was ambling toward the house, looking not at all like someone who had just been in jail. Behind her, Terp's car was heading out the driveway.

Charlie's first reaction, not a noble one, was relief. Anita would be so furious about Terp, she might forget to ask who had posted bail. Only secondarily did he take in the rest of the story, that the dinner interview with a reporter had lasted until morning.

Charlie could think fast, when thought might avoid conflict, and he instantly recognized that his interests and Dryden's coincided. If they both pretended she'd been released from jail this morning, they could save themselves a lot of trouble.

Nor would they have to lie. They could simply neglect to mention a few facts.

When Dryden came in the door, Anita wasted no energy on motherly embraces.

"This is too much!" she said. "Do you have any regard for the good of your family?"

I'd have been tempted to reply, "Define family." Dryden just smiled and said, "I'm sorry. Is there something you couldn't find in the cupboards while I was gone?"

"You know perfectly well what I mean," Anita said. "Cozying up to the media like this."

"I like him. He plays the upright bass. We've been jamming a little."

"The bass! Is that supposed to be a joke?"

Anita stared at Dryden, looking for a hold. Dryden looked straight back, still with that unworried smile.

Suddenly Anita's expression changed. In a tone of certainty, she said, "You've slept with him, haven't you?"

Dryden shrugged. "That, too. But so what?"

"So what!" Anita exploded. "It's no wonder this blasted story won't die. Charlie, did you know about this?"

So much for the mutual defense pact, he thought. The tacit agreement that a few key facts could go unmentioned. He should have known it would be useless in the face of Anita's infrared intuition. When in his life had he ever succeeded in fooling her?

The only strategy that occurred to him now was irrelevance. If they stayed on the subject of sleeping arrangements, Anita would remember his trip to get a newspaper.

"About the bass?" he said. "No, I didn't know but I can't see the harm in jamming..."

He chattered on about jazz until Anita's glare brought him to a halt. There was a moment's silence, a moment in which he could already feel Anita's thought processes headed in the direction of when and how Dryden had been released from jail.

Then Dryden spoke up in an offhand way, pursuing the topic of music.

"I agree with Dad. The world would be a better place if more people played a musical instrument. Lower blood pressure. Less hostility. It occupies the time when you might be vandalizing property."

She'd been gazing out the window, dreamily. Now she turned to look at Anita.

"I think the saxophone is one of the best things that ever happened to me."

Charlie winced. Why did Dryden always say the thing most likely to provoke Anita? Even now, after twenty years, his wife was still furious about the saxophone.

He stayed silent, but inwardly, he was wishing some power existed that would stop them goading each other.

"You are pitiful, you know that?" Anita said.

For a moment, he thought she was speaking to him. It seemed so fitting. Then he saw that she was facing Dryden.

"You'll sell our family's privacy to get a little attention. Do you think that guy gives a damn about you? What a joke. He's laughing all the way back to his keyboard. He got a screw and a story both and you're fatuous enough to think it's love. God. It's beyond pitiful."

Her certainty was relentless and it all sounded so plausible: that Terp was like every other reporter, a smooth talker who would exploit his own mother to get a story. Dryden was good material and the sex was gravy, something to be grabbed because it was there.

Charlie ventured a protest. "I don't think that's quite—" he began, but Anita swept onward, answering him without bothering to look in his direction.

"Of course it's about the story. Somebody like that can lie as soon as breathe and Dryden is so naïve, she's a sitting duck."

Dryden hadn't moved. She was still looking at Anita, her body upright and strong, but her stillness had changed. The calm and happiness were gone. Her muscles were braced, trying to resist a force that could not be met with muscles.

I had no window into Dryden's mind, but I didn't need one. I could guess at the army of thoughts she was fighting not to think: that her mother despised her; that her father's love was so feeble it was meaningless; that she'd been a mere convenience to Jonathan.

To whom could she look for the certainty that she was loved? Noah's fondness she would credit to his attachment to me. As for Otis, the only value he acknowledged publicly was her usefulness. His softer feelings he kept as secret as he would the most shocking of family scandals and she had not witnessed his presence at the protest meeting.

Then there was me. I had loved her, beyond anything in my life, but had I ever said so? How easily she might think she'd been a convenience to me, too, a useful hand with a wrench. And if she did know how I felt, I was dead and my affection was no use to anyone.

She never found any words to answer. She stood for a long time in rigid silence, then strode out of the room and headed upstairs, taking the steps in leaps. A moment later she was back, carrying all three of her saxophone cases. Still without saying a word, she went out the door. Scollay scooted out at her heels and she didn't stop him, or even seem to notice. Her face looked like a death mask.

Charlie sidled over to the window, expecting to see her take the truck and leave. Instead she went into the workshop, a choice that puzzled Charlie but worried me. The shop had a lot of tools of destruction.

He wanted to go after her, to talk, but Anita might insist on coming and he couldn't imagine stopping her. Better to wait, he thought, and retrieved his book.

Under other circumstances, I'd have been glad to lose myself in the lives of John and Abigail Adams, but now I wanted Charlie's ears and I cursed the excellence of the biographer's prose. I strained to hear the periphery, hoping to catch the sound of a saxophone. I wanted to know that Dryden was doing her usual thing and venting her mood through her horns. Instead I heard only Anita's voice, talking on the phone with her office.

Eventually, Anita needed papers from her luggage. When she put down the phone and disappeared up the stairs, Charlie closed his book and put on his coat.

Outdoors, it was very quiet, quiet enough that I could hear the scrape of his shoes on gravel. Not a good sign, the silence. When Dryden wanted to blow off a bad mood, she was likely to play for hours. Destruction, on the other hand, took no time at all. At the workshop door, Charlie stood still and listened, trying to hear what might be happening inside. There was nothing to hear, except his own breathing. Cautiously, he opened the door.

The first thing he saw was wreckage. Across the room, under a blazing fluorescent light, the workbench held scattered piles of metal, the fragments of a dismantled horn. Dryden was standing with her back to him, staring at the mess.

Her hand moved toward one of the piles and Charlie leapt forward, crying, "No, wait!"

At the sound of his voice, Dryden jumped and a tiny screw slipped out of her hand and disappeared into a shadowy corner under the bench. She cursed and dropped to her knees to search for the screw. Charlie halted in confusion. Belatedly, he noticed the neatness of the piles and saw the delicate tools, brushes, and polishing cloths laid out nearby. This was not destruction at all. This was the balm of work. She was seeking solace the same way her Aunt Fay would have done, with a screwdriver, a bottle of lubricating oil, and a task that demanded all of her attention. Dismantling, oiling, and adjusting all the finicky little mechanisms of her horn.

Now that the scene was in front of me, it all made perfect sense. I'd seen Dryden do this job many times. Usually she took the instrument apart on the dining room table, away from the grease and grit of the lawnmowers, but today her mother was in the house and the dirt of the workshop was the preferable alternative. The dirt she could manage with a clean sheet of plastic.

Dryden fetched a flashlight and found the screw she'd dropped. She picked up a key mechanism and began to thread the screw, still without having said a word to her father.

Charlie began to back away. "Sorry. Didn't mean to interrupt. I thought you might want..."

If he was hoping Dryden would ask him to stay, she didn't oblige. She shrugged and said, "It doesn't matter," and continued with her task. He felt briefly hurt, but he also felt relief. He did not have to attempt a delicate conversation. He could leave her to work through her feelings in her own way, with her hands.

I, on the other hand, did not need a stomach to feel sick. This was not the moment when she should have been taking apart her saxophone. For as long as I'd known her, she had chosen the dullest of days for working on her horns. It was I, not she, who had used intricate mechanical tasks as a refuge when humankind threatened to make me feel more than I wanted to.

In the past, if Dryden was in a passion, she didn't tinker with her horns. She played them.

Don't go down this road, I shouted. Don't retreat. Don't keep everything important at a safe distance. Whatever you do, don't be like me.

But how was I to stop her? Monkey see, monkey do. I was her role model.

When Charlie emerged from the workshop, he met Anita headed for their rental car.

"If you're coming with me, let's go," she said.

Only when they were on the road did he ask where they were going.

"The police, obviously. If that man has talked her into bed with him, then for sure he's wormed it out of her, about the body."

"But you've already told the police."

"Yes, and I'll bet they haven't even talked to the man. They're so worried he'll wave the constitution at them."

"Suppose they ask and he won't tell them," he said. "Then what?"

"Then he should be in jail for contempt."

When they reached the police station, they saw a protester at the far side of the parking lot, walking slow figure eights in front of the town hall. His breath made clouds in the cold air. He held a large placard, its surface so packed with important messages that none of the text was legible from a distance. The protestor, however, was recognizable. It was Otis.

Anita scowled at the sight of him. "I thought these people were famous for minding their own business," she said.

They are, I said. For Otis, this was equivalent to dancing a tango in public. I'd have kissed him if I could.

As Anita headed for the police station, Charlie lagged behind, drifting closer to the sign to read the messages and say hello. Otis seemed unsure whether to smile or growl at Charlie, but the first thing that came out was embarrassment at being so conspicuous.

"I didn't write this stuff," he said and wagged the sign. "I'd have stuck to 'Don't be so damn foolish.' Not that it'd do any good."

"Probably not," Charlie agreed.

They paused a moment, contemplating the general hopelessness of the world, and then Charlie said, "She's out on bail, you know."

"She shouldn't have been in to start with." The bite in Otis's tone conveyed the rest of his thought: "If you had any balls." He asked who bailed her out.

Charlie hesitated. Would Otis talk to Anita? He made a non-committal gesture, hoping that would suffice, but Otis kept waiting, as if it was a test. Could Charlie give a simple answer to a simple question? Could he ever lean into the yoke and pull straight ahead?

"It was me," Charlie said finally.

"Took you long enough."

Charlie had no answer, because he agreed.

They were silent again. Without either of them saying anything, they turned a little and gazed across the parking lot at the door where Anita had disappeared. Now that Otis had said his piece, he seemed inclined to welcome Charlie back into the brotherhood of men for whom marriage is an uncharted bog.

After a while, Otis said, "So Dryden'll be doing her own chores again, I guess."

The remark reminded Charlie that he should thank Otis for his help at the farm. From there the conversation ambled onward to more comfortable topics, such as whether pigs were more or less likely than chickens to eat something disgusting from the back of the refrigerator. Neither of them wanted to talk about family, marriage, or any of the issues on Otis's sign.

They were still chatting when another car pulled up. The driver was Noah and he seemed strangely reluctant to get out of the car. He was looking at Otis and Charlie, who were unavoidably in his path to the town hall.

When he finally did open the car door, the reason for his hesitation became apparent. He was carrying Eloise's baking pan, covered in foil to protect its contents. Rather than returning it clean and empty, he had baked something as a return gift, and now he was going through gyrations, trying to make a ten-by-fourteen-inch baking pan less noticeable.

The effort to be casual was as good as an announcement. He must feel more than a polite interest in Eloise or he would not have worried what other people would think. Especially not Otis and Charlie, who were unlikely to look beyond the surface meaning of a pan of brownies.

Almost as soon as hellos had been said, Otis gestured toward the pan and said, "Whatcha got in there?"

"It's chocolate chip brownies. For the people in the office."

"You forget to pay your taxes or something?" Otis joked.

"No. It's just... you know..." Noah ended with a shrug of confusion.

"Christmas season," Charlie offered.

"That's it," Noah said quickly.

Such an obvious explanation. It was the time of year when anyone could give anyone a gift of baked goods and not cause comment. Noah must be far gone not to have thought of it.

"Cold's making me hungry," Otis said. "Maybe I'll come inside with you, see if they'll share their brownies with the taxpayers."

He propped his sign against a railing and made an invitational arm sweep, as if by rights everyone in town deserved a share of the brownies. Noah looked dismayed, but he had no choice except to smile and let himself be caught up in the fellowship of the season.

As he and Otis headed inside, Charlie hesitated. Brownies in the town hall looked a lot cozier than a visit to the police, but he knew Anita would be irritated by his absence, whether she needed him or not. He turned and started a slow trudge toward the police station.

He was halfway across the parking lot when I was abruptly bounced elsewhere. In the space of a second, Charlie's mood of dragging reluctance gave way to a butterfly whirl of amazement, joy, and inopportune sexual arousal, all doing their best to keep up a front of ordinary politeness.

From across the width of Eloise's desk, I saw Noah holding out the pan of brownies. While he wasn't brimming with laughter, he wasn't prostrate with grief either. His expression had a particular intentness that I recognized. It was the same look I'd seen in the early days of our love affair, when our eyes communicated meanings we did not want our neighbors to notice. Seeing that look, I had no doubt. If not for the lingering impediment of a husband, Eloise would soon be in his bed.

Reaching to take the pan, she placed her hands in a way that allowed their skin to touch and he did not immediately let go. His hands stayed on the pan as if to steady it and from that small point of contact, waves went rippling up her arm and into her body. She kept talking all the while, maintaining a stream of banalities, but the waves kept piling up and the more she worried they might be noticeable, the more her tension heightened them and sent new ones pouring in from different tributaries. Finally, she pulled the pan out of his hands and set it down and then stood there, stupidly, trying not to look at him too directly.

She could feel the stares, from Glynnis, the town treasurer, and from Belinda Boyle, who had been using the public copy machine. She couldn't see a safe way to deflect their curiosity. Her face felt hot and her mind had gone blank. Noah wasn't helping either. He just smiled, nervously, and shuffled his feet, offering no pretext for hanging about.

Having the advantage of detachment, I suspected Eloise was giving her neighbors too much credit for insight. Odds were, they thought Noah was lonely and Eloise was politely trying to cheer him up. But for Eloise, reality had shrunk to the width of the desktop that separated her from Noah.

She was saved by Otis, who throughout their subliminally lustful interchange had been staring with equally lustful intentness at the baking pan. Seizing the gap of silence, he said, "You gonna cut into those brownies while they're fresh?"

At the sound of his voice, the waves in her body began to recede and she saw that Glynnis and Belinda were also casting hopeful glances at the pan.

"Of course. Yes. Definitely," she said. "I'll get a knife."

I, meanwhile, was contemplating how magnificently selfless a person could become when the lack of a body made it impossible to be anything else. Without a body, there was no territory to defend and nothing to fight with either. Combat became a comic absurdity, as did jealousy, ownership, prowess, or any other notion of power. It was humbling, but also entertaining, to see how much of human behavior became merely ridiculous in the absence of flesh.

Why shouldn't I wish Eloise godspeed in her pursuit? I had nothing to gain by wishing her a trip to the antipodes. There was nothing Noah could do for me now, except be happy.

Perhaps in time I would be graced with oblivion. Perhaps I was a traveler with an error in my papers, halted in transit. Perhaps if my body got buried, I would be sent on my way, my eyes finally closed forever. But how could I know?

This might be what eternity looked like.

Chapter 33

"What the—! He knows where the body is and he's just sitting on it?"

Randall bounced out of his chair and paced around his office, probably as an alternative to unleashing a stream of expletives. The public was present, in the form of Anita and Charlie, and decorum had to be maintained.

Evidently Anita's visit to the police department had not been fruitful. Now, having decided to try the newspaper, she had finally found the one person whose outrage might be equal to hers, though for different reasons. Randall had the look of a man who discovers his dog won't hunt. Seething but stymied. If the dog won't, he won't, and no force can make him.

Which didn't mean the dog wouldn't hear about it, scathingly, at the first opportunity.

In the meantime, Randall had Anita and Charlie to deal with. He stopped pacing and sat down, assuming an air of cool skepticism. "Are you absolutely sure about this?" he asked.

Anita matched his coolness. "I didn't see with my own eyes, but she did say she's sleeping with him and he did take that trip up north."

Charlie was slumped in his chair. There's nothing Anita won't do, he thought, and he couldn't stop her.

"Do you have any other information that should be part of our coverage?" Randall asked.

"Only what I've said all along. That our family is one hundred percent Christian and all this vaporing about tolerance is irrelevant. The plain fact is, my adopted daughter is lying."

"May we quote you?" Randall asked.

"As long as you don't misquote, you may. And kindly make it clear that that girl does not have a drop of Kirkwood blood in her veins."

Charlie's slump turned to squirming discomfort.

"Is that really necessary?" he put in.

"Unfortunately, for Spenser's sake, I think it is. We can't have people thinking he might be like her."

"But he is like—"

She cut him off sharply. "Not in this he's not. People do understand about adoption, that parents can only do so much and some patterns are innate. Blood will out."

"It certainly will," Charlie muttered.

Much as he'd have liked to stand his ground and claim his daughter without qualification, he couldn't do it. He told himself it would be unseemly to start a family fight in Randall's office, but the truth was, he didn't want an audience. Not because he and Anita would yell and throw things. Because they wouldn't. Because he would be temperate and open-minded and the confrontation would end as it always did, with him retreating and placating.

An argument would be a pointless display in any case. Randall was going to print whatever he felt like printing, within the limits of the law. Other than a few non-committal remarks about "seeing what he could do," he had made no promise to look out for the interests of the Kirkwood family, however those were defined.

In the car, Anita was exultant. "God, what a relief to see somebody in this frozen mudhole get angry. Maybe she'll finally be forced to turn over the body."

Without an audience, Charlie felt a little bolder.

"What would you suggest they do to force her? Start pulling out fingernails?" he said.

"It's tempting."

"I don't understand you! Why can't you think about her for a change? She's family."

"Family!" Anita spat. "She doesn't know the meaning of the word—"

If their argument broke any new ground, I missed it. In the middle of a sentence, I was grabbed by a stronger feeling. Car, road, and Anita vanished and I saw typewriting on a computer screen, a story about Dryden's release from jail.

The story, too, had stopped in the middle of a sentence. The cursor hung flashing at the end of the word 'but,' and I heard Randall's furious voice on the phone.

"For Christ's sake Terp, what's going on here? You got your brain caught in your fly? I can't believe you'd sit on a story like this just to get laid. But I guess in a way, it's good news. I was starting to think you can't write and I can't do shit to fix a bad writer, but if you're just a horny bastard with no ethics, maybe I can kick your butt. I'd have thought you knew better than to stay on a story when you're screwing the subject. But what really kills me is that I've had a week's worth of boring, watered-down crap to print when the whole time you've got hold of a piece of information most guys would trample little old ladies to get their hands on."

Terp was tempted to point out that he wouldn't have that precious piece of information if he hadn't been screwing his subject, but he took a deep breath and stopped himself. He didn't want to get sucked into an argument in those terms. In any case, Randall would recognize the point for himself, once he calmed down, and when he did recognize it, he'd be hard put to find any moral high ground in the situation, not the way he was framing it. Which was worse, to use sex as leverage to get information, or to use information as leverage to get sex?

The one possibility that had not occurred to Randall was the truth. That Terp was in love and didn't care what would make the best story. Nor did Terp mean to tell him. The feeling was still too new and strange and he really didn't want to talk to Randall about it.

Probably Randall had taken his measure, accurately, when he hired him. That he was changeable and out for fun, a clever chameleon who could argue any point of view without ever committing himself to an actual belief. A man who really could approach the impossible ideal of journalistic objectivity, because he had no convictions strong enough to make him try to reshape the news into polemic. Starting with that assessment of his character, Randall's conclusion was logical: if Terp was passing up the chance at a killer scoop, he must be hard up for the sex.

So let him think so, Terp thought.

"This crap may be boring but it's the truth," he said. "There isn't any other story here."

"I've just had Anita Kirkwood in my office, insisting that you are withholding material evidence in a homicide case. Why would she say this stuff if there's nothing there?"

"Because she's in a fight with her daughter, OK? This whole thing is about personal feelings, and just because one person wants to use the police and the media to help her win a family argument, that doesn't make it a matter of public concern."

"I don't buy that, Terp. Nobody could have it in for her kid that much. I mean, maybe in the middle of a yelling match, sure, but this lady was cool as a cucumber. And the husband didn't contradict her. You're saying they both have it in for the girl?"

"Look, Randall, the woman's a frigging Humvee. It doesn't mean anything that her husband didn't say peep. I bet he didn't say anything to back her up, either."

That gave Randall pause, briefly. "No, that's true."

"Exactly."

"But he did come with her," Randall said. "And it wasn't like he talked about anything else, either. I'd say he's just a doormat by nature."

"There's no knowing what his nature is. Anita Kirkwood could turn a Doberman into a doormat."

"It just doesn't add up, Terp. I mean, suppose you're right, that the mom is just pissed off and there wasn't any murder. Then why the hell can't you tell the police where the body is and get this thing straightened out? It must be some screw you're getting that you won't let go of your hold on it."

"Think what you want. The point is, if a source tells me something off the record, I keep it off the record."

Terp crossed his fingers as he spoke. His understanding with Dryden had been personal, not professional. He'd never promised, explicitly, as a journalist, to keep anything off the record. He'd only promised, without words, as her lover, that he would keep her secret come hell or high water. Technically, his silence had no more legal or institutional protection than any random joe hearing drunken confidences from a buddy over the barbecue grill.

"I don't know that we can back you up on this, Terp. If it's a homicide investigation. I can't see what larger interest you're defending by helping her hide a dead body."

"Larger interest? Isn't it in the constitution, that we can think whatever nonsense we want to about death and the hereafter and the government can't tell us we're wrong?"

"Somebody might hear the voice of God telling them to sacrifice their infant son, but it's still murder if they do it."

"Sure and what she's done is a crime, too. She didn't get the right pieces of paper. If they want to charge her for it, I expect she'd plead guilty. But she's not going to turn over the body. For all I know, she might be stubborn enough to stand trial for murder first, but it will be a travesty if it goes that far."

"Even if you're right, Terp, you know I can't keep you on the story. I'm sorry, but you've completely lost perspective. I've got to get somebody who can see straight."

"I figured that. So what am I on instead?"

"I haven't thought that far. Maybe that public hearing on the new landfill. But first, we'll have to see if the police want to talk to you. You might be tied up."

As if in answer to the thought, Terp heard the beep of a call waiting. He was willing to bet it was the police, because when it came to knowing how the system operates and being a jump ahead of it, Randall was world class.

He and Randall both were right. The caller was Sergeant Mayhew of the state police, who said he understood that Terp had information relating to the whereabouts of Fay Kirkwood.

Instinctively, Terp responded with a joking sidestep, the first that came to mind.

"From what I hear, if you want to know where Fay Kirkwood is now, you should ask a priest, not me," he said.

There was a pause on the other end of the line. With a bit more edge in his voice, Mayhew said, "I think it might be best if we proceeded with a more formal interview. Would it be convenient for you to come to the police department in Leonardston later today?"

"What time?"

"Say six o'clock. No, better make it seven."

"You work long hours."

"Longer than they ought to be, in this particular case. But perhaps you can help us with that, if you're prepared to share the relevant information."

"The information I have to share, I put in the newspaper. It's what I do for a living, share information."

"You do understand, I hope, that you have an obligation to assist in the pursuit of justice and there are legal consequences if you fail to do so. And naturally, you're permitted to have legal counsel present, if you wish."

"Do I need it?"

"That is your decision. We much prefer to have witnesses come forward willingly."

"I'll see you at seven."

Terp hung up and looked at the half-finished story on the screen. From habit, he saved the file, even though it wasn't his story anymore. Now what? He needed something to do, to keep from thinking too much. He wasn't like Dryden. He didn't have the ability to tune out the details of reality, such as concrete block walls and steel bars and the company of inmates who were not well-intentioned liberals in jail by choice, as an act of civil disobedience.

He picked up the phone and called Randall back.

"What time is that landfill hearing?"

"Seven o'clock."

"That figures. I gotta be at the police station at seven. You got some other little thing I can do between now and then? To calm my nerves?"

"There's a lady over in Hewes Corner who slid her car off the road into a pond. You could talk to the guys who pulled her out."

"Thanks, Randall."

"Look, don't be stupid about this Kirkwood thing, OK?"

Chapter 34

The woman's skid into the pond turned out to be less of an emergency than it sounded. The water was only three feet deep and the rear of her SUV was less than five feet from the bank. No lives had been at risk, although the farmer across the road had risked his comfort, wading through floating fragments of ice to help open the door. The most notable piece of the story was that rather than waiting for a wrecker to come, the farmer had waded back into the pond with a chain, secured it to her towing hitch and hauled the SUV out of the pond himself, using his tractor and a come-along anchored to a tree.

Sitting in a warm kitchen with a cup of coffee, the farmer was glad to share every detail, down to the length of the chain, the horsepower of the tractor, the kind of tree, and the betting odds on whether the woman and her husband would rethink their recent decision to move from North Carolina to Hewes Corner. By the time Terp had written his story, it was late enough that he had to hurry to get to the police station.

On the way there, he could no longer avoid his own thoughts. The whole situation seemed surreal. Could they really cite him for contempt or obstruction of justice if he refused to talk about a minor crime? The only evidence of homicide was Anita's assertion that there must have been one. It wasn't evidence at all, but that might not matter. Dealing with someone like Anita, who was relentlessly willing to pressure people to get what she wanted, reasonable people often bent an unreasonably long way to keep the peace. Reasonable people reasoned the way Randall had, that a mother would not accuse her daughter of murder without some basis.

Was it really so vital, to defend the beliefs of a dead person? If he told the police what he knew, Dryden would be off the hook without having gone back on her word. Could that be what she was hoping for? If so, she'd given no hint. But she wasn't really the type to drop hints, either, and that left him with his own intuition, which felt like a doubtful instrument.

The interview room was pale green and glaringly lit by fluorescent bulbs. Mayhew was there, in plain clothes, along with a stenographer, a video camera and a uniformed policeman with a gun, handcuffs, radio, and some other mysterious items that looked electronic. Terp knew the uniformed cop from previous reporting. His name was Burt Elman. He was a muscular six-six, the most physically imposing officer on the Leonardston force, although placid in temperament. Since Terp was hardly a risk for violence, presumably the display of handcuffs and weaponry was meant to remind him where he could end up if he failed to cooperate.

He still didn't know exactly what he was going to say. He would see how things went, like a gunslinger waiting for the opponent to draw his gun first, on the theory that reflexes were faster than conscious decisions. The theory might or might not be true, but it fits Terp's instincts.

Mayhew gestured to him to sit. There were two chairs available, so the first question was which to choose. One chair was closer to the stenographer and the video camera. The safeguards. The other was closer to Mayhew. The interrogator. Was this happenstance or was it an intentional test of his attitude and probable truthfulness? He chose the chair closer to Mayhew, not from boldness, but because even in a situation of personal jeopardy, he was ruled by curiosity and Mayhew was the most interesting object in the room.

We don't need any heroism here, I said to him. We don't need anyone else going to jail over a sack of meat and guts. Just tell the policeman where my body is and we can all go home. Dryden will get over it and she might even be glad. It will get bloody Anita out of the house.

So said my judgment, but my heart still felt a sneaking hope that he would be foolish and gallant and try to play the knight errant for Dryden's sake. When in her life had she ever had a champion?

I heard Mayhew clear his throat. He turned to the stenographer and signaled for recording to begin. He spoke a short introduction, giving the date and the names of the people present. Then he turned back to Terp to begin the interview.

"Could you state your full name, please?" he said.

"Lionel Turnbull Jones," Terp said.

I didn't hear the next question. Before Mayhew could ask it, I was gone.

In front of me was a plate of spaghetti, but Charlie was not eating it. His stomach was churning and the thought of food only made it worse. Across the table from him, Anita was winding spaghetti onto her fork as she talked.

"Now we'll find out how much your precious reporter cares about your cause, when it's his own backside on the line," she said. "I'll bet he tells them what they want to know so fast your head would spin. I'll bet he's already drawn them a map."

Dryden didn't argue. She just kept chewing her food, the dinner she'd cooked for everyone in the house, welcome or unwelcome. It was a custom of rural life, to feed the people who happened to be under one's roof at dinnertime, and I'd held onto it, even though the isolation that gave rise to the custom was a thing of the past.

You don't owe them dinner, I said. The principle doesn't apply to people who use kinship as an excuse to act like vipers. You ought to toss them out on their ear.

Not that she'd ever do it. How many people ever can say to their family, "Buzz off and don't come back until you can treat me at least as well as you would a stranger in an elevator."

Dryden didn't say that or anything else. She chewed methodically and her gaze rested, unfocused, on a spot near the saltshaker. Her silence wasn't an active resistance, not this time. She had withdrawn into a state of indifference so profound, one wondered whether she'd bother to get out of her chair if the house was on fire.

Charlie felt deeply uneasy, but Anita was too caught up in her own irritation to analyze Dryden's behavior. She wanted a reaction and she would keep hammering until she got one.

"You think you can wear everybody down with your stubbornness," she said, "but this time you won't get away with it. Do you think that reporter is going to risk his job and his freedom for this nonsense of yours? Because he lo-o-o-oves you? What a pathetic self-delusion!"

Dryden stopped eating and a flush darkened her face but she still didn't say anything. Her silence only goaded Anita, who went on talking and talking, in an escalating fury. It almost seemed she couldn't stop herself, as if the need to master her daughter had become an obsession and she no longer counted the cost.

"You make a show all right, playing the tough girl... telling us to go to hell... And then some guy gives you a wink and you roll over like a lap dog... it's an embarrassment, the way you let him manipulate you... But I suppose it must not happen very often, that a man shows an interest..."

Her words had no visible effect on Dryden, but Charlie finally let out a wail of protest.

"Anita, stop! Please! What harm has she done, really?"

"What harm! This thing is wrecking Spenser's career! He's got the press after him, the churches after him..."

"But that's not her fault! She didn't do anything..."

"I can't believe you're defending her when she's trying to ruin your son's future! How can you possibly justify what she's doing! It's pure wanton destructiveness. She's a misfit, she's malicious and you're putting her ahead of a son who's everything a parent could ever hope for."

Anita paused for a moment, like an orator who wants a telling point to sink in. The room was dead quiet. No one made any move to eat. Dryden was so still, she looked like a carved object. Charlie's whole being was roiled by outrage but he didn't know what to say that would make any difference.

Their mute immobility was not enough for Anita. She wanted a tangible surrender and she didn't yet have it. In a tone of dismissive scorn, she added one last dig.

"She's not even your own blood, for Christ's sake!"

Dryden made no voluntary movement, but a tremor passed the length of her body and then she began to shiver, uncontrollably. Seeing her distress, as wordless as an infant's, Charlie's rage finally topped its banks.

He could see his opening. Anita had offered it to him, blindly confident that he wouldn't take it, that shame would stop his mouth, but watching Dryden, he no longer cared about his personal shame. His failure as a husband seemed inconsequential compared to his failure as a father. If he could for once open his mouth to make amends, at least it would be one small thing.

He spoke in a desperate rush, as if he feared that this was his one chance. In a moment, the opening would close again and his courage would fail.

"She may not be my blood," he said, "but she damn well is yours. If blood is what counts, then you're the one who should defend her. You're the only blood she's ever had. You're the one who chose her father and gave her birth. You're the one who put her where she is—"

"No, you're the one who put her where she is. You're the one who wouldn't let her go and be with her own people."

"Her own people!" Charlie's voice was a shriek. "You're her people! She's a walking replica of you. Do you think she got that stiff neck from that sweet puppy-dog of a kid you—" He stopped abruptly. A little more calmly, he finished, "From Mariano?"

The image clicked into place. The handsome laughing boy, pausing from mowing the lawn to run around the yard with a soccer ball. The masculine version of Dryden at seventeen, brown-eyed and nimble. Except that he was slight and quick, while Dryden had Anita's broad-shouldered, heavy-boned Saxon frame.

"Of course I didn't let her go," Charlie cried. "She's your daughter. I wanted her. How could I possibly let her go?"

For once in her life, Anita seemed to have no idea what to say. She had always been the axis of certainty, the one who knew what she thought, was sure she was right, and spoke with corresponding self-assurance. She didn't know what to do with ambiguity. Her mind did not have the elasticity that had allowed Charlie to bend himself around her infidelity in order to love her child. She'd spent most of thirty years barricading herself against embarrassment, pouring more concrete into her belief that she'd been right to lie. When the ground shifted, she couldn't shift with it.

Charlie was silent, too, his burst of energy spent. He'd said what he needed to say and now he waited, drained and nervous, to see how Dryden would react. The only sound in the room was the hum of the refrigerator.

For a long time, Dryden just stared at Anita, trying to process the information. Her skin was the same bloodless dun color it had been when she found my body, but from her expression, I couldn't tell if she felt anything except shock.

Finally, she gave her head a shake and murmured, "You're my mother...?"

Speaking the words seemed to make it real to her and her reaction was straightforward and succinct. She leapt from her chair and bolted toward the bathroom. Her gut was faster than her brain, however, and halfway to the door, she doubled over and began to vomit, explosively, onto the linoleum of the kitchen floor.

Chapter 35

In the present situation, one could not have asked for a more socially useful reply. For several minutes, no one needed to talk because they were busy with the mundane necessities that arose from a pool of vomit on the floor.

The first concern was Scollay, who by instinct was drawn to the sound of retching. Dryden was still bent over, waiting for the heaves to subside, when the dog poked his nose in to see if she had regurgitated anything worth eating. Her heaves halted immediately as she grabbed his collar to pull him away.

When the dog was safely out in the yard, she fetched a basin and scooped up the worst of the pool. Anita wiped up the remnants with a mop and Charlie followed with paper towels to dry the floor. By the time Dryden returned from emptying the basin and washing her face, everyone was calmer.

Without saying anything, they mutually agreed they had no desire to finish the congealing remains of their dinner. Instead, Charlie gathered the dishes to wash, while Dryden put away the leftover food. Anita, who had a great gift for effective action, good or bad, put a kettle on the burner to make a pot of tea.

They didn't hurry to be done with work. When the tea was brewed, they drank it on the move, still finishing with dishes and wiping counters, choosing this moment to scour rubberized grease spots off the back of the stove and empty the crumb pan under the toaster.

It felt silly to talk about small things, and most of the big things were obvious. Dryden did not have to ask the reason for the pretense: Anita and Charlie had had a social position to maintain. With one small adjustment to the facts, Anita's infidelity vanished and they became saintly rescuers of a child in need.

They could easily persuade themselves that it was in Dryden's best interests as well as their own to have the doubtful circumstances of her conception attached to some abstract and absent people. The social stigma of the truth would have been immediate. The emotional consequences of the fiction were hypothetical, off in the future, and in Anita's view, very likely overstated by self-indulgent, touchy-feely types. Rational humans were meant to operate on a level higher than mere chromosomes.

Neither parent had looked Dryden in the face since the truth was spoken. Anita was still busy with a sponge and cleanser, putting a shine on the sink, while Charlie was reorganizing the spice rack. Eventually, Dryden put aside her dishtowel to ask a question.

"Who was Mariano?"

There was a brief hitch in Anita's scrubbing stroke, which she masked by pausing to dump more powder onto her sponge. Charlie stopped alphabetizing spices and started fidgeting with the papers near the telephone. When it became clear that Anita was not going to answer, the tempo of his fidgeting increased.

"Mariano was a k—" He caught himself and paused to revise. "He was a young man who did yard work around the neighborhood. He was very..." He stopped again. Every word that came to mind might suggest to Dryden that her father had been a sophisticated playboy. Charming. Handsome. Lively. Playful. How to convey the reality, that he had been basically still a kid at seventeen, a wiry, cheerful young man who could shovel a mountain of topsoil one minute and bounce around like a Golden Retriever the next, who laughed at his mistakes in English and was taking night courses at a technical college and seemed to need almost no sleep.

"Nice," he said.

"Nice?"

"Yes, he was a nice k—guy."

"That's all? Nice?"

"He liked soccer. And he played the—"

"He's also dead," Anita said abruptly.

"He is?" Charlie gaped, his own train of thought forgotten. "But how do you—? I thought we'd lost track..."

"I kept track. In case it ever mattered. Which it hasn't. He was in a car wreck."

"When? Why didn't you...?"

"It was a long time ago. Probably fifteen years."

"Fifteen years... so he was only..."

He felt strangely grieved and realized that along with the still-vivid memory of the boy he'd actually known, he'd been carrying another image, like a shadow, his idea of what the boy must have become. A middle-aged man. Possibly balding or heavier. Possibly with a wife and children. An imagined person that turned out not to exist anymore.

He shook his head. "I can't believe it. He was so..."

"Nice. Yes. But what can it possibly matter now?"

"What did he play?" Dryden asked suddenly.

"Play?"

Charlie was mystified. He didn't remember what he'd been saying earlier.

"You said he played something."

"That's right... the harmonica..."

"He didn't play, he doodled," Anita said. "So if you're imagining he was some sort of genius, don't. The simple fact is, he was not a person of any great consequence."

"How can you say that!" Charlie protested. "He could have become anything..."

"Well, he didn't. He became nothing whatsoever. He was a groundskeeper."

"Why the harmonica?" Dryden persisted.

"What?"

"Why the harmonica? How did he decide?"

"How should I know?" Anita said irritably. "Maybe because he could carry it in his pocket. Maybe he had something else at home."

"He liked Bob Dylan," Charlie said. "I remember he said that once."

"Ah." Dryden pondered a moment, then murmured the name again, like new vocabulary she was studying. "Dylan."

After that, she was silent, seemingly not interested in any other information. In less time than the opening scene of a play, her biological father had been introduced to her, dismissed as a nonentity and killed off. Probably the harmonica was the only part of him she could make real to herself. She quickly swallowed the last of her tea, put on her coat, muttered something about taking the dog for a walk, and went outside.

As soon as she was gone, Anita turned on Charlie.

"What the hell was the point of that!" Anita said. "You think she's out there dancing with delight at the news? She's never wanted to be one of us. She hates us. Especially Spense. And you've just handed her another way to make trouble. If the papers find out…"

"Find out what? The truth? And all this time you've been pushing for the truth at all costs. Saying that it can't do any harm."

"But how can you not——? He's your son…"

"Indeed. So he is. One of my very own children. How could I ever do anything to hurt any of them?"

He shrugged himself into his coat and reached for his boots.

"I'm going to get some air."

Outdoors, the wind stung his cheeks, but he didn't mind. His breath poured out clouds and his heartbeat felt stout, quickening as he walked.

He had half a thought that he might find Dryden and he started with a circuit of the farm buildings. He wanted to tell her he'd back her up, no matter what. He wanted to say he thought she was beautiful from the day she was born.

In the chicken coop, the hens shifted on their roost, edging away from the open door with soft coos, still half asleep. In the barn, the air was warmer, and the pigs made a steady rumble of contentment, grunting and nudging for position. Everywhere else, the farm was still and the only sound was the wind.

Leaving the farmyard, he walked out the driveway and along the road past the first bend. There, too, he saw no sign of Dryden. He supposed she must have gone off into the fields with the dog and could be anywhere. His body was starting to shiver. His coat was too thin for the season and his gloves were only for dress. Reluctantly, he turned to go back to the house.

Chapter 36

For a time, after Charlie returned to his book and immersed himself in the intricacies of John and Abigail's marital correspondence, I enjoyed a rare interlude of peace. Before long, though, I began to hear whispers, fragments of phrases, voices that multiplied and grew louder and louder, until I was engulfed in a cacophony of argument, pontification, and prayer being uttered by people, mostly strangers, who were sure they knew what God had in mind for me.

In the confusion, I lost track of time, but I did winnow a few facts out of the chaos of voices. The proliferation of prayer was largely due to a broadcast by a prominent televangelist whose followers had more zeal than they did clarity about why he wanted them to pray for me. Some of them asked that the world be protected from my blasphemous example and my innocent niece retrieved from my corrupting influence. Others asked that my innocent corpse be rescued from sacrilege and my blasphemous niece punished for her sin. For me, the key fact was that there were a large number of faithful and it seemed I had to listen to all of them.

The nighttime prayers were succeeded by daytime oratory and argument. Anticipating a future run for state representative, Payson Satterthwaite had sent a leaflet to the voters, calling himself a voice for law and order. From a parking ticket to high treason, he declared, the law was a single edifice and permissiveness at any level was a crack in the structure. Satterthwaite didn't mention Dryden by name, but the neighbors discussing his leaflet had not missed the implication. The fault lines in their debates weren't linear, however, since some of the same people who wanted plenty of cops and tough jail sentences were not necessarily eager to have the local game warden enforce every line of the law.

Farther afield, in Arizona, Spenser's two prospective opponents in next year's primary had seized the opportunity to identify themselves as the candidates of Christian values. After having jointly declared the name Kirkwood to be anathema, they were now engaged in a decorous but fierce dispute about which of them had the more clearly Christian position on the issue of my burial.

The barrage of disagreement was bad enough, but I learned there could be worse when a TV talk show host had the bright idea of linking my name to the old Monty Python routine about eating one's dead mother. Within minutes, interspersed with the prayers and political rants, I was hearing the same three jokes, repeated by a countless legion of people with an email account and a generous wish to share the laugh.

When the jokes began, I knew it was all over. The issue had moved from religion and politics to pop culture and there was no stopping it. By now it didn't matter whether Anita kept pushing for action or not. Too many wheels were already turning. I was no longer an obscure rural curmudgeon whose fate was the object of near-universal indifference. I was a rich woman from an influential family and my corpse was a fresh excuse for people to hurl rocks and jokes at each other across the ravine at the center of American culture.

I was trapped, cut off from everyone I cared about, drowning in noise and conflict and repetitive stupidity, and I could no longer tell how long I had been in this state. It could have been as little as an hour or as much as a week. To me, it felt endless.

And then, quite suddenly, the cacophony died away and I was dropped, like jetsam, in one particular place with only the sights and sounds of that place, which now felt like an oasis of serenity compared to where I had been.

The wind was rattling branches and whipping a few scattered pellets of sleet slantwise through the air. Outside the town hall, Dulcie Sullivan was at her post, bundled in a knee-length down coat and holding her placard on behalf of freedom of religion. Her only company was a large thermos of hot chocolate and a portable radio playing oldies at low volume.

She was not alone for long, however. Within minutes after I arrived, a van and two SUVs pulled up and eight people got out. They clustered in a semi-circle across the walkway from Dulcie. They were holding placards proclaiming that respect for human life included respect for the afterlife and that those who were most helpless, such as the dead, had the greatest right to protection by our laws and institutions. The out-of-state-plates on the van and one of the SUVs indicated that their occupants had driven more than a thousand miles to make their views known. The only people I recognized were Inchkeep and one of his parishioners.

The arrival of the counter-demonstration was soon followed by the arrival of two news vans, one from the local TV station and one from a national network. As background, they filmed views of the town green and collected quotes from Dulcie, Inchkeep, and one of the out-of-town visitors. Then they hovered, hopefully, waiting to film the first dramatic confrontation between the protestors and the local populace.

Like a border collie, I thought, waiting for the faucet to drip.

Even on a busy day, the traffic into the town hall was sporadic. On this particular day, most of the local populace had telepathically decided it was not a good time to transact their town hall business, which was rarely urgent anyway, except on the deadline days for property taxes and dog licenses.

If the civil liberties placard had been in the hands of Lawrence Buell, he might singlehandedly have provided the drama, but Dulcie's passions were more governable. Rather than hurling newsworthy epithets, she walked over to the opposing group to commiserate on the coldness of the day, offer them a pour from her thermos of hot chocolate and remark how great it was to live in a free country.

She carried herself with the graciousness of sovereignty. Her banner declared the ruling principles of tolerance and liberty; her opponents' messages were those of minor fiefdoms who, in the absence of a stronger principle, would be cutting each other's throats. Though Dulcie might not have articulated it as Eames could, she understood by instinct that my freedom to leave my body in the woods depended on other people's freedom to say that a member of *their* church would be damned for doing what I'd done.

Also, she had deep familiarity with the concept of getting along.

Her offer of hot chocolate was declined and before long, the out-of-town visitors grew weary of polite coexistence. They put their heads together and decided that their demonstration should move itself to a more populated location in the hope of finding someone who would argue with them. After alerting the news vans to their intentions, they decamped to Leonardston, to the building that housed the courthouse.

The location suited their purpose much better. The courthouse was adjacent to the business center and the two shared the use of a municipal parking lot, so the protestors had a reasonably steady audience. Better still, since Dryden and I were not known in Leonardston, except by way of the media, their audience was more likely to be swayed by their message.

Within a fairly short time, a forty-ish couple in Patagonia jackets stepped out of their Thule-rack Subaru and into the encounter the protestors sought, a loud-voiced exchange between "blind medieval ignorance" on the one side and "godless liberalism" on the other. A few passersby stopped to watch, the cameras rolled, and pretty much everyone but me was happy.

As it turned out, this farce among strangers was just the prologue. The volleys of catch phrases were still flying back and forth, when suddenly the doors of the courthouse swung open and a knot of people came spilling out. At the center of the knot were Terp and the massive policeman from the interview room. In front of them, another policeman struggled to clear a path through the onlookers, while a local newspaper reporter shouted questions and a still cameraman snapped photos from the perimeter.

When the group from the courthouse and the group with the placards caught sight of each other, everything came to a stop. Clearly, neither group had been aware of the other's presence and their convergence was pure coincidence.

The TV news reporters were the first to react, instinctively turning toward the freshest scent. With a wave to their cameramen to come along, they raced toward the courthouse steps. Seeing the placards and TV cameras, the large policeman grasped Terp's arm and braced himself, bringing the whole group to a halt at the bottom of the steps.

A moment later, I heard a thought, *Damn, I wish I could write this story*. Terp.

I could feel the policeman's fist clamped on his bicep, the bodies jostling him on all sides and the voices barking a confusion of questions in his ear but what I felt more than anything was contentment. My own contentment. The contentment of a hermit crab, finding the right-shaped shell. I was back where I most wanted to be, in the company of this entertaining young man, who seemed to love Dryden and possibly would make a better job of it than I had done.

The first questions from the TV reporters were a slightly loftier phrasing of "what the hell is going on?" but gradually, the essence of the situation became clear. Terp had refused to say where my body was, he had been cited for contempt and he was presently being taken to jail to consider whether he wanted to change his mind.

To most of the reporters' questions, his answer was a shrug, conveying the obvious. If he hadn't given information to the police or the court, why would he give it to the media? One question he did answer: no, he was not going to change his mind.

His own thoughts were divided between two tracks.

Exactly how bad would jail be?

Exactly how much of the irritable swiftness with which the judge had cited him could be attributed to a story he'd seen in that morning's *Herald*, a small inside paragraph reporting that the judge's nineteen-year-old son had lost control of his parents' Ford Explorer and skidded into an oncoming Honda Civic and although the drivers were unhurt, both vehicles had been totaled?

Only when he was away from the melee, alone in a cell in the county jail, did he let himself think about the question that really bothered him.

Where was Dryden? Why wasn't she talking to him?

He had called several times. He had left messages with her parents when they answered and on her machine when they didn't. He had emailed. He even had driven by the farm, only to have Anita tell him, brusquely, that Dryden had gone out somewhere with the dog.

It was inexplicable. When he'd last seen her, it was to drop her at the farm after a lazily blissful morning in bed. He had thought they understood each other. He had thought his own feelings were unmistakable and that he was not misreading hers.

And then, nothing. Not even a word to say she felt regrets or had changed her mind.

It seemed a long time ago that he'd made the decision to stay silent. At the time, he'd felt no doubts. Dryden's well-being was his own well-being and the moment his decision became a concrete action, in the police interview, he knew it was what he wanted to do. At the time, he almost wanted to be sent to jail, to make his action all the more definite.

His messages had been careful not to push her too hard, not to reveal too much to her parents. Although he was itching to say that he loved her madly and was going crazy not hearing from her, he had held back. He could tell her those things in person. He'd said only, "I'm hoping to talk to you, call me."

But she hadn't called, and he didn't know why not, and then events began to move on their own and he had to decide if the choice he had made for the police was his choice for the court, too, with or without any more word from her.

So here he was, with time to think and no distractions, apart from the post-nasal snuffling and hacking of his nearest neighbor, who was awaiting trial for possession of narcotics.

He looked around at the cold concrete, the deadening flatness of the lighting. If he'd been sure of her, he could have felt heroic and taken pride in not caring about the dreariness of his surroundings. But he didn't feel sure any more. Her silence spoke doubts.

How bravely he had said he wouldn't change his mind when he was outdoors in the open air and people were watching. Now, alone and confined in a place designed to be grim, he wondered if he'd been fooling himself about her. He jumped up from his cot and began to pace circles around the cell, as if movement might bring clarity.

You can't change now! I yelled. She'll never trust anyone! From her first breath, her mother wanted her to be someone else. Her mother's there now, the invisible worm, chewing on her mind, trying to make you into someone else. If you line up with the worm, she'll pull inside and seal herself off until doomsday.

Change later, if you have to. Move on later, if you have to. Be unreliable later, if you have to. Just not right now, please!

Somebody help me here! Somebody tell this guy, if you can't be stalwart, then at least sit tight. If you can't be courageous, then at least be cautious. Believe me, Dryden's happiness depends on your persistence.

Think of yourself as a guard dog, trained to your task. Be diligent and patient, like a well-mannered German shepherd. Don't analyze. Just sit! And stay!

And if you need a bone to keep you busy, try reading that book you brought.

Terp was still pacing the cell, wondering if it was simply not in his nature to choose one path and stick to it, wondering if his propensity for seeing alternatives made him incapable of fortitude.

And then, wonder of wonders, his eyes wandered to the book lying on a corner of his cot and he thought, maybe that's the next best thing to fortitude. To distract himself and let inertia keep him on course. If he was reading, he wouldn't be envisioning alternate realities. The reality he'd already chosen would go forward, for good or ill.

He sat down and picked up the book. It was a good fat one, a history of the Civil War. If the prose was passable, it might keep him occupied long enough for my purposes. He read a page, then another. The prose was better than passable. He adjusted a pillow and stretched himself full length on the cot. Before long he was far away, in another century, with only his body still stuck in a cell.

Yes! Good dog! Stay!

Chapter 37

In the morning, two headlines topped the front page of the *Leonardston Herald*. **Protest Sparks Confrontation. Local Journalist Cited for Contempt.** The stories were the subject of a lively discussion at the diner, where the unifying sentiment was that a whole lot of people had taken leave of their senses, although there was disagreement as to exactly which people.

Gradually the array of opinions sifted themselves down to one: that the situation was a waste of police time and public money but at least offered the pleasures of comedy. That view belonged to Jim Jorgensen, whose copy of the newspaper was tucked under his arm as he carried a Danish and a cup of coffee from the diner to his cruiser. He was unperturbed by the prospect of continued silliness, which made me think that his romantic life must be proceeding smilingly.

At his office, he settled in to eat his breakfast and read the news articles more carefully. His own opinion hadn't changed. He was still convinced that Dryden was telling the truth. He didn't say this to his superiors, however. It would only irritate them and nothing would change. Within the confines of his job, he did what he was told, and what he'd been told was to provide all possible assistance to the state police in their investigation.

At this point there wasn't much assistance to be given, because they had no leads. They had scoured the farm and turned up nothing suspicious. No human blood. No signs of struggle. No weapon or poison, beyond the usual inventory of hunting rifles, utility knives, ropes, wrenches, hammers, crowbars, chainsaws, axes, insecticides, disinfectants, and veterinary medications to be found on any farm in the county.

None of the potential weapons looked freshly cleaned. The dust on the poison containers was undisturbed. Of the rifles, only the .22 appeared to have been fired in the previous year, and even that discharge was judged to be weeks or months old, most likely from the summer, when woodchucks were abroad. As for witnesses, there were none. Or rather, the two most relevant, Otis and Noah, both swore that Dryden got along fine with her aunt.

For the moment, his task was to document his part in the farce by typing up a report of everything he'd done from the moment the case began. This would take a while, not because he was a slow typist, but because he could tell that Mayhew wanted maximum detail, as if being thorough in one's implementation of stupidity could make it less stupid.

He was well into his second cup of coffee, this one from his own drip pot, when his door banged open and Dryden burst in.

"Thank god, no bloody pinheads here! I need your help."

He started to ask what he could do, but she wasn't waiting for questions.

"My fucking mother is bullshit!" she said.

She saw the newspaper on his desk and gestured at it in disgust.

"My mother's the one who ought to be locked up, not Terp. He hasn't done a thing. This whole thing is bullshit!"

This time Jim kept his mouth shut and waited, figuring she'd eventually define bullshit without his asking.

"If nobody was murdered, he'll be free to go, right?"

She pointed at the headline again.

"I believe that's true. Any charges would be dropped."

"OK, I'll show you where she is."

"Right now?"

"If you're not too busy."

"No, definitely not."

He clicked the sleep button on the computer and stood up to put on his jacket.

"We can do this, just the two of us, if you want," he said. "But I'd rather get hold of the state police and have them send their team, too. So there won't be any question whether there was proper handling of..."

He hesitated. The words he could think of sounded either gruesome or sanitized.

"The evidence," he said.

She winced. She was quiet for a while, but in the end, she shrugged.

"Sure, call whoever you want. Call the Marines. It's already a circus. Why not have a few dancing poodles, too. Just let me clear out of there before they start their act."

"Of course. I'll make sure of that."

"And before we go anywhere, I want Terp out of that place."

Terp, at the moment, had just put aside his book and was lying on his cot, staring at the ceiling and considering whether his principles were worth the price.

For most of a day, he had blocked out the details of his own situation by immersing himself in the much graver sorrows of the Civil War. Then, in the last hour, he had come to a chapter on prisoners of war, and even though he could feel a rational gratitude that the county jail had none of the filth, disease and deprivation of the Civil War prison camps, he could no longer avoid the awareness of where he was. Nor could he keep reading. However clean, safe and well-fed he was, a cell was still a grim prospect and it wasn't consoling to know that imprisonment could be infinitely worse.

He had some blank paper with him and he made a couple of tries at writing a letter to Dryden, but each time he gave up, because he was no longer sure what they meant to each other. Was she his lover, the closest companion of his heart? Or was she a chance encounter, their connection as transient as the circumstances that brought it about?

The only thing worse than thinking about being alone in a cell was thinking he might have been alone in his feelings for Dryden, so after a while, he put the letter paper aside. He had the means to his release right there with him in his head, the memorized instructions to the dead body, but he left them unspoken. If his reading about the Civil War had given him no comfort about the prospect of prison, it had at least given him a yardstick of suffering on which his twenty-four hours in a clean, warm jail cell would barely register. For the moment, his capacity for self-mockery took the place of courage in keeping him steadfast.

He was still lying on his cot when a guard appeared and opened his cell door.

"You're out of here," the guard said.

"What happened?" Terp asked.

"I dunno. I just do what I'm told."

Terp quickly gathered his things and followed the guard. Coming into the reception area, he saw Jim Jorgensen standing near the desk, talking to another officer.

To Jim, he repeated his question, "What happened?"

Jim didn't answer directly. Instead, he smiled and nodded in the direction of the entrance door. "Out there," he said.

Terp stood still for a moment, wanting to fix a sensation in his memory. He knew what "Out there" meant. He knew Dryden was there and he knew this could happen only once, this first sudden certainty that he was loved.

Outdoors the air was biting and Dryden was walking to keep warm. When she saw Terp come out the door she didn't say anything. She just came over and put her arms around him and kissed him. They stood a long time, not talking, feeling one another's warmth.

Finally Terp stepped away a little and said, "You don't have to do this, you know. If it's important to you to leave her be, I'll go back in there."

"Are you nuts?" she said. "There's no way she'd want you in there."

They looked at each other and started to laugh.

"OK, so I'm not consistent, but that's tough," she said. "Fay will have to deal with it. Let's just hope things have gotten so crazy that she'd be laughing, too."

That she would be, darling girl. That she would be.

Epilogue

Watching the team of uniforms following Dryden through the woods to my earthly remains, I wondered once again if changing the state of my body would change my status in the hereafter. Would I finally leave behind the living and experience the torment or ecstasy that so many institutionalized religions would say I had earned?

Or would I finally be granted the oblivion I had always thought I wanted?

Torment. Ecstasy. Oblivion.

Damn.

I didn't want any of those. I wanted to stay right where I was. But the choice was out of my hands, because I didn't have any.

My questions were answered soon enough, starting when the pathologist took apart my skull to look at what was left of my brain and ending when the box containing my ashes was buried in the family plot.

The police had recovered most of my body, all but some of the tiniest bones. Joints were dismantled, guts and muscle halfway eaten, but the parts were there, strewn about like engine parts in the repair shop. The pathologist found more inside my skull than I might have guessed. The remaining tissue was nicely frozen, preserving the essential fact: "Massive cerebral hemorrhage. No evidence of trauma or toxicity."

After the autopsy, I was cremated and the ashes were buried, quick before the frost went too deep. I watched these events and they made not a particle of difference. Nor did the memorial service that Anita organized as proof of the Kirkwood family's Christian devotion. Burned, buried and blessed I was, and nothing changed. I was as present and helpless as ever.

The service was led by Reverend Eames, who did not demand either religious belief or pleasant behavior as a precondition to the consolation of a funeral. His preaching voiced a happy confidence that god and Jesus cared for me, which was more than I deserved, based on any allegiance I'd given them when I had the choice. I figured he was just giving a name to his own kindness and his words didn't bother me.

Within days after the service, I would be right there in the town hall as Royce Palmer, over a cup of coffee, offered the opinion that the Kirkwoods might be the strangest family he'd ever met in all his years of police work.

Eloise concurred, although she was in a mood of generous tolerance that prompted her to add, "You know, it takes all kinds to make a world."

Her mood was the natural result of two happy occurrences. First, Gerald had suggested, amicably, that they proceed with the divorce forthwith. Then Noah had used the pretext of asking for a recipe to send her an email and that seed had blossomed into a correspondence of such warmth and frequency that her computer was now the object of continuous fluttering anticipation.

"Yup, it takes all kinds," she repeated contentedly and went back to composing an email.

Within the month, I would see Anita ask her lawyer if her sons had grounds to challenge my will and hear his opinion that Joe Lambeth had been scrupulously careful and her sons would probably lose. I also would learn that with my name gone from the newspapers, Spenser's re-election campaign had returned to the issues of more immediate concern to his constituents, such as immigration and gas prices, and he had surged back into the lead in the polls.

Closer to home, I would see Otis concede that ibuprofen and crankiness were no longer sufficient remedy for the knees that had troubled him for the last ten years. I was dead and Dryden was moving on. He had no family who wanted to farm. It was time to lease out his land and make himself a useful retirement driving tractor and helping with chores for his neighbors, when he felt like it.

And so it continued. My return to obscurity ended the pinball ride among strangers with a passing interest in me, but I still had a livelier social life than I'd ever had when I was alive. Mostly, I went where Terp went and he enjoyed touching feelers with the whole human colony. Thanks to him, I would learn that Payson Satterthwaite had lost the election to the state legislature but that Millicent Gray had won a seat on the school board, where she would work tirelessly to cut the school budget. I would hear that Dulcie Sullivan's nephew from Minnesota had been killed in the invasion of Iraq, that Belinda Boyle was struggling to raise an autistic son, and that Coral Hoskins had persuaded Singing Wolf to offer a spiritual retreat in a nearby ski resort town.

In time, I would see the acquaintance among Terp, Dryden, and Jim Jorgensen become an everyday friendship and thus I would be in attendance when the Reverend Eames performed a ceremony of union for Jim and Gerald. Shortly thereafter, I would hear that Reverend Inchkeep had told Gerald his services as organist were no longer required.

The latter event was less devastating to Gerald than might have been expected. When the news became public, the Episcopal Church in Leonardston, which also had a very fine organ and was about to lose its organist to a husband's job relocation, made discreet inquiries as to whether Gerald would consider changing his religious affiliation. He replied that yes, he would, although in truth he would be worshipping in the same way he always had.

For myself, I was content, and a day would come when this no longer surprised me. The watching was plenty, it turned out. I was old and tired and it was remarkably peaceful to know that if I couldn't prevent foolishness and misery, I also couldn't cause any. At most I could offer helpful suggestions, some fragments of which might be dimly apprehended by the person to whom they had been offered.

While still alive, I never imagined I would someday look at a broken fence and be glad to think, "That's not my problem." But so it was.

I was settled where I wanted to be, with the person who loved Dryden, and I liked his company as well as I'd ever liked my own. He made Dryden happy so nothing else he did could bother me.

As for the rest of humankind, I saw about as much of them as I could bear.

Acknowledgments

This book was a long time in the making and I am grateful to the friends, family, and even strangers who read the manuscript, offered suggestions, or cheered me on. My particular thanks go out to Sally Brady, Peter Collier, Victoria Dillman, Marguerite and Will Graham, Mary Hensley, Marjorie Matthews, and Charlotte Wunderlich. I also want to thank the talented folks at Rootstock Publishing who are making the book a reality: Samantha Kolber, Jennifer Gennari, Vance Kiviranna, Cynthia Brackett-Vincent, and Eddie Vincent. It has been a pleasure to work with them. Finally, above all, I say thank you to my beloved spouse Ruth, who read and critiqued the earliest draft of the story and lived with it for quite a few years.

About the Author

Edith Forbes grew up on a family ranch in Wyoming. She graduated from Stanford University with a degree in English, which served to launch her on a career in computer programming. When she found herself trying to write poetry in Pascal, she abandoned computers in favor of less reliably logical pursuits, including farming, house renovation, and writing. Her primary interest is fiction, but she also has tried her hand at essays, poetry, screenplays, a cookbook, and, most recently, a memoir. Her four novels, *Alma Rose, Nowle's Passing, Exit to Reality,* and *Navigating the Darwin Straits*, were published by Seal Press in Seattle. For many years, she lived on a small farm in Vermont, where she could see from her office window that her cows had broken through a fence. In 2018, she moved into town and now she can see from her office window that her chickens have escaped into the vegetable garden. Visit her website to learn more: www.edithforbes.com.

🍃 We Grow Our Books in Montpelier, Vermont

Learn more about our titles in Fiction, Nonfiction, Poetry and Children's Literature at the QR code below or visit www.rootstockpublishing.com.

www.ingramcontent.com/pod-product-compliance
Lightning Source LLC
Chambersburg PA
CBHW030338120226
39577CB00034B/342